KATAKI

An evil has survived World War II. The Black Dragon society has risen intact from the devastation of Hiroshima and Nagasaki.

KATAKI

Now, forty years later, the secret society has found the perfect instrument to carry out its plan. His name is Matt Bancroft, an American raised in Japan and scarred by the death of his family. He can move freely among whites, yet obeys a samurai's creed. And he is sworn to Kataki: a blood oath of vengeance.

KATAKI

They have chosen their target. He is a man who once fought in World War II and who is now Vice-President of the United States. He is George Bush. And his death will avenge yesterday's defeat—and insure tomorrow's triumph . . .

"AS WITH ALL CLASSIC SUSPENSE ROOTED IN HISTORICAL ACCURACY, THE IMPOSSIBLE SUDDENLY SEEMS ENTIRELY PLAUSIBLE!"
—*Booklist*

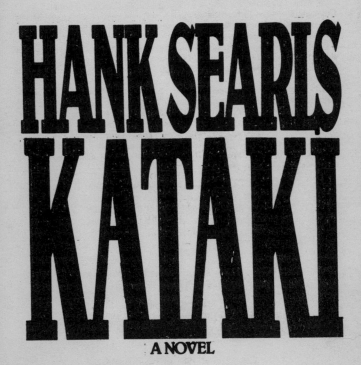

HANK SEARLS
KATAKI

A NOVEL

BERKLEY BOOKS, NEW YORK

Grateful acknowledgment is made to the following for permission to quote from
previously published material.

"Oh What a Beautiful Morning," by Richard Rodgers & Oscar Hammerstein II.
Copyright © 1943 by Richard Rodgers and Oscar Hammerstein II. Copyright renewed
and assigned to Chappell & Co., Inc. International copyright secured. All rights
reserved. Used by permission.
"There's a Star Spangled Banner Waving Somewhere," words and music by Paul
Roberts and Shelby Darnell. Copyright © 1942 by MCA Music Publishing, a division
of MCA, Inc., New York, NY. Copyright renewed. Used by permission. All
rights reserved.
"Bless 'Em All," words and music by Jimmy Hughes, Frank Lake and Al
Stillman. Copyright © 1940 by Keith Prowse and Company, Ltd., for all countries.
Copyright © 1941 and 1969 by Sam Fox Publishing Company, Inc., New York,
N.Y., for the United States of America, Canada, South America, Central America,
China, Japan, Hong Kong, the Philippine Islands, Mexico, Cuba, Puerto Rico,
and all other countries of the Western Hemisphere, except Australia and New
Zealand, and by Keith Prowse and Company, Ltd., for all other countries. All
rights reserved. Used by permission.

This Berkley book contains the complete
text of the original hardcover edition.
It has been completely reset in a typeface
designed for easy reading and was printed
from new film.

KATAKI

A Berkley Book / published by arrangement with
McGraw-Hill Book Company

PRINTING HISTORY
McGraw-Hill edition published 1987
Berkley edition/October 1988

ISBN: 0-425-11252-7

A BERKLEY BOOK® TM 757,375
Berkley Books are published by The Berkley Publishing Group,
200 Madison Avenue, New York, NY 10016.
The name "BERKLEY" and the "B" logo
are trademarks belonging to Berkley Publishing Corporation.

PRINTED IN THE UNITED STATES OF AMERICA

10 9 8 7 6 5 4 3 2 1

To Nathaniel Savory, of Massachusetts, whose hope—that his descendants could live as Americans forever in the Bonin Islands off Japan—was dashed by history.

To those of his island seed—Jerry Savory and the present-day Nathaniel—who helped me unwrap the story.

To Colonel—now General, retired—Presley M. Rixey, United States Marine Corps, first U.S. island commandant, and Major Robert Shaffer, head of his board of inquiry, both of whom doggedly pursued the guilty.

And to the victims of Hiroshima's *pika-don*, including you and me.

Author's Note

Although this is a work of fiction, Chichijima Island, only five hundred miles south of downtown Tokyo in the Bonin Islands, is of course real. So are its American whites, citizens of Japan.

Its monsters, unfortunately, were real too: General Yoshio Tachibana, Imperial Japanese Army, island commander at the time of Hiroshima; the Japanese poet-admiral Kunizo Mori, Imperial Japanese Navy; and Major Sueo Matoba, the savage giant.

But for astonishing luck and a passing U.S. submarine, Vice President George Bush, shot down at the age of twenty as he dove his TBM Avenger at Chichijima's radio tower in 1944, would have fallen into their hands. Neither of his two crewmen survived their mission.

The general, the admiral, and the major were tried for the murders of downed American airmen—and for a crime so bizarre that it violated no written law—along with ten other officers and men of the 17,000-man Chichijima garrison. They were convicted by a U.S. Navy War Crimes Commission on Guam in 1946. Some were hanged and some live in Japan today.

The prewar history of the colonists on Chichijima is real, although Matt and Alicia and Lorna and Lemuel are not. Vice President Bush's wartime experience with the island is true.

All historical characters appearing under their own names are real. All others are fictional. Any resemblance they bear to living persons, though gratifying, is coincidental.

Hank Searls
Newport Beach, California
1987

kataki: revenge; "death for a death"

O wretched sons of men! Why do ye get you weapons and bring slaughter on one another? Cease therefrom, give o'er your toiling, and in mutual peace keep safe your cities. Short is the span of life . . .

—Euripides
The Suppliants
410 B.C.

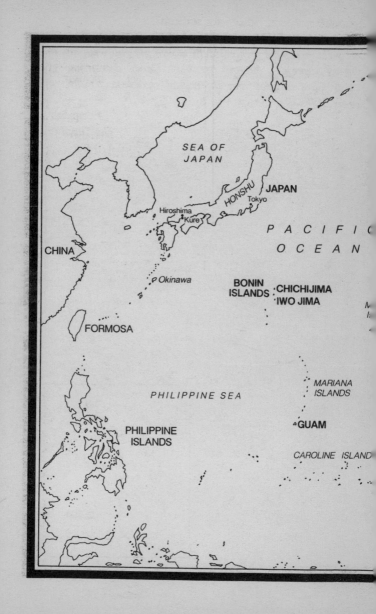

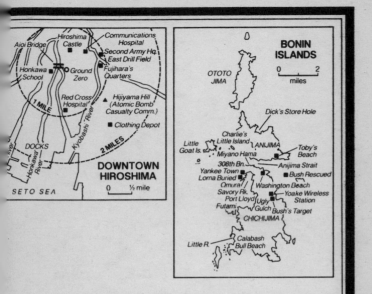

DOWNTOWN HIROSHIMA

Aioi Bridge
Hiroshima Castle
Communications Hospital
Second Army Hq.
East Drill Field
Fujihara's Quarters
Honkawa School
Ground Zero
Red Cross Hospital
Hijiyama Hill (Atomic Bomb Casualty Comm.)
Clothing Depot
Kyobashi River
Honkawa River
1 MILE
2 MILES
DOCKS
SETO SEA

0 ½ mile

BONIN ISLANDS

0 2
miles

OTOTO JIMA
Dick's Store Hole
Charlie's Little Island
Little Goat Is.
ANIJIMA
Toby's Beach
Miyano Hama
Anijima Strait
308th Bn.
Bush Rescued
Yankee Town
Lorna Buried
Washington Beach
Omura
Savory Rk.
Yoake Wireless Station
Port Lloyd
Ugly
Futami
Gulch
Bush's Target
CHICHIJIMA
Little R.
Calabash
Bull Beach

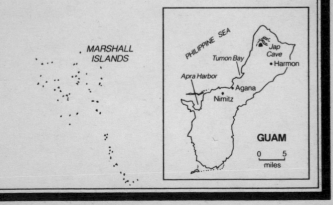

• Wake Island

MARSHALL ISLANDS

GUAM

PHILIPPINE SEA
Jap Cave
Tumon Bay
• Harmon
Apra Harbor
Agana
• Nimitz

0 5
miles

PART ONE

Child of the Pika-Don

CHAPTER 1

If you are an intelligent man, wish to kill the Vice President of the United States, and plan to die immediately thereafter, you may of course succeed.

If additionally you are to dine with him at a speakers' table as a member of a foreign trade delegation, cleared by the State Department, the Secret Service, the FBI, and the National Security Agency, your chances are actually quite good. Even the Secret Service admits it.

Christopher Hart—born Matthew Calbraith Bancroft—so wished, and had an appointment to breakfast with him today.

He answered a wakeup call in his suite in the Washington Hilton Hotel. He had slept perfectly.

These last months had been devoted to planning the assassination. He was sure that he would not fail. Too many things had fallen providentially into place for him to doubt that his gods at last were with him.

He was tall and lean, tanned from tennis, and seemed younger than fifty-five. He had a graying mustache and quizzical lines at the corners of his emerald eyes.

He swung his legs from the bed, moved to the window, and checked the weather by cracking the venetian blind. A beautiful summer day: here, and probably at home. The *sakura* festivals, starting in southern Kyushu, had swept northeast as the cherry blossoms fell: now the summer festivals

3

were following: Hiroshima's, on the banks of the languid Ota, had begun this week.

It was seven A.M. and traffic below on Connecticut Avenue had hardly begun. The trade breakfast was at ten.

He shaved and dressed, picking a tie that he had bought last year on vacation in Kyoto, with this day in mind. It was a Countess Mara—or a reasonable Oriental copy of one—with a pattern of tiny imperial chrysanthemums, in gold, on silky navy blue.

The tie pin was a miniature Yamagawa XL-15 sports car in eighteen-karat gold, Yamagawa's New Year's gift last year to its top executives. It had been presented him by Osamu Takahashi, foreign sales director, at the annual stockholders' meeting in Hiroshima.

All appropriate, all as it should be.

Now, the gift for Vice President George W. Bush, to be handed from the peak of the Japanese auto industry to the heights of political power.

Carefully, he lifted an exquisite World War II Grumman Avenger aircraft model from its felt-lined nest in a rosewood case. It was gold-plated, cast in the Yamagawa model shop by the best automotive model makers in the world.

For a moment he studied it, sparkling in the slanting morning light.

It was only eleven inches long, but of intricate detail from its embossed navy stars to its tiny rivets. Its wings were folded back along the fuselage, as if for stowage on a hangar deck, and even the control surfaces, he had noted, moved when the tiny stick was touched.

The present had been invoiced to Yamagawa's International Sales Division at five thousand dollars, nearly three-quarters of a million yen. It was his own idea. He had proposed it at the corporate conference table in Hiroshima at which the trade mission had been discussed with other members of the Japan Automotive Manufacturers' Association: Nissan, Honda, Toyota, and Subaru. All had shared in the cost.

Their careful, deliberate consensus was that it was an inspired tribute, once he had explained that Vice President Bush had flown this very plane in World War II, and convinced them that an American politician would hardly notice a certain irony in the gift.

He felt a twinge of pity for his fellow executives, who had unknowingly approved it, and for innocent officials at the speakers' table who were bound to feel its force.

Those of his colleagues who survived the blast would doubtless be tendering resignations tomorrow if not actually contemplating suicide. For the gift was not what it seemed.

Delicately, he unpacked from his suitcase a carefully engineered charge, well padded by shirts and socks. It had been devised to his specifications from the cartridge of a World War II Japanese twenty-five-millimeter antiaircraft shell. Cylindrically shaped, and of gleaming brass, its case was scored with deep lines, like a grenade's, and it weighed just under a pound.

Carefully, as the explosives expert who had made it for him had instructed him, he pulled a safety device from a slot in the shell case. He unscrewed the model's nose, slid the shell case into the fuselage, and replaced the engine-nacelle. Now the airplane was armed and would explode when the wings were unfolded, as planned, by the Vice President for display on the speakers' table.

On its pedestal was inscribed: TO VICE PRESIDENT GEORGE H. W. BUSH, IN RECOGNITION OF HIS STEADFAST SUPPORT OF FREE TRADE BETWEEN NATIONS. That was certainly true: two years ago the vice president had convinced President Reagan to seek voluntary export limits on Japanese autos rather than to push for import restrictions.

He wiped the tiny plate with his handkerchief, and repacked it in its fitted case.

Before he had left Hiroshima, he had toyed with the idea of a short-bladed *wakizashi*, to take his own life afterward. But though the model had been shown the Secret Service, and was expected, a dagger in his briefcase was emphatically not. So he had given up the sword, abandoned Bushido for a cyanide capsule.

Dreams of glory were fine, but reality was harsh: the capsule was safer. Professional spies and foreign agents, he imagined, had to forgo heroics all the time: the mission was the thing.

He gazed at the pill for a moment.

Better to die from a capsule than from a machine-gun slug dealt from on high, or in a burst of turquoise light above a city.

He placed the capsule in his handkerchief. He would down it when the vice president began to unfold the model's wings: if he waited for the blast, he might wake up helpless in a hospital bed, powerless to kill himself.

He checked his briefcase: speech, notebook, graphs of import quotas in the event that the breakfast meeting turned from form to substance.

Finally, a yellowing picture of his mother, himself, and Alicia clowning on the beach at Chichijima. He put in another of his father, clownish too as a Caucasian in his high-peaked Imperial Army hat on Iwo, and a photo of his beloved Mickey-san, also in uniform. He added a newspaper clipping from the *San Diego Union* and a yellowing Japanese army intelligence report to explain his actions. The photos would be something for the Secret Service to puzzle over, and possibly leak to the press: the clipping and report, he knew, they would suppress, but he could not help that.

All was in order.

Suddenly he felt his hands turn clammy.

He pressed his palms together, closed his eyes, and concentrated, as Mickey-san had taught him, forty years ago.

A lily, floating serenely in a mirror-pool of green.

As always, he grew calm.

A functionary at the Japanese embassy had briefed them yesterday on vice presidential protocol. He had warned them that the limousines would pick them up at nine. It occurred to him suddenly that they would embark at the same hotel entrance at which Hinckley had tried to kill President Reagan.

He looked at his watch. Eight forty-four.

He bade farewell to his last hotel room, walked down his last hotel corridor, and stepped into his last elevator.

To all of these things, sayonara: "since it must be so."

CHAPTER 2

"Christopher Hart" had lived his childhood years as Matthew Bancroft, of almost pure American blood and one of the few white subjects of the emperor of Japan.

In 1932, a Year of the Monkey, he was born on the island of Chichijima, five miles long and three miles wide, five hundred miles south of Tokyo.

The Bancroft clan were citizens of Japan. The household was one of a dozen English-speaking Chichijima families, bilingual descendants of a colony of Yankee and English farmer-traders which had landed on the uninhabited island in 1831, before the Japanese—settling by the thousands—had come.

Matt's name was duly entered in the 1932 parish records at the Anglican church in Chichijima's Omura Village, capital of the Bonin Island chain. He was named for Commodore Matthew C. Perry, USN, who had anchored in the island's harbor during his voyage to open up Japan with his "black ships" and befriended Matt's great-great-grandfather, Elias Bancroft, in 1853.

In 1861, the first Japanese colony had landed. By 1912 there were only seventy-nine non-Japanese—Bancrofts, Savorys, Robinsons, Webbs, and Gonzaleses—on Chichijima, and Tokyo presented them with an honor and an ultimatum: become naturalized citizens, or leave. The elders of Yankeetown

7

conferred. To save their homes and farms, they became subjects of the emperor.

The white skin of Matt and his cousins had caused him little grief with classmates in elementary school, although the Yankeetown colony's archaic English—untouched by twentieth-century slang—was forbidden in the classroom.

But on the day in 1941 when his emperor's fleet struck Pearl Harbor, everything changed in an instant.

By the next morning, emerald eyes and fair hair were no longer a joking matter. To discuss the matter away from the womenfolk, Matt's father Lemuel asked him fishing off Miyano Hama Beach.

Matt, at nine, was honored and astonished: to go fishing on a school day was unheard of.

They drove their farm truck north to Anijima Strait, continually forced to pull from the dusty road to make way for army lorries. Above the sand, the flanks of Mt. Mikazuki, headquarters of the 308th Battalion, swarmed with troops. They trundled his Uncle Noah's dugout from the palms and pushed off.

All morning they bobbed in the warm sunlight. His father sat moodily, wide-brimmed hat pulled over his eyes, lanky frame draped over the stern sheets.

At last his father raised the brim of his hat and looked into his eyes.

"Believe I'd best join the colors, son."

Matt felt his world collapse. "The Imperial Army?"

"Appears I truly have no choice. They'll only conscript me."

"You're too old!"

His father smiled. "I'm only thirty-six."

Lemuel uncapped two bottles of Asahi beer. Moving gracefully, like any island boatman, he balanced along the narrow thwarts and handed one to Matt. It was the first beer he'd ever offered his son. Their eyes met as they raised their bottles: *"Gombei . . ."*

Matt did not like the taste, but he was thirsty. And in a few moments it brought a warmth to his body, taking the sting from his father's announcement.

"Will you be an officer?" Lemuel was a graduate of St. Joseph College, in Yokohama.

His father shrugged. "Not from the way they treated me in

Omura last night.'' When Lemuel had entered the village bar, the police chief, a lifelong friend, had called him *keto*—''hairy barbarian''—and stalked out.

His father poked in the compartmented *bento* box. The meal was *fugumeshi*—a blowfish dish Matt loved. His father squatted in the thwarts, at Matt's level, with the box between them, hashi sticks in hand. ''Eat, son!''

''I can't.'' Suddenly he couldn't control himself. ''Daddy, don't go! Don't go to war!''

Lemuel patted his son's knee. ''Matt, don't fret. I doubt they'd trust a white in a combat battalion. *Gunzoku* labor battalion, more likely, with a passel of Koreans. But I have to join.'' He studied his beer. ''I do declare, Matt, I wish we'd fished more often, just you and I, like this . . .'' He looked up. ''No matter. For the nonce, you'll protect your mother and your sister till I'm back. You're very near a man, now, and a fine one. You're most dear to me. I'm proud.''

He reached into his trousers and took out his fishing knife, essential tool of any islander. It was wooden-handled, worn with use, but sharp as a whetted razor. ''I won't be here for your birthday: keep this sharp, Matt, and it's yours.''

Awkwardly, his father squeezed his knee and retreated to the stern.

That night Matt's mother Lorna, a beautiful gray-eyed woman with an easy smile, enshrined her husband's fingernail clippings, a lock of his hair, and his last will and testament in an urn in the *tokonoma* alcove in the main room of their farmhouse, as if he were already dead.

She was only one-eighth Japanese, and a good Christian, but this was the island way.

Within a week Matt, through tears of pride, was waving his father good-bye at the quay.

CHAPTER 3

Crouched behind a *latte* stone on a mountainside in Guam, First Lieutenant Josh Goldberg, U.S. Marine Corps Reserve, was a thoroughly frightened man.

Under no circumstances must he show his fear to his platoon of selected regimental misfits, who were close to panic themselves. They were afraid they had a tiger by the tail.

Goldberg was a thoughtful officer with a square jaw, deep-set gray eyes, and the build of a college wrestler. In this tropical climate he had his black hair cut in a butch. He had graduated from law school at UC Berkeley and left his new job as a deputy district attorney in San Francisco three years ago for Officer Candidate School at Quantico.

He was due to be relieved at noon to return to his battalion near Agana, fourteen miles south at the waist of the peanut-shaped island.

He was in love and he wanted to live, though he suspected that even if he survived the morning he was carefully scheduled to die before the war was over, probably trying to take a beachhead on an obscure island named Chichijima, off Japan.

He was drenched with sweat. It was dripping from his two-week beard onto the bolt of his carbine, and trickling from his brow into his eyes. Surreptitiously he pulled off his helmet and blotted his forehead against its camouflaged cover.

No one noticed. The eyes of his gum-chewing sergeant, his tubby nisei interpreter, and his rat-faced radioman were all riveted on the mouth of an overgrown cave in the hillside, and on the marine inching downward toward it through the jungle vines above.

Josh had established his command post behind one of the strange oblong monuments, relics of an ancient race, that dotted the rotting jungle like the blue stones of Stonehenge circle.

He was safe enough personally here, even if the Japs were in company strength in the cave, as an army L-5 lightplane had estimated when it reported Japanese holdout movement in the area.

The cave certainly seemed big enough for a company. And if they sortied, Josh's section would be overwhelmed. Last week three marines in another mop-up detachment had died under a banzai charge.

For a week he had been stirring up wasp nests, and he was sick of it. This morning he had considered calling for help from Battalion, but discarded the idea: he was in poor enough favor with the battalion commander already, and if the cave was empty, he and his black sheep would be a laughingstock.

He wished that he could stay behind the stone but knew that with his sorry detachment of rejects he could not. He would simply have to lead them or they'd fail.

He had a squad deployed in the tangled growth above the entrance, with a fair field of fire from the rotting mango logs and mottled shade, and another section hidden in reserve below him on the slope.

He took a breath to steady his voice. He exhaled, feeling no better. His crotch stung with jock itch and his toes itched with jungle rot. He felt in the breast pocket of his jungle-green jacket for a pack of Luckies and an olive drab Zippo lighter embossed with the globe-and-anchor emblem of the corps. The pack was soggy with his sweat. He lit a cigarette, never taking his eyes from the man descending toward the entrance to the cave. The cigarette tasted stale.

It was time for the usual useless palaver through his interpreter with the always-hidden Japs.

"Tell 'em how it is, Corporal," he ordered the nisei, projecting nonchalance.

His nisei corporal poked his head around the stone. He

pointed the loudspeaker at the cave and blared: *"Honorable brothers in arms! I am Lieutenant Colonel Akira Kuramoto! General Obata surrendered the island to the Yankee Third Marine Division over a week ago!"*

He paused. His voice echoed from the cliff above.

Laughter issued from the cave, and a guttural voice shouting rapid-fire Japanese.

Shit! They were in there, all right.

The nisei corporal, a grocer's son from Pullman, Washington, yawned. He was bored. And safe: he was too valuable to waste. Besides, he was army, on loan from the Allied Translator and Interpreter Section, and Josh had given him permanent orders to stay in the CP, no matter what.

"What did he say?" asked Josh.

"He says I lie, Lieutenant."

He lied, all right. Hardly any Nips had surrendered, certainly not General Obata, whose stinking body was found after a night kamikaze attack, sprawled on his back in a cloud of flies with the hilt of his samurai sword pointing toward the sky.

Ten thousand Japanese had died on beaches and in the jungle before the island was "secured" last week. From a census of the dead, there were supposed to be five thousand still alive in these northern hills, but you couldn't trust the body counts: half the Jap corpses rotted undiscovered in the jungles, dead of starvation or malaria.

Negotiation with the holdouts was a waste of time. No one ever talked them in. The only soldiers Josh had captured all week long were a half dozen Korean labor troops, dying of TB.

A Japanese shouted again, from deep within the cave.

"He says they're Yamato Squad, ready to die, but we must come and get them."

Yamato, according to the interpreter, was untranslatable, but meant something like "the spirit of Japan."

Whatever it meant, its men—commanded by a legendary Captain Wada—were more than holdouts: they were kamikaze fanatics, attacking from the jungles, finding victims every night.

This was all Josh needed, on his last day in the bush.

"Finish it up," he told the nisei.

"General Obata has ordered that you surrender. He says

his men are being well treated.'' He sounded like the barker outside Sally Rand's fan dance, at the San Francisco Fair. Josh was beginning to understand some of the words, by now. *"We have water! If you will surrender, as all of your honorable comrades have, we shall give you rice and fish and beer!''*

That, at least, was truth. Josh would gladly have given them steak, champagne, and thrown in his jeep, if only they would quit and let him go back to Agana and the woman he loved.

The sergeant was studying him coldly. Like Josh, he was a regimental outcast, victim of some screw-up on the invasion. Josh dimly remembered hearing that he'd led a squad into a minefield.

Josh dragged at the cigarette. By the standards of the corps, he had earned his group of oddballs. He was in disgrace. Last week, on the cliffs of Chonito, he had flatly refused to risk his platoon to bring in the body of his dead company commander.

Josh was a stubborn man, and the confrontation with his slim, handsome battalion commander, Colonel Hodding, was eye-to-eye, in front of witnesses.

His punishment could legally have been far worse, and he realized it. His father, a San Francisco police captain with a nightschool law degree, had taught him to follow orders under fire, and it had not been easy to rebel. With a mind honed at Boalt Hall in Berkeley, Josh had easily led the class in Naval Courts and Boards at Quantico. He understood better than anyone that if he'd been court-martialed, he'd have faced a naval prison term.

Instead, the battalion commander had merely given Josh's old platoon—carefully trained and honed with him in battle on Bougainville—to a second lieutenant fresh from Annapolis. He'd saddled Josh with the misfits.

The penance, though potentially lethal in combat, was mild, imposed by a superb leader whose pride had been badly bruised.

Still, it was enough. He'd been too long in the bush. Everyone else was established in the base camp, resting after the campaign. No one on Guam cared if he lived or died. Except Corky. He tried to summon her presence.

She had promised to avoid night duty in the ward tonight,

and expected him back in Agana. She had ingratiated herself with the staff legal officer for him, and asked him to try for a legal billet to get himself out of the bush. He had agreed to ask for it, and to hell with his sad sack platoon.

And if a company of zealots was preparing to charge from the cave? Then hoist a stinger for me at the bar, Cork, I love you, yes I do.

"Well, Lieutenant?" his sergeant brought him back. "Don't look like these slopeheads want to join the marines."

Why would anyone?

His own answer lay in a photo and an ivory-handled sword. Both were legacies of his mother's godlike older brother, killed at Château Thierry four years before Josh was born.

His uncle Josh Anderson, the grandson of California pioneers, had volunteered the day that Congress declared war upon the Kaiser. He had grinned at Josh from his mother's dresser all his life, the globe-and-anchor gleaming on his high Marine Corps collar.

His uncle's dress sword glittered above the study desk in Josh's childhood North Beach flat; Josh had learned the saber manual-of-arms with it at eight. His father, who called the uncle Joshua the First, claimed Josh spent more time polishing the sword's ivory handle than his Latin.

Those were the seeds that had brought him here, and his mother doubtless rued the day she'd planted them.

Right now, Josh did too.

He exhaled a cloud of smoke. He couldn't delay any longer.

He had communication with the corporal above the cave, although he could not see him. He yanked the handset off the field radio strapped to his radioman's back.

"Jessup, your BAR guys set?" His voice was trembling, as he'd feared. The corporal had two men with automatic rifles hidden in the brush somewhere above.

A crackle of static blasted the jungle. Damn! If he lost communications he was shafted.

The corporal answered, beneath the garbled hash.

"Yes sir, all set." Corporal Jessup, for once, sounded cool. Still, he was a fuck-up like the rest.

"Ten seconds, tell 'em."

"Aye-aye, sir."

"*I'm* ready, sir," the sergeant grinned, trying to pressure him.

"Ten seconds, you guys!" yelled Jessup unexpectedly, from above. "Mac! Little Abner! Heads up!"

The sergeant groaned and the nisei, who suspected that the mysterious Captain Wada spoke English, clapped his hand to his forehead and groaned. Josh squeezed the button on the handset: "*Handsignals*, asshole!"

The sergeant glanced at him quickly, not criticizing, just evaluating him, as usual. Josh cringed inside. The sergeant was right: you couldn't talk like that to a corporal in the hearing of his men.

"Aye-aye, *sir!*" gabbled Jessup on the radio, sounding aggrieved.

The marine above the cave had wrapped his left hand in a hanging vine. He was fumbling with his grenade. He almost dropped it: Josh tensed. The man hung on. Josh put out his cigarette, unclipped the silver bar from each collar and slipped them into his pocket. He nodded to the sergeant. The sergeant moved from behind the *latte* stone, and made a sudden chopping motion with his arm.

The marine pulled the pin with his teeth, spat it out, waited interminably, and leaned away from the slope, hanging from his vine. Suddenly he hurled his grenade into the black gaping void, then began to scramble up.

"Four, five, six, seven, eight . . ." Josh chanted softly. He was suddenly trembling. He did not want to leave the stone.

The grenade went off with a muffled *boom*, sending a shower of dust into the tropical morning, as if the mountain had sneezed.

"Move out!" he yelled. He found himself in bright sunlight, with the cave infinitely distant. He was moving in slow motion with the awful conviction that he was all by himself: he had never had this feeling on Bougainville. Was he *alone?* No, he could hear the crunch of the sergeant's boondockers behind him.

He looked up and saw the lone marine grab at a tree root, slip, and twist, clutching at anything on the cliffside, then begin to fall.

Shit, shit, shit . . .

Faster and faster slid the marine, white-faced and grimac-

ing. He struck with a thud at the bottom of the entrance, tried
to rise, and crumpled to the moist black earth in plain sight
and easy range of the cave.

Josh refused to look at him. His eyes, as he charged up the
slope, were on the entrance. There were rocks placed like
teeth in the mouth of the cave, placed there recently, not like
the blessed *latte* stone, but placed by modern men with
modern weapons, as savage as any ancient race.

If the Japs had one machine gun laid between those teeth,
just *one* . . .

He was halfway across the clearing now, still running. His
chest heaved. He needed air. The private who had fallen was
trying to roll for cover behind a growth of scrub. Smoke was
drifting from the entrance to the cave.

Josh twisted as he ran, looking for the sergeant, spotted
only the top of his helmet, barely visible behind a hummock
in the open space commanded by the cave. The sergeant had
gone to earth: his carbine barrel was poked feebly into the
sunlight, pointing up.

Chickenshit sonofabitch . . .

Zigzagging, Josh sneaked a glance down the slope. The
section from down the hill, which was supposed to be halfway across the clearing behind him, was still trickling from
the brush in two snail-paced columns, as if facing a hundred
mortars on a beach.

The marine who had fallen from the cliff wailed piteously:
"Lieutenant . . . Broke m'leg!"

Josh dropped to cover him, carbine steady on the entrance.
He saw movement behind the smoke, they were coming,
coming, shit, shit, *shit* . . .

A bedraggled, bearded Japanese in a loincloth and peaked
khaki hat, bandoliers over his bare chest, staggered from the
cave. He held two cylindrical grenades, one in each hand. He
blinked in the sunlight, spotted the fallen private, put one
grenade down, and tapped the other on a rock to arm its
picric-acid fuse. Grinning, he gauged the distance to the
fallen marine.

Ineffectually, Josh fumbled with his gun sight. Fifty yards,
seventy-five? No time to set it anyway. He settled for the
battlesight, dead on the bare belly. He got off a round and
missed: he had jerked. *Squeeze!* He slammed another round
home.

Where were the BARs? Where was his support?

The Jap whirled at the shot, spotted him in the clear, and tossed the grenade at him instead of the private. It arced in the morning sunlight, hit on the soft moist earth, and rolled toward Josh. No time to reach it, hurl it back.

Corky, Corky, Corky . . .

Josh jammed his face into the soggy earth and waited for eternity.

Nothing . . . a dud!

He heard a burst of automatic fire from above, and slowly raised his head.

The Jap was writhing outside the cave, clutching his second grenade. It exploded in a ruddy shower, cutting him in two.

For a long moment nothing moved. Josh heard footsteps behind him, and the sergeant passed him at a cautious walk, clumping ponderously up the slope, skirting the dud in front of Josh, taking cover at the side of the entrance. He hurled a phosphorus grenade inside, pulled back, then tossed in another. The booming echoes were split by a single scream, and then all was quiet.

Josh arose.

The sergeant turned. "Jesus, sir, is the Lieutenant trying to get the Silver Star?"

"You trip and fall?" Josh growled. "Or were you covering me?"

"Why, *covering* you, Lieutenant," grinned the sergeant. *"Semper fi."*

Josh watched his navy corpsman splint the private's ankle. The injured marine had been clumsy, but *he* was the one who deserved the Silver Star. Josh would write the commendation, but he'd never get it for him. He was the wrong CO.

He looked at the cave. He felt a glorious lightness in his gut. He wanted to cheer aloud. He was sure that the Jap who'd killed himself and the one that had just screamed were the sole occupants. The others had probably spotted the L-5 circling and abandoned their refuge long before Josh arrived.

About that, they'd know more in an hour or so, when they crept in behind more phosphorus grenades—flame throwers were too heavy for these slopes. Until then, with the BARs commanding the outside and everyone covering the entrance with carbines and M-1s, they were safe.

Sure enough, when they sidled into the cave, they found rice enough to sustain a company for a month, but only one more body, and no ammunition at all.

Yamato and Captain Wada had fled to the gorges below before they even came.

They poured gasoline on the rice and torched it. This afternoon, from Agana, he'd send a burial team of Filipinos and a few Seabees up to dynamite the tunnel.

Back at the bivouac he posted double pickets, in case Japs had followed them.

He took down his mosquito-netted hammock from beneath the palm trees he had grown to know so well. He looked up at the jungle growth, through which the stars had flirted, remembering the nights when he had been afraid to sleep. He chambered a round into his carbine in case of ambush and climbed into his jeep. The sergeant was mustering his men for the trip home. Josh would move out before the sergeant had them loaded into the trucks: he traveled fastest who traveled alone.

Ahead, until the next patrol, lay safety, and Corky, too. He beeped the horn in farewell, and looked back.

There was excitement at the ration cache at the other end of the clearing. Men were cocking their pieces, moving cautiously into the bush. Faces were turning in his direction. With a premonition of ill, he pulled off the road and drove back across the bivouac. The sergeant was shaking his head in disgust.

"Lieutenant, we found C-ration cartons missing. And I think we got a problem: we can't find Pappas."

Josh's presentiment darkened. Pappas was just eighteen. Josh liked him, though he was a terrible marine, the butt of the platoon, a credulous, tubby kid with a gentle smile who thought that Josh was God and would have followed him to hell. He had been a sponge diver in Key West. The sergeant, who loved to haze him, had last night enticed him into a singalong: "There's a Star Spangled Banner Waving Somewhere," a redneck country-western, the ballad of a cripple trying to enlist in the marines.

The song had become a parody of dime-store patriotism on Guam, but not for Pappas. As the rest of the platoon doubled in silent laughter, he had ended the song alone, tears streaming down his face:

Though I realize I'm crippled, that is true, sir,
Do not judge my courage by my twisted leg!
Let me show my Uncle Sam what I can do, sir,
Let me help to bring the Axis down a peg!

The target of all humor, he seemed out of place in the jungle, like an overturned crab on the beach.

The sergeant had posted him as picket this morning—probably to keep him out of the way—to guard their rations while they hit the cave.

Shit, shit, shit . . . Couldn't once, just *once*, this platoon do it right?

"Jesus Christ!" someone screamed from the perimeter. "Sergeant! Look at this!"

Josh bailed out of the jeep and crashed into the bush behind the sergeant. He found Corporal Jessup, ashen-faced, hand over mouth, and a dozen other shaken men.

Bound to a palm, bloody from face to GI boots, sagged Pappas. His jungle greens were slashed in a dozen places. He had been bayoneted slowly. His pants were down, circling his shoes, and his crotch was a gory hole.

Flies were buzzing at his mouth. Josh felt his stomach churning. He must not vomit, not here, in front of the men. He wanted to order them to cut the corpse down, but when he looked at their faces he was afraid to test their discipline: he'd have to do it himself.

He held his breath against the smell, and drew his combat knife. He began to saw through the tent-ropes binding the corpse. In a moment the sergeant joined him. Then, with the navy corpsman, they laid the bulky body down.

"Poor fucker," said the sergeant. "Probably never heard a sound."

And at the end, had been expecting Josh to charge to his rescue like the star in one of the war movies he seemed to think were real. Josh would have bet on it.

Hopelessly checking his carotid for a pulse, the corpsman moved Pappas's head. Something fell out of his mouth.

"What's that?" grunted Josh, engulfed in nausea.

"Hell, Lieutenant," said the sergeant nonchalantly, standing up, "they made him eat his balls. If he hollered for us, he hollered soprano. What you want to do now?"

Josh arose. He drew the sergeant aside: "Deploy, Sergeant. I want a thousand yards of bush searched, before we're relieved. North, south, east, and west.''

The sergeant started to protest: ''A thousand—''

''A thousand fucking yards by noon. Or Sergeant?''

''Yes sir?''

''I'll feed *your* balls to you.''

The sergeant looked into his eyes for a long moment. Then he saluted sharply, like a battleship marine.

''Aye-aye, sir. I do believe the Lieutenant, indeedy, yes I do.'' He glared at the waiting men. ''Get a litter, assholes! Haul him back and then fall in!''

By noon Josh and his men were torn, tattered and exhausted, but the thousand-yard perimeter had been searched. They had, of course, found nothing, but at least they had survived.

A lieutenant and his platoon arrived to relieve him. Josh was grateful: Let *them* chase the little bastards down, not that they ever could.

He climbed into his jeep and led his platoon south to Agana.

The sight of poor Pappas had changed his mind. He was staying with his outfit. The regiment was scheduled for a landing on Chichijima, a flyspeck in the Bonins off Japan.

When he told Corky, she'd probably toss him back the globe and anchor he'd given her to wear.

Corky had got billeted in a room alone in the temporary Quonset they'd built for the nurses—God knew how, as an ensign, she'd worked that—and had foresightedly removed the window screen so he could crawl in and avoid the bitch head nurse.

The golden moon lit up the tiny cubicle. On her creaking bunk, he stroked her hair. ''Come here,'' he whispered. ''Come here, you.''

She had got quite drunk at the club, and her amber eyes had blazed when he turned down the legal billet, but now, all at once, it was right, better than ever before, and she was tossing, writhing, with her wrist jammed in her mouth because the head nurse was quartered in the next room, and for a long moment they were one . . .

For the first time in months he slept, really slept, deeply and fully.

At dawn he heard a rooster crow from some *chamorro*'s shack, and the rumble of thunder at sea.

Corky slumbered, face innocent, black-Irish hair wild on the pillow.

He wanted her again, but it was almost 0700 hours, and he could not stay. There was a briefing in Colonel Hodding's tent at 0745, on the Chichijima landing. He crawled out the window like a thief.

Chichijima?

It sounded like the vector for a tropical disease.

CHAPTER 4

The boyish lieutenant (jg) squirmed uncomfortably in the leather ready-room chair. The compartment was a small one, for the carrier *San Jacinto* was tiny, built hurriedly after Pearl Harbor on the hull of a light cruiser. The air was choked with cigarette smoke and clammy with drafts from air-conditioning ducts that spewed more noise than ventilation.

The jg's name was George H. W. Bush. One day he would become Vice President of the United States.

Son of a Wall Street investment banker, he had joined the navy straight out of Phillips Academy in Andover on his eighteenth birthday. A year ago, when he had won his wings at Corpus Christi, he was nineteen and had been the youngest commissioned pilot in the U.S. Navy.

Now he had just turned twenty. He was a skinny young man, over six-feet three, a poor fit for the ready-room chairs, more comfortable in the cockpit of the enormous single-engine torpedo bomber he flew.

He had blue eyes and untamed hayrick hair. The back of his khaki flight suit was dark with sweat. On his chest, navy wings stamped in gold had gradually disappeared from a scuffed leather namepatch, leaving only their outline.

He was taking notes on a knee pad strapped to his right leg, and nothing in the briefing from the stubby air intelligence officer with the brush-cut hair on the podium was calculated to increase his own confidence, or that of his squadron mates.

Task Force 58, under Admiral Marc Mitscher, was heading north toward Iwo Jima and the Bonin Islands off Japan. Bush had flown against fortified islands before, in the prelanding strikes against Guam, but most of his missions lately had been uneventful antisubmarine patrols.

He had recently survived a ditching with his two-man crew, slamming into the sea riding four five-hundred-pound depth charges. He and his men had narrowly escaped the explosion by rowing their raft away from the sinking fuselage before the charges detonated at depth. He had spent two days on the USS *Bronson*, the destroyer that picked him up, then flown a new TBM back to his carrier.

Bush christened the new plane after Barbara Pierce, daughter of the publisher of *Redbook* and *McCall's* magazines, a coed at Smith and his longtime sweetheart and wife-to-be. He had BARBIE stenciled on the nose. His two crewmen—John Delaney and Leo Nadeau—followed suit, painting their own girls' names at their stations.

Now they were ready to take up the war again.

When the briefing was over, he felt a hand on his shoulder and turned. Lieutenant (jg) William G. White—called "Ted" —was aboard the carrier as a squadron gunnery officer. White was a family friend, older than Bush—everyone was. He was a Yale graduate from St. Paul, Minnesota.

"What you hitting up here, George?" he asked Bush.

"Iwo Jima. Later maybe Chichijima, in the Bonins."

For weeks White had been asking Bush to take him on a combat mission, in place of his gunner, Nadeau.

"This time, George?" he begged.

"These are supposed to be tough islands," Bush warned him.

"George?" pleaded White. "Please?"

"You'll need the skipper's permission," Bush said reluctantly, and let it go at that.

They were scheduled to turn south again in a few days to support the invasion of Peleliu in the Palaus, so the strikes might not happen at all.

CHAPTER 5

In the spring of 1944, at the white-plastered headquarters of General Yoshio Tachibana's First Mixed Brigade on Chichijima, Major Michihiko Fujihara presented his temporary orders to the brigade engineering officer.

"Were you able to quarter me with some whites?" Fujihara asked.

"It is so arranged, Major."

The colonel bowed lower and longer than necessary.

Major Fujihara shifted uneasily. He was a quiet, gray-haired man, an architect in civilian life. He had the fine, slightly hooked nose of the Japanese aristocracy. He wore a ready smile. He was well built and carried himself with great dignity.

He wore on the red tabs of his collar only the dark brown metal badge of the Engineers Corps, warranting no special consideration from the likes of the colonel. But his accent held traces of the palace, for his mother had been the daughter of a viscount and his late wife a baroness.

He was modest, and actually regretted that his manner of speech and bearing seemed to humble army seniors, though he himself was the son of a mere army general and bore no title.

His father had won fame in the assault on the German forts at Tsingtao when Japan joined the Allies in 1914, but the major sometimes felt like an impostor when his superiors in the service became obsequious.

As a young university graduate in the twenties, he had worked under Frank Lloyd Wright on the plans for Tokyo's Imperial Hotel, in which his family—along with the imperial house—had invested. He had helped to change downtown Tokyo from a gawky provincial village to one of the world's great cities.

Volunteering for the Engineer Corps after Pearl Harbor, he had gained a reputation—unwarranted, in his own eyes—as an expert on field fortifications.

Years ago he had read the history of Nathaniel Savory and Elias Bancroft's outcast colony. He had once lectured on earthquake-proof architecture at the University of Hawaii and his English was excellent. But one could always improve it, and he was grateful for the opportunity to live temporarily among Chichijima's whites.

Now he discussed his engineering mission on the island with the colonel and left. At the headquarters motor pool, the transportation sergeant offered him a driver for the battered scout car the colonel had arranged for him. But the major declined and drove it himself.

He eased along Omura's single dusty road, under a cliff that bristled with gun emplacements and was pocked with tunnels. One of his missions was to inspect their shorings, and he would begin tomorrow.

There was a tropical smell to the air and a scent like Hawaii's. He left the village and continued along the shore toward the head of Futami Harbor, to Yankeetown, as the general's chief of staff had called it.

He parked under a palm in front of the Bancroft house, the largest Western-style cottage at the head of the bay. He noted the neat stone pathway, the clean clapboard porch, and the newly thatched roof.

Good. Most people who lived on islands, he had observed, were less than tidy, even the Japanese.

A tall brown-haired *gaijin* lad with vivid green eyes—no, not *gaijin*, he remembered, but probably naturalized Japanese—trotted down the pathway, wearing a kimono, a sash, and a blue-visored school cap. The boy saluted, bowed deeply, introduced himself in perfect Japanese as Matthew Calbraith Bancroft, and asked if he could help him with his field chest.

The major, amused, returned the salute and put out his hand, Western-style. The boy glanced at it uncertainly, then grasped it and bowed deeply again. He reached suddenly into the backseat of the scout car, lifted out the major's sword, and handed it to him reverently.

In his steady green eyes the major read courage, and a certain smoldering unease.

Unlike most officers, the major seldom wore his *tachi* sword except on formal official visits. But with the emerald eyes watching him expectantly, he found himself buckling it on.

Mrs. Bancroft and her daughter Alicia were kneeling at their door to welcome him. As he drew closer, he was startled to see that both were lovely, in the Western sense, with tawny skin and soft, golden hair. The sister had the emerald eyes of her brother. The mother's eyes were gray, and calm as the Seto Sea.

He recalled that his father once told him that at the turn of the century, when the army first began its climb to ascendancy, Bonin women—*chamorro*, Hawaiian, and white blood mixed—had been selected for their beauty to serve in officers' brothels in Tokyo. Now he could see why.

In the mother's face he saw intelligence and curiosity. She frowned as she glanced at the sword. He removed it, wishing that he could tell her that he had only worn it to please her son. He drew off his brown leather boots, and slid into woven straw *waraji* sandals.

He was stirred by the woman's beauty, and the open smile on her daughter's face.

A lonely widower on this fragrant, forgotten island, he had found a home.

On Chichijima, Major Michihiko Fujihara had been assigned several engineering missions, but one was overriding. In a ravine behind the seaplane base, he was to make a study of the shoring and construction of a huge cave, excavated long before the war. Inside it was an immense concrete revetment, shaped like an American Quonset hut. It was airtight and—incredibly—lined with sheet copper, more valuable to Japan than gold.

General Sumi, head of 2nd Field Army Intelligence in Hiroshima, had told him that if Chichijima escaped assault, the National Archives of Japan would be shipped by cargo submarine to Chichijima after the Kyushu landings and stored in the Copper Cave.

Fujihara doubted that the archives would ever get this far, but he strengthened the shoring and engineered artillery emplacements around it, placing them with care, for the Yankees were coming on inexorably.

By June, as a huge amphibious fleet carrying the 2nd and 4th Marine Divisions clustered off Saipan, U.S carrier aircraft bombed Chichijima and battleships shelled it.

In the Palau group, to the south, his only son Tohru was a lieutenant in the 14th Infantry Division on Peleliu, with thirty thousand crack troops under General Sadao Inoue. Everyone in Chichijima headquarters was sure that Peleliu's time was near. After that, the Americans would land on Iwo Jima and perhaps here, and then the main islands of Japan.

Fujihara spent little off-duty time in the officers' mess but much with the Bancroft family. He learned from Alicia to pick island hymns on Elias' ancient banjo, and taught her tunes from Tokyo. He became Matt's mentor in all things, teaching him to slice a serve on the garrison's tennis court and cheering him at the school's baseball diamond when he pitched.

He struggled with his feelings about Matt's mother as best he could. She was after all the wife of a fellow soldier and of tainted blood, only one-eighth Japanese. But when she served him his evening meal, with her curves moving softly beneath her light *yukata*, his blood heated. So he would think of a lily floating in a clear, unruffled pool, and his passion would recede.

One golden Chichijima evening he returned from a day in the tunnels at the southern end of the island. He found her kneeling on the porch, with a little wicker basket beside her, darning socks that he had intended to have mended by the mess servant at headquarters. Gently, he removed the darning egg from her hand and set the basket aside.

Matt, an acolyte in the church, was with Reverend Gonzales cleaning the church's silver. Alicia's bicycle was gone from below the porch steps: she must be shopping in the village. The ancient fisherman who helped Lorna tend her little truck garden was digging nearby. The major gathered

his courage and said, in English, "Lorna . . . It is all *right* to
call you Lorna?"

She smiled, and his throat tightened. She had strong,
straight teeth, dazzling white, and her cheeks dimpled when
she laughed. Her sea-gray eyes held no hint of her Japanese
blood. They shone softly. "Of course."

"It is a beautiful name. Though I have trouble with the *l*."

"My father liked the novel *Lorna Doone*."

"Then you must call me Mickey, as Matt does."

"Mickey-*san*, you mean," she grinned. "Respectful, but
terrible Japanese."

He chuckled, and then grew serious. "Lorna, it is strange,
the guilt I feel at being here. This war, which is bringing you
such loneliness . . ."

"Not so much, since you have come . . ."

He found his cheeks going hot. "You are too kind. What I
meant to say . . . I have been alone in life, since my wife
died, I am used to it, war or peace, but now women like you
are lonely, and other men die for me." Her eyes fell. Why
had he said that? The presence of her husband, three hundred
miles away on the unspeakable moonscape of Iwo, with the
Yankees bombing every day, intruded. He swallowed and
charged ahead: "I feel bad, because I have such pleasure here
with you."

She was suddenly serious. "Don't feel bad." Her eyes
were level on his. "You did not start the war."

"Nor did your husband," he blurted miserably.

The sun had set, and she shivered. "His eyes died when he
stepped on that boat," she murmured. "He knew he was
doomed, and I know now."

Yes! On that island, under Kurabayashi, all would perish
when the Yankees came. The general himself had left the
samurai sword which had been in his family for generations at
home in Tokyo, along with a saber presented him by the
emperor when he graduated from staff college. Kurabayashi
knew his garrison was finished, and so did everyone else.

Nevertheless Fujihara, disgusted with himself for wanting
another's wife, refused to accept her husband's doom as fact.
"He is not dead *now*. You must hope."

"He will die on that rock," she said mistily. "You know
it, and I. Only the Reverend and the children can hope."

"He is not dead yet," the major insisted. "And he suffers,

while I . . ." He sucked in his breath. "My father was a fighting general! What is *he* thinking in the world below, to see me living as a prince?"

She smiled again, and waved her hand at the little truck garden, the thatched barn. "Scarcely a prince, Mickey. Not here, with holes in your socks." She reached for the basket, and held his eyes. "A baron, mayhaps, if you let me mend them?"

He longed to take her in his arms. "No, that is not for you to do."

Her eyes grew tender. "Your bath," she murmured. She had never bathed him, though one might have expected a hostess to do so; he had of course never commented, as a matter of delicacy, assuming that some Protestant ethic handed down through the generations inhibited her. Because she had so far hesitated, the anticipation aroused him. Heart pounding, he drew off his boots and followed her into the house.

As steam curled from the enormous pinewood *ofuro* tub in the family bath behind the kitchen, he sat naked on a wooden stool. She poured water down his back, lathered him with the last bar of prewar soap in the household. She rinsed him clean, then soaped herself, rinsed, and followed him in.

In the bath, he looked into her eyes, and her gaze never wavered, and he knew that she would be his. Emerging, they dried and he led her to his bed—which had been Matt's—and after they made love he murmured in English of things he had never dared to speak to his wife in Japanese.

She had never known such calm, she said, and he believed her, for he had known none either so beautiful as this.

In the weeks after that, though they slept together frequently, they were circumspect, and Matt would never know, though the major was sure that Alicia suspected, and accepted what she sensed.

Matt called him *sensei*—teacher. Fujihara told him of meeting the crown prince, now the emperor, with Frank Lloyd Wright, in the glorious days when their Imperial Hotel, floating on its fluid foundations, had confounded all their critics and survived the Great Earthquake.

The boy was fascinated with tales of old Japan, perhaps because his own roots lay in such porous ancestral soil. One morning at breakfast, which the two shared as they kneeled at the *kotatsu*, they agreed that the true samurai was gone. But his spirit and his code lived on. The modern samurai—like the Anglo-Saxon knight—was courageous, just, benevolent, polite, honest, loyal, and compassionate. But—regardless of how those in the West scoffed at his chauvinism—he chose death always before surrender.

"And so he will win in the end, sir?" asked Matt. "He will win, if he's willing to die?"

It was August 1944. Peleliu would soon be under attack, and the major's thoughts dwelt forever on his son.

"I think we will not *always* win, Matt," he answered. He added, in English, "On Peleliu, we shall not."

Matt's eyes widened. "In *Japan,* though, if it comes to that? We shall win on the home islands?"

For a long while the major was silent.

"I think not," he said.

Matt seemed shocked. But the war *was* lost, though few in the army admitted it, and none ever spoke their doubts. The major was not worried, though. Matt was too bright to repeat his words.

The emperor, though partly responsible for the war himself, was intelligent enough to recognize defeat. But he had fallen into the hands of fools and madmen.

Still, samurais must perish for the imperial honor, however doomed their cause.

"Matt, does it matter who 'wins'? If we are willing to die before we surrender?"

The boy considered this for a long time, and finally shook his head. "No, sir, I fancy not."

CHAPTER 6

*B*y 1944, air raids had become part of the Bancrofts' family life. They spent long days and nights huddled in the hillside caves, and Matt cheered with his classmates when they saw U.S. planes shot down.

At six P.M. one cool evening, after a carrier raid, Alicia was alone, spading the onion rows in their truck garden. She was tired from the excitement, and famished. She wanted only to finish and get into a hot tub.

A motorcycle with an empty sidecar, driven by a private, roared up the road from headquarters. To her astonishment, it pulled up beside her, motor clucking quietly.

"Do you know English?" the driver demanded.

"A little, sir," she mumbled cautiously. What did he want?

The man patted the sidecar. "Climb in, young girl. My colonel has need of you."

Alarmed, she said: "My mother will be here soon. She expects to find me home."

The rider twisted his throttle, shattering the quiet. "The colonel expects *me* to find someone who speaks English! Now!"

She shook her head. She could not meet an officer in her baggy *monpe* pantaloons, like a peasant from the fields. She

31

invoked Mickey-san: "Major Fujihara quarters here, sir! I must prepare for his return today!"

He slammed his palm on his sidecar and began to dismount. "Do I have to put you in myself?"

Hurriedly, she climbed in. In a cloud of dust and a roar of power, they raced for the eastern peaks.

The private slammed around the curves on the dirt road. He twisted through the ridges north of Mount Asahi, like a stunt rider in a cinema show. The wind was raising havoc with Alicia's hair, but she lost her apprehension in the thrill of the sliding, jolting turns.

They crested the backbone of the island and began to wind down the hairpin curves toward Washington Beach, spraying rocks and dust behind them. To her left she glimpsed concrete gun emplacements, commanding the narrow, five-hundred-yard-wide strait to little Anijima—Elder Brother Island—on the north.

She and Matt had often taken this road before the war, pushing their bicycles up, coasting gloriously down. She recognized a crippled white oak where they had paused for water from his canteen. At the end, they had swooped down through this breadfruit grove, parked their bikes, and raced barefoot along the golden strand.

Here on the leeward side of the island the surf was unexciting, but there were plenty of abalone to bring home: reds (so tender you could pry them out and chew them raw, right there) and greens and pinks. You ignored the tough little blacks. And you didn't even have to dive: the abs were in plain sight, three feet deep, their shells like muddy cow dung from above, clinging to the tidal rocks almost everywhere you looked. This beach had been their treasure chest.

But now, in the pandanus scrub fringing the strand, were lines of tents, and behind them, hidden in the foliage, tunnels into the hillside. A company of Korean labor troops was lined up at a huge *kimchi* pot. The smell of their garlic and unwashed bodies was enough to turn a Japanese stomach sour, the private said, parking his motorcycle. He switched off his engine, which died with a gurgle and a bang.

He motioned her to follow him and started for the beach. She spotted ammunition bunkers everywhere, like prostrate bodies hidden in the brush.

A long thatched hut, once a boathouse for Charlie Washington's canoes, was a mess hall now. Outside sat ranks of empty army shoes; inside, scores of soldiers, rice bowls in hand, squatted on mats at their evening meal.

She was famished. "What do you want me here for?"

The private only ordered: "Follow me."

They emerged from evening shadows onto the beach. She stared at their special cove. There were ugly tank barricades—six-foot rails welded together at their centers to form monstrous child's pickup jacks—tossed as if by giants along the golden strand.

Beer and sake bottles were everywhere, and rotting food. A half dozen soldiers squatted over a slit-trench latrine where Matt and she had picnicked: shocked, she looked away quickly, but the odor of night soil was heavy in the air.

She followed the private along a path skirting the edge of the scrub. A knot of soldiers was gathered ahead, sucking on beer bottles. They stared at her, astonished, and one of them laughed and made an obscene gesture with his finger and his hand. She felt her cheeks go red.

All at once she noticed, tethered by his waist to a tree, a big black-haired American pilot sitting in the shade. On his flight suit she saw golden wings. When he saw her he rose incredulously to his feet. His knee was bound tightly in an oily rag. He had a gold tooth, which flashed in the dim light.

"What the hell! You some goddamn kind of *spy?*"

A soldier shoved him with a rifle butt, pointing to the sand. The pilot sat slowly down, and she could not meet his eye.

A weathered telephone pole stood near, on sandy soil near the edge of the trees. From a ten-foot-high crosspiece dangled two canvas dummies filled with sand. They were bayonet targets, she knew; there was one at the Turihama drill field, too, where the school drillmaster had taken the students, girls and all, to practice with bamboo spears.

Across the nearest dummy someone had painted characters for "MacArthur" in *katakana* characters and smeared the whole with red. The dummies were well used, with patches everywhere.

Behind the pole, in the darkening shadows of a bamboo grove, stood a thatched frame cabin with open *shoji* screens. From within came a deep voice, cursing in Japanese. The private told her to wait, and entered the hut. He emerged with a bald, erect sergeant, who stalked past the gathered men, ignoring their bows.

The sergeant walked to the painted dummy. He drew his sword, ran his thumb along the cutting surface, measured his distance, and swung. The blade arced in the fading light. The dummy, its rope cut only inches above its top, dropped with a thud. The line hardly quivered. The sergeant barked an order, and one of the men pulled the dummy away.

"Bring the other *gaijin* bastard out!" roared the sergeant.

There was a commotion at the shadowed door of the hut, and she squinted into the fading light. Her heart was beating violently. A lean Caucasian stumbled along the path, followed by a stocky private with a bayoneted rifle.

The prisoner seemed much younger than the black-haired pilot, hardly older than she. He was cradling his left arm in his right hand. He had brown hair, which escaped in every direction, like that of a child's doll. His nose was raw and sunburned. He wore a tan flying-suit. It was sweat-soaked and the left sleeve was ripped off. A grease mark slashed across his neck. On his forehead was a clotted cut.

She had a sudden impulse to go to him and clean his wound. Roughly, the private shoved him under the dangling rope. As she stared, the sergeant grabbed the Yankee's hands and hoisted them.

"Agh . . ." yelled the American, wincing in pain and pulling free. "Shit!"

She gasped as the sergeant slapped him across the face. The prisoner staggered. The sergeant and the dispatch rider lifted the man's arms again, tied them tightly with the rope, and left him standing, hands raised as if in supplication.

"Sir," called the sergeant, back toward the hut. "The radioman's ready!" He looked at Alicia. "Are you?"

"For what?" she muttered. She felt faint. "What are you going to do?"

"Ask him some questions."

A corporal, sucking on a beer bottle, was staring her angrily in the eye because she was white.

They all stiffened suddenly, throwing their shoulders back, hands extended along their trouser legs. The corporal dropped his beer bottle.

An officer walked heavily along the path leading from the hut. He was in a light tropical uniform of mustard khaki, as if fresh from Southeast Asia or the Philippines. He wore leather boots. A curved *tachi* sword with a diamond-laced hilt dangled from his tunic. A pistol-holster strap crisscrossed his Sam Browne belt. He wore an open white shirt and a tan pith helmet. On his unbuttoned tunic collar glittered three stars on red-and-gold tabs.

She recognized his rank and corps: *kempeitai*. She had heard of him: Colonel Kondo. Yankeetown rumor had it that he was not a good man to cross. He had a receding chin and narrow, glinting eyes. A scar from cheek to chin gave him a devilish look, twisting his face into a grimace, like a *myo* idol stationed by Buddha to guard a temple.

As he stepped from the shadow of the mountain, he paused for a moment, fingers caressing the hilt of his sword. He surveyed the scene: soldiers, prisoner, fallen dummy. His eyes fell on Alicia. He seemed amused.

"A girl?"

"The only person home, sir," said the dispatch rider.

The colonel smiled faintly. "Well, I'm Colonel Yasushi Kondo, of General Tachibana's staff."

She bowed deeply. The silly *monpe* pantaloons made her feel like an *eta* beggar. She raised her eyes: "I am Alicia Bancroft, sir. Major Michihiko Fujihara is quartered with my family." Ashamed that she had slighted her father, she forced herself to add: "I am the daughter of Superior Private Lemuel Bancroft, Imperial Japanese Army."

"And you speak English?" His voice was soft, not at all like the sergeant's growl. "You look as though you should."

"Yes sir."

Her mother was probably frantic. Suddenly she hated the dispatch rider, the soldiers, the ugly, velvet-voiced colonel. But she stood frozen before them, hands moist with sweat, wishing she had brushed her hair.

"Good," said the colonel. His eyes flicked away and he mumbled: "I speak not one word." Somehow she did not believe him: in translating, she must be careful, in case he did. He took her arm and guided her toward the prisoner. He had a steely grip. "Ask him his name."

The American was staring at her in confusion, through blue-gray eyes.

"He wants to know your name," she squeaked, and cleared her throat. "Your name," she repeated, more calmly.

The prisoner nodded and licked his lips. He glanced toward the pilot and swallowed. The words tumbled out in a drawl that she could hardly fathom: "Hamilton. Jerry Lee Hamilton. Aviation Radioman Third Class, U.S. Naval Reserve. Service Number 389 984."

She repeated it, and translated rank and service number into Japanese. The colonel reached for the ID tags dangling from the prisoner's neck. She flinched as he ripped them off, leaving a welt on the skin. He handed them to Alicia. "The same?"

"Yes sir."

The colonel peered at the tags. "Nothing else?" She whiffed sake as the colonel pointed to a letter "O" below the serial number. "What does that mean?"

"Just the English letter *O*, sir, I don't know."

"Well, ask him!"

She asked.

"My blood type," the prisoner said. "Are you . . . Are you a prisoner too?"

She found herself blushing. What must the young man think? It was mortifying. She turned to the colonel. "His blood type," she translated.

"Ask him his ship, the carrier he flew from?"

She repeated the question.

"I can't tell him that! You gotta make him understand, I can't tell him that." He stared at her. "What are you? A German?"

"I am Japanese!" she quavered. She was trembling. She must get herself under control or her family would lose face.

She heard a slither of steel at her side and a thump as the flat of the colonel's sword lashed the radioman across the chest. The American grunted and his knees buckled. Prevented from falling by the rope, he hung awkwardly for a moment, his knees barely touching the sand. Somehow he struggled erect.

"He will *answer*," murmured the colonel. "Not talk to you. And *you* will not talk to *him!* Now, the name of his carrier!"

"Yes sir." She looked at the prisoner. He met her gaze stubbornly. She was confused. He had already surrendered alive, forfeiting his honor. Why was he now balking? He was only provoking the colonel, couldn't he see?

"Your ship," she urged, "please! You must tell him the name of your ship!"

The young man swallowed, his Adam's apple bobbing.

"Hang in, son," called the pilot. "Hang in, Jerry-boy."

Colonel Kondo whirled on the officer, started to speak, then turned to the sergeant. "You will spear the officer first," he muttered, "and then this one will talk!" His eyes narrowed at the radioman. "Your ship, I asked!"

She winced as the sword slammed the American again. This time the radioman took longer to straighten his body, and when he did, she read fear in the blue-gray eyes. Her throat tightened. He was only a few years older than Matt!

"Ask him again," the colonel murmured patiently.

"Mr. Hamilton . . ." she began.

But "mister" didn't seem right: he seemed too young. Astonished, she felt tears rising to her eyes.

"Please!" she faltered. "You must needs give the name of your ship!"

The sailor's lip trembled. His voice broke, but his eyes never wavered. "I don't 'must needs' give a fucking thing! He gets my name, rank, and serial number. And that's all. Under the Geneva Convention!"

"Geneva?" muttered the colonel in Japanese. "Did the *gaijin* say *Geneva?*"

She didn't answer.

The colonel's voice rose. The scar on his face turned red: he jerked a thumb toward the other. "His pilot was strafing a fishing boat when the 308th shot him down! One of his friends dropped a booby-trapped fountain pen for a child to pick up!" The soldiers stirred angrily. "Their ships are shelling women and babies on Saipan! Their flamethrowers roast our soldiers in their caves! Geneva? Girl, tell him I want the name of his carrier. Now, or his pilot dies!"

There was dead silence. The smell of the latrine drifted on the evening breeze. A seagull cawed from the glistening beach, gull and sand both golden in the quickly setting sun. The tide was going out.

"Jerry Lee," she begged, terrified, "you better . . . better . . ."

All at once she was crying, and could not speak. The colonel whirled toward her. "Stop bawling, girl! You're not a child!"

From the road came the squeal of brakes, and the sound of sliding tires. Alicia turned.

Mickey-san appeared from the grove of beach-side trees, striding along the strand.

Thank God . . .

His head was high, his shoulders back, iron-gray hair riffling in the breeze. He wore neither hat nor sword, and his tunic was unbuttoned, but he looked more soldierly than the colonel with all his trappings. A private, writing a letter at the edge of the pandanus trees, arose and saluted as he passed. The major did not even nod.

He marched straight to the colonel.

The colonel eyed him coldly. "Yes, Major? What is it?"

Mickey-san barely bowed. He put a hand around her waist, and she could feel the fingers trembling with anger.

"This girl is just seventeen!" the major blazed. His precise, aristocratic voice was heavy with scorn. "She must not be involved!"

"Is that a fact?" The colonel tapped his sword against his boots. He motioned the major away from the troops. Alicia heard him quietly ask: "And who are you?"

"Major Fujihara, chief engineer, Second Army Headquarters."

"You're a long way from Hiroshima, Major," murmured the colonel. "You should remember that. But Fujihara is an important name." He studied the major. "Perhaps you bear a title. Baron, viscount? Surely, not a prince?"

"I have no title."

"But are close to many, I would say," mused Colonel Kondo. "Unhappily, you're a long way from the Imperial Palace, too."

"And you, sir, are a long way from General Tachibana and the island headquarters! Where your prisoner should be!"

The colonel beamed. "You have much to learn about General Tachibana, and island headquarters, too." He slammed his sword into its sheath. "The prisoners belong to Major Matoba of the 308th on Mikazuki Mountain. His machine-gun company shot them down and captured them and this unit bought them for a case of dynamite. But he is mine to interrogate as long as necessary. And he will be interrogated here, away from headquarters. Therefore, I need the girl."

"She's of American blood."

"Obviously." The colonel smiled. "And so, disloyal?"

"She's quite loyal. Nevertheless, she should not be here. It does no credit to the army, nor the emperor." Mickey-san held the colonel's eyes. "Colonel, I speak English. I request to relieve her."

For a moment the two stared at each other. Finally the colonel shrugged. "Granted. *You*, at least, won't cry."

The major bowed and said: "Wait in the scout car, Alicia." His voice dropped. "Speak to no one of this. When the Americans come, it could haunt you."

She ran to the car, fearful of what would happen to the young American and his officer. She did not fear the Americans, if they came. She had been forced to translate, it was not her fault.

But she was full of shame. She was sure that she had failed the army and the emperor and lost her father face.

Major Fujihara watched her start back to his car. He was sick with fear. If American occupying forces learned that a beautiful white girl had questioned a prisoner for the *kempeitai*, only the gods knew what they would conclude.

He moved reluctantly back to the interrogation. The radioman refused to give the name of his carrier. Fujihara could not be sure if the colonel's rage was real, or an interrogation technique, for he glanced continuously and quite coolly at his watch, as if he had an appointment.

"Ask him the name of his ship once again!" the colonel demanded tersely.

"Mr. Hamilton, your carrier?"

The boy, tight-lipped, shook his head. Kondo strode closer, boots creaking, and slapped him across the face. The pilot shouted a protest from the tree. Kondo glanced at him scornfully and thrashed the flat of the blade across the radioman's chest.

Fujihara had had enough. Quietly, so that the troops would not hear, he quoted to Kondo the Japanese Regulations for Handling Prisoners of War, Chapter I, Article 2: "Prisoners of war shall be treated with a spirit of goodwill and shall never be subjected to cruelties or humiliation."

Kondo laughed and ordered his sergeant to fix his bayonet. "Ask him the name of his carrier!"

"Son, your ship!" begged Fujihara. He had an awful feeling of doom. "You must!"

"I . . . I can't!" sobbed Hamilton.

"Bayonet the bastard," Kondo ordered. "In both legs."

"Do not touch him!" barked Fujihara.

Kondo whirled on him, raising his sword in the classic *kendo* position of attack. "Silence, Major," he growled. He nodded at the sergeant. "Do it!"

The sergeant winced, lunged at the boy and bayoneted him in the right thigh, then quickly in the left. The young man screamed in pain and shouted: *"Hornet! USS Hornet!* Oh, my God!"

Fujihara's heart sank. Everyone knew that the *Hornet* had been sunk in battle long ago. "Bind his wounds!" he ordered. No one moved.

"The *Hornet* was sunk," smiled Kondo, "in 1942. Tell him that."

Fujihara translated sadly. The boy's eyes closed in agony. "All right," he moaned. *"Enterprise,* the USS *Enterprise!"*

"Hai!" growled Kondo, without waiting for a translation. "That answer we shall test throughout the night." He turned to the sergeant. "Your men will fix bayonets. They shall line up. Each shall stab him lightly. And the one who finally kills him shall be beaten!"

"I cannot!" a soldier cried, bolting for the shadows. He was clubbed down by another, and dragged to Kondo, who slugged him to the ground, kicked him once, and left him retching on the sand.

The soldiers began to jab carefully at the radioman with their bayonets. He screamed, and his officer, howling curses, struggled to be free. Colonel Kondo picked a bamboo spear off the pile lying near the structure. He handed it to a superior private, and gestured toward the officer.

"Run him through!"

The private took the spear, approached the pilot, closed his eyes, lunged, and speared him through the chest. The officer fell backward with a belly-wrenching groan. He writhed endlessly, gurgling, with blood rushing from his mouth, and after an eternity lay still.

The air-raid siren began to moan from the other side of the mountain. Kondo ordered all personnel to shelter, except the soldier he had beaten, who would stand guard on the radioman. "If he survives this raid, you will be the first to spear him. He will be our dummy, and you will all use spears, for that is what we shall have to use when the Americans land."

Fujihara could hear the drone of aircraft in the dusk, and the first faint bursts of antiaircraft from the southern tip of the island.

He broke from the group and trotted down the beach to Alicia and his car.

Alicia had waited an hour under a lopsided moon by the time the air-raid siren wailed and Mickey-san came running. He took the road savagely, whipping through the turns like a race driver. Neither spoke. When they reached the tunnel entrance, he reached across her and opened the door.

He warned her again to say nothing to anyone but her mother. He felt a great dread that for her, the killing on Washington Beach was not over.

"What shall I say to Matt?" she asked.

"That I drove you down to see the bomb damage. Say that."

She bowed her head. *"Hai."* She started to get out. "Mickey-san?"

"Yes?" In the light of the dashboard, her face seemed pale.

"What will happen to the Americans?"

He could not tell her that one was dead and the other doomed. "They are brave men. They will be sent to Japan, of course. To a camp. And when the Americans release them, will speak of how they were treated." He hesitated, looking at her strangely. "What did you *think* would happen to them?"

"Colonel Kondo said he'd *kill* the pilot."

He swallowed. "Bluffing."

"Will they torture that boy tomorrow? He looks hardly older than Matt!"

"And younger than my son." Mickey-san reached across and touched her cheek. "Sleep well in the tunnel, my daughter. Rest your mind." His eyes grew thoughtful. "No one will torture him."

He watched her as she pounded on the steel tunnel door. When it opened, he drove off toward her house.

• • •

In his room, Major Fujihara strapped on his sword. Then he sped to island headquarters, seeking General Tachibana. Little Captain Ohta, one of Tachibana's aides, told him that the general was dining at Colonel Kondo's house on the beach on Anijima Strait, as he did almost every night. Major Fujihara's heart sank, but he could not abandon his mission now.

He found the house by moonlight, a well-constructed wood-and-plaster structure as fine as the general's itself. He took off his boots and entered. Colonel Kondo stood with his cook at a simmering sukiyaki pot. Kneeling at the table, hashi sticks poised, was General Tachibana, stubby and square-jawed. He was bleary-eyed, sweating, and obviously drunk. Major Matoba, a shaven-headed giant who commanded the 308th Battalion, kneeled opposite him.

Fujihara saluted the general, who replied with a wave.

"You have come about the events on Washington Beach?" Kondo smiled. "You could not wait to go through channels?"

"There seems no time." Fujihara bowed to the general, took a deep breath, and blurted: "Sir, you should know that a violation of army regulations has taken place. A prisoner has been killed and a radioman wounded . . ."

Matoba, chewing with massive jaws, asked Kondo: "The two *we* shot down earlier?"

Kondo nodded. "Yes."

Matoba grinned. "The Washington Beach detachment bought them from me, General, for a case of dynamite. They lost two soldiers in this morning's raid. Their commander wants to raise their fighting spirit."

General Tachibana lifted his sake cup. "I applaud that."

Fujihara wondered if he was having a nightmare. He licked his lips. "But the officer's *already* been killed, sir! And the radioman wounded! The Prisoner of War Bureau has ordered that prisoners must be sent to Japan!"

"Not these, certainly," the general belched. "That would dishonor Matoba, for he has already sold them!"

Kondo lifted a piece of meat from the pot with his hashi sticks. "Have a drink, Fujihara, and try this. It will make your stomach stronger."

"Go ahead," chuckled Matoba. "It is turkey-liver."

Fujihara looked at it curiously. It could not be turkey. So far as he knew, there were not a dozen turkeys in all Japan.

He was surprised that Matoba, an uneducated thug, had ever heard of one.

All at once he had an awful thought. Americans, everyone knew, referred to their big navy torpedo bombers as "turkeys," as did Japanese identification pamphlets and the flash cards spotters used.

No. Ridiculous . . .

"My surgeon," Kondo grinned, "cut it from a fat American bird Matoba shot today."

He stared at them. They were insane!

Then he whirled and left the house. He knew what he must do.

Fujihara stumbled along the moonlit sand of Washington Beach. The mess tent had been hit and it was burning. He could hear the radioman groaning. He had expected trouble with the guard, but the guard had fled. The body of the pilot lay half in darkness, half in moonlight. The radioman hung writhing, his flight suit soaked in blood.

The major unsheathed his sword. The keen *katana* blade, two hundred years old, cut the rope as if it had been a string drawn taut. The boy sank to the bloody sand. Helplessly, Fujihara tried to ease his legs.

"Water?" the American moaned. He seemed to recognize Fujihara.

Fujihara spotted a half-filled bottle of beer on the beach and held it to his lips. The boy drank it and began to cry.

"They coming back?"

"When the raid is over." The sound of antiaircraft was dying. He had not much time. He felt the boy's pulse. It was strong, and very fast. "I have a son, older than you, on Peleliu."

The boy squirmed in the sand. "I just can't stand no more."

Fujihara kneeled beside him and lifted his head. "Do you want *me* to do it? Now?"

Faintly, from over the mountain, he heard a series of blasts, over and over again. "All clear," murmured Fujihara.

"Oh, God," the boy muttered. "Yes!"

Fujihara clapped his hands twice to attract the attention of the gods. He bowed, then arose. The diamond pattern of his sword hilt was warm in the palm of his hand. He wondered which of his ancestors had wielded it when last it tasted blood.

Lorna had taught him a Christian prayer, and he began it now, for the lad.

"Our Father, Who art in Heaven," Fujihara faltered. "Hallowed be Thy name . . ."

The boy struggled to his knees. Fujihara took a double-handed grip, and stared at a spot three inches above the base of his neck.

He heard a distant shout above the surf. They were returning.

"Thy Kingdom come," murmured the boy, "Thy will be done . . ."

Fujihara tried to think of the lily, floating on green water, took a breath, swung with all his might, and it was done.

CHAPTER 7

At dawn Lieutenant (jg) George H. W. Bush scrambled up the fuselage of his huge torpedo bomber on *San Jacinto*'s flight deck.

He wore a yellow inflatable vest over his sweat-stained khaki flight suit. The earflaps of his summer-issue helmet were whipping in the wind. In a shoulder holster he carried a short-barreled .38 Smith & Wesson.

His unit, Torpedo Bombing Squadron 51, had struck at the radio tower perched on Yoake Peak on Chichijima yesterday, September first. They had found it heavily protected with antiaircraft crossfire from the mountains. They lost a plane, and when they left, the Japanese transmitter was still sending.

The carrier task force was turning south in a few hours, but the Chichijima radio station, an essential link in Japanese trans-Pacific communications, must be knocked off the air before the U.S. Marine assault on Peleliu.

Bush and three other pilots from the squadron were to try again for the transmitter, during a strike on Futami Harbor by torpedo and dive-bombers from the heavy carrier *Enterprise*.

Bush was almost too tall to pass his flight physical but he was dwarfed by his aircraft. The TBM Avenger of World War II was the largest single-engine plane the world had ever known. Weighing eight tons loaded for bear, with a fifty-foot wingspan, it towered sixteen feet above the carrier's deck.

The aircraft was armed and ready. It hugged four five-hundred-pound bombs in its closed torpedo bay.

Here, fifty miles east of Chichijima, the morning was warm and humid. The little carrier—only twenty thousand tons—was churning along at twenty-five knots. Already she was turning to launch, into a northwest breeze which would bring the wind along the flight deck up to almost forty.

In the moist, artificial gale, Bush had to cling tightly to the recessed fuselage handgrips and to place his feet fully into the inset footholds to keep from being blown to the flight deck. He checked to see that the greenhorn "gunner"—Lieutenant (jg) White—who would ride behind him, was properly installed in his aft-facing ball turret suspended above the rear seat. White had prevailed on the skipper to ride on the mission: Bush's regular gunner Nadeau was safe at breakfast below.

The gunner's chest chute hung outside the turret: the turret was so small that it could not be worn inside. If they had to bail out, the radioman from the tunnel below—who had room to wear a chute—was supposed to assist the top gunner into his straps before both went over the side. Bush's ordinary crew was quick at this, from drills, but there had been no time to practice with White, who had little flight experience.

That morning, in the ready room, White had been exuberant. Bush saw no problem, for he needed no rear seat gunner: it was not a strafing mission and he expected no fighter opposition from the island's tiny airstrip, knocked out the day before.

Now Bush, hanging into the rear cockpit in the shadow of the folded wings, plugged in White's intercom for him, and shouted down into the tunnel compartment to check on his radioman, John Delaney, a cheerful little Irish youth from Rhode Island, who would man the aft-facing machine guns in the belly. Then Bush hoisted himself into the cockpit high above the rolling deck, shrugged into his chute straps, and snapped his shoulder harness to his lap belt.

He got a thumbs-up from the brown-shirted plane captain below and started his engine, adding his own huge prop to the other blades whirling shards of early sunlight along the flight deck. He taxied forward through a hell of engines, loudspeakers, and rising wind. His fuselage bobbed as he worked his brakes. He was passed by hand signals from one red-shirted taximan to another, spreading his wings as he went. Two blue-shirted planepushers darted under his wings to check the wing-locks. They gave him a thumbs-up, and he was hooked to the catapult.

The cat-shot was as frightening as ever: an explosive jolt, then the normal, breath-squeezing ride toward the void beyond the flight deck. The TBM was so heavy that one always wondered if it would really get airborne, or plop down in a sheet of spray under the carrier's bow.

Suddenly he was flying, tucking up his gear. His wingman, Milton Moore, slid into position to his port. Bush labored up to join his squadron commander, Don Melvin, a veteran who had earned his license in 1929 and his navy wings of gold in 1937. Melvin was circling at fifteen hundred feet.

High in the distance, to the west, Bush could see eight Helldivers and a dozen more TBMs from *Enterprise*. They would bomb and strafe the island while *San Jacinto*'s four planes went for the transmitter.

Higher still circled a dozen Hellcat fighters to escort them all.

In twenty minutes he could see Chichijima's jagged peaks, and, across a narrow strait, Anijima's lesser bulk.

He armed his bombs as the other squadrons began to dive on Futami Harbor, behind the mountains to the west.

CHAPTER 8

*L*ong before dawn, Matt awoke in the tunnel. The all-clear had not yet sounded, but he stepped to the steel door, avoiding prostrate bodies and belongings spread everywhere.

His cousin Jonathon was standing outside, watching the fireworks from the tunnel entrance. The Yankee pilots dropped flare after flare, until Futami Bay looked like the background for a newsreel.

Guns pounded distantly from the slopes of Mount Asahi, and he could see their rosy flashes, like lightning before a typhoon, silhouetting the ridges to the east over Washington Beach.

Great orange bursts lit the eastern sky, followed in a few moments by the thunder of their blasts.

They heard rumbling far at sea as a force of U.S. battleships and cruisers began to slam the island with sixteen-inch and eight-inch shells. The yellow flashes of their great guns were visible on the horizon but they seemed to be firing only at military installations, so Matt dared Jonathon to join him for a better look. Together they climbed to a secret aerie near the peak of Mount Asahi, "Peak of the Rising Sun."

In the darkness, the shells arched red-hot, flying toward them from the eastern skyline, two- and three-round salvos waltzing together, first one leading, then another. They approached like cherries, with invisible stems attached to each other, tossed by a demented giant. Sometimes, from the perspective of the mountain peak, they seemed to circle each other in flight.

As the sun rose, the hurtling cherries turned to black dots. They seemed to climb forever, then drop suddenly on fortifications by the bay behind them. Matt could hear the rumble of their passage overhead. He was imagining himself crouched on Peleliu with Tohru, or Iwo Jima with his father, when all at once the thought struck him that if a single round went astray and landed on the tunnel below, his mother and Alicia would die.

The all-clear sounded while he was bolting with Jonathon down the trail, full of fear and anger at the guns, and at himself for leaving his family. His mother only looked at him with her gentle gray eyes, touched his cheek, and led them home.

There were letters on the *kotatsu* table in Mickey's neat handwriting, in English, one to each of them.

Sick at heart, Matt read:

> I must fly back to Hiroshima. There is no time even to go to the tunnel to bid you farewell. A headquarters clerk is picking up my kit and will leave these letters for you. As you read this I am winging north like a pigeon to his roost.

Matt's throat tightened. The writing blurred before his eyes.

> I have heard at island headquarters that civilians will be evacuated today if air raids continue.
>
> So, Matt, there is an English saying: "Turn about is fair play." And I have invited your mother and you and Alicia to share my unworthy quarters in Hiroshima when you are made to leave. I should be most honored if your mother accepts.
>
> Sayonara, dear young friend.

The letter was signed "Mickey-san." The major's *hanko* personal seal, in red, was smeared, as if he had stamped it hurriedly.

He looked up. His mother had finished reading her letter. Astounded, he saw that she was weeping. He squeezed her to his side. He was as tall as she, he noticed for the first time. Her hair smelled of lilac.

He missed Mickey-san already. "We'll stay with him in Hiroshima," he asked, "when we're evacuated?"

Her eyes met Alicia's, and Matt felt left out.

Alicia smiled, and seemed strangely older. "Father wants us safe," she murmured, looking deep in her mother's eyes. "God knows *how* they'd treat us adrift in Tokyo, or Nagasaki!"

His mother seemed grateful and pressed her hand. "You are my sweetness," she murmured.

"So we *will* stay with him?" Matt insisted.

She smiled, a little sadly. "In truth, it seems God's will." She moved to the open window and looked out at the sky. The raids frightened her. "If we could only *go!*"

By now Matt blazed with hatred for the Americans who were trying to kill his mother, his sister, and himself, and would kill his father some day on Iwo Jima. He decided that he would join the army, as his best friend Susumu already had.

But by noon that dream was dead, and he was sitting on a suitcase on the Omura quay, in the shadow of a rusty island freighter. Alicia roughed his hair.

"Once upon a time," she said, "a samurai warrior saw an old crone drowning in a river, while his enemy dared him to cross—"

He shrugged her off. "Don't want to hear your silly stories! I'm not a goddamn child!"

"Language! So instead of fighting, he rescued the old lady—"

"Alicia, just leave me *be!*"

She drifted off. He looked up at the ship. Paint flecked from her hull: he wondered if she would make it north through the choppy seas. He almost didn't care.

He had given up hope of enlisting when his mother unsealed his father's testament and showed him a letter addressed to him, ordinarily not to be opened until after his death.

"You shouldn't," he had cried. "He's *alive!*"

"In this case, he'd want me to."

My dear Matthew,

   You must protect your mother and sister with all your strength, for there are those of our countrymen who will abuse them—and you—no matter how hard you labor in the emperor's cause . . .

It was enough. He was beaten.

Susumu Sasai had managed to get leave for an hour from his basic training at the garrison, to bid his own mother and little brothers sayonara. He lolled nearby, swallowed in his uniform and self-consciously carrying his rifle. Matt's throat was tight with envy, but he could not utter a further word of argument to his mother.

Now, sitting on the pile of their possessions, the Bancrofts waited for a *kempeitai* military policeman to stamp their exit passes. When he did, they followed the line of refugees up the gangway, signed aboard, and started down evil-smelling ladders to the hold below, loaded down with their possessions.

They spread their eating utensils and bedding in a corner of the compartment in which they would sleep and eat, an immense, hundred-mat area spread with moldy futons and littered already with the bedding of scores of other families who would share it. It would be a miserable, rolling, three-day voyage north.

When they had laid claim to their own territory below, Matt left his sister and his mother and went topside, to watch the undocking and to wave good-bye to Susumu.

As he stepped into sunlight he heard a shriek from the air-raid alarm at the Omura Naval Base. Simultaneously, the freighter's whistle, high above him, began to blast, in angry gut-wrenching roars that set the deck to dancing under his feet.

A gun on the bow began to bark. From the bridge, he heard the staccato pounding—*pom-pom-pom-pom*—of an antiaircraft piece. He could hear the familiar popping of guns from Mount Asahi.

He whirled to go below for his mother and Alicia, struggled through the deckhouse door against a river of civilians.

He could not fight his way against the rising tide. He felt the shock of the bow gun jolting the bulkheads.

Pushing, grunting, he struggled against the human flood. Finally, an officer, one arm in a cast, cursed him and slammed him in the face. He found himself rushed back on deck. Dazed, he heard a short burst of metallic clangs and realized that the freighter was being strafed.

The gangway was choked with fleeing passengers, and troops on the quay below were firing at the sky. He saw Susumu banging away with the rest, cringed as a plane roared overhead, felt its shadow fall on his face.

A second flight of TBM Avengers was roaring across Futami Harbor, heading for the ship.

He dropped behind a deck ventilator, rolled into a ball, closed his eyes, and waited.

Circling at five thousand feet, Lieutenant (jg) George Bush watched his skipper and his skipper's wingman dive on the radio tower perched on the slope of Mount Yoake, far from the village of Omura and the island's only dock. The squadron commander pulled up in a ravine, and Bush noticed a crossfire of tracers probing at the attacking planes, but neither seemed hit. Then the skipper's five-hundred-pound bombs struck the transmitter and its surrounding buildings in a burst of orange flame.

It was his own turn now. He nosed into a gentle thirty-degree dive, with Milt Moore flying wing. He used no evasive tactics: he dove straight for the tower, for accuracy.

He was hit almost instantly. The shell ruptured an engine oil line and a fire started. Black smoke belched from the nose, pouring along the wings, approaching his gas tanks. He finished his run, pickled off his bombs, and felt that he had scored.

He could no longer see his instruments. He switched his transmitter from the squadron frequency to 4475 kilocycles, to notify any U.S. submarine in the area that he was hit and was going to jump. He got no reply. He turned out to sea.

He shouted on the intercom for White and Delaney to bail out. Squadron mates heard him repeating it, over and over, on the radio. His wingman Moore closed in but when Bush lost power completely, Moore went sliding by ahead. Moore's gunner, facing aft, yelled: "Chutes!"

Then Bush bailed out. Hurtling over the side, he hit his head on the tail and pulled his rip cord too soon. The chute snagged the elevator but tore free. Stunned by the blow on his skull, he still remembered to unbuckle his harness in the air.

He plunged from twenty feet above the water straight in and saw his chute blowing off toward Chichijima. He pulled the toggles on his CO_2 flight vest, inflating it, but his seat-raft was nowhere in sight.

An *Enterprise* Hellcat dived from out of the sun, repeatedly, pointing his raft out to him. He thrashed toward it and struggled aboard. The wind was pushing him toward the island. He drew his pistol to see if it was working.

He heard engines overhead. His skipper and wingman had spotted him, were undoubtedly radioing his position. Suddenly they banked and flew away, apparently afraid that if they stayed they would pinpoint him to Japanese on the island.

He was seasick already, and groggy with fatigue. He had seen no other chutes, and wondered where White and Delaney were. He was uncertain whether one or both had actually bailed out.

Less than two miles away, off the island, two Hellcat fighters and an Avenger flown by his squadron mate Doug West were strafing Japanese boats that were heading to pick him up.

The Vice President-to-be did not know this.

He was vomiting and trying to paddle off to sea.

CHAPTER 9

Matt Bancroft, crouched behind the freighter's ventilator, heard the firing cease as a wave of fighters passed. He began to crawl out. Then another wave came, and another, and soon he was cowering in a ball, drenched with sweat and shivering in fear. Finally the attack seemed to stop.

Slowly, drained and half paralyzed with fright, he emerged to find his mother and his sister already on deck. His mother seemed calmer than he, but let him lead them down the gangway to the quay. They could see that the little village had been wrecked; flames and smoke were everywhere.

As they reached the dock, Matt heard the *crump* of antiaircraft guns. Another wave was approaching. A huge torpedo bomber—a TBM Avenger—was skimming the harbor water. It banked, paralleling the quay, and he saw the ball turret at the rear of the cockpit swing abruptly, winking orange flame. Tracers slammed into the freighter's superstructure, whined across the landing, ricocheted from the stone seawall.

Lorna, Matt, and Alicia took cover behind a pile of military crates. Matt peered from behind their shelter and saw the pilot banking. His head was tiny in the cockpit, his white face was staring down. The roar of his engine beat against Matt's ears, rose to a crescendo, and faded as the plane thundered away across the harbor.

Panting, he hurried his charges from behind the cache of supplies toward the Omura tunnel a thousand yards away, tugging at his mother's hand.

She wore a blue kimono, tight across her legs, and she could not run. His visored school hat jounced off, and he let her go and paused to pick it up. He heard the rising throb of an engine from over the bay and swung around to look.

The Avenger was returning. His fear was swept away in anger. He found himself alone on the street, fists raised to the sky, tears streaming. "Bastard!" he howled. "Bastard! Bastard! Bastard!"

He heard Alicia scream. He whirled and saw her beckoning anxiously behind an army scout car, but his mother, kimono held high, was running back to drag him from the street. She was calling, but the roar of the returning plane drowned out her words.

He shouted a warning and flung himself down on the street, hands to his ears. Tracers were slamming everywhere, raising great puffs of coral cement. Dust filled his nose and eyes. He got to his knees, peered into the choking cloud. Dimly he saw his mother reach toward him. Then she flung up her hands and collapsed.

The Avenger roared overhead. Matt crawled to his mother, hugged her close. Her kimono was soaked in blood. A trickle of it ran from her lips. Her gray eyes met his. She tried to speak, and touched his cheek. Her fingers were icy. All at once Alicia was with them, eyes round and empty.

Speechlessly, they looked at each other. Alicia sobbed once and ran to the tunnel for help.

When she came back, with two medical corpsmen and a litter, their mother was dead.

Matt peered into his sister's eyes. He heard himself saying, quite seriously: "My cap, I had to get my cap. I had to get my cap."

It was as if someone else had spoken, and afterward, he was dumb with shock.

Late that afternoon Matt stood with his sister at the side of the brush-tangled family plot in a tiny glen. It lay on Mount Mikazuki, behind Omura, far above the smoke from Futami Bay.

There would be a short ceremony only, for the freighter, which had sustained minor steering damage, was being repaired and was scheduled to leave before dusk. He watched as his mother's body was lowered into the moist volcanic earth. She would lie near the crude gravestone of his great-great-grandfather Elias, with scores of other Bancrofts and Robinsons along the mountain path.

Holding Alicia's hand, he heard dark-skinned Reverend Gonzales intoning, in English: ". . .till thou return unto the ground, for out of it wast thou taken . . ."

He was suddenly seven years old, playing follow-the-leader along the dusty Omura road with Susumu and some of the village children near the caves that the army had begun to enlarge. The leader crawled into a drainage pipe under the road, hardly a foot in diameter. Matt followed Susumu.

It was thick with debris inside, pitch-black, and so tight that he could hardly move. He inched along, with Susumu's tiny *getas* in his face, grunting and squirming. By far the largest of the troop, he was suddenly jammed, and the sound of Susumu's body scrunching further and further under the road grew faint.

To show alarm would be to lose great face, so he worked at the problem, scrabbling at the sand that was blocking him, burrowing a few feet forward, heart racing. He had better back out before it was too late . . .

He could not. He was trapped. Too late, he yelled into the void. Ahead he saw a sudden gleam of light: Susumu was through, probably chasing after the rest. If he noticed that Matt was missing, he might be afraid to tell, for they were on army property, and might be beaten.

He was suffocating. The pipe seemed to grow smaller by the moment. He fought and screamed and cried and prayed as the light at the end of the pipe faded. The sun had gone down. Finally, exhausted, he lay panting in the fetid air.

They would never even find his body.

Perhaps he fainted, or merely slept. But he awoke to his mother's gentle voice, calling from far behind. "Matt, sweetness, what have you got into?"

Susumu must have got her. "Mama," Matt sniveled, "I can't move . . ."

"Of course you can, Pumpkin." Her voice was music. "An inch at a time."

Calmly, she insisted that he try.

She sang to him as he worked himself back, the songs that she plunked on Old Elias' banjo: "Amazing Grace," and "In the Sweet Bye and Bye," the Japanese "Coal Miners' Song," even "Jesus Loves Me, This I Know, For the Bible Tells Me So."

She did not even try to help him when she could have grasped his legs. She had sent home Susumu, so when Matt emerged filthy, with knees and elbows scraped, there was no one to laugh at him. She had only praise for his calm and courage for trying the pipe, and on an island which gloried in gossip and ridicule, he had never heard a word about the incident from Susumu or anyone else.

"Dust thou art," chanted Gonzales, "and unto dust shalt thou return."

Just before the funeral, Susumu—trying to get him to talk—had told them an Avenger had been shot down. A chute had been seen to open. The airman had been sighted only two miles off the island, in his raft on the open sea. Two boats that had been sent to pick him up had been strafed, and a sailor killed, and so they had turned back.

Now the Yankee was paddling uselessly with his hands, and said to be blowing ashore. The orders to troops on Washington Beach were simply to watch and wait; through binoculars, the American seemed tall and strong, but he would be no match for the Spirit of the Wind.

Matt assumed it was the same plane.

Let the pilot who had killed her pray to Jesus: Matt had another god: the wind of Chichijima, blow. Divine wind—kamikaze—*blow*. High on the ridge, it ruffled his hair.

In his mind he saw Susumu and the others, waiting for his mother's murderer drifting slowly to the beach.

It was said that prisoners were sent to Japan. Perhaps he could find him there. He knew that he would find him somewhere, someday.

In the carpenter's deserted workshop near the quay, Uncle Noah Bancroft, tall, gentle, dark as a Hawaiian, had carved an inscription on the horizontal member of the unpainted wooden cross: LORNA ROBINSON BANCROFT, BELOVED WIFE OF LEMUEL, ADORED MOTHER OF ALICIA AND MATTHEW. BORN CHICHI-JIMA, AUGUST 8, 1906. DIED SEPTEMBER 2, 1944.

Now, as the funeral party left the graveyard on the ridge, Uncle Noah, arm around Alicia's waist, was moving down the trail with the rest, while Matt loitered at the grave.

When he was alone, he clapped his hands quietly, twice, to attract the gods' attention. He pressed his palms together, as before a Shinto shrine, and bowed his head.

In a rush he felt *kataki-uchi*, the blood-deep need of a samurai to avenge a parent's wrong, and he welcomed it. *The soul of the samurai is the sword.* Some day his own would flash.

He unclasped the fishing knife his father had given him. He dropped to his knees. Slowly, carefully, on the vertical member, he scratched in Japanese, with the razor-sharp blade, *Killed by a Yankee flier. His soul will burn in hell. Her only son*, he added, *forever swears* kataki-uchi *on her grave.*

He arose and bowed. *I will never forget you, Mama, until the day I die.*

He took a bottle of sake from a nearby Japanese tomb, and placed it by the cross.

Her great-grandfather had been Japanese. She had always claimed a secret taste for sake.

Unavenged, it was said, her spirit could not rest. When revenge was taken, perhaps the sake would speed her on her way. With the pilot drifting ashore, vengeance lay in the wind on his cheek, and his mother need not wait long.

America's future Vice President paddled with his hands for two hours, into the spanking breeze. He never stopped vomiting. It seemed the end of the world to him. Fighting the wind, he did not know if his crewmen had survived.

Suddenly, four minutes before noon, he saw a periscope a hundred yards away. He was paralyzed with terror, thinking that it was Japanese. Then the hull broke the surface, and he saw American sailors racing down its deck.

In moments he was aboard. The sub was the USS *Finback*. Bush stood dripping on the conning-tower, facing the skipper, Commander R. R. Williams.

Bush was still seasick and trembling with shock. "Sir! Is there word on my crewmen? I never saw their chutes!"

Williams knew nothing of any chutes. He quickly had Bush hustled down the hatch for medical attention and took the sub below. *ME—TOM KEENE & CREW*

In the tiny wardroom, while a corpsman treated his cuts, Bush found the pilot, gunner, and radioman from a USS *Franklin* torpedo bomber, rescued the previous day. They told him that he faced a month's war-patrol off Japan: *Finback*'s tour as a planewatch rescue vessel would be over when today's strikes were finished. She was loaded with torpedoes, and could not return simply to deliver navy pilots to their carriers.

At seven bells on the wardroom clock—three thirty P.M.—less than four hours after Bush's rescue, *Finback* received word from an escorting Hellcat fighter that it had sighted a man in a rubber raft. Bush made his way to the control room. Perhaps it was White or Delaney.

Finback rose to periscope depth and searched, directed by the fighter. The skipper finally sighted a downed airman on a raft just over a mile from the beach. He was being shelled from shore.

Afraid to surface so close to the coastal batteries on Anijima and Tatsumi Shima, Commander Williams dived to fifty-five feet, maximum periscope depth, and made a run on him submerged. Bush, certain now that it was one of his crewmen, squirmed and sweated at his side.

The submarine missed the raft, backed and filled. Williams began to ''stalk'' it, as he put it to Bush, issuing quiet, incomprehensible orders: ''Blow forward tanks. . . . Flood aft. . . . Blow negative to the mark. . . . Starboard engines ahead two-thirds.''

Through the scope, Williams could see the flier perfectly, and at last he reported that the airman had an arm around the periscope. He could not risk his submarine by surfacing so close to land, so the downed American clung to the scope while he tried to tow him away from the island at two-thirds speed.

The airman was out of his raft now, but would not let it go. He was trying to tug it along while he clung to the periscope with the other arm. The raft finally pulled him free of the periscope and the whole agonizing drama began again, while Bush stood sick with fear.

NOT-BECK MAN
-KEENS ONLY

Five miles out, Williams finally felt it safe to surface to get the airman aboard. But he was neither White nor Delaney: He was Ensign James W. Beckman of the *Enterprise*. He stated that only one man had parachuted from Bush's plane—presumably Bush—so the search for Bush's crewmen was discontinued.

Before she left Chichijima waters, *Finback* picked up one more TBM pilot, who had been strafing the Omura dock. His crewmen had disappeared too.

Then she turned north, with Lieutenant (jg) Bush and the rest of her guests. Just after midnight, sixty miles northwest of Chichijima, her SJ radar picked up an enemy plane. She dove. In a bunk in a clammy torpedo compartment, far beneath the surface of the sea, Bush tried to sleep. The diesels throbbed and the bulkheads trembled. There seemed hardly enough air.

From here on he knew that *Finback* would be stalking enemy ships, not American airmen. And she would be under radio silence. There would be no way to find out what happened to Ted White or John Delaney until he got back to the *San Jacinto*, if he ever did.

Alicia waited for her brother at the bottom of the ridge. She asked what had delayed him but he would not speak. On the dock, Susumu ran up to them. His squad had just been trucked back from Washington Beach.

The gods, he said, had failed them. The downed airman had been almost within rifle range when an American submarine had surfaced, snatched him up, and sunk scornfully from sight.

Matt only stared into Susumu's flat brown eyes.

"I'm sorry, Bancroft-san." Susumu bowed in shame, as if it were his fault.

Matt's roar of anguish echoed from the freighter's rusty hull.

Matt could not sleep the first night out, but the second night he did, and for the first time had the deathless dream that would plague him all his life.

His mother was alive, she had not died, and he was with her in the narrow coffin, with her wounds still bleeding and her lungs whining for air. She pounded feebly at the lid, the sides, and no one heard but him. She begged for the Other World, but could not die until her murderer was killed, and no one knew but Matt, who was with her but was not.

Dust thou art, and unto dust shalt thou return . . .

And she could not return!

Her rest throughout eternity was up to him!

NOTE: THIS SHOWS HOW AN AUTHER CAN TRY TO MAKE MONEY.

Dan

CHAPTER 10

The stucco quarters of Major Michihiko Fujihara, staff engineer of Second Army Headquarters, lay sleeping at dawn in the Hakushima district near Hiroshima Castle.

On Monday, August 6, 1945—the day that half the city would vanish in a burst of azure light—Matt and Alicia Bancroft had lived in Hiroshima for nearly one full year.

The solid European-style residences along the street had been the homes of merchants and bankers ever since the Meiji Restoration had opened up Japan, but now they billeted senior officers of the Fifth Engineer Battalion and Hiroshima Military Barracks. The major's house was the smallest, but each of the other buildings on the street was occupied by more than one officer, while Major Fujihara lived alone, with only a body-servant, cook, and his two young Caucasian wards.

The day dawned crystal-clear on the Seto Sea. As the rising sun burst suddenly on the city from over the crest of Hijiyama Park it turned the branches of the Ota River into paths of hammered brass.

Until the tides of war had changed, the city, with a third of a million inhabitants, had been an embarkation port for the troops that won Japan the Far East. But the heroes had long departed. The Hiroshima garrison of twenty-four thousand youngsters and aging reserves were willing but untrained. In

ill-fitted uniforms, uncertain in bearing, they seemed unready
for the Yankee landing that everyone knew would come.

Hundreds of doomed navy launches, packed with explosives for kamikaze attacks on American landing craft, lay
creaking side-by-side in the tide at the city's piers.

At Kure, guarding the entrance to Hiroshima Bay, lines of
tiny two-man submarines heaved in the swell of the Inland
Sea. Those naval volunteers who had been selected to pilot
the launches and trained to operate the submarines knew that
in the end their lives would go for nothing.

But "Better to Die Than Seek Ignominious Safety" and
"One Hundred Million People Die in Honor" were pledges
that even landlubber civilians were making. The remnants of
the Imperial Navy, stung at Midway, battered in the Marianas, and finally defeated in the Battle of Leyte Gulf, were
honor-bound to perish in the inlets of Japan.

The air services seemed to be holding themselves in reserve, too. The army was saving its remaining pilots as
kamikazes to fight the landings; the Naval Air Force had been
fatally mauled in the Battle of Midway. Antiaircraft fire
seemed futile: the B-29s that daily passed Hiroshima heading
north were flying six miles high. The city seemed to have no
air defenses.

The few antiaircraft shells Hiroshima residents saw nowadays, stacked by the sandbagged guns, seemed always to be
cast of a grayish pot metal; brass and steel had somehow
disappeared.

Hiroshima Harbor, sewn with American mines dropped
from "Mr. B"—the B-29s—had been empty of transports for
a year. The Ota River's branches were nowadays almost bare
of tenders and tugs. Though little stills had been constructed
in the forests to produce wood alcohol for motor fuel, there
was none to spare for small craft. What few supplies were
needed on the desolate, empty wharves were trundled in from
factories and railroad depots by charcoal-burning army lorries, spewing the foulest smoke.

Matt Bancroft, sprawled asleep on his straw tatami floor,
popped awake as a beam of sunlight struck his face. He had
been aroused by Mickey-san to a screaming air-raid whistle
just after midnight, had spent half the night in the neighborhood air-raid shelter, and had only crawled back into his own

futon at three. But with dawn streaming through his open *shoji* screen, he was wide awake.

He threw aside his quilted *kakebuton,* waddled to the wall on his knees, and knocked to awaken Alicia, who slept next door in the only Western-style room in the house. He folded the futon and stowed it with his tiny *makura* pillow in the cedar cabinet along the side of the room. He drew on the tan uniform of the Student Labor Force, wrapping his puttees tightly so that Captain Tasaka, the one-legged officer who would drill them with wooden rifles at morning assembly, would not swipe at him with his crutch as an example to the others.

Matt worked swiftly, criss-crossing the puttees in the distinctive old-army style that Captain Tasaka had taught them: if he got dressed in time, Mickey-san would probably let him drive the staff car as far as Hiroshima Castle, where he could walk the rest of the way to school.

Monday . . . school . . . and afterward, hours of shoveling with the short-handled spade, made for boys much smaller than he, in the East Drill Ground, under the Student Labor Service Program.

Yesterday, he had spent his Sunday helping Mr. Suzuki, the baker, destroy his little shop, which stood in the path of a projected municipal fire lane. He inspected his palms. They were raw and blistered from tugging at beams and joists, and now he faced an afternoon digging under the blazing August sun, like a peasant in the fields.

Suddenly he burned with guilt. In the skies over Tokyo, when the invasion began, fifteen-year-olds would be slamming their fighters into U.S. bombers. He saw himself as an army pilot, soaring into the morning sun to battle Mr. B.

Faintly, he heard Alicia's radio, tuned to Radio Guam, spouting American propaganda. *From Guam,* the speaker blared: *Carrier reconnaissance aircraft from the U.S. Third Fleet confirmed yesterday that the Japanese battleships* Haruna *and* Ise *were on the bottom at their anchorages off Kure.*

Kure lay less than ten miles south.

The radio was too loud. What if a passing Thought Policeman heard the American voice? If he entered the house, Mickey-san would lose face.

Returning carrier pilots, the voice crackled, *reported that the* Hyuga, *a modern battleship converted to a carrier, lies at anchor with water washing over her main deck. Meanwhile, B-29s from the Twentieth Air Force last night bombed six out of seven Japanese cities that had already been warned that they were on a list for destruction.*

Matt had heard the list. Hiroshima was not on it. He stepped swiftly into Alicia's room.

She was sitting at her mirror in her light summer *yukata*, brushing her golden hair. He clicked off the radio.

She glared at him in the glass. "Matt!"

"Your radio's too loud."

"Pshaw, no one will hear!" She shrugged, and held his eyes. "Did you dream last night?"

"There wasn't time," he grumbled. "Did you?"

She nodded. "Of you. You were flying an airplane in the Kamikaze Corps."

"But only in your dreams," he muttered savagely.

"Yes, and I'm glad."

In her mirror he caught his own reflection: tall for thirteen—taller than she—with the Bancroft eyes of emerald, and wavy hair, darker than hers. He could easily pass for fifteen. If it weren't for her and Mickey-san, he'd lie about his age and volunteer.

He sat down on her bed as Alicia began to talk about her best friend, Yuko Imagawa, a dumpy, cheerful seamstress who worked in the Army Clothes Depot at the machine next to hers. Tomorrow Yuko was moving back to her village on Miyajima Island, a few miles down the coast from Hiroshima. Alicia would miss her. "Her grandfather thinks they'll firebomb us here."

Matt shrugged. Many in Hiroshima had grown nervous at the firebomb raids on Tokyo and Osaka.

Hiroshima, despite its huge population and army headquarters, had been lucky past all belief. During all the spring firebomb raids on the home islands—which were rumored to have gutted Nagoya, Kobe, Osaka, Yokohama, and Tokyo, not sparing even the Imperial Palace—only two small bombs from a flight of U.S. Navy raiders, and another ten from a high-flying B-29, had fallen in the city. In all, only twelve citizens had died. Yuko's grandfather apparently saw no reason why Hiroshima's luck should last, and was fleeing with his family to the countryside.

Matt tried to make Alicia feel better. "Miyajima's not far. We'll go there next Sunday."

But he saw that her eyes were wet. When their mother had been killed, Alicia had been stronger than he. Now he had become the protector.

"It's so *silly*," she continued. *"No* place will be safe when they land. Even Mickey-san says that!"

He considered himself her mentor in all things military. "We'll fight them off," he promised.

"With bamboo spears?"

"And *yamato*. Spirit is stronger than guns."

"Well, we shan't," she said recklessly. "We can't."

They were arguing, suddenly, and he didn't want to. In Hiroshima, she had become his best friend. Here, even more than on Chichijima, they were alien. *More* alien, with their round eyes, damned height, and white skin, than the American-born Japanese students one saw in class.

The nisei children had been sent by their parents back from America to high school and trapped here by the war. They were probably neutral, or worse, in their twisted Yankee hearts, and could hardly speak Japanese. But at least they *looked* like everyone else. He and Alicia, loyal to the emperor, looked to everyone like *gaijin* American gangsters in the streets.

He felt the walls of her bedroom closing in. He wished he were anywhere but in this forgotten backwater. He cursed his age. He pictured himself crammed into the cockpit of a Mitsubishi with his *hachimaki* headband gleaming white, in a screaming dive toward a U.S. carrier, flinging the emperor's name to the wind. With all his heart he envied little Susumu on Chichijima and the Junior Air Cadets he saw on the streets, swaggering with their seven brass buttons shining and everyone bowing to them.

He looked across the city. It was very quiet. He could see a portion of East Drill Field, Hiroshima Military Barracks parade grounds, between two buildings. Troops were mustering for morning roll call.

A corporal found fault with the set of a man's cap, and slapped him; the hat went flying and the private, bowing deeply, left ranks to pick it up. Faintly, Matt could hear a hidden sergeant's voice: "Turn to the northeast!"

The ranks did a half-right-face, toward Tokyo, 350 miles

away. "Revere the Imperial Palace!" The men bowed, sliding stiff palms down their thighs, until their backs were horizontal. "Return to attention! Recite the Five Imperial Doctrines!"

The ranks straightened. In the hoarse, breathless voices taught them in training, they began to chant.

Matt found himself murmuring along with them: ". . . third, the soldier respects martial courage; fourth, he values truthfulness; fifth, he remains austere."

In the whole war, he had done nothing for the emperor but shake his fists and get his mother killed. He wished that the B-29s would drop a few bombs as they passed. If they dropped, he was ready. He saw himself shielding Alicia with his body as the firebombs crunched nearby, directing frightened neighbors to the *bokugo* shelter at the corner, grabbing a pistol from a fallen officer in the shelter's entrance to shoot at a strafing Hellcat.

On East Drill Field the bugler sounded colors. Matt stiffened to attention. The flag of the rising sun, fluttering high over Hiroshima Castle, was jerking upward, following the sun itself.

His throat grew tight. Alicia was right. His country was doomed. The Americans would soon wash ashore, sweeping all before them.

Alicia glanced at her brother in her mirror. He was so mature, in some ways, and such a child in others. He was braced up like a soldier, flying with some squadron of the Divine Wind, perhaps, or going down with the battleship *Yamato*.

"*Banzai*," she giggled, prodding his tensed-up belly.

He blushed and glanced at the distant flagpole. "It's a beautiful flag," he pointed out. "Our father died for it."

She thought of their white-bearded grandfather Adam, slim and erect, hanging *another* flag, the Stars and Stripes, over the fireplace on some long-ago Fourth of July, while the family sang—she could not have been over three years old when he died—what was the song? "My country 'tis of thee . . ." The last time she had seen *that* flag, two of her uncles were straining arrowroot through it, to use in a turtle stew.

Alicia joined Matt at her window. In the courtyard below, Private Ono, Mickey-san's batman, was washing the major's

staff car. Mickey-san was teaching Matt to drive it, doubtless
to the consternation of pedestrians. Seeing a barbarian at the
wheel with a Japanese major in back, they must think that the
Americans had already landed.

She wished that Mickey-san could somehow arrange to
drop her at work on his way to the castle, but she would not
dream of asking. The daily streetcar ride to her job was
torture, with everyone staring at her. She was too tall, her
nose too big, her eyes too round, and *green!* She knew she
would be pretty in London, Sydney, Berlin: *beautiful,* Mickey-
san said. Here in Hiroshima she was a comic strip cartoon.

And her feet! Japanese shoes—whether *geta, setta, zori,
waraji*—were impossible to find in wartime, even for Yuko,
and never in her own size any more. As if the feet themselves
were not big enough, she had been forced last week to wear a
discarded pair of Matt's Western-style sneakers to her job.
And once at her sewing machine, she could hear the giggles
of her co-workers all day long.

Alicia was still irritated that Matt had turned off her radio,
so she murmured: "Ono says Mickey-san's losing the car."

It worked. Matt turned to her, face bleak. "Why?"

She shrugged. "Gasoline. You have to be a colonel or
above."

He frowned suspiciously. "We've been burning *alcohol* for
the last six months."

"Alcohol, too."

He peered into her eyes. "Bullshit."

"That word's not nice," she decided. "Leastwise, I don't
think so."

He shrugged. "Okay, give me a synonym."

"Use *bunkum,*" she suggested proudly. That was what
their father—and granddaddy—would have said.

Matt regarded his sister with amusement. Her English, he
suspected, was as old-fashioned as his own. It was not their
fault. Even the novels they had devoured in Reverend Gonzales's church library had been archaic: Dickens, Sterne, Field-
ing, Melville. Kipling, by Yankeetown standards, was a
modern writer.

" '*Bunkum*'?" he grinned. "Well, all right."

He would humor her now. But for an instructor in American slang, he would find somebody else.

He was actively trying to scrub nineteenth-century English from his speech, for by the time the invasion came, he wanted to sound like an American soldier. He had a plan of battle. It would horrify Alicia and Mickey-san if he told them, so he held it close to his heart, dreaming of it at night when first he settled on the tatami mat under his warm *mofu*.

When the Americans landed, he would somehow steal one of their uniforms. While his countrymen battled the invaders in the hills and paddies and streets, he would pass among the Yankee soldiers as a young GI himself.

Somewhere among them he would find his mother's murderer and kill him.

At 7:25 A.M., waiting by the car for Mickey-san, Matt noticed a tiny speck high over Hiroshima, dragging a contrail toward the west. The early haze had moved inland on the breath of a morning breeze, stripping brown gauze from the sky.

Matt's hand rested fondly on the major's staff-car headlight. They were late, but he was still hoping for a chance to drive. Alicia had turned on her radio again; he could hear it way down here.

He looked up and found the silver speck. He watched it move away from the roof-gutter. His heart sank. If the B-29 triggered another air-raid alarm, he would not get to drive. Sitting in the shelter, he'd miss school, and arrive just in time to march to his afternoon agricultural duties with the Student Labor Force.

But as he watched, the B-29's wing flashed in the sunlight, banking to the left. Its lazy arrogance infuriated him. As always, it would be unchallenged by fighters and the outdistanced antiaircraft guns would remain silent. The plane rolled from its turn and began to inch east again, toward the Inland Sea and the ocean beyond.

He decided that it was a reconnaissance plane, photographing the shoreline for the landings, or maybe checking the weather for the other B-sans waiting to begin the day's assault on Tokyo.

Mickey-san suddenly appeared, immaculate in his mustard-colored uniform. He was hurried, apparently late for an appointment. He was disappointingly swordless as usual, though his

well-worn leather belt was polished to a glitter. The single
silver star of his rank shone on each red tab at his tunic collar.

Private Ono snapped to attention, sucked in his breath, and
bowed from the hips. Matt bowed too.

"Shall I be allowed to drive, *sensei?*" he asked. Mickey-
san glanced at his watch.

"*Hai,*" he nodded.

Ono opened the door for the major, then slipped into the
passenger seat beside Matt. Carefully, Matt put the car into
gear, looked both ways, and slid smoothly from the curb.

From Alicia's window, faintly, he could hear music:

Oh what a beautiful morning,
Oh, what a beautiful day . . .

He looked up to see if she was watching him drive. She
beamed down and gave him a thumbs-up.

I've got a beautiful feeling
Everything's going my way!

They would hear it all over town! He motioned her to turn
it off. She shook her head and laughed. Then she blew him a
kiss.

His annoyance fled. He had a strange and vacant feeling.
His throat tightened.

"Put out your hand," Mickey-san reminded him softly, in
English. "You have to signal, Matt-san."

Matt stuck out his hand and pulled carefully into the stream
of bicycles. To Alicia, he hadn't even waved.

There were hardly any taxis or autos any more, but the
streets, as always at this early hour, were streaming with
bicycle traffic. The streetcars clanged past, heavy with passengers. Hangers-on clung to the cow catchers at the rear.

Matt eased the car into the shadow of Hiroshima Castle,
housing of the Chugoku Regional Military Headquarters in
the center of the city. The huge feudal redoubt, built in 1589
by Lord Mouri Terumoto, was named Carp Castle for the fish
in its sapphire moat. Like a massive, broad-based pagoda, its
tenshu tower soared in clean white splendor five stories above
the barracks and headquarters clustered at its feet. Its graying,

ancient timbers were offset by gleaming plaster trim. Each of its ascending levels was of smaller area than that below, and each was faced with the peaked, sweeping gables of ancient Japan. At the ends of its roof beams broached a pair of golden dolphins with lion heads—*sachihoko*—to protect the castle from fire.

The uppermost story, a perfectly square white house set upon the rest, was crowned with a green-tiled roof. In ancient days this level had been the headquarters of the castle, riddled with *jugan* loopholes for guns and *yumihazama* slits for bowmen. Here the *joshu* lord of the castle resided under siege.

It had a narrow balustrade outside, on which Matt pictured samurai patrolling, in helmets and leather armor, bows all strung and ready, to protect their master to the death.

At the massive stone gate guarding the moat, he stopped the car and got out. He took his lunch box, his rucksack with his books, and quilted air-raid hood. Ono slid into the driver's seat.

Matt slung his book bag over his shoulder and threaded along the crowded sidewalk at a half-run. By eight o'clock he had crossed Aioi Bridge and was lined up at attention, towering over his classmates, his wooden rifle at present arms, his breath still heaving, and his tan shirt already soaked with sweat.

Captain Tasaka, their military-science instructor, with one trouser-leg pinned up and leaning on his crutches, led the school anthem:

> *The evening rain is white*
> *Over Hiroshima Castle.*
> *Faded is the flower*
> *That was at its height.*
> *Springtime departs with the flowing Honkawa . . .*

He glanced up. Two new B-29s were tracing contrails, scribing ruler-straight lines across the cloudless sky. They were so high that they could not be heard above the hymn. They seemed to ignore the city, which ignored them in return.

Like a schoolboy's palm outstretched for punishment, Hiroshima lay waiting on the shore. Its fingers were etched by the branches of the Ota River, flowing from the generous mountains to the north. Wharves and docks of the Imperial Army Supply Depot dangled like fingernails awash in the Seto Sea.

At 8:06 a volunteer plane watcher at the Matsunaga lookout station in the hills to the east of Hiroshima sighted two high-flying B-29s heading northwest toward the city. He picked up his phone and was reporting them when he sighted another, following miles behind. He added that one to the same report.

Downtown, the streets teemed with life in the hot morning sun.

CHAPTER 11

Major Michihiko Fujihara alighted from his staff car inside the main gate of Hiroshima Castle. He acknowledged Private Ono's bow. Striding to the door of the old Imperial Headquarters Building, a relic of the Sino-Japanese War in the shadow of the castle tower, he returned the salute of the sentry there and paused, struck by a charitable thought.

He would have no further use for his vehicle this morning, for he had a conference scheduled in his office with General Toshio Sumi, Chief of Second Army Intelligence, who would head the underground arm of the National Volunteer Fighting Corps in Hiroshima Prefecture after the Yankee invasion. The major's own car would only rest all morning in the garrison garage.

He walked back to the auto and told Ono to return to the quarters and drive Alicia to work. Ono's peasant face fell. He had been anticipating his morning nap. The major sympathized: his driver had been up half the night, like everyone else, and could probably use the sleep. And auto fuel was very scarce: to waste it seemed unpatriotic.

But he had been feeling strangely nostalgic, and a little apprehensive, since he arose from his futon at dawn. Something was in the air. Ever since the horrible morning he had left Chichijima, he had prayed to the Sun Goddess before the little shrine by the pool in his garden. On most days, the prayers had given him tranquillity, and strength to face the world. But today his heart had grown even heavier. He sensed that with the coming invasion, a phase of his life was hurtling to an end.

When he had invited the Bancrofts, mother, daughter, and son, to Hiroshima, he had been certain that their father, like all the rest, would die on Iwo Jima. It had sorrowed him and filled him with shame, but since it must be so, he could not help but dream of the day he would marry the woman he loved.

Since she was gone, at least he could ease life for her daughter, whom he loved as a father would. She had spent half the night in a bunker; today she should not have to fight her way onto a jammed streetcar and sustain the daily gawks and stares. A war widow, she told him once, had yanked at her hair, "to see if it was real."

The major entered the building and climbed to his second-floor office. The room was a small one, facing west. It was occidental in decor, and he had replaced the army furniture with some he had kept from his Tokyo architectural loft. A photo of Matt and Alicia, on the beach at Chichijima, and some family pictures of his son and late wife taken in happier days, hung above a draftsman's table placed in the window's light.

The place was scrupulously neat. Though not a fussy man, the major strove as a Shintoist and Zen Buddhist for a clear, uncluttered mind. He aimed for perfection in every task, and disliked all sloppiness.

He looked at the German wall clock above his files. It was nearing eight o'clock, and General Sumi should be here.

He opened his window. He could smell night soil, richly spread as fertilizer, wafting from beyond the ancient castle wall. Over the gray mortised stones he could see the fields—now turned to truck gardens tilled by students—of Asano Park. Beyond it flowed the Kyobashi-gawa, green with glints of polished bronze, dancing in the early sun.

He was looking out at hereditary lands—the palace garden, in fact—of the great Asano family, a setting in the finest legend in Japan, that of the leaderless samurai, the "Forty-seven Ronin."

Three centuries before, the ruling lord of the Asano house, Asano Naganori, *daimyo* of the province, had traveled to a state ceremony at the shogun's palace in Edo with forty-seven of his soldiers. Here the lord had been insulted. One Kira Yoshihide, the court chamberlain, thinking him a yokel, had tried to instruct him in the etiquette of the shogun's establishment. Drawing his samurai sword, the prince had slashed at the functionary, wounding him severely.

In his trial, it was found that he had doubly sinned: for drawing his *katana* in the palace, and for assaulting the shogun's official. He was allowed to commit hara-kiri. Before his forty-seven grieving samurai, he killed himself as ordered. His samurai, evicted from the palace, were suddenly *ronin*, soldiers without a leader.

But their dead lord had been dishonored by the wounded Kira, and must be vindicated. They pretended to accept the verdict, and for two years waited patiently. On the snowy night of February 7, 1703, the Forty-seven Ronin saw their chance. By ruse, they silently invaded the mansion of Kira and killed him.

Then they gave themselves up. They were allowed to commit seppuku themselves, joining their *daimyo* in death. The very Japanese-ness of it all had turned the Forty-seven Ronin into national deities.

From his window, the major could see the family temple where the Asano clan and the family of Oishi Yoshio, leader of the raid, were buried. The tale was embedded in Japanese culture. The major was amused that as an educated man, flawed by the modern West, he was touched by the savage legend. But he felt his throat grow tight with admiration for the loyal *ronin* when he saw the story reenacted on kabuki stage or cinema screen, or heard one of its versions on the air.

Let Americans laugh at our chauvinism, or scorn it; it is a fact they ignore at their peril.

Standing at the window now, he had only to close his eyes to see shadowy figures, cloaked in snow, stealing across a castle moat. Each of the forty-seven was one with the other; each was one with his master, who, adrift in eternity, was waiting for revenge.

The flash of *katanas*, the grunt of combat . . . Then seppuku, the shining dagger into one's tense belly, the jerk from right to left . . . For *those* samurai, all had come right in the end.

The West had its Three Wise Men: Japan had forty-seven

dutiful *ronin,* who had grown to eighty million now, warm in
the emperor's love. Such was the glue of a culture, as the
Yankees would find out.

High above Asano Park crawled a tiny silver speck. Another B-29. He found himself thinking of its crew.

*Die as my son did, in battle, since it must be so. But do not
trust my countrymen to spare you, if you fall into their hands.
Men who wear my uniform have twisted the people's minds . . .*

The Propaganda Ministry had painted the Yanks in dripping blood: they would rape, pillage, murder, and extermi-
nate Nippon. In railroad stations stood posters of U.S. Marines
bayoneting helpless women.

Fujihara knew that the posters lied, that Americans were a
kind, if mindless, breed. A Nazi military attaché, stranded in
Japan after VE Day, had told him of the mercy that the Yanks
were showing Germany. But even if the general population
were allowed to hear of it, it would prove nothing to them. It
was to be expected: *Germans* were white, after all.

Matt and Alicia would lose his protection, for he was to be
engineering chief of staff to General Sumi and finally would
become the fighting man his father had wished him to be,
blowing bridges, setting charges, repairing bunkers. He turned
abruptly from the window. He could not bear to think of
Alicia and Matt alone against the mobs.

He heard the rattle of rifles in salute below. The general
was here. He hoped that the interview would concern itself
only with engineering problems in the last-ditch redoubts
above Kure. But he had a premonition, from his last meeting
with Sumi, that intelligence matters—dealing with his wards—
were on the agenda too.

He called to his clerk—a slight, bespectacled sergeant who
had studied at Kyushu University—to prepare tea, and arose
behind his desk.

General Toshio Sumi entered hurriedly. He was a chunky
officer, not yet forty, of peasant stock, one of the new
generation of imperial staff officers who had arisen from the
ranks in the Army of Kwantung. On this stifling day every
other officer in Hiroshima army headquarters was wearing an
open shirt collar outside his jacket, Burma-style. The general's uniform was rumpled and he was sweating already, but
he had his collar properly buttoned, high on his thick bull

neck. To the major he evoked a faint scent of the rice paddy where, he was certain, some of his family toiled today.

The general bobbed his head impatiently, removed his sword, and took his seat. He opened his dispatch case.

In his best moods, he was as polite as any colleague. Sumi had served the major's father as a young lieutenant in Manchuria. Though Sumi had been cited for bravery by the old general, his father had always spoken of the young man with a kind of amused contempt, suspecting that he was a member of the Order of the Carp, the espionage branch of the ultranationalist Black Dragon Society.

In the last months Sumi had been saddled with a task too hard for any soldier. Under the secret General Defense Plan of the National Volunteer Fighting Corps, he was to form an underground in Hiroshima and Kure. From a cadre of reservists quite ignorant of military art, he was to organize a military force. The strain had made him irascible. Anything was enough to trigger a tirade against lukewarm patriots in the Diet or traitors in the House of Peers.

The major bowed deeply and seated himself. "Honorable General, my clerk will serve us a certain pale and tasteless tea: Would you do me the honor of drinking it?"

The general nodded impatiently. "It is I who am honored," he said, without enthusiasm.

When the clerk served him tea, the general sipped it swiftly, meanwhile briefing the major on those roads and bridges of the prefecture that he thought they should demolish, with their ill-trained guerrilla forces, after the invasion. From his dispatch case the general drew a large-scale topographic map of the Islands of Kyushu, Shikoku, southern Honshu, and the Inland Sea. He moved behind the major's desk and traced with his finger a series of crimson, arrow-headed prongs: the Imperial General Staff's concept of the coming Yankee invasion.

When he was through, the general growled: "We may not be allowed to fight. There are those in Tokyo who advise the emperor to surrender."

And they are right, the major thought.

The general's eyes were filling with tears of anger. He inhaled with a hiss, his jaw tense. A gold tooth glittered in the morning sunlight. "They are asking the *Russians* to mediate. There are *traitors* in our cabinet. We should kill them!"

And you may, thought the major sadly, before the army's done.

The general noticed the picture of Fujihara's son—dressed in the high-collared uniform of a military academy cadet—above the drafting table. To ignore it would have been a breach of courtesy.

"A fine-looking boy. *He* would not surrender. I believe he gave his life on Peleliu? Under General Inoue, with the Fourteenth Infantry?"

Surprised, the major nodded. "He would be pleased that you knew of him, sir. As *I* am."

The general smiled. "It is the duty of an intelligence officer to know what he can." He was inspecting the picture of Alicia and Matt. "Your two young *gaijin* wards?"

Alert, the major said cautiously: "Yes sir. Not *gaijin*, though. As I told you when last we spoke, they are citizens of Japan."

The general moved closer, put on glasses, and peered at the photo more closely. "So you said. Loyal subjects of the emperor! It seems quite impossible, does it not?"

The major shrugged and said that he thought not, with five generations in the warmth of the emperor's sun. "Their mother's grandfather was Japanese."

"They do not look it. 'Bankloft-o Mitsugu,' " mused the general, using Matt's Japanese name. He commented that it seemed curiously disloyal to use his Western one. "And quite illegal, under Japanese law, as well."

"It is to honor his father," Fujihara said stiffly, "who died under the name Bancroft on Iwo."

"So you told me." The general mused for a moment. "The boy speaks good English?"

"Yes sir," the major said cautiously. "At least, he *can.*"

"And he works . . . where?"

"With the Student Service Corps, on alternate days."

The general's lips tightened. He was suddenly hostile. "So you have left him still in *school?*"

The major didn't like the trend of his questions. He had purposely placed Matt and Alicia himself, fearing American anger after the war. If he had put them in sensitive jobs, the Yankees might accuse them after the invasion of disloyalty or even treason when they found out about their American blood.

"He is just thirteen, sir, too young for military conscription."

"But not too young for certain more valuable civilian

work. I have children of twelve on my switchboards." The general thought for a moment. "And the girl?"

"She is a seamstress at the Army Clothes Depot." He sensed danger.

"She speaks English too?"

"Why, yes."

"One wonders why they are not already in some code room in intelligence?" The general bent and snapped closed his dispatch case. "Or in the Propaganda Ministry, broadcasting?"

The major found it demeaning to lie, and his face, he felt, was flaming, but he tried. He explained that he had felt that his wards should work humbly with their hands for the emperor: "I did not think of their value as translators."

"Well, *you* are their guardian: the choice was yours. I'm afraid it no longer is." Sumi produced his handkerchief and blew his nose like a barbarian: a habit picked up in China, perhaps; Americans did it too. The major hid a shudder: one should dab, not snort like a hog.

"What do you mean, sir?"

"When last we spoke I suggested that we might have the boy volunteer to join the Yankee ranks as an interpreter."

"No," the major said. "He speaks an English frozen in time a hundred years ago." He forced a smile. "Could the *ronin* infiltrate the castle today, mouthing the ancient tongue?"

The general lit a cigarette and fanned out the match. "Why not?" He dragged at the cigarette. "Major, I must tell you that I have visited my document section." He bent, shuffled through his suitcase, and found a rice-paper envelope. He drew out a green passport, emblazoned with the eagle of the United States. He opened it, stepped back to Matt's picture, compared it, and tossed it onto the desk. Astonished, the major saw Matt's face, as it appeared on his entry pass from Chichijima, staring up at him from the page. He picked up the passport: *Christopher Hart. Birth Place: Tokyo, Japan. Birth Date: January 11, 1932.* It carried a 1941 prewar endorsement by the American consul in Tokyo, and had undeniable authenticity.

"A good selection, Major?" murmured the general. "Even the age is close."

"Who is Christopher Hart?" muttered the major.

The general shrugged. "The son of Episcopalian medical

missionaries. They stayed in Tokyo, when the *Gripsholm* sailed. All very Christian, it was. The mother was a nurse, I think. They were tending American POWs at the Kagawa Christian Fellowship House POW camp." The general grinned. "They were incinerated by their own firebombs on March 10. The *kempeitai* had, of course, their passports. This one needs young Bankloft-o's signature, as Hart."

The major chilled. He must be careful, very careful, not to fight too hard, but to fight just hard enough.

"Sir, you would find my ward most willing. It is *I* who have doubts."

"What doubts?" smiled the general.

"The moment he contacted American authorities, he'd be repatriated. What good would that do us?"

"They will *need* interpreters. I think they will let him stay."

"But he's untrained! When they caught him, he'd be shot as a spy!"

The general walked to the window. Softly, he said: "But not . . . beheaded?"

There was a deadly silence. The major could hear his clerk typing. A telephone rang.

"As the young radioman was," continued the general, "on Washington Beach?"

Outside, the major heard troops falling in. The guard was changing.

"What do you mean?" His mouth felt dry.

"Your Bankloft-o is thirteen." The general turned back. "How old was the American on Chichijima? The radioman?"

The major could not answer. He had suspected, when he left Chichijima, that Kondo would investigate the radioman's death. Now he only wondered, if the general knew he had killed the prisoner, how many others did.

Sumi scanned his face, amused. "Colonel Kondo, my liaison officer on Chichijima, found your departure rather strange."

"Strange, sir?" He felt ill.

The general's eyes focused distantly, as if he were reading invisible charges in the air. "You were sent to Chichijima on temporary duty. You carried an Air Priority arm band, 'Special Class.' Wearing the arm band, you returned on a Kawasaki-56 regular morning courier flight."

"That's right, sir." He licked his lips. His heart began to pound.

The general's voice rose: by noon that day Colonel Kondo at Chichijima Fortress Headquarters had radioed Second Army, asking if a certain Major Fujihara had returned to Hiroshima and querying as to why he had simply left. "There is no record of your having properly got your orders endorsed by their engineering chief of staff. Nor by fortress headquarters. Nor of your making a courtesy call to bid farewell to General Tachibana's Mixed Brigade. Is this *true?*"

Calm, calm, he cautioned himself. *Calm as a pool of midnight water, stay calm no matter what.*

"Probably I forgot, sir. I was finished my work. They *had* my recommendations." He managed a smile. "A small breach of regulations, at any rate."

The general shook his head. "Your father was a general. You completed staff training. You've been a field-grade officer for four years." Surely the major realized that when one's temporary duty was completed, one didn't simply climb in a plane and *leave*?

Fujihara steadied his voice: "There was confusion, that day on Chichijima," he explained. "The Americans bombed us the day before, again that very morning—"

The general smiled. "Yes. An American Helldiver was shot down. A pilot and radioman were captured and interrogated. In fact, *you* translated. After the young Bankloft-o girl tried and broke into tears." He puffed at his cigarette. "You'll be sad to hear, Major, that both prisoners were found to be dead at dawn."

Sumi was no longer a peasant in general's uniform: he was Buddha with a hundred arms and a hundred thousand eyes.

"One speared, one beheaded," mused the general. "Beheaded before Kondo could learn what carrier they flew from. Now, who could not wait for orders to kill him? Or permission to do the deed?" The general seemed lost in thought. "I wonder. . . . The criminal would have to be bearing a sword. Some lieutenant wandering by, perhaps, who lost his wife in the Tokyo raids?" The rock-hard eyes bored suddenly into his. *"Or an angry officer of poor judgment, about to lose his son?"*

The major could only stare.

The general picked up his cap. "Knowing this thing, I picked you for my staff."

The major gazed at him in shock. Sumi placed a hand on his shoulder. The general seemed to grow in size. A vein throbbed at his temple. He smiled paternally, and the gold tooth flashed. "I can forgive a lapse in judgment, in an officer with zeal. I *need* men who will kill in anger! And die in anger, too."

He could not permit himself to be seen in so dishonorable a role: "General," he murmured dazedly, "I must tell you that it was not anger—"

The general raised his hand and glanced at the clock. "Explanations are not necessary. There will be plenty of time to discuss young Bankloft-o's mission. But he will sign his passport tonight." He put the passport on the desk. "Convince him of his duty to use it when so ordered by my staff."

The major understood. Sumi would use the Chichijima execution as a sword against him.

"As you know," the general continued, buckling on his sword, "the action on the beach was quite in violation of the Imperial Army Operations Handbook." He smiled. *"Whoever* performed it. Sayonara, Major Fujihara, I am late."

The major found himself too shocked to bow. When the general left, he sat down behind his desk, his mind blank.

His clerk stuck his head in the office. "A call from Prefecture Air Alert, sir. There will be an alarm very shortly, if the Yankees do not turn back."

The old Imperial Headquarters Building always received advance notice, to enable officers to put their classified material into their safes.

"Go ahead," he told his clerk dazedly. "I'll follow."

He began to open his safe, then changed his mind and put the passport in his tunic pocket.

By the cobbled road at the castle gate sloped the steel doors of an ancient cellar, shelter for headquarters personnel. Ancient stone steps led down to an arsenal, a wartime storehouse for the artifacts of the castle's military museum. The shelter was crammed with leather samurai chest plates, helmets, and sturdy spears.

His thoughts whirled. General Sumi had seemed to approve of his killing the radioman, but that only made it worse.

A samurai was compassionate. The major had acted out of

mercy, but who would realize that? Not even his ancestors in their graves. The Fujihara name hung in the balance. Now he could not fight to save Matt from a mission which seemed suicidal, or Sumi might charge him before the world.

Suppose *Alicia* learned what he had done?

He started down the bunker stairs, past a private tugging at the door to close it. On the third step he turned to glance at the deep blue sky, begging tolerance from his father, understanding from his son. In the Other World, only the poor young radioman knew the truth.

With the silent impact of a hot flashbulb in his face, the heavens turned to white. A blast of heat struck his cheeks, as if the door to hell had opened. He flung his hands to his eyes, recoiled, missed his footing, and crashed backward down the stairs.

CHAPTER 12

A Japanese army private manning earphones at the Nakano searchlight battery's sound-detection equipment, near Hiroshima, had picked up the drone of aircraft engines at 8:14 A.M. Training his huge mechanical ear, he reported that unidentified aircraft were approaching from Saijo, fifteen miles east of Hiroshima, and heading for the center of the city.

At 8:15 two planes were sighted by the antiaircraft spotters of a battery on Mukay-Shima Island in Hiroshima Harbor. They were B-29s, one following the other, but separating rapidly. As usual, the aircraft were too high for accurate ranging. Ammunition was so short that the acting sergeant commanding the battery decided to hold fire and the gunners could only watch.

The two aircraft acted oddly. When the first was almost a half-mile ahead of the other, it banked violently toward the right. At the same time, the second aircraft banked left: below it two tiny parachutes blossomed white against the blue.

Puzzled, because they had not fired and knew of no one else who had, the men in the Mukay-Shima battery nonetheless let out a cheer: obviously, the second plane was in some kind of trouble and the crew was bailing out.

Most of them were still staring upward, forty seconds later, when the sky over Hiroshima turned for an instant to a pure and dazzling light.

They were lucky. They were over five miles from the flash, past the range of the burns which would turn the faces of some of the least-scorched of the city's survivors a permanent walnut color—the "Mask of Hiroshima."

But the antiaircraft gunners would all be blind for hours.

In the precise center of Hiroshima, the Ota River split into two branches: the Honkawa, flowing southwest past the Honkawa Middle School, and the Motoyasu, flowing southeast. Both continued for some thirty blocks before they passed the Hiroshima shipyard and army docks and spilled into the Inland Sea.

Crossing the Ota River where it split was a concrete four-lane bridge carrying a streetcar line. The bridge was the Aioi, and in its middle, at right angles to the main structure, another span jutted south to the teeming Tenjimachi District in the fork of the two river branches.

Thus Aioi Bridge was T-shaped, unmistakable on a clear day through a bombsight from thirty thousand feet. Its unusual plan, in the middle of downtown Hiroshima and less than eight hundred yards from Second Army headquarters and the Hiroshima military barracks, made it a perfect aiming point—almost a crosshair itself—for "Little Boy."

The "T-Bridge" was a godsend to Major Thomas Ferebee, *Enola Gay*'s bombardier, a poker-playing Southerner with a huge mustache. He was a veteran of Berlin raids, no longer given to great enthusiasms. But when first he had been shown the bridge on a reconnaissance photo on Guam, Ferebee called it the most perfect aiming point he had seen in the entire war.

Little Boy—the bomb he would drop—was torpedo-shaped, ten feet long, and just over two feet in diameter. Armed with its 135-pound uranium core and plug, it weighed almost four and a half tons. On its khaki-colored body armorers on Tinian had scrawled the usual graffiti in crayon: *Fuck Tojo, For the Emperor,* and *Nip the Nips.*

One of the ordnance men had scribbled on the fins a memorial to the dead sailors of the cruiser *Indianapolis,* which had delivered the core of the bomb to Tinian last week, then sailed south to perish, torpedoed by a Japanese sub. Tinian Island rumor had it that nine hundred of her twelve-hundred-man crew had died in the shark-infested waters of the Philippine Sea before the navy knew she had been hit: the bomb might help to avenge them.

Inside Little Boy's case was a half-ton six-inch gun barrel, six feet long. At one end was a charge of TNT and a uranium plug: at the other end the uranium core. Firing the plug into the core would create an instantaneous critical mass and an explosion variously estimated to be equivalent to five to fifteen thousand tons of TNT. The system—unlike that of the plutonium bomb tested three weeks before in the Trinity shot at Alamogordo—had never been tried.

Enola Gay, wallowing under the weight of Little Boy, was preceded by a weather plane and accompanied by a laboratory plane, both B-29s. The laboratory plane parachuted two transmitting canisters of recording equipment—monitored by the plane—just before *Enola* dropped: it was these canisters which misled some Japanese who saw them to believe that a crew had bailed out, and others that the bomb was dropped by parachute.

By 8:13, Major Ferebee, at 31,600 feet and making 285 knots due west, had Aioi Bridge ahead, the T squarely in the reticule of his bombsight. Just after 8:15 he pickled off his load, only seventeen seconds late. Little Boy arced silently down for forty seconds, toward the seventh largest city in Japan.

At a height of 1,850 feet, directly above Shima Hospital in downtown Hiroshima and only 800 feet horizontally from the center of Aioi Bridge, it exploded. It exceeded—by two thousand tons of dynamite—the Manhattan scientists' most optimistic estimates. They had calculated its charge at fifteen kilotons: its actual power was seventeen. It destroyed sixty thousand of Hiroshima's ninety thousand buildings, but less than twenty-six percent of its industrial and military capacity, since industrial plants and army depots were on the periphery of the city.

Three hundred twenty thousand men, women, and children were within forty blocks of Shima Hospital at 8:15 A.M., including 3,200 American citizens of Japanese ancestry—mostly students—who were in Hiroshima, trapped by the war.

The flash from Little Boy temporarily blinded all who were watching the parachuting instrument canisters. Its heat vaporized some unprotected residents near ground zero and liquefied others, melting their fatty tissues as lard is rendered into soap.

Farther away, it scorched the design of clothing onto human skin, as photographic images are transferred from negatives to prints. The half-second shock wave—equivalent to a one-thousand-pound air hammer striking the human body at sonic speed—disemboweled some, ruptured ear drums of others, turned bodies into projectiles, filled the air with flying glass, and stripped virtually all unsheltered victims of their clothing.

Seventy-one thousand Japanese died instantly. Few of them would ever be identified. Hiroshima's elementary and middle schools, unlike her factories, were downtown, so some twenty thousand of those who were killed were children. Within four days the total dead would reach 118,661, as the mortally wounded died of burns, lacerations, and the early stages of radiation sickness.

Thirty thousand, five hundred twenty-four citizens were severely injured but survived; 48,806 were only slightly injured. About 100,000 were physically unhurt.

Ten American B-29 crewmen captured July 27 in Kyushu died in their cells five miles from Shima Hospital. Thirteen other American POWs, in various military prisons throughout the city, died too.

Aioi Bridge—Ferebee's aiming point—survived. On its concrete balustrade, Little Boy sketched its own graffiti: two striding human figures and a cyclist, hurrying to work.

In a line of his fellow students just inside the entrance to Honkawa Middle School, Matt Bancroft bowed to a closed door. Beyond it hung the school's portrait of the emperor, never displayed except during school assemblies.

He bowed likewise to the statue of a fabled Japanese peasant boy, his back stacked with wood and reading from a scroll, purportedly so anxious to master his *kanji* characters that he studied even as he delivered his cords. The statue was to be found at the door of every middle school in Japan.

Matt headed for a seat at the back. Though academic achievement entitled him to a first-row chair, whenever he took one he blocked the view of shorter students behind him, so he had been assigned to the rear with the oafs.

Already the morning was growing warm, so he crammed

himself into the tiny seat nearest the open window above the schoolyard, setting and locking the writing platform on the chair, though it was really too short for his arm. He glanced out the window. Captain Tasaka, who would supervise their digging later, was swinging across the basketball court on his crutches, probably heading for the East Drill Field.

Their teacher had not yet arrived. Two years ago, the class would have been unruly. Now, everyone was so tired from alerts and weak from wartime rations that hardly anyone talked, and no one had the energy for horseplay. In front of Matt sat a boy—whose uniform seemed to grow larger every week—already nodding in his chair.

Matt's nisei friend across the aisle, Tomoyuki, was from San Francisco. He had never learned half the *hiragana* characters he needed. He had been assigned Friday to prepare to read aloud a passage from "A Forest in Full Flower," by Yukio Mishima, a startling young writer hardly older than they. Now, waiting for their teacher, Tomoyuki picked up the book and leaned closer across the aisle. He pointed to the page. "What is this character, Bancroft-san?"

Matt turned away from the window to look at the page. "Sea god," he said. "Like Neptune, in English. God of the—"

Time suddenly stopped. Forever afterward, Matt would have the impression that even before the flash, everything had turned to black and white: Tomoyuki's face, furrowed in concentration: then, next to Tomoyuki, Daiji Sakamoto, a noodle merchant's son, fat as a miniature sumo wrestler: past Daiji, a bespectacled boy named Akira Kuramoto, frozen in time through all eternity, picking his nose.

A silent, vermilion light bathed the classroom. There was a blast of heat from outside. Tomoyuki's eyes, facing the window, turned to gold. Then the room went black, as if the sun had gone out.

"A bomb?" someone squeaked uncertainly in the dark from the front. "In the schoolyard?"

All at once the world caved in with a crash of shattered glass. Matt felt plaster, roof tiles, timbers raining on his shoulders; instinctively, he covered his head with his hands.

Then, in a cacophony of squealing boards and shattering glass, he was hurled to the floor and blacked out.

•   •   •

He awoke on his side in the dark, alone. His hips seemed squeezed in one mighty vise, and his shoulders in another. He caught a horrid stench of moldy cement and sewage. He knew suddenly that the roof had collapsed on him and he was imprisoned in rubble, dank and cold. Still there was no sound. He tried to move his legs, but they were trapped. He could move his left hand and his left arm, but not his right.

He squirmed uselessly. He was coughing dust. All at once he smelled smoke, more acrid than the awful smell of the disemboweled building, and the first wisp of it drove him frantic.

The drainage pipe: "Mama, I can't move . . ."
"Of course you can, Pumpkin. An inch at a time . . ."
"Tasukete kudasai!" he grunted. "Help me!"

But now there was no reply, no sound at all. He was utterly alone. He began to scrape with his left hand at the coarse plaster and clay. With all his strength, he pressed upward against the timbers crushing his hips. He was strangling, coughing, retching, while he struggled like a buried ant. He shrugged out a space from around his shoulders, then got his hands down to his hipbones and worked loose a space in the rubble there.

He became conscious of light—or a certain absence of darkness—a few feet from his face. Scratching and clawing, using strength he never knew he had, he squirmed toward it, until it turned into a triangle gleaming a few feet from his face.

Two roof timbers were angled over a tile. One of them moved. He pried it loose and squirmed forward. His head emerged into daylight. The smell of smoke was worse. Panicked, he made a mighty effort and crawled to his feet.

He was outside the building, in a darkened world. To his amazement, he was on the ground floor. A giant hand had shoved over the structure, which had simply folded like a house of cards. He had ridden it down and now it was flat. Nowhere did the rubble of the two-story building seem taller than himself. He peered about.

Three willow trees by the schoolyard entrance, erect a moment ago—or an hour ago, he had no idea—were bowed like branches in a wind. The wall around the school was down, though the concrete entrance with its open iron gates remained. It stood as a lonely monument, all that was left of the place. No one was around, no one and nothing. The basketball backboards were gone, but something was burning near the gate. He stumbled over and looked.

It was one of Captain Tasaka's crutches. But where was the captain? He must have panicked and deserted them, somehow hopped away without it. The captain *deserved* to lose his crutch, but nevertheless he had better try to save it.

Angrily, he picked it up by the arm-pad and beat it against the earth, until he snuffed out the flames and they turned to smoke.

The sun seemed gone forever. A black cloud, reflecting orange lights, hovered over the schoolyard and extended far beyond. He was alone on a darkening plain; there was no one, simply no one, to explain to him what had happened.

He turned back to the rubble. Where was Tomoyuki? Where were they *all?*

He noticed that a dozen little fires were burning in the wreckage, fanned by a sudden gust of wind.

He screamed his classmates' names: "Tomoyuki!" he shouted. "Daiji! Akira!"

The wind was rising. He ran toward the ruin and began to pry at the mess with the captain's crutch. He got nowhere, so he began to scrabble in the jumble with his bare hands, oblivious of splinters and tiles and jagged shards of glass.

It was useless, stupid. Had he not been at the corner of the building, in the last row, toward the window, he would never have survived the collapse. Had he not turned away from the window, he would have been blinded.

Everything was flattened: A direct hit, though he saw no crater anywhere.

The B-29s must have seen them drilling at morning assembly, and come back to wipe them out. He looked up at the darkened sky, remembering Omura's shattered street, and his mother in his arms. Would they *never* quit?

"Bastards!" he shrieked in English. "Bloody, rotten bastards!"

The wind ceased suddenly. A raindrop, huge in size, splatted on his forehead, and another on his arm. He stared at the mark on his khaki sleeve.

It was rimmed with black.

Astonished, he cupped his hand. He studied the water in his palm.

Black! The rain, like the world, was black!

The evening rain is white
Over Hiroshima Castle.

What had happened, to turn rain black?

He threw back his shoulders. He was a good Japanese. Unlike the captain, he would not panic. There was a military police sentry box at Aioi Bridge, only two blocks away, though hidden in the smoke and dust. He must tell them that the school had been bombed: they would dig his classmates out.

He began to run toward the gate. Passing between the gate columns, he noticed that the left one had been scorched black. Startled, he paused.

As if sprayed on the column stood the white shadow of a human body.

He found himself trembling in the haze.

He was conscious of a new smell. It evoked Alicia's hair curlers, used too hot, or his grandfather's plucked chickens, singed on the open fire for the Yankee Thanksgiving.

Burned flesh, burned hair?

His eyes darted about, stinging from the smoke. Ten yards beyond the gates lay the other crutch, charred on one side, untouched on the other.

Near it, face-up in the gutter, he could see a body through the smoke. Reluctantly, he drew closer. Its right side was naked and black, its left side seemingly untouched. The left pant leg was pinned up, and the crease was undisturbed.

He had found the captain!

Involuntarily, he yelled. The head moved toward the sound, blindly, and the scorched arm rose. Then the body shuddered and was still. Matt knelt by the captain's head, holding his breath against the smell. One eye was seared closed, and the other stared whitely at the darkened sky.

Tiredly, Matt got up. Flames were rising from rubble across the street, where a row of shops had stood. He was overwhelmed by thirst.

For the first time he noticed that his right forearm was cut. From it projected an inch-long splinter of glass. It did not hurt at all. Carefully he plucked it out, then noticed that the back of his right hand, which had been toward the window, was reddened, exactly to the sleeve-line, as if he had worked too long spading beneath a blazing sun. This *did* hurt, excruciatingly.

He rolled the sleeve away from the burn and began to trot toward Aioi Bridge. Inside, in time to his steps, his mind sang words that would not leave.

> *Faded is the flower*
> *That was at its height.*
> *Springtime leaves with the flowing Honkawa . . .*

The black rain stopped abruptly. In the distance, across what had been buildings, he could see the bridge. He slowed and began to walk. He noticed that there was no more military police kiosk. Perhaps they had torn it down yesterday, for a fire lane.

All right, he would cross the span, catch the tram, and find a policeman somehow, if he had to ride all the way to Hiroshima Castle.

Suddenly he stopped.

Aioi Bridge remained, but it was swarming with naked, walking corpses. They moved slowly in two columns, one inching east, one west. Each corpse—he could not tell the men from the women—was holding its arms extended from its body, like Jesus on the cross, fingers dangling limply in the wind.

He could smell the scorched, wandering ghosts a block away. Nausea swept him. Whatever had happened, he would never cross *that* bridge: he would swim the Honkawa first.

Tramping across hot, smoking roof tiles from what had once been riverside homes and stores, he scrambled down the bank.

He paused again. More walking dead—crowds of them—stood by the river, crouched at its side, lay in its shallows.

No one spoke, no one cried.

A child, fully clothed and unburned, was leading its naked mother—or father—by the hand.

A mother squatted in the rushes, trying to nurse her baby from a scorched and bloody breast.

He sidled through the mob. Keeping his eyes from the survivors, he slipped off his shoes, tied them together, and slung them around his neck. He was wading into deep water, scooping up a drink, when a body, bloated and black, bumped into him. Caught in the swift current, he could not fight his way clear of it. Finally he shoved it mightily, dodged it as it passed, and began to swim.

Just short of the other side, a schoolgirl in underwear, who had ventured in too deep, held out her hands to him. She was horribly burned. He grabbed at her forearm and lost his grip when her skin peeled off like a glove. She did not even grimace, but lost her footing and was swept away before he could grab at her again.

He gazed after her stupidly.

He had always thought that he would be a hero, given the chance. But he had no strength to swim after her, and hardly enough to save himself. She would probably die anyway; her eyes had been seared to slits and her face looked like a boiled tomato.

He struggled up the bank. At the top he vomited yellow bile.

Finally he straightened up. Tired or not, he must report the bombing of the school. And somewhere telephone Mickey-san and Alicia to tell them he'd survived.

Thank God they had been far from the school and the river when the Yankee bomb had struck.

CHAPTER 13

General Toshio Sumi's staff car, with rising-sun emblems fluttering at its fenders, began the ascent of a rise on the Hiroshima-Kure coastal road.

The general sat stolidly in the rear seat. The half-hour trip to Kure was to inspect Fujihara's work in constructing their final bunker above the Kure naval base.

Between the seat and the general's boots sat his briefcase. He kept it always with him nowadays.

In it lay the records of his sacred charge, the roster of the Order of the Carp. When finally he moved to his command post, he would lock it in his safe, deep in the mountain.

It would rest securely there until the end. By the time the Americans destroyed his redoubt he would be dead. The empire, its outposts, the order, and the Black Dragon Society itself would have perished for the emperor. He would burn the roster, first, as a memorial to the spirits of brothers who had gone before.

He sat back and lit a cigarette. A good morning's work, with Major Fujihara, already. He had waited for the proper moment, and sufficiently intimidated Fujihara, he hoped, so that he would volunteer the Bankloft-o youngster as a spy.

The major was the key to his *gaijin* ward, and the lock had needed lubricating, that was all.

He exhaled a cloud of smoke. Matt Bancroft was, for all

intents and purposes, a recruit of the Order of the Carp already. With his white skin and round eyes, he would be worth a regiment in the guerrilla actions to come.

Suddenly the general felt a warmth on the back of his neck. The pine trees by the road and the wooded islands on the Seto Sea flashed into purple. His driver shouted: *"Wah?"*

"Stop the car!" Sumi craned backward. Over Hiroshima, an immense white thundercloud was rising, as large as the city itself.

An explosion at Ujina ammunition depot? No, far too large.

A meteor?

As the car crunched to a stop on the roadside gravel, the general scrambled out.

The top of the cloud churned and flashed with vermilion flame. Now it hovered over the entire basin of the Ota River.

He heard an immense sigh from the wooded mountainside, and a mournful wail, like wind in a ravine. He clung to the car door as a hot gust slammed up the road, raising a cloud of dust. He heard his driver clap his hands to summon his family gods.

He did the same. He burned with shame. Perhaps they had not fought hard enough, failed Amaterasu, the sun goddess, and she had turned against her people. Only her descendant, His Imperial Majesty, could save them now.

The wind had died, but to return to the city was useless: Hiroshima castle was floating somewhere in the cloud.

It was time they manned the bunker on the peak.

CHAPTER 14

Lieutenant Josh Goldberg left the Naval Air Transport Service Quonset at Harmon Field on Guam and stepped into blazing heat. Carrying a secret packet, he returned to the jeep he had parked in the shade of the building. He discovered that more vehicles had arrived, some of them flying flags with stars. He wondered what was happening.

It was 1000 hours. He and other duty officers had come to pick up revisions to Olympic—the invasion of Kyushu and the feints against the Bonins—from the courier flight from Hawaii. Packets from Commander in Chief, Pacific Fleet, had been arriving almost daily for months. With the landing only four months away, training for Olympic had begun on the southern beaches of Guam, and new changes had to be integrated before every exercise.

He was climbing into his jeep when he heard someone drawl, in a flat Australian accent: "So where's your bloody bus?"

He looked up. A lanky, redheaded man, chewing at an unlit pipe, had emerged from the NATS Quonset and was gazing down the road to Agana.

He was freckled. His jutting nose was sunburned. He wore an Australian bush hat and khaki shorts. He showed no rank, but on his shoulder was a patch: CORRESPONDENT.

He was the first war correspondent Josh had ever seen, and a very impatient one. His pale blue eyes were cold and icy, and his lips were tense. He had a thirty-five-millimeter camera slung over one shoulder and a jungle-green sea bag over the other. In one hand he carried a portable typewriter and in the other a gnarled and varnished cane. He favored his left leg, leaning heavily on the jeep.

"Bus? I don't know," Josh said briefly. The correspondent had obviously just arrived from somewhere, with an air priority probably higher than that of half the colonels milling around inside.

The man continued to stare down the road. "I just hooked a ride from Tinian in a navy TBM. They told me inside there was a shuttle bus to Agana." Obviously, he was hinting for a lift. The pale blue eyes flicked to the papers in Josh's hands. "Olympic?"

Josh started the jeep. "What's Olympic?" he asked coldly. My God, Tokyo Rose would have it on the air, next.

The redhead put a hand on the door handle.

"A little wager, mate. If I tell you where you're landing will you give me a lift?"

"No," he said, "but I may be able to get you shot." He wondered how much the man really knew. Curious, he shrugged and said: "Oh, hell, climb in."

The Australian tossed his gear into the rear and settled himself in the jeep. "Let me guess. Fukushima! Essex Beach? Ford Beach? Franklin? No, I think Ford."

The journalist should never have heard of any of them, but at least he hadn't mentioned Chichijima. Josh wheeled onto the road. "On *this* island, friend, don't toss those beach names around, or you'll end up in the brig."

The correspondent didn't answer. He was regarding the passing rubble of Agana. It had been bombed and shelled strenuously before and during the landing.

"You bloody finished *this* place. And *it* was your own colony. You plan to do this to Japan?"

"Whatever it takes," said Josh. Bitterly, he added: "Did you see Pearl Harbor?"

"Once or twice," nodded the Australian. He stuck out his hand. "Rab McGraw, here. UPI and Reuters, out of Melbourne."

Josh shook hands. "Josh Goldberg. USMCR, out of San Francisco."

McGraw looked at him with interest. "Not too many Jews make it through Quantico."

He was right, but Josh didn't have to explain the corps to every civilian asshole that he met. "Not too many Aussies stay out of uniform, either," he observed. "Where did you want to go, McGraw?"

They were nearing Commander Marianas headquarters. Everything was becoming clean and neat.

"Com Marianas press shack." McGraw lapsed into thought as they wound up Com Marianas Hill along a twisting coral road. Finally he smiled again. "You're a right touchy wallah, Lieutenant. And worried."

"Who *isn't?*" He jabbed his thumb at the Aussie's shoulder patch. "Unless he's wearing one of those?"

"Hardly fair, mate," grinned McGraw. "I mean, Ernie Pyle just bought the farm on Okinawa."

"Pyle didn't *have* to make landings."

The Australian chuckled. "Neither do you."

Josh glanced at him, puzzled. The man must be some kind of socialist nut, trying to spread doubt and dissension. He was Australian, after all. Look what Harry Bridges had done to the San Francisco docks.

Carefully, he asked: "I *don't* have to land? Why not?"

"It's off."

"What's off?"

The Australian didn't answer. Josh pulled in front of a Quonset marked: PRESS SECTION, COM MARIANAS. Something was going on inside: through the open screen door he could see that the shack was as crowded as the NATS terminal had been. An Air Force captain was gesticulating outside with a man, dressed in Army officer's tropicals, but without bars of rank. *Another* correspondent!

"Damn," the Aussie muttered. "That's Lawrence of the *New York Times.* In a bloody brouhaha! Appears we can't file here, either!"

"What's off?" Josh demanded again. McGraw opened the door, put a leg out of the jeep, then turned back and tapped him playfully on his shoulder with his cane.

"Olympic, my friend, will be scrubbed."

"Horseshit."

"True." McGraw smiled, almost sadly. "You've dropped a single bomb on a place called Hiroshima, and from what I hear you've won the bloody war."

He slung his gear over his shoulder, picked up his typewriter and cane, and stumped toward the press Quonset.

CHAPTER 15

Major Michihiko Fujihara had somewhere lost consciousness in his wild fall backward down the stone steps of the shelter.

Now, swimming into awareness, he found himself lying on some kind of tatami. He could see nothing, and the air was fetid. He heard no ventilator. They must have lost electrical power.

He heard his clerk talking to someone: "The major was looking at the sky at the moment of the *pika-don* . . ."

Pika-don . . ."Flash-boom."

A new word, but instantly clear to him. "Sergeant!" he called. "I cannot see! Where are we?"

There was a moment of silence. Then, his clerk's voice: "Here in the shelter, honorable sir. We have been here half an hour."

"And what happened?" His voice sounded reedy in his ears. He must calm himself, evaluate their plight when his eyes accustomed themselves to the underground gloom.

"We don't know, sir." His clerk's voice was shaking. "We think—well, parachutes were observed, Private Hashimoto says. A Yankee bomb struck the castle directly—without a sound. Hashimoto peeked outside. The castle is destroyed. And the wreckage burned."

He could not believe it. He sat up in the dark, fighting nausea. "The *castle?*"

"Ruined!" Private Hashimoto broke in. The major recalled his voice: he remembered a wide, flat face and a sturdy, dependable air. He was rumored to have been an explosive expert with a squad of bangalore torpedo men, who had survived the Mukden Campaign to be invalided home. From his accent, he seemed to be from Hokkaido. "And a black rain falls outside, sir. Can it be a poison gas? We have shut off the ventilator."

The major tried to gather his senses. "Turn it on, or we shall smother. And the lights."

There was silence. He heard his clerk draw in his breath. "But honorable sir?"

"Yes?"

"The lights *are* on. They flicker, but we have power."

Blinded! He found himself shaking. He was suddenly nauseous; there was no up, no down, he was alone in a void. He retched, felt his clerk cleaning the vomit from his tunic.

The ventilator began with a wail. The sound of it cleared his head. "And above, is there still fire?"

"Only smoke. And the rain . . ."

He asked how many were here: the shelter was enormous, with room for three hundred men.

"Just us three, sir. You and me and Private Hashimoto, from the portal guard—"

"Just *three?*" He could not believe it. Two hundred men— clerks, military policemen, a detachment from the Second Army's intelligence section, radiomen—and almost a hundred officers, staff and line, had been working in the castle and in the Old Imperial Headquarters Building. *"Three?"* he repeated dazedly.

"Prefectural Air Raid Warning sounded no alarm," said his clerk.

He suddenly remembered the general. "General Sumi?" demanded the major. "He passed safely through the gate?"

"Yes sir," answered Hashimoto. "Five minutes before the *pika.*"

So his secret was abroad.

With the ventilator on, the major smelled a scent that he had known when a childhood toy, whirled to make sparks for New Year, had been too energetically used, or the smell near a streetcar when its trolley antenna, sliding loose, swung groping in a shower of tiny stars.

Ozone. Perhaps the bomb had been some sort of electrical device. Well, ozone was not lethal: it was time to get out. He told Private Hashimoto to go up and check for fires.

There was the sound of hobnailed boots shuffling up the bunker steps and the creaking of iron hinges as the bunker door swung open. For a moment there was silence, and all at once he heard Hashimoto bellow: *"Gaijin!* Halt there, where you are!"

Gaijin? Paratroopers? Surely not yet!

He had an awful thought. "What *gaijin?"* he called in alarm.

From somewhere above, he heard Hashimoto's rifle bolt slam shut.

A distant voice piped plaintively, protesting in Japanese: "Don't shoot!"

"Stop him!" he grunted. Groping toward the stairway, he tripped and fell against a rough stone wall. He heard his clerk brush past, running up the steps. "Hashimoto!" the sergeant yelled. "Put down your piece!"

The major pulled himself to his feet, stumbled up the steps, and felt a hot wind on his cheeks; flames crackled somewhere; he heard someone, far away, crying for water.

"I am here, *sensei,"* he heard Matt say. "The school was bombed and fire and smoke are everywhere."

"Matt-san . . ." The major opened his arms, and suddenly the boy came into them. He was wet: how strong his back seemed: he wondered if he'd ever see his clear green eyes again. "We must try to find Alicia."

To be a blind architect was to be dead. Once he knew that his other ward was safe, seppuku itself might be very sweet indeed.

Matt, hands shaking, bound Mickey-san's eyes with a handkerchief. The flames of the city were coming toward them. With Private Hashimoto, the clerk, and the major, he started for the wide refuge of the East Drill Field, half a dozen blocks away across the Kyobashi River.

They found a mob of patient, tattered refugees damming the western end of the Kyobashi Bridge as they waited to cross. Guiding Mickey-san through the outskirts of the crowd, Matt heard a commotion behind him.

Four men—communications workers, from their armbands—

were bulling their way through the crowd. "Make way, stand clear! We have the emperor's picture!"

Behind the four staggered a fifth. On his back was a huge lithograph of Emperor Hirohito, in a golden frame. A chuffing little motorboat, ready to cross with refugees, removed a mother and three little children and took the five aboard. In state on the bow, the emperor chugged across the Kyobashi, choked with bodies like the dolls one floated down it New Year's Day, carrying one's troubles to the sea.

As the portrait approached, the crowds on the far bank all bowed in reverence.

Matt, the major, Hashimoto, and the clerk crossed the bridge, Hashimoto shoving civilians aside to make way for them. Matt had seldom in his life passed through a crowd without enduring the stares of bystanders: now he felt free, for these people were too dazed to wonder at the color of his hair and eyes.

They passed the ruins of the barracks, picking their way through debris to the parade ground beyond. The field lay under a pall of heavy black smoke, drifting from the central column behind them on the breath of a southeast wind.

The vegetable plots that Matt and his classmates had sown were gone, trampled already by the mobs. Bodies lay in furrows they had tilled.

Everywhere Matt heard the cry: *"Mizu, mizu . . .* Find me water, please!"

Matt and Hashimoto would try to find Alicia at the major's quarters. In the thousands of refugees pouring onto the drill field, Hashimoto somehow found a place in the shade of an oak for the major to rest and wait for them. They promised to return with the major's swords and an urn with the fingernails of his son.

Matt jogged swiftly through the chaos of the Nigitsu District with Hashimoto at his heels. Smoke seared their lungs. The neighborhood was a huge blast furnace. When the wind would shift to the south, they would take shelter behind stone walls bordering the narrow streets; when it would change suddenly to the north, he and Hashimoto would race forward, like soldiers attacking a pillbox, until the next onslaught.

The concrete, Western-style residences had withstood the blast well enough, although there seemed not a single pane of glass in any window that had not blown out. Matt could see that the approaching fire would level them very quickly.

Every few yards they passed some bleeding victim huddled against a wall, crying for water, or simply staring up at the oily, heaving sky.

After a while the wounded were gone, and there were only bodies. Matt glimpsed the boards and piles of Mr. Suzuki's little bake shop, which he and the baker had stacked so neatly yesterday. The debris was already smoking, and the baker's garish three-wheeled push-cycle, still chained to a lamp post, was lying on its side. The gold characters on the cycle's red bread box, advertising fresh rice cakes, had peeled from the heat.

"It's no use," panted Hashimoto. "I'm not going to fry for a *gaijin* woman! We have to go back."

"No! We're there." Matt could see almost to the end of the block. Mickey-san's quarters still stood, though flames were soaring from the second floor: the staff car sat outside. He ran faster, leaving the private grunting in his wake.

"Alicia," he yelled. "Alicia!"

He opened the gate, and ran up the stones of the pathway to the front door. All the windows were blasted away, but he could not see inside; the smoke was too thick.

Under the portico, Ono's army boots, and his own scuffed sneakers—Alicia's work shoes—stood side-by-side.

She had not left for work!

"Alicia!" he screamed. *"Alicia!"*

A gust cleared the portico of smoke. He crashed through the door, crunched down the hallway on broken glass. Through the door of the cooking room he saw Ono's body crumpled by the oven, staring upward with dead eyes. One hand was nearly severed by a shard of glass.

From above he heard a sudden high-pitched scream. He raced for the stairs. A blast of wind drove a river of smoke down the stairwell, engulfing him. He recoiled, coughing. He felt Hashimoto grab his arm: "The swords? The urn?"

Coughing, Matt pointed toward the major's room, by the back garden. The smoke retreated up the staircase, returned again on a gust from the rising gale. Matt dropped to his belly and began to snake upstairs.

"No!" shouted Hashimoto, from the *shoji* screen at the major's room. *"Baka,* don't go up there!"

Matt ignored him and slithered up one step, two. He grasped a banister post and tugged himself up a third. The heat was unbearable. The posts seared his palms. A red-hot roof tile crashed beside him and tumbled downstairs in a shower of orange sparks.

"Alicia!" he croaked up the stairwell. "Come down!"

The world was turning dark. He was going to die . . .

All at once he was grabbed by the ankles and yanked down the smoldering steps. He protested, clinging to the banister: "My sister!"

Hashimoto had a grip like steel. He hurled him toward the front door, stooped and picked up the major's swords and burial urn.

Matt fought him at the entrance, found himself shoved down the path, started back, dodged Hashimoto, and was almost to the door when the house collapsed in a creaking of timbers and a burst of blazing joists.

She was gone!

He heard Hashimoto's footsteps behind him, and felt a blow on the side of his head. Groggy, he struggled in the private's arms. When he could think clearly, he was in the backseat of the staff car, lying on broken glass. The car was jerking and bucking down a side street. Flames were everywhere. Hashimoto, clinging to the wheel, was peering into the smoke, jerking along in low gear. He tugged the wheel to avoid a body, yanked it back as a timber fell in an explosion of flaming embers. Then he stalled.

For a moment he tried to start the engine, then began to curse in gutter Japanese.

Matt scrambled out. Behind them rose a funeral pyre. The fire was approaching fast, but he could not forget Alicia's scream: like a moth he was drawn toward the flame.

"Where are you going?" the private called, above the roar of the wind.

"Back there!" His eyes were full of tears.

"*I* cannot drive!" barked Hashimoto. "Am I to *outrun* the fire?"

Matt looked at the embers. She was dead. He stalked back to the car. He slid behind the wheel, started the engine, and raced through the blazing streets toward the East Drill Field.

She had blown him a kiss from her window this morning. He had not even waved good-bye.

• • •

They found the major in the shade of the oak. His rank and bearing had somehow kept the spot clear of refugees. He looked up blindly when he heard Matt's voice.

"Sensei . . ."

"Was she there?"

Matt took the swords and laid them across his lap. He placed the urn in his hand. "They killed her!" gulped Matt. "They killed Alicia!"

Mickey-san folded him into his arms, and for a long moment they embraced. He heard his mentor murmuring: "Think of a lily, a water lily . . . afloat in a dark mirrored pool. All is quiet, all is still . . . Her spirit's at peace, like the lily, floating at peace, in the calm, dark pool . . ."

The voice droned on forever, and finally Matt grew heavy-eyed and slept.

CHAPTER 16

*T*he fires of Hiroshima burned all night.

At dawn the ruined city, flattened from the docks in the south to the foothills in the north, lay hidden from the sky under a blanket of greasy smoke. By eleven A.M. the mountains to the north had heated, drawing a breeze from the Seto Sea which unveiled the wreckage of the city to three U.S. Navy pilots.

Flying stubby Hellcat fighters, they were returning to their ship from a raid on the naval base at Kure, ten miles south, where—for lack of better targets—they had just strafed the drowned hulk of the carrier *Amagi*. She had been on the bottom for the past two weeks, with her flight deck awash and listing forty-five degrees in the oily harbor swell.

In their carrier's wardroom the night before, they had heard on a newscast of Hiroshima's "atom bomb," and had detoured now to take a look.

Incredulous, they peeled off like startled bumblebees to buzz the wasteland. Except for the shells of a half dozen downtown buildings, nothing was left over ten feet tall, so they flew their pass at fifty feet.

As the third pilot roared from the eastern edge of the ruins and tossed up a wing to bank, he glimpsed a grassy field. It seemed carpeted with people, thousands of them—*tens* of thousands—most of them prone on the turf. The sight reminded him of a Texas ant colony, found under his barracks window at Corpus Christi. Sprayed with insecticide, its inhabitants had fled to die in the sun.

He pressed his mike button to break radio silence, and then changed his mind.

Not ants: people.

His leader might want to strafe them.

He rejoined the others silently, and they headed out to sea.

Matt Bancroft watched the American Hellcat roar away from East Drill Field, cursing him silently, but happy that he had apparently not seen the hospital tent, or the crowds of refugees. Sweat dripped from his face. He brushed a fly from his cheek.

With all of the buildings gone, the city seemed very small and close. Matt could see across the leveled ruins all the way from the drill field to the towering shell of the Fukuya Department Store far downtown. Built to withstand earthquakes, it was the only structure standing between the drill field and the army docks.

An awful guilt swept over him. He was alive, and almost unhurt. Everyone who had not died seemed in agony.

He had heard from a military policeman that not one single other student at Honkawa had lived. By surviving he wronged even the bullying seniors, murdered at their desks.

Men of his blood had killed them all: classmates, mother, father, Alicia. If there was a spirit world below, their souls were watching.

The gods had spared him for revenge.

Matt finished his bowl of rice in the cave. He and Mickey-san had arrived after dark at General Sumi's hidden command post, a wooden-shored shelter in the heights above Kure. It was huge, rough-hewn, with dirt walls and a kitchen, a man-made grotto in the soaring peaks.

Matt glanced around the bunker. Despite pain and nausea, Mickey-san was kneeling before an ammunition crate his clerk was using as a desk, and the clerk was reading him dispatches under a bare lamp bulb.

By a door cut into solid rock a sentry stood: presumably this was Sumi's lair. Matt had not met or seen him yet.

The air was heavy with charcoal smoke. The cave had been

designed by Mickey-san last year, and was prepared so that
Sumi could take over regional command when American
forces cut communications at Kure, far below. Radios were
powered by soldiers pedaling bicycle generators; telephone
lines lay everywhere on the earthen floor. Ammunition was
stacked by the entrance. Far in the dim interior, a line of
young girls were manning a switchboard.

Matt was assigned a crude straw mat as a bed, with twenty
off-duty soldiers snoring nearby. A half-dozen prostitutes for
the soldiers slept with the off-shift telephone girls in an
adjoining chamber hewn from rock.

After eating the evening *gohan* Matt collapsed on the damp
straw mat on the earthen floor, and slept like the dead.

When he awoke, sunlight was pouring through the open
entrance to the bunker. The place was noisy with conversation, the switchboard was busy, and an army cook was la-
dling rice into the bowls of soldiers squatting on the floor.

The major seemed not to have moved. He was sitting on
his heels by the crate, chanting. On the crate was the urn.
When he was through, Matt served him tea.

Mickey-san looked up blindly, fumbling for the cup. "I
was praying to Amaterasu-Omikami," he murmured. "For
Alicia's safe journey to the spirit world."

Matt bowed gratefully. "Thank you sir."

The major shrugged. "Amaterasu may not listen. The Americans made their own sun goddess." He touched his eyes and
smiled faintly. "Mine may be angry that I looked her in the
face. Still, I shall pray."

"Good, because I can't."

Mickey-san looked sad. "You must believe in *something*."

"What does Bushido say?" Matt asked bitterly.

Mickey-san did not answer.

"To avenge a wrong!" Matt reminded him. *"Kataki-uchi.*
As the Forty-seven Ronin did." He took the major's wrist.
"Sensei?"

"Yes?"

"I want to kill Americans. That is all. And I want to kill
one in particular very much."

The major's clerk was staring past Matt, arising. Matt
turned.

General Sumi had wandered from his lair and was standing
behind him. He looked very tired, and his high-button tunic

was poorly pressed. He nodded to them and handed the clerk a dispatch. His eye fell on Matt.

"I too want to kill Americans," he said softly. "I, too, young *gaijin,* want that."

The general turned and went back to his lair.

Matt wandered outside. A squad of soldiers lounged by an army lorry, pulled under a camouflaged canvas. They were passing around a cigarette. They must have heard of the major's Japanese *gaijin,* for no one even stared at him, and their corporal offered him a puff.

He inhaled it, fighting not to cough.

The sun was high in the pine trees. A bird trilled somewhere, as if yesterday had never happened and tomorrow would never come.

His stomach felt better, and his injured hand hardly hurt. At last he was a part of the army, where he had always belonged.

He hoped that Alicia and his mother were looking on him with pride.

CHAPTER 17

On August 8, 1945, Miyajima Island—"Shrine Island"—basked in summer sunshine two miles off the western shore of Hiroshima Bay. Two days before, Hiroshima had died, and was still hidden from the island beyond a shroud of smoke.

Alicia Bancroft sat shivering on a porch in the hot summer sun, high above the island's jammed main street. She wore her best friend Yuko's heaviest kimono, and had slipped a padded air-raid hood on her head and around her shoulders, for warmth. The horrible burn on her shoulder, bandaged in linen and salved with fish oil, pained her beneath the weight of her clothes. She had been cold for two full days.

Alicia had watched Matt drive away with the major a half hour before the *pika-don,* and gone downstairs. Baba-san handed her the *bento* lunch she would eat at the clothes depot and told her that she had decided to forgo the morning with her sister, clean the house instead, and take the next day off.

The old cook begged Alicia not to wear Matt's tennis shoes to work. It demeaned the household and shamed the major. She herself would not need her worthless *zoris*; she would be in the house all day. Would Alicia deign to wear them, *kudasai?* Tomorrow, she would try to find her something better.

To refuse the loan would be unthinkably impolite. For one

day, at least, Alicia decided, she would escape the giggles at the clothes depot and the laughter on the tram. Outside, she managed to cram her feet into the *zori* straps and shuffled to the streetcar stop. She squeezed onto the tram and was standing in line at the clothing depot time clock when the bomb lit up the northern sky and the world she knew was destroyed.

Now a soft breeze jingled the wind chimes on the porch. At the end of the alley below her, the ferry from Miyajima-Guchi, across the channel, was nosing into its berth, bouncing from piling to piling in a screech of tortured wood. Every forty minutes for two days it had arrived, jammed to its gunwales with refugees, some bandaged, all grimy. Evacuees had slept last night, it was said, in streets and alleys, below in the great *torii* of Itsukushima Shrine, the pagoda, and even on the holy floors of the Hall of a Thousand Mats.

She wondered how so small a town, on so tiny an island, was going to hold them all.

She was lucky to be here, though she was very sick. She had no idea what ailed her. It seemed a disease spread by the *pika-don*, for many showed the symptoms.

The Army Clothes Depot had been nowhere near the explosion. Though hundreds of girls had been hurt—and God knew how many killed—by flying glass at their sewing machines, Alicia had been spared the hell inside.

She and Yuko had just arrived and were standing in line outside, protected by the building from the glass, but not from the flash or the blast which followed it, and something in the one or the other had made her very ill. Last night her stomachache had been unbearable.

It was four o'clock in the afternoon, and a chill entered the air. Nine miles away the outlines of the Hiroshima docks took on a golden hue. Yuko's grandfather shuffled to the porch, a white-haired, nervous gentleman in a black kimono, with a scraggly Van Dyke beard. She had always disliked and feared him. Following her gaze, he said irritably: "It is most unfortunate when the young pay more heed to their friends than to their elders."

A naked accusation, disguised in *haragei* "belly-language," that she had somehow asked Yuko to risk a trip back to Hiroshima to inquire after Matt. Alicia's eyes filled with the injustice of it. Much as she wanted news of her brother, she had begged Yuko not to go. He knew this already, for he had heard them quarreling about it. She did not answer, though. One did not confront so old a man in argument: her silence was enough.

He peered across the water.

"I was right to move," he announced suddenly. "The city is gone."

Not Honkawa School, she screamed silently.

She struggled to her feet. She was dizzy, and almost threw up. She moved to the railing. "I see Fukuya Department Store! See? Above the rest?"

He shielded his eyes. "The Fukuya, yes. But there is no 'rest.' "

Baka! The old fool's vision was failing, his eyes were growing weak!

She saw Yuko on the street below, climbing the hill from the ferry. Yuko looked up, shook her head, and burst into tears. Alicia clasped the railing and was very sick.

CHAPTER 18

*T*hree days after Hiroshima, Major Charles Sweeney, a happy-go-lucky pilot flying the world's second atomic bomb over Japan, circled his objective.

In the last few moments, he had become a very nervous man. He had just discovered that due to a faulty fuel pump he had six hundred gallons of unusable gasoline trapped in his bomb-bay tank. He had no target in sight below. He had already been orbiting above the overcast for three-quarters of an hour.

His bomb was named Fat Man. It was shaped like a barrage-balloon, much stubbier and shorter than Hiroshima's Little Boy. Its charge was plutonium, whereas Little Boy's had been uranium. And where Little Boy's detonation over Hiroshima had been problematical—no uranium bomb having been tested prior to the drop—Fat Man's was assured. The bomb that Manhattan Project scientists had detonated in the first atomic explosion at Alamogordo, New Mexico, less than a month ago, had been exactly like the one he carried today.

The date of Sweeney's mission, originally August 20th, had first been accelerated nine days, to August 11th, by General Leslie Groves, U.S. Army, the obese, irascible head of the Manhattan Project. But a five-day spell of bad weather was forecast, beginning on the 10th. And Russia had declared war on Japan yesterday, as she had promised she would all along. If the second atomic bomb were dropped today—August 9th—it could prevent the Soviets from claiming a real part in the victory. It might even warn the Russian ally of the future dangers of too vociferous an appetite.

After Hiroshima, Groves was anxious to see that "the Japanese would not have time to recover their balance." Though decoded diplomatic cables a month ago had shown that the Japanese had ordered their ambassador in Moscow to ask the Russians to act as mediators for a surrender, Groves was a West Pointer, not a diplomat.

President Truman had decided that additional atom bombs were to be dropped "as soon as made ready." The Japanese had, after all, been given a full seventy-two hours since Hiroshima to surrender.

Without further White House consultation, Groves made a second sudden date change: August 9th. So come hell or high water, the second bomb would be dropped today.

But now, over Kokura, Sweeney was running out of gas, and smoke from factory chimneys obscured his aiming point. He had been forbidden to bomb unless he had a visual target. He had made three passes, hoping that the smoke would clear. It did not.

He had no desire to return to Tinian and attempt a landing with the bomb aboard; in fact, it was against his orders. If he crashed on Tinian's North Field, he might blow up half the island.

He'd been gently reminded by a senior naval officer prior to takeoff that Fat Man had cost twenty-five million dollars, and warned to "get our money's worth." The navy man's estimate was low by many orders of magnitude—together with Little Boy, Fat Man had actually cost over two billion—but Sweeney did not know that, and even twenty-five million dollars swinging in his bomb bay seemed astronomical to an officer who drew less than four hundred dollars a month.

As he circled, Kokura remained covered below. His alternate target, listed as Nagasaki Urban Area, was reported under clouds, but perhaps it would clear. He gave up on Kokura and headed for Nagasaki, which he understood to be a much larger city of a quarter of a million.

By the time he reached it he had fuel for only one pass. He decided to violate his orders and begin the run by radar. Through an opening in the clouds, his handsome bombardier,

Captain Kermit Beahan, spotted a stadium he recognized and pressed his pickle-switch.

Fat Man was released three miles off target, but at least they had complied with orders: Beahan had seen the ground.

The bomb exploded at 1,500 feet above the Urakami district of the city, where factories, schools, and residences were concentrated, thirty-six blocks from its intended point of detonation.

The mistaken ground zero lay at the center of a five-hundred-yard circle on which sat Nagasaki University Hospital, Urakami Cathedral, Shiroyama Primary School, Urakami Prison, a Mitsubishi Foundry, and the Chinzei Middle School. An eight-hundred-foot ridge protected the militarily more important part of town—the Nakashima district—where prefectural, municipal, and other governmental offices were located.

Though Fat Man managed to destroy almost fifty percent of Nagasaki, Beahan's bombing error was expensive: the ridge which had protected the other half of the town saved tens of thousands. Only seventy thousand Japanese were killed outright or would subsequently die, and the per capita cost of annihilating a man, woman, or child in Nagasaki—however one calculated Manhattan's budget—was almost twice that of destroying one in Hiroshima.

Sweeney struggled back to his alternate field on Okinawa, and landed so low on gas that he could not taxi in. Despite his bombing error, the 509th on Tinian and General Groves were happy: the mission could have fared a good deal worse. Without Sweeney's skill and luck and Beahan's sharp eye, Fat Man might have been wasted entirely, or they might have lost the plane.

Before the mission, Dr. Louis Alvarez, an atomic scientist working in Tinian's bomb hut, had Scotch-taped a personal letter onto one of the telemetry cylinders which was to be parachuted to transmit blast-data to Sweeney's escort plane. Presumably, it would land undamaged on Japanese soil. The letter was addressed to a Japanese physicist who had studied under him at the University of California Radiation Laboratory before the war.

"We deplore the use to which a beautiful discovery has been put, but we can assure you that unless Japan surrenders at once, this rain of atomic bombs will increase manyfold in fury.''

Propaganda pamphlets warning of conventional bombings had been dropped on Japan for months. Tomorrow, leaflets prepared with the help of Japanese POWs and printed on Tinian Island would flutter down on Tokyo, Osaka, and Kyoto, urging Japan's surrender. At last the leaflets would mention the atom, as U.S. broadcasts had been doing for three days. The doctors of Hiroshima and Nagasaki, and the man in the street in Tokyo and Osaka, would finally learn that the *pika-don* contained not dynamite or poison gas, but the power of a minor sun.

Conceivably, though it was not spelled out in the leaflets, they might learn to stay out of the radioactive rubble and survive.

Matt Bancroft squatted inside the entrance of the bunker above Kure, as close to the radio as he could get. At exactly noon the emperor himself would speak. At his lips he held a tin rice bowl from a battered mess kit. He shoveled tough brown *gemmai* rice into his mouth with his hashi sticks. He crouched in a circle of hungry second-line troops—old men, mostly, of forty or fifty, or boys not much older than he—just out of recruit training. Rations were growing short, and the convoy of supply trucks expected from the naval base below had not arrived today.

He had heard rumors for the last few days of a second *pika-don* dropped on Nagasaki. Mickey-san thought the emperor's message might be a call for a fight to the death when the Yankee invasion came.

A steady drizzle fell outside the bunker, dripping from the pine trees onto the camouflaged truck covers in the motor pool. The bunker thrummed with activity. The communications section, in the rear, was swamped with messages, and Mickey-san, as one of the few Second Army staff officers who had survived the bomb, was busy with dispatches. He seemed to have shrunk in size, and his face was scored with lines of age that Matt had never noticed before.

Just before noon, a lieutenant called attention and everyone rose. The officer tuned in to NHK, in Tokyo. Static from the storm outside peppered the announcer's words: *"This will be a broadcast of the gravest importance. Will all listeners please rise?''*

Matt, hands moist with excitement, could hear almost nothing. But a high-pitched, nervous voice in the accent of court Japanese began to speak. In these tones, Matt had read, he addressed his subjects as the high priest of Shinto, as well as emperor of Japan.

"Despite the best that has been done by everyone . . . war situation . . . not necessarily to Japan's advantage. In order to avoid further bloodshed, perhaps even the total extinction of civilization . . . have to endure the unendurable, to suffer the insufferable . . .''

Next to Matt, a gray-haired private in an ill-fitting uniform moaned. Matt twisted in the circle of soldiers and glanced at the major, standing at attention with his clerk and Hashimoto. He was far to the rear of the bunker. He had removed his bandage and there were tears in his eyes. His clerk beckoned Matt.

Matt sidled through the dazed troops and joined him. He still did not understand the emperor's speech. And the voice had been so thin and reedy, so unlike that of the god that he had imagined, that he could not believe it had really been the emperor.

"What did it mean, that voice?" murmured Matt. "I did not understand."

"It is over!" Hashimoto's voice lashed out. "He said it was finished! We must turn in our arms!"

The major reached out his hand.

"Matt-san?"

"Here, sir." He took the hand. It was cold as death. "It is *done?*" Matt asked. "The *war?*"

Mickey-san squeezed his fingers. "Done, my son. All done."

Stunned, Matt could not speak. What of his plans for revenge?

Mama and Alicia! Father. And look what they had done to Mickey-san! The Americans must pay!

He took a deep breath. *He* would not cry. Though others were sobbing, he would show himself a soldier of Japan.

"I'll kill the first American I see!"

"I'll hold him so you can," growled Hashimoto.

"No," murmured Mickey-san, "you won't, for the emperor spoke." He glanced at Matt. "Lead me outside. We have been too long in here and I need air."

Major Fujihara—*ex*-major now, he supposed wryly—stepped for the first time in days from the bunker into bright sunlight. He felt Matt's hand on his elbow, guiding him.

The emperor's reedy voice had shaken him. He remembered the shy young man who had visited the Imperial Hotel more than twenty years before, to praise Frank Lloyd Wright and his staff on the clean, spare beauty of line and form.

Behind the words "bear the unbearable," Fujihara had heard a plea for them all to build a new Japan that would triumph in the end.

Matt would be a part of it, he would not.

The rain had stopped. For a moment he covered his eyes against the glare. When he took his hand away, he gasped. He could see dim outlines of the pine trees, as if through a film, straight ahead. And from the sides of his eyes he could see even better. He pulled away from Matt and drew close to a low-hanging limb. Each pine needle held a tiny glittering drop of water at its end, clear as a sphere of crystal above a Tokyo ballroom.

"Matt-san! I can see!"

He stumbled toward what he perceived as a line of vehicles. He put out his hand toward his staff car, touched its wet and muddy window.

"Mine?"

"Yes, sir!" Matt's face, blurred in his eyes, was shining. "Sir, you *can!*"

So the gods had pitied him. Standing by the car, he felt a drop of rain from a pine, sensed the blessed glitter of light on the Inland Sea, far below.

He smelled gasoline on the wind, and smoke. Matt told him that the cove at the foot of the mountain was full of suicide torpedo boats, all burning. Their crews had heard the emperor's speech.

Fujihara had not really come out for air, but to warn Matt. The boy was volatile as a stick of blasting powder, left too long in the sun.

"You spoke of killing Americans. You must watch your tongue. They will be here very soon."

Matt lowered his eyes. "Yes, *sensei*."

"Watch what you say, and hide what you feel."

"I feel *kataki-uchi*," murmured Matt, "and my mother cries for revenge."

He looked into the boy's face. "Look ahead, not behind. The past is for your elders, not for you."

Matt did not answer.

General Sumi's clerk stepped from the bunker and saluted. The general wanted to see Major Fujihara immediately.

The general's quarters, which Fujihara had gouged months ago from the bedrock inside the main cave, had walls of solid granite. The general sat behind a folding map table. In the dim light, the major perceived that Sumi was dressed in a ceremonial *montsuki* kimono, with deep sleeves. It was of cheap material and lacked even the ordinary family crest. A hibachi glowed at his feet, but the chamber was cold, and clammy as a vault. A drab olive file cabinet, open and obviously just emptied, sat near the desk. A battered briefcase was stuffed with papers.

On the desk before the general lay his short-bladed *wakizashi*.

One of the prostitutes was folding his futon. She laid it carefully in a corner, glided to the door, bowed deeply to the two of them, and was gone.

The general stared at him from across the table. "You are not well."

"Who is, sir, who saw the *pika-don?* But my sight is returning."

The general reached for a bottle of sake and poured two cups. "*Gokenko-o*," he toasted.

Fujihara lifted his drink. "To your health, sir."

"I expected us all to be killed in this bunker. And now I am considering taking my life." Watching him closely, the general asked suddenly: "Do *you* intend seppuku?"

Fujihara certainly did not. But if the general himself was considering suicide, to laugh it off would be a dangerous affront. "I am not sure I should have the courage," he said carefully.

"We did not fight hard enough, and lost. Some would say we must atone to the emperor. One need not come from a samurai family to know that!"

"I am not sure that His Majesty would want us all dead," he said.

"Is it true you know him?"

"I met him once, as crown prince."

Sumi studied him. "And your father? Would General Fujihara counsel seppuku?"

"Perhaps. He lived in another age."

Sumi smiled. "Is he laughing at me, from the Other World? That I consider seppuku when his own son does not? A peasant, aping a samurai?"

"He had always the greatest regard for you, so far as I know," said Fujihara charitably. "Or he would not have cited you for bravery."

Sumi sipped his sake. "Your father was my *sensei*. He made my career." He grinned, and the gold tooth glittered. "His spirit saved you from a court-martial in the matter on Chichijima. Whether you know it or not."

Fujihara bowed. He had no doubt that it was true.

The general continued: "He thought in Manchuria that I had joined the Order of the Carp." He lit a cigarette but failed to offer one to Fujihara. "He did not approve of that."

"I am glad he was mistaken," Fujihara said delicately. "It would be a dangerous affiliation when the Americans land."

The general shrugged. "To its enemies, the carp is a dangerous fish." Sumi's eyes were on Fujihara's, and they never wavered. "It is blessed with good luck, and lives forever."

Fujihara met his glance. "Still, the Hiroshima Castle carp are dead in the fortress moat, young Bancroft saw them there."

"A pity," said Fujihara. "Some were so old, people say, they were fed by the Asanos themselves."

"There are other carp," murmured Fujihara. "I hope the city will be rebuilt."

"And the castle, rebuilt too?" Sumi's eyes held steady. "The army?"

"Not the army," Fujihara blurted angrily. "The army has destroyed Japan!"

The general's eyes flashed and his hand moved toward the hilt of his sword. "The army is His Imperial Majesty's will!"

Fujihara tensed, but Sumi regained his composure. Coldly, he told Fujihara to evacuate the bunker and destroy it.

"I want no one on my staff available for debriefing—or torture—by enemy counterintelligence. So my orders to you are the same as to the other officers. You are to burn your records and return to your home prefecture. It is Tokyo?"

"*Hai*. The boy and I shall depart today."

He bowed and turned to leave.

"Wait! Have you given him Hart's passport?"

Fujihara felt a bolt of alarm. He turned, sucking in his breath.

"It is destroyed. It was on my desk," he lied, "where you put it, sir, before the *pika-don* went off."

The general's eyes went dead. "Send him in. I want to talk to him."

Fujihara distrusted Sumi thoroughly. "Might I ask the reason, sir?"

Sumi glared at him. "Because it is I who command this bunker! You are still in uniform, are you not?"

Fujihara bowed. He found Matt outside the shelter and passed on the general's order. "Do not trust him and promise him nothing," he murmured. "Remember, the war is done!"

Matt nodded nervously and went inside. Ill at ease himself, Fujihara watched him go. Then he put Private Hashimoto— his only explosives expert— to work setting cordite charges under the timbers shoring the cave.

Matt moved through the empty bunker. It seemed much bigger, now that it was deserted, and much colder already. He rapped on the door.

"Enter."

General Sumi was sitting behind his desk, his *wakizashi* blade unsheathed on the desk.

Matt bowed deeply. "I am Matthew Bancroft, sir. You called for me?"

The general smiled. His gold tooth gleamed.

"I thought we should talk. Of all who leave here, you and I alone want to kill Americans. The emperor will not let us. What are we to do?"

Confused, Matt mumbled: "I don't know, sir."

"Perhaps we should stay in this bunker, you and I."

Matt stared at him, suddenly frightened. Drunk? Or a true samurai? "Not I, sir."

The general nodded. "Why not? Because you have a better thing to do?"

How could he read his heart? Matt nodded.

"I know," Sumi muttered. "And I have too." The general sheathed his blade. He sipped his cup of sake, studying him. "I'm told you saw the castle carp, all dead in the castle moat."

"Yes sir."

"A brave and stubborn fish, the carp." He looked deeply into Matt's eyes. "Did you know it is the only fish that won't shrink from the fisherman's knife?"

Matt nodded: "I have heard."

"Well, their *pika-don* did not kill them all." He rounded the desk, and let his hand fall on Matt's shoulder. "There are thousands more in the rivers and lakes, the Americans will learn. In *our* rivers and lakes, and *theirs* . . ."

"I don't understand, sir," muttered Matt.

"Some day you will." He began to leaf through his briefcase. "Your mother died on Chichijima?"

Matt nodded. Mickey-san must have told him.

The general pulled out a file. "From a Chichijima *kempeitai* report: 'Killed by a Yankee flier. His soul will burn in hell.' "

A shiver raced down Matt's back. He was speechless.

The general looked up, then continued: "'Her only son forever swears *kataki-uchi* on her grave.' " Sumi's eyes burned into his. "In your heart is still *kataki-uchi?*"

"I'll kill that pilot," Matt whispered, "if it takes me all my life!"

The general snapped the briefcase shut.

"Tell no one what we talked of here. But I shall find you in Tokyo and we'll speak of this again."

Fujihara saw General Sumi drive away. Hashimoto slammed down the plunger of his detonator and they watched as the mountain peak vomited out their bastion in a great brown belch of earth. The choking smell of cordite hung sharply in the air.

Within minutes after the explosion, Matt was at the wheel of the staff car. With Private Hashimoto to help them if they ran out of fuel en route, they were gone on the battered highway to Tokyo, where by imperial order they would have to turn in the auto and all their arms.

The roads and paddy paths they passed were clogged with soldiers, bedraggled, weaponless, slogging homeward: afoot, on bicycles, hanging from trucks and motor buses. Three million landless *ronin,* masterless and lost, were on the move, for the most part bound toward the broken heart of the homeland and the emperor's ruined capital, burned nearly to the ground.

Matt volunteered nothing of his meeting with Sumi, and finally Fujihara asked him in English what he and the general had discussed.

The boy seemed reticent. "Carp, *sensei.* Mostly carp."

Fujihara's heart plummeted. "The Brotherhood of the Carp?"

Matt glanced at him in the mirror. "No, sir. Just carp: *koi.* How brave they are, not to flinch."

"Or stupid."

Matt seemed puzzled. "What is the Brotherhood of the Carp?"

"A *kempeitai* branch of Black Dragon, which the Yankees will try to stamp out. Those who truly love the emperor must hope that they succeed. I think Sumi is a member."

Fujihara sat back, troubled. Sumi had planted a poisonous weed, and Matt was fertile ground. He must somehow get him out of Japan, before the seed could grow.

In his inner pocket rested the passport of Christopher Hart.

His own life was over. Somehow, the bomb was draining it away. But for Matt the passport in his pocket was the key.

PART TWO

The Forty-eighth Ronin

CHAPTER 1

Josh Goldberg, promoted last week on Guam to captain, USMCR, leaned weakly against the rail on the wing of the destroyer's bridge. He hated ships, and the voyage north had been a rough one. He studied the wooded slopes and soaring peaks ahead.

It was October 6, 1945, seven weeks after the emperor's surrender speech. The USS *Trippe,* a battle-weary 5th Fleet destroyer, was five hundred miles south of Tokyo, slicing through mountainous swells off Chichijima under fat lead-bellied clouds. She carried the newly designated commander of U.S. Occupation Forces for the Bonin Islands—Colonel Presley M. Rixey, USMC—and his staff of six officers.

Josh liked Rixey. The colonel was a big man, ruddy, courtly and mustached. Fondling a swagger stick, he was a throwback to the days of the old corps. His forebears had been regular navy and Marine Corps officers since before the Civil War. His great uncle, as surgeon general of the navy, had established the Navy Nurse Corps.

Rixey had been born in Yokohama while his father served in the Far East. Brought up in the Orient, he knew the strange history of the island they were approaching. At dinner in the wardroom last night, he'd recounted it to Josh in his deep Virginia accent.

According to Rixey, *Bonin* was a corruption of the Japanese word for "Islands of No Men," and had been uninhabited when white colonists, led by one Nathaniel Savory and Elias Bancroft, had settled it in 1831.

Nathaniel Savory had deserted his father's farm in 1828 and shipped on a British merchantman. On the square-rigger, he lost a finger when a fifteen-gun salute to a British man-of-war misfired. His captain left him in Hawaii for surgery, under the care of the British consul to the Sandwich Islands.

Nathaniel was energetic, ambitious, and a leader. In Honolulu, he saw transplanted Boston merchants making fortunes under King Kamehameha from trading with whalers. He decided that he could do the same thing on one of the uninhabited islands off the coast of Japan, opening up a whaling port and later, perhaps, a coaling station when trans-Pacific steamship travel became practical. He organized a party. Elias Bancroft, a Boston minister's son of some education, was his lieutenant and confidant.

The British consul outfitted a schooner for them and, in an attempt to make sure that the Bonin chain became a Crown colony, appointed an illiterate Genoese, who had served on British men-of-war, as governor.

Nathaniel and Elias sailed from the Honolulu wharf in 1830. With them were Aldin Chapin, a fellow Yankee from Massachusetts; Richard Millinchamp, an Englishman; Charles Johnson, a Dane; twenty Hawaiian men and women; and the Genoese, Matteo Mazarro.

Savory and his colonists landed on Chichijima in a harbor named Port Lloyd by an early explorer. They found cliffs towering over the harbor's beaches, and verdant subtropical foliage, thick as Hawaii's or Guam's. They discovered streams and even trees with trunks that, when properly stripped, gave water to the thirsty traveler. They found land more fertile than that of their various homelands, and cleared it. They caught fish offshore and two-hundred-pound sea turtles that would feed a household for a month.

They became voluntary castaways, the sole owners of a mountainous, wooded archipelago a stone's throw from the sleeping enigma, Japan. Here Nathaniel Savory established an agricultural community on Chichijima's rich volcanic soil much like that of his *kanakas*' native Hawaiian islands.

"Old Nat" and Elias were much loved in the western Pacific. On their plantations they raised tobacco, sugar cane, and vegetables. Their onions—valuable in fighting scurvy at sea—were the best in the Far East. They smoked ham and made rum, sold their goods to visiting whalers, and accumulated cash, cattle, and pigs.

Seamen from some of the passing whalers jumped ship and settled: Americans, French, British, and Portuguese.

In 1849, the crews of two visiting American whaling-ships ran amok, forcing Nathaniel and his colonists to hide in caves in their hills, and taking their livestock and common-law wives. The Hawaiian women, tempted by a wider world, went willingly, Nathaniel's "wife" having thoughtfully led her captors to his accumulated cash, two thousand dollars hidden in his barn.

Governor Mazarro, who had once tried to murder Nathaniel, had died an alcoholic, and Mazarro's child-bride widow Maria, a *chamorro* from Guam, had refused to run off with the whalers. Nathaniel married her. He, a God-fearing Protestant, and Maria, a Catholic, raised ten children.

When Commodore Matthew Perry, during his voyage to open up Japan in 1853, steamed his flagship *Susquehanna* to the harbor entrance, the island had still been called Peel, after an early British ship captain. Nathaniel piloted him into the bay and had him drop his anchor at Ten Fathom Hole.

Nathaniel was fifty-nine and Elias fifty-seven when they met the commodore, and had lived on the island for twenty-four years. Nat was tall and slim, white-bearded, with a direct gaze and stiff bearing; Elias was a mild, introspective man. Perry, portly, convivial, a New Englander himself, liked them instantly.

Perry stayed on Peel Island four days. He and Nathaniel conferred over glasses of Perry's port and Nathaniel's rum in Perry's flag-quarters. The commodore regarded them through heavy-lidded eyes. He was a thoughtful man, who saw the Bonins as U.S. possessions, and seemed angry at the colonists' sufferings from the piracies of 1849. He encouraged Nathaniel to seek protection from Washington and promised his support.

Here on the island Perry decided to establish a U.S. Navy coaling station, warehouse, and dock. Nathaniel sold him a thousand yards of waterfront land for fifty dollars, which the commodore took from his own funds, since he had no authorization from the Navy Department to make the purchase. He helped Nathaniel write a "constitution," gave him the flag from the truck of the *Susquehanna*, appointed him his agent, and left for Japan.

For Nathaniel and Elias, the Bonins were U.S. soil. Now, under Perry's "constitution," Nat was chief magistrate. For the next twenty years, when ships would enter Port Lloyd, the American flag with its thirty-one stars flew from the simple wooden plantation house that he built in Yankeetown at the head of the bay.

Eight years after Perry's visit, in 1861, the first Japanese colony was landed. Nathaniel respectfully wrote to the U.S. Secretary of State, pointing out that if America did not move to annex his island, as Commodore Perry had promised, the Japanese might seize his own and other settlers' property and expel them.

Hamilton Fish, secretary of state, denied Washington's obligation and ruled that Nathaniel, never having received explicit promises of protection, had expatriated himself.

Nathaniel died next year, heartbroken, but still a patriot. Elias survived his old friend by a year.

The first Japanese colony failed: the island soil was not good for rice. But in 1875 a Japanese steamer arrived with troops and commissioners to lay official claim to the island chain. That night the flag of the rising sun flew over the village by the entrance, which was now Omura. Henceforth Peel Island was Chichijima—"Father Island." Hog Island to the north across a quarter-mile strait became Anijima, or "Elder Brother." And the chain became a Japanese family.

The other islands were suddenly Younger Brother and Grandson: to the north lay Bridegroom, Matchmaker, and Bride; to the south, Mother, Elder Sister, Younger Sister, and Niece. The Paps, a mountain on Chichijima so named by the Americans because its peaks were shaped like a woman's nipples, became Asahi Yama—Mountain of the Rising Sun.

And the white colonists, so far as Colonel Rixey or U.S. naval intelligence knew, had simply disappeared. Perhaps they had lost their identity and language in intermarriage with Japanese. Perhaps they had been bodily exiled in the early 1900s. Perhaps—if any had lasted until Pearl Harbor—they had been interned somewhere in Japan. Their only legacy lay in the destroyer's wheelhouse, English names on an ancient harbor chart: Bancroft Rock, Savory Rock, Bull Beach, Little Calabash, Welcome Rock.

Josh shivered on the bridge. The bomb-ruined harbor of Futami Bay was sliding into view. The storm had passed and the swell eased, but Josh noted without enthusiasm that the wind was whipping whitecaps across the expanse of the anchorage. The devastated village of Omura crept from behind Cape Zohana.

The 3rd Marine Division had offered Rixey a regiment to occupy Chichijima and Naha Jima forty miles south. But the colonel had refused it and brought only his personal staff. With a supply officer, a medical officer, an operations officer, a language officer straight from the navy's translator school in Denver, an intelligence officer, and Josh as his legal beagle, he was sure that he could handle the preliminary arrangements for a formal surrender. The regiment would land to troop the colors in a month.

Seventeen thousand Japanese troops—impatient and hungry—were waiting on Chichijima for evacuation to their homeland, and had been for almost two months. Another eight thousand occupied Naha Jima and the other islands in the Bonin chain.

A thousand yards off the village's bombed-out quay, *Trippe*'s anchor rumbled down.

Josh's heart began to pound. In a few minutes, he was to meet officers in the wardroom to arrange the logistics of the Japanese surrender, the same men who would gladly have given their lives in the caves and ravines to kill him two months before.

Rain began to fall. As Josh scrambled down the ladder toward the wardroom, a blast of thunder sounded from behind the mountain range. He flinched and glanced into the hills, half-expecting to spot the flash of artillery.

As if in agreement, the guns above him whined as they turned toward the island. The control officer of the forward five-inch battery, sitting atop a steel turret high above his guns, was slewing his mounts to starboard. The guns elevated, quivered for a moment, as if sniffing for danger, and finally trained forward again.

Josh felt better. Someone else besides himself was jumpy.

The meeting in the wardroom went well enough for the Japanese until Colonel Rixey dropped his bombshell.

Part of their mission was to try to track down rumors of downed American airmen. As legal officer Josh was responsible for bringing charges if the team found Japanese misconduct toward POWs. He had already been bucked a letter from a young ex-navy pilot named George Bush, now a student at Yale. Son of a politically prominent investment banker, Bush inquired about the fate of his two crewmen, shot down over the island a year ago.

Colonel Rixey sat at the head of the wardroom table, below an open porthole. By his side sat his interpreter, a navy lieutenant named Jones.

Across from Josh sat Captain Toyozo Ohta, ex-Imperial Japanese Army. He was small, immaculate, correct, and very bright. He represented General Yoshio Tachibana, commanding Japanese troops on the entire Bonin Island chain. The captain, who spoke fair English, was trying to remain poker-faced, but he was nervous.

Colonel Rixey had warned his staff to assume that all of the Japanese spoke English: the Japanese would often feign ignorance, preferring to work through interpreters to give themselves time to think.

A fresh-faced naval cadet named Ichikawa, who had lived in Hawaii as a child, was the Japanese contingent's official interpreter. He sat next to Josh.

But it was Colonel Yasushi Kondo, wearing the red tabs of the *kempeitai* military police, who silently dominated the Japanese liaison group. Kondo had somewhere had part of his jaw shot away and wore a scar from his cheek to his forehead. From his glinting, narrow eyes, the Americans could not tell whether he spoke English or not, but it was clear that he was listening to every word. When his eyes met Josh's, Josh saw humor, contempt, and a scornful challenge to do his very worst.

The sonofabitch, thought Josh, is laughing at us!

The wardroom had grown stuffy with cigarette smoke. Next to Josh, Cadet Ichikawa, who seemed almost too young for tobacco, was looking for an ashtray. Josh shoved over his empty coffee cup and saucer. The boy bowed, smiled gratefully, and ground out the butt.

"Mr. Ichikawa," Colonel Rixey drawled suddenly, "tell me, son: eighty Americans were shot down attacking these islands. What became of the ones you captured?"

"Sir?" Ichikawa swallowed. It was obvious that he had never expected to be asked to answer a question himself.

"The *Americans* you captured?" smiled Rixey, shooting in the dark. His voice was soft and gentle. "You haven't told us what happened to *them*."

There was a deadly silence. The clock on the bulkhead chimed: *ding-ding, ding-ding, ding-ding, ding-ding*. Eight bells, time for lunch. Josh heard a clap of thunder from the mountains.

Ichikawa's eyes flicked to Kondo's, but the colonel smiled blankly and said nothing.

Captain Ohta cleared his throat. "Yes. We captured six. Two were sent to Japan." His eyes fell and he added softly: "The last four, unfortunately, you killed in an air raid against these islands in March."

"Who was in charge of POWs?" Josh cut in abruptly.

The captain spoke to Kondo. Kondo's shattered face beamed with goodwill.

"He says he was fully responsible," Ohta said.

"Why weren't they in shelters?" Rixey demanded.

When Ohta translated, Kondo chuckled and spoke eagerly to Colonel Rixey.

"He says," fumed Jones, "they were safer outside. 'The civilians would mob them, because a child had been hurt picking up a booby-trapped pen after a previous raid.' "

"What were the prisoners' names?" growled Josh.

"He claims he's forgotten," said Jones.

"Ranks? ID tags?"

"All lost, in the bombing."

"And where are their bodies?"

"He buried them," interrupted Ohta, "with customary honors, in a common grave in the graveyard above the village."

Josh had questioned scores of witnesses in court, and sensed a lie in any language. He glanced at Rixey. The colonel nodded.

Josh arose and motioned Ohta to accompany him.

"I want to see that goddamn grave, right now!"

Josh Goldberg clung to a velvet strap in the rear seat of the Japanese staff car as it wound up the jungle road. The squall had passed and the sun blazed down. USS *Trippe* dozed peacefully in the harbor below, riding her anchor buoy.

The roof of the auto was peppered with holes—bomb fragments, he guessed. Omura Village, glimpsed fleetingly below through the broad palm trees, was a hopeless wreck.

Captain Ohta stopped the car by a break in the foliage and led him up an overgrown path to a tangled little graveyard, badly neglected. Crude gravestones, slabs, and crosses rested by the side of the trail. Most of them were surrounded by carefully placed beer and sake bottles, and plates of ossified food.

Some had Japanese letters and carved Buddhas, but most were crosses with English names: Washington, Robinson, Gilley, Webb. Josh fell behind the captain and read the gravestones curiously. He spotted one that interested him: ELIAS BANCROFT, B. WALTHAM, MASS., JULY 28, 1794, D. PORT LLOYD, PEEL ISLAND, APRIL 7, 1874.

Next to the patriarch's grave stood an unpainted cross. In block-letters across its horizontal member were carved the words: LORNA ROBINSON BANCROFT, BELOVED WIFE OF LEMUEL, ADORED MOTHER OF ALICIA AND MATTHEW. BORN CHICHIJIMA, AUGUST 8, 1906. DIED SEPTEMBER 2, 1944.

A white on the island? As late as last year?

Leaning against the base stood a sake bottle with a faded label. It was full. Down the vertical member of the cross were Japanese characters. Curious, Josh ordered Ohta to translate them.

The captain seemed embarrassed, but complied: " 'Killed by a Yankee flier. His soul will burn in hell. Her only son . . .' "

He hesitated.

"Go on."

" 'Her only son forever swears *kataki-uchi*—' "

"What's that?"

Ohta thought for a moment. " 'Revenge for parent'? Yes. 'Her only son swears revenge for parent on her grave.' "

The cross disturbed Josh, but he had another reason for being there. The captain drew him to another grave just a few short yards away.

It was bordered with small rocks. It had been recently raked. All was neatly arranged. Raised precisely in the center of the plot was a cross, exactly squared off, made from two-by-fours. Captain Ohta apologized that it was not painted: there had been no paint on the island for a year, even for the boats. There was no inscription, either: just a bare, unpainted cross.

Josh inspected the cross. It looked new. Certainly not ten months old. He sniffed at the top of the vertical post. Fresh wood. He rubbed his thumb across the grain. Sawdust. The galvanized nail heads were still bright, shiny as new dimes.

The cross had only been up for a day or two. And if Ohta had lied about that, then what else?

There would obviously be human bones beneath it: the Japanese were not stupid. A Graves Registration team and its medic might determine whether they were large enough for American bones, and whether they had been shattered by bombs or—he remembered poor Pappas on Guam—by samurai swords or bayonets.

He would summon a team from Iwo Jima today.

CHAPTER 2

*O*ne night six months before Hiroshima, in the spring of 1945, Tokyo had become a crematorium.

After dark on March 8, General Curtis LeMay's aircraft had come in force. Three hundred thirty-four B-29s pounded in at less than five thousand feet. They were unopposed: Japanese fighters—the few that remained—stayed on the ground, reserved as kamikazes for the invasion of Kyushu. Out of the velvet sky, the bombers dropped hundreds of thousands of six-pound M-69 incendiary bombs. The bombs were filled with a slow-burning, gelatinous gasoline just developed by the Army Chemical Warfare Service and tested at Dugway Proving Ground in Utah.

The new substance was called napalm. Ignited, it burned everything it touched. The tiny M-69 was designed to explode on impact and hurl the jelly in all directions. The firestorms it started in Tokyo were fanned by a heavy breeze.

As the fires spread, entire rows of wood-and-rice-paper houses burst into flames simultaneously. Two hundred sixty-seven thousand homes were leveled, 2,300 city blocks incinerated. Firefighting forces were overwhelmed. Men, women, and children struggling to escape the flames plugged narrow alleys and Tokyo's humpbacked little foot-bridges, where their charred bodies remained piled for days. Beneath the bridges floated corpses boiled in canals which had bubbled from the heat.

Eighty-three thousand Japanese civilians perished. Another 41,000 were wounded. Over a million slept homeless in the ruins.

The raid was the most destructive man would know for ten weeks, when, on May 23 and May 25, the B-29s struck again. The area set afire was even greater. Japanese guards allowed sixty-two American POWs in the Tokyo Military Prison to burn, while four hundred Japanese prisoners were saved.

Despite the city-wide holocaust, the Japanese went on, preparing for the *ketsu-go* guerrilla war they would mount with their civilians when troops landed on their shores.

While the war dragged on, the Imperial Army hid the results of the fire raids from the rest of the nation and the enemy. Afterward, as with Hiroshima, MacArthur's censors strangled the press and confiscated newsreel footage. It would be decades before the files were opened and the world would truly know.

In the autumn of 1945, Tokyo was still a junkyard and an open grave, a jungle to the living. Matt Bancroft and former Major Michihiko Fujihara, in the weeks they had been there, had barely learned to survive. Mickey-san's own home in the Marunouchi District near the palace had been burned to the ground, along with a good portion of the imperial residence itself. The Imperial Hotel, in which Fujihara owned stock, had been confiscated by MacArthur for VIP billets. Because former Japanese commissioned officers were not allowed on the premises, he could not have got a job there as a busboy.

He and Matt—and ex-Private Hashimoto, who had no wish to return to his starving village in Hokkaido—moved onto Fujihara's mother-in-law's property not far from Tokyo University in the Bunkyo-ku district. Her home, an old-style residence with a walled garden, had burned and the old lady had died in the flames. A sleeping room and some of its stone foundations still remained.

Hashimoto built another room against the foundation. It was a hovel constructed from stolen Imperial Army packing cases, with a galvanized tin roof, windowless and dark.

Fujihara could find no employment. Even if the Occupation had not forbidden ex-officers to hold executive positions, there were simply no jobs to be had. He was too weak to work, anyway, and the taint of the atom bomb was on him: *hibakusha* were welcome nowhere, as if the sickness they carried were contagious.

Though his eyesight had improved, he was losing his hair: great hanks came out while he was brushing it a week after their arrival. He knew that the poison of the atom bomb was deep in his bones. He ached continually, felt fevered and chilled, and was sure that he would not survive the winter.

For a while he insisted that the three of them live in *sekihin*—poverty, but honorable and legal—on their rice allotment, but the city's rations failed and the allotment was replaced by a "caloric equivalent" in rotten yams and stale barley, which they found inedible.

He had dysentery. The government ration of toilet paper was twelve sheets per week, per family.

They tried to plant beans in what had been the old lady's garden. It was the wrong season: Fujihara knew nothing of truck gardening; Hashimoto had been a miner; Matt was clumsy: in the Bancroft vegetable garden in Yankeetown, spading had been women's work.

For a month Fujihara supported Matt and himself—Hashimoto refused all financial help—by peeling off his remaining assets as one peeled a bamboo shoot: the "bamboo-shoot life," as people were calling it. He auctioned a family rice paddy outside Yokohama, an interest in a store he had designed in the Shinjuku district, and finally a pearl necklace that he had given his wife before the war. Within four weeks he had sold all of his possessions for a song to black marketeers and *yakuza* gangsters just to feed himself and Matt.

Forced to the black market themselves, they found that a riceball cost forty times its price before the war. A pair of American shoes—the only footwear obtainable—sold for seventy-five dollars in a store and six dollars in yen on the street.

Hashimoto—who had taken on the role of the major's retainer, and slept across the door to their hut—began to steal from black marketeers, despite the major's objections. One night he was chased and cornered and had to half-kill his pursuer in an alley.

Three-quarters of a million ex-soldiers, repatriated from the former empire, poured into the city. Civilians shunned them. Whole and maimed, in ragged army uniforms, they begged in the streets. Hundreds froze, as winter approached, in ramshackle huts erected in the parks.

Fujihara grew weaker day by day.

As Christmas approached, Tokyo grew colder. Only Americans, swaddled in woolen khakis in their jeeps and staff cars, seemed to Matt Bancroft to be warm.

Once he saw a U.S. naval officer driving a gray jeep through the streets, jaunty in a blue uniform, white-visored cap, and flier's wings of gold. That night, shivering on the earthen floor, unable to sleep, he fantasized. The officer stopped and asked for directions to navy headquarters. Matt volunteered to guide him but lured him into a blind alley instead. With Matt's father's fishing knife at the pilot's throat, the aviator admitted that he was the one who had strafed the Omura quay. He died begging for his life and Matt's mother passed gratefully to the World Below, her struggles done.

As the weeks dragged by, Matt scavenged burned-out houses for fuel. Late one evening he went adrift looking for an address Hashimoto had heard of, where one could find wood scraps for the hibachi.

Matt was lost because the U.S. Army had replaced Tokyo street signs with its own. To the Japanese mind, house addresses around an intersection should be numbered in the order in which they were built, like members of a family. But MacArthur had renamed the streets in Western grids: First Street, Second, A, B, C, and numbered from one end to the other.

Passing the Marunouchi Hotel near Fourth and Y—a corner on which a GI could buy a *pan-pan* girl for a pack of cigarettes—he was stopped by an MP, the first American he had ever met. The soldier gaped at his Japanese army tunic.

He questioned Matt. Was he a military dependent, playing games? A U.S. Army brat? A young GI in disguise?

Matt remained silent, as if he did not understand. The GI, who wore a pair of brown leather gloves Matt would have died for, tried pidgin English, finally grinned, shrugged, and offered him a stick of gum.

Matt shook his head, but when the smell of the gum hit his nostrils, he grew dizzy and almost went down in a heap. Fighting nausea, he spun on his heel and strode off, shoulders back and head held high. That night, huddled at the feeble fire in the hibachi, he told Mickey-san that he had grown faint because Americans—who notoriously smelled of butter—made him sick.

Mickey-san disagreed: "No, your diet is too poor. The scent of sugar made you ill. You have lost too much weight. The time has come to try to get you out."

"*Out?*"

"Out of Tokyo. Out of Japan. Out of this hell we are living."

Matt did not understand. "Go home? The Americans have stolen Chichijima. I read it to you from *Mainichi*. No more Japanese."

Mickey-san shook his head. "Not to Chichijima, to America!"

Matt could not believe his ears. "*America?*" He sneezed. "They won't even let their GIs *marry*, for fear they'll bring home the girls!"

Their breaths were steaming in the pitiful glow from the embers. They were burning dry bamboo that Hashimoto had stolen, probably from the nearby temple grounds. Mickey-san, trembling with weakness and aging every day, dug feebly beneath the layers of protection he wore: a shabby army blanket over his army greatcoat, his tunic under that. When he reached his pocket he was panting. His eyes held Matt's as he handed him a little green booklet.

Outside, the rain splattered endlessly. Matt's nose was running: he seemed always now to have a cold.

He held the booklet close to the light, studying its cover. He could hardly believe what he saw. On it was stamped PASSPORT, over a golden eagle.

United States of America?

Matt opened it and peered inside. His own photo, somehow lifted from the evacuation pass he had been given at Chichijima, stared back at him. *Christopher Hart. Birth Place: Tokyo, Japan. Birth Date: January 11, 1932. Eyes: Green. Nationality: United States of America.*

Such a forgery—to some in Tokyo—would be worth a million yen!

He licked his lips. "Is it permitted to ask where you got this, *sensei?*"

"From General Sumi," Mickey-san said, "the morning of

the *pika-don*. The general had some scheme to infiltrate you behind enemy lines in the battle for Japan.''

Matt sat back on his haunches. Strange! Precisely what he'd dreamed of, in Alicia's bedroom, a million years ago. He would have become a ninja, cloaked not in black but in their own khaki, slitting their flabby throats. Now it could all come true in a different way.

''Why 'Hart, Christopher'?'' he asked curiously.

''The passport is real enough. Hart was a missionary's son: they were killed by the firebombs in March.''

''Good,'' growled Matt. ''What will I tell the Americans?''

''That you were trying to help the survivors of your father's flock, but now you want to go home.''

Matt put a hand on Mickey-san's knee. It was like touching blanket and bare bone. As much as he wanted to go for his own reasons, the major needed him.

''I can't leave you, *sensei*. You know that!''

''You shall do as I say,'' Mickey-san insisted.

Emaciated, the major's face in the wavering shadows seemed a living skull. His head was bald. He began again the struggle toward his tunic pocket, and produced a treasured drawing pen. This, and his father's samurai sword and the short-bladed *wakizashi*, illegal now and hidden beneath their piled futons, was everything he owned.

''I fear I'll leave *you*, soon enough.''

''No! You cannot!''

''Sign the passport, in your own hand.''

Matt took the pen. On the line marked *Signature of Bearer/ Signature du Titulaire*, he wrote the name: ''Christopher Hart.'' As the pen moved on, a strange feeling of lightness and freedom washed over him, as if he had wings to fly. He shivered.

He handed the passport back to Mickey-san. ''I'll never use it, *sensei*,'' he insisted, ''so long as you are here.''

''The time will come,'' his mentor promised. ''And it is not far off.''

CHAPTER 3

Josh, at attention behind Colonel Rixey, stood with the staff before the regiment watching the Japanese troops swing off to their camp. For the first time in seventy years, the Stars and Stripes flapped openly over Chichijima.

Josh watched General Tachibana waddle along, swordless and head held high. Tiny Captain Ohta strode behind him, erect and shoulders back. Vice Admiral Mori marched stiffly away, leading the naval forces. Captain Ohta had told Josh that the admiral was a talented amateur poet, well known in Japan.

The tallest Japanese Josh had ever known—a shaven-headed bully and drunk—was Major Sueo Matoba of the 308th. He swaggered off, towering above his battalion staff.

Their samurai swords lay stacked on a table on the beach. Colonel Rixey had decreed that enlisted marines would have first choice.

Colonel Kondo, of the *kempeitai*, Tachibana's intelligence officer, strode behind the general. For a moment his eyes met Josh's and the colonel grinned.

All right, Laughing Boy, I'll get you yet . . .

Josh had been digging here for information on downed airmen for a full two months. The grave on the hill had indeed contained bones of men: their condition was consistent with bombing injuries. He had learned nothing—of Lieutenant Bush's crewmen or of any other American airmen—from any of the Japanese officers or men passing before him now.

He had grown to hate them all. Their stories were too precise, their memories too exact. Each told exactly the same tale, in exactly the same terms. They had memorized a script, written by someone they feared. They were lying to him, to Rixey, and to everyone else. He sensed that the author of the script was not General Tachibana, but Colonel Kondo. Soon they would all be on their way back to Japan, as fast as the leaking island freighters could repatriate them.

He thought of poor Private Pappas in Guam, tied to the bloodsoaked tree, screaming at his tormentors in the empty, steaming jungle.

There were murderers leading these mustard-colored ranks, and murderers in them too.

And he was letting them escape.

When their samurai swords had been distributed to the officers and men of the 3rd Marines, Josh returned to his office in the "White House," a stucco building not far from the dock, which the Occupation used as headquarters. He shoved his swivel chair from the desk, swung around, and looked out at Futami Bay. A rusty island freighter from Tokyo had anchored a few hundred feet from the quay. The ship was the first of many, he hoped, that would clear the island of Japanese troops so he could go back to Guam.

He was depressed. Corky had been right. She had told him to wait out his discharge in the legal office in Guam. Yet here he was, trying to develop murder cases eight months old on an island no one had ever heard of, or ever would hear of. He had given the corps enough.

The mail from Guam had arrived this morning. Nothing from Corky, for the second week running. What was she doing there, anyway?

He moved to his window, lighting a cigarette to calm his nerves. His eye was drawn to a confrontation on the dock below. A huge marine MP had stopped four men in Japanese uniform. They had obviously disembarked from the island freighter. There was something strange about the four.

Josh reached for a pair of field glasses he had traded from a Japanese artillery lieutenant. He put them on the group below. The MP was a strapping mountaineer from West Virginia, but the four Japanese soldiers were lanky men, too: one of them as tall as the American. And though they wore the high-crowned cloth cap of the Japanese infantryman, they had removed the yellow stars from them and made themselves as civilian as they could. Perhaps the uniforms were the only clothes they had.

Startled, he focused the glasses more carefully. Though the men had the mahogany skin of Hawaiians or *chamorros*, they had Caucasian features. They were obviously white, or mostly so.

He trotted downstairs, crossed the street, and joined them on the quay.

"Cap'n Goldberg," the MP announced, "these jokers claim they *live* here!"

The youngest of the four was a handsome man of perhaps thirty, with an oval face and gentle green eyes. He would have passed as a southern California surfer or a ski instructor tanned on the slopes.

He was looking at Josh anxiously. He bowed in the Japanese fashion and said: "I'm Noah Bancroft, Captain. Noah Joseph Bancroft. These are my brothers: Harlan, Abner, and Isaiah."

He spoke with precision: there was a trace of New England in his words, and something Victorian. To Josh, he seemed to have stepped out of history. He seemed at ease, but the other three were nervous, glancing up toward the head of Futami Bay, where Yankeetown had stood.

"Bancroft?" Josh said. "Descendants of Elias?"

The tall man nodded. "Yes sir. We were forced to leave this island just last year."

Had Josh not seen the woman's grave on the ridge, he would never have believed that whites had survived on a Japanese fortified island through the 1930s, let alone throughout three years of war.

"You're Japanese citizens?" asked Josh.

"But of American blood. I was conscripted into the Imperial Japanese Army."

"Jesus, Captain," gaped the MP. "They're *traitors!*"

"No," Josh murmured. "But no Japanese citizen is permitted to land on any Bonin island. You're in violation of an order from Supreme Commander Allied Powers, right now."

"Sir, this is our home." Bancroft drew from his tunic a typed rice paper, and handed it to Josh. "We were asked to

represent the other families, too. A petition to return, for the
U.S. island commander.''

Josh skimmed it.

He found himself touched as he read a plea that the younger generation be exposed to Western education:

> We will try to build again a model community as
> visualized by Nat Savory and Elias Bancroft (our Ameri-
> can ancestors). . . . The love we bear for the Bonins
> will help us to reconstruct what has been erased by the
> devastations of this war. . . .
>
> Most of us do not have the necessary backgrounds to
> mix in the highly competitive life of Japan proper.
>
> Our last and strongest reason is that all of us
> want to live under American rule, by which we
> know every man is a free man and everyone will have
> a fair chance of making a better living in a fair
> world.

It bore the signatures of a hundred Bancrofts, Savorys,
Gilleys, Webbs, and Robinsons. Some of them, from the
childish writing, were apparently very young.

He folded the petition and put it into his shirt pocket.
Suddenly Bancroft was staring down the dock with fear in his
eyes.

Colonel Kondo was climbing from a staff car. The driver
was unloading his field chest from the trunk. Behind him, a
column of Japanese soldiers was forming to embark for Tokyo, spreading out their gear on the beach for inspection by
the marine MPs. Obviously, Kondo was returning to Japan
with the first draft.

"Sir," muttered Bancroft quietly, "I must speak to you
about that officer. In private.''

"Colonel Kondo? Why?''

"About his treatment of American prisoners of war.''

Josh felt his pulse quicken. He told the MP to take the
other Bancrofts to the guard shack, and led Noah to his
office.

As they passed Kondo, the colonel's eyes narrowed. Bancroft stopped, spat at his feet, and went on.

Josh and Noah Bancroft arose from the table as Colonel

Rixey entered the deserted officers' mess in the headquarters building. Bancroft bowed deeply, and snapped a salute.

The colonel motioned them to be seated, poured them coffee, and served them. He had a marvelous effect on anyone who had shared his own background in the Far East. To the Japanese he seemed clothed in robes of power, though he never raised his voice or showed them anger.

He read Bancroft's petition without comment. "But you served in the Imperial Army?"

"Here, at home. In a noncombat company. As a stevedore."

Rixey looked into his face. "Your people came from Massachusetts. So how did you feel about that?"

Bancroft's eyes did not waver. "Sir, my great-grandmother Jenny and my great-grandfather Elias flew Commodore Perry's Stars and Stripes over their house until 1875. Every Fourth of July, when I was small, we shot firecrackers."

"That's what I mean."

Bancroft swallowed. "In 1865, America did not want us. *Last* Fourth of July, the U.S. Navy bombed our homes! America had forgotten we were here."

Rixey nodded. "Go on."

"Before I was born, my family became Japanese citizens. We had to, or leave our island. All we knew was here! Many had married Japanese. In Massachusetts, our own relatives called us 'Japs.' "

"I see, Mr. Bancroft," murmured the colonel. "And you were drafted?"

"Some of us. Lemuel volunteered, or he would have been conscripted. I *had* to enlist, or I would not be here now!"

The colonel seemed to accept it. "Captain Goldberg says you have stories to tell us, Mr. Bancroft?"

Josh glanced out the window. The homeward-bound draft had formed in a long line at the pier: an ex-*kempeitai* military policeman was checking them off a list. They would be under way for their homeland this afternoon. Kondo was boarding the launch now.

Bancroft took a deep breath. "Yes, sir. From Korean worktroops I served with, *gunzukos*, who hate the Japanese. Not nice stories, at all."

Bancroft was greatly disturbed. He told them he had heard that several American pilots had been beheaded, in front of assembled troops and naval forces.

He gulped: "And Colonel Kondo . . ."

He looked too shaken to go on.

"Go ahead, son," urged Rixey. "The colonel?"

"Colonel Kondo made his surgeon cut out the fliers' livers . . ."

"Jesus," breathed Josh.

"And had them *cooked* . . ."

"Christ!" Josh felt sick.

"Yes?" probed Rixey.

"And they *ate* them! At a party!"

Rixey's eyes narrowed. *"Who* ate them, Noah?"

"Colonel Kondo. Major Matoba. General Tachibana!" Bancroft's cup rattled as he set it down. "They *ate* them, as if they were meat!"

There was a long silence. Enlisted chow call sounded from the marine battalion camp. An ex-Japanese PT boat, brought to life by marine mechanics for water-skiing, was droning in the bay.

"The general, too? Hard to believe. Do *you* believe these stories, son?" asked Rixey.

Bancroft looked into the colonel's eyes. "Sir," he said miserably, "Japanese are my kin. I have their blood in my veins! They are not cannibals! But our army? Colonel Kondo?" His eyes dropped. "Yes," he whispered, "I do."

"And your brothers from the freighter? They heard these stories too?"

"Yes, they did."

Colonel Rixey arose. He squeezed Bancroft's shoulder. To Josh, he said: "Quarter them in *our* camp. I don't want them near the Japs."

Josh stood up. "Aye-aye, sir."

He called down the hall for an MP, and watched him escort Bancroft out the door.

When they were alone, Colonel Rixey said: "Pluck Kondo off that *maru* out there."

"Yes *sir!*" Josh beamed.

"Arrest his surgeon. And Matoba. Get General Tachibana, too, and Admiral Mori: he was senior officer. Put them in a stockade, no visitors. Take precautions against suicide."

"Aye-aye, sir," exulted Josh.

"Convene me a three-member board of investigation under Naval Courts and Boards. Make Major Shaffer senior member. Put Lieutenant Caskey on it. I want the navy in it, too: make Dr. Poutasse a member, and Lieutenant (jg) Parcell recorder. Pick the best typist in Headquarters Company for reporter."

"Aye-aye, sir. And me?"

"Find us witnesses. You're my legal officer: Keep it legal."

"Yes, sir."

Sorry, Corky, thought Josh. I won't be in Guam for Christmas.

His first task was to get Kondo, before the freighter sailed.

He stopped at his Quonset, slipped a clip into his forty-five, and strapped it on.

For Kondo, he didn't even want an MP along. He picked up Cadet Ichikawa as an interpreter, commandeered the Japanese launch embarking the repatriates, and chugged out to the *maru* in the bay.

On the dirty, rusty bridge he found the colonel, looking back at the island and laughing with the skipper. He approached him and touched his shoulder.

The colonel whirled. His lips tightened, and hate glittered in his eyes.

"Tell him," Josh ordered Ichikawa quietly, "that he didn't say good-bye!"

CHAPTER 4

Alicia Bancroft stood in the cramped toilet of Yuko's family home on Miyajima Island, peering at the hairbrush she shared with Yuko. It was their only one. She drew several golden strands from the bristles. Thank God, no more.

Four months ago, a week after the *pika-don,* when she was sickest, she had lost her hair in handfuls, leaving her bald. "Like a great white egg," Yuko's grandfather had grimaced.

When she got better, it had grown back as luxuriantly as before.

She joined Yuko on the porch. "Alicia," Yuko warbled, in English, "Cholly-san come to the store today! He has two-day pass over Clistmas—"

"*Came* to the store," corrected Alicia. "*A* two-day pass. And *Christmas.*"

Cholly-san was an Australian soldier. Yuko hoped to marry him when Occupation rules relaxed. She saw herself as a Melbourne lady in flowing skirts, playing croquet on the lawn, with an icebox full of milk. She was truly in love. Though still dumpy, she seemed prettier than before.

Now she took Alicia's hand. "There is to be a party," she bubbled, "in a room at the *hoteru.* On their Christmas . . . *Your* Christmas. You must come."

Alicia turned away. The ferry to Miyajima-Guchi was pulling from the dock, on its last trip of the day. On Hiroshima

Bay lights of fishing boats were dancing, and beyond, the feeble glow from the shattered city.

"No."

"You still hate them? It is your brother?"

And father, and mother, too. "Perhaps."

"My own father will never return," murmured Yuko, "but Cholly-san killed no one. And what is done is done."

"I cannot forget."

Yuko swallowed. "Then you will die single," she warned. They were *hibakusha,* touched by the atom, lepers. Even the carp had died in Hiroshima Castle moat, and every matchmaker in town made it her business to find out how far from ground zero a prospective bride had been. Stories of deformed babies abounded.

"At least," Yuko added, "the *gaijin* are not afraid of us!"

"Perhaps," Alicia suggested cruelly, "because they do not intend to marry Japanese girls anyway."

"Because they *cannot!*" Yuko choked. "It is forbidden by their superiors!"

"Good. *I'd* sooner marry a devil."

In the light from the *shoji* screen Alicia saw the tears start up in Yuko's eyes. "I want to go to the party, Alicia-san."

"Then go."

"You know I can't, alone."

Alicia stared across the roofs below. Much as she hated her prison here, she disliked the streets even more. Scarcely anyone in Miyajima had not lost a friend or a relative in the bombing: for this, when she went on some errand for Yuko's mother or grandfather, their sullen eyes blamed her.

She wavered. At least, surrounded by Caucasians at the party, she would not be a freak. And Yuko had defied her grandfather to go and hunt for Matt.

"Christmas?" she asked.

Yuko's eyes lit up. "The night before."

"All right," sighed Alicia. *"Hai."*

The little hotel on the street leading to the five-story pagoda was Miyajima's only Western hostelry. It had the town's sole neon sign, a glaring prewar creation in purple and gold. Unlike the island's *ryokan* inns, the hotel had a lobby and even a tiny bar.

Alicia and Yuko, dressed in their kimonos, paused in the

lobby while Yuko applied lipstick, which she seemed to think essential. Alicia borrowed her compact, glanced at her face. To use it or not? She never had.

A big American marine lurched from the bar. Passing them, he muttered to Yuko: "Merry Christmas, baby-san." He glimpsed Alicia, behind the compact. His eyes snapped open. "What the *fuck?*"

Face flaming, she followed Yuko down the hallways. With a jolt, Alicia realized that Yuko must have been here before, alone.

A hubbub greeted them as they rounded a corner. At the end of a long corridor, a room door was open. From it came the sound of singing, and the giggles of the street girls. Yuko hesitated. Then Cholly-san appeared, a curly-haired, powerful youth with bleary eyes.

"Yuko!" he grinned. He stared at Alicia. "And who in bloody hell is *this?*"

"Alicia Bancroft," murmured Alicia.

Ignoring Yuko, he took her arm and pulled her into the room.

A sudden silence fell. Alicia looked around. There were half a dozen street girls—"butterflies"—dressed in Western style, some in the arms of Australian soldiers on the bed, some kneeling with their men on the carpet, drinking beer. "An American sheila," an immense, potbellied sergeant belched. "All dressed up to kill!" He arose and stumbled toward her. "What's your name, lady? I'm called Rhodes."

Cholly barred him with an arm. "I brought her, mate, I keep her," said Cholly.

"No need to shove *me*, laddie," the sergeant said tensely. "Bloody company clerk!"

"Cholly-san!" whispered Yuko, stricken, "she no butterfly. Same as sister! She is my friend!"

"Then she stays away from this old bastard," Cholly grated.

The sergeant summoned a steely-eyed corporal with a jerk of his chin. The corporal lurched forward and grabbed Cholly from behind. The sergeant dropped a shoulder and slugged the boy once, in the pit of the stomach. Cholly grunted and went white.

"Mates!" he retched. "Lend a hand!"

"Fourth Armored!" yelled someone. "Down the hall!"

A phalanx of soldiers from an adjoining room crowded in. All at once there was chaos. Alicia heard the splat of knuckles against flesh, the thump of elbows against ribs, the roar of a soldier kneed in the groin.

She grabbed Yuko's hand and ran from the room. In two minutes, as two big Australian MPs screeched up to the hotel in a jeep, they were back on the street again.

"He wanted *you!*" whimpered Yuko, on the way home.

Alicia squeezed her hand. "A drunken pig, and the rest are too."

In the early dawn, as she lay sleeping on the tatami between Yuko and her mother, Alicia heard Yuko crying softly.

From that night on, Cholly was a memory and her friend spoke only Japanese.

CHAPTER 5

Captain Josh Goldberg awoke in his bunk on Christmas Eve, an hour after he had drifted into a drunken, restless sleep. He had staggered home early from a party at island headquarters: he had received no Christmas letter from Corky, and finished half a quart by himself before he quit.

Outside the Quonset he heard a low voice muttering in Japanese. His mind flashed to insurrection. There were still fifteen thousand Japanese troops on the island, and only five hundred marines. He lunged for his forty-five, hanging in its holster on his folding wooden chair. He chambered a round, glancing at the empty bunk of his hutmate, a navy paymaster. The party at the White House mess must still be going on. Someone rapped lightly. "Noah Bancroft, Captain. Can we speak to you?"

Josh put the gun back into its holster and opened the door. Noah Bancroft had with him a Korean *gunzoku* corporal, from one of the labor battalions. He introduced him as Corporal Kim Hong Yong, and said he had information. He was a tall, intelligent man with sparkling light-brown eyes. He was Christian, educated in a mission school outside Seoul, and his English improved by the moment.

"Captain," he said with a bow, "first I ask you promise I will be removed from the Japanese bivouac. There may be *kempeitai* among the troops."

Josh nodded. "Okay."

Kim bowed and took a deep breath: "I was with work party on Washington Beach. June 15th, last year. After evening *gohan*, the Japanese brought two American airman to the sand, an officer and a radioman."

He said that the officer had been murdered on Washington Beach by Colonel Kondo's order, and his crewman tortured with bayonets.

"A young American girl was forced to translate. She was crying."

"Wait," said Josh. He got a legal pad from his field kit and a pencil. "A young *American* girl?"

"My niece," offered Bancroft. His eyes were bleak. "It could have been no one else."

"And you saw Kondo?" pressed Josh, his head clearing fast. "You can swear to it?"

The Korean looked scared, but nodded.

"Go on," murmured Josh.

"I could not hear, but soon a major of engineers came to translate, and the girl was sent to his car."

"Who was the major of engineers?"

"Major Fujihara. We worked on his tunnels."

At last he was getting somewhere. Hand shaking, Josh wrote down the name. "Then what?"

"The crewman was left alive when we all ran off in an air raid. The next day we found him with his head cut off. He was very young."

The board would sit for the first time the day after tomorrow. Noah Bancroft was scheduled to be called, but he had only hearsay. At last they had an eyewitness.

"And your comrades?" he asked Kim.

"Repatriated to Japan. By now, perhaps to Korea. I am the last one on Chichijima."

"And Major Fujihara?"

Kim believed that he had left the island the next morning: they had never seen him again.

Bancroft said sadly: "He returned to Hiroshima, and was killed by the atom bomb."

Josh's spirits fell. "What about the girl?"

Bancroft sighed: "Her mother was my sister-in-law Lorna. Lorna was killed on your raid of September second . . ."

The day Lieutenant Bush lost his crewmen, Josh remembered. He poured them bourbon, in navy coffee mugs.

"I saw her cross in the graveyard," he told Bancroft.

Bancroft blushed bright red. "And did anyone read you what was carved in Japanese?"

"The curse by her son? I know."

Bancroft sighed. "He was out of his mind, but he should not have defiled her memory with a curse! Last week, I planed it off!"

"And what is your niece's name?" Josh asked.

"Alicia," Bancroft said softly.

"And where is she?"

Bancroft stared into his glass. "I sent them both to Major Fujihara, as my sister planned. They too were killed by the bomb. We have found no trace."

"I'm sorry, Noah."

He would check anyway, with SCAP counterintelligence in Tokyo.

He thanked Bancroft and Kim.

It didn't seem appropriate to wish them Merry Christmas, but they'd given him the only present he would get.

In the early light of dawn, Josh sat tiredly at his desk, a legal pad before him. He stared at the scarfaced colonel. Colonel Kondo gazed back impassively.

It was a hell of a way to spend Christmas morning.

Lieutenant Jones, Rixey's language officer, sat sleepily at the side, drinking coffee. A tall MP stood at the door, watching the colonel carefully, a forty-five holstered on his white webbed belt.

"Tell him to cut the bullshit," Josh said wearily. "Tell him we know he killed American airmen. And ate their flesh."

Jones translated, and Kondo roared with laughter.

"He asks 'Are Japanese cannibals, now, as well as murderers?' " reported Jones. "And wants to know who is your witness to this?"

"I'll bet he does." Josh felt himself slipping into anger, the mortal sin of a good DA. "Tell him we know he remembers the name of every POW he interrogated. *We want those names!*"

"He says, 'All Yankee names sound the same to me. I could not pronounce them if I knew them.' "

Josh sat back, defeated. "Tell him we'll try him in Guam, and hang him if he's guilty."

Jones spoke in Japanese and translated: "He says, 'American kabuki theater? I will try to learn my part.' "

The phone rang. It was Colonel Rixey, with a dispatch from Supreme Commander Allied Powers in Tokyo.

Colonel Rixey skidded the dispatch from SCAP across his desk.

SECRET: FROM CIC SCAP TO COMMANDER U.S. FORCES BONIN ISLANDS: RE UR REQUEST FOR INFO ALICIA BANCROFT CIVILIAN AND/OR MICHIHIKO FUJIHARA FORMER MAJOR IMPERIAL ARMY: AUSTRALIAN OCCUPATION FORCES HIROSHIMA UNABLE FIND SUBJECTS X BE AWARE 118,661 CIVILIANS LISTED KILLED AND 3,677 MISSING THAT CITY AS OF 8/30/45 X MILITARY CASUALTIES UNKNOWN

Josh stared blankly at the communication. No casualties remotely like this had been published, anywhere. He couldn't believe them. The numbers were simply too great.

The colonel tapped a cigarette out of his pack. A distant clap of thunder made the windowpane shiver.

"With that many missing, Josh, how do *they* know who survived? Maybe you should go to Hiroshima. Can I spare you?"

Josh had trudged through the wreck of Agana when they hit the beach on Guam: one ruined city was enough. If a hundred thousand had died in a single ball of fire, he didn't want to see the rubble now. But he remembered Kondo's taunting eyes, and took a breath and said: "You can spare me, Colonel. Yes."

That afternoon he bounced from Futami Bay into the drizzling sky. He rode in a transparent plastic blister behind the wing of an amphibian PBY that sounded as if the Wrights had built it. They lumbered, in and out of scud, past the Bonin Islands, one by one.

All but Chichijima had already been evacuated.

Before Nathaniel Savory landed, *Bonin* had meant "the Islands of No Men" in Japanese. Now the islands would, it seemed, be empty of Japs once again.

CHAPTER 6

*H*iroshima, as 1945 drew to an end, had endured not one but two disasters.

On the sultry night of September 17th, a month after the emperor's surrender speech, as survivors slept in hovels thrown up in the city's rubble, the Makurazaki Typhoon had swept up from the east China Sea. It brought torrential rains and hundred-knot winds. It could not have pounced upon a more helpless community at a more vulnerable time.

When it struck, Japanese medical teams from army hospitals in Yamaguchi, Hamada, Kokogawa, Fukuchiyama, Okayama, Kokura, and Fukuoka were still giving burn treatments to dying survivors of the *pika-don.* Until the emperor's surrender, army hospitals had handled forty-five thousand casualties. Then the military hospitals disbanded. So did the troops which kept order.

The Ujina Army Hospital, on an island off the dock area, had alone handled eighteen thousand victims and buried the ashes of 2,600 of them. A Japanese scientist, from study of fogged X-ray films found after the bombing, had deduced that the weapon had been atomic, and that the victims were suffering the same effects as highly overdosed X-ray patients. Radiation sickness was slowly becoming known to doctors and nurses alike.

Almost fifty percent of the pregnant women who somehow

survived near ground zero were bearing microcephalic babies: those fetuses which had been in utero closest to the center of the blast seemed to have the smallest heads.

Word of these things passed only by rumor: under MacArthur's Press Code, no mention of them was allowed on the air, in newspapers, or in scientific journals.

Meanwhile, two invisible diseases had been born in the moment of the *pika-don*. They came to be known as "keloid of the heart" and "leukemia of the spirit." For in the shock of the bombing, in one of the most familial cultures in the world, hundreds of fathers had deserted trapped sons, children had run off from parents, and husbands had abandoned wives, seeking only to escape. Now those survivors, mostly injured, suffered deadly guilt. (No mother had to endure remorse: apparently a Japanese mother would perish before she left her child to die.)

The Makurazaki Typhoon finished the carnage the Americans had begun. It swept away the Ono Army Hospital, killing all ten scientists from a Kyoto Imperial University team who were attempting to evaluate casualties. Floodwaters destroyed half the city's bridges, leaving only boats to cross the Ota's seven branches. With most of the city's police and firemen killed five weeks before in the bomb blast, there was no organization to rescue typhoon victims. There were few maintenance crews to repair dikes, or to clear rail lines deluged with dirt and silt. The bomb had left no city hall to coordinate relief.

Hiroshima Red Cross Hospital, a mile south of the hypocenter near the Army Clothes Depot, had lost eighty percent of its staff to the bomb in August, including 408 student nurses. Half its patients had perished or were wounded. Its main building was severely damaged and its secondary buildings burned down. But it survived the typhoon, and became a source of information to relatives looking for survivors of the blast.

By Christmas, it had nearly been repaired.

Captain Josh Goldberg stared up at the hospital. It was of concrete construction. It alone, out of all the public buildings he and his interpreter had visited today, seemed as if it would continue to stand in a high wind. It was his last hope.

Above it fluttered a Red Cross flag, and a new Australian Union Jack, sporting the Southern Cross.

His jeep driver was a nisei GI from Utah, borrowed, like the jeep, from the U.S. Army G-2 office set up in the ruined Japanese navy yard in Kure. Josh had landed at Iwakuni Marine Air Base and spent the night in the BOQ. Marine G-2 wanted nothing to do with him: Hiroshima was coming under Australian supervision and no one at Iwakuni knew how to search for a survivor, anyway. He hitched a ride in a navy launch across Hiroshima Bay to the Japanese navy base at Kure, where the U.S. Army, in the process of turning over Hiroshima Prefecture to the Australians, still had a liaison office.

The Army G-2 outfit was moving out. The officers seemed primarily interested in seeing that their files were properly packed. He was passed politely from the adjutant down the chain of command to a lieutenant, without results. He finally came to rest in the office—which looked as if it had belonged to a Japanese admiral—of a laconic master sergeant in the Counter Intelligence Corps.

At first the sergeant only chuckled, chewing on a toothpick.

"Find an ex-major of engineers? In that mess over there?"

He moved to his window and looked across the water toward the flattened city, twenty-five miles away. "And a *white* Japanese? I never *heard* of a white Japanese."

"Well, they had them on Chichijima. Can you help me?"

"For a war-crimes trial?" mused the sergeant. He sat down, put his boots on his polished desk, took the toothpick from his mouth, inspected it, reversed it, and began to chew on the other end. "Accused? Or witnesses?"

"So far, material witnesses."

"What happened?"

He told the sergeant of the Chichijima executions, and pulled out his trump card: "Some of those poor bastards they *ate!*"

He expected shock, and found none. The sergeant merely shrugged. "Saw that in the Philippines. Mountains north of Davao. Japs had Formosan porters, used 'em like pack animals. When the Japs got hungry in the hills, they'd hack off an arm or leg."

Josh stared at him. "Are you serious?"

"Got pictures." He nibbled on the toothpick. "Sometimes, if they liked the guy, they'd even kill him first."

"You're bullshitting me, Sergeant," smiled Josh. The sergeant looked at him gravely, poked into his drawer, and tossed a photograph across the desk. It was faded and mottled with heat. Tied to a long bamboo platform, stomach down, head craned back and buck-toothed, was the remnant of a man. His eyes were open and seemed full of pain. He had bushy hair and a faint mustache. The stump of his nearer arm was roughly bandaged, the other intact. His feet had been raised, tied somewhere out of sight, and the nearer shinbone had been stripped of flesh.

"Oh, God," breathed Josh. "Oh, my *God!*"

"It's hot in the bush above Davao. Their medics must have done the amputations. They'd been feedin' him to keep him fresh."

"He's *alive?*" Josh's hand shook.

"Until I cut that bandage off. Alive and jabbering. Tough babies, Formosans. Hard to kill."

"Jesus!" Josh dropped the photo and turned away. "What did we do to the Japs?"

"Shot 'em. Comin' down the trail to surrender, after the emperor quit. General said 'No prisoners for thirty days.' We shot every fuckin' one. Didn't need no war-crimes trial."

Josh swallowed. "Well, it's a little late for that on Chichijima." He was sweating. He tried to get hold of himself. "So can you help me?"

The sergeant regarded him for a long moment. Finally he nodded. "Goin' to give you a jeep, and interpreter. And call CIC in Tokyo. If either your major or the girl's the head of a family, they're on a ration-book list."

Josh stood up. "Thanks. Anything I can do for you?"

The sergeant thought for a moment. He reversed the toothpick with his tongue, picked up the phone, and looked into Josh's eyes.

"Matter of fact, there is."

"What's that?"

The sergeant glanced at the photo and tossed it back in his drawer.

"Just see the bastards hang."

Now, outside the Red Cross Hospital, Josh climbed from the jeep. They had found no records anywhere else: but with the last card in his hand, he would see what he could do.

Josh followed his interpreter through a succession of over-worked Japanese hospital administrators, who helped the nisei check their admission records. They found no Bancroft, or Bankloft-o, or Fujihara, either: no one remembered ever having seen a Caucasian, victim or otherwise, in wartime Hiroshima.

It was cold and damp in the dark, unlighted wards. They passed through rooms jammed with beds of victims, horribly scarred and mutilated, separated by blankets hanging from I.V. racks. They found a sign: U.S. ARMY MANHATTAN DISTRICT ENGINEERS: SURGEONS INVESTIGATION TEAM.

Josh dismissed his interpreter, knocked, and entered.

An American doctor sat at a desk. Behind him stretched a deserted laboratory. He was a lieutenant colonel, thin, gaunt, and very bitter. A Toledo radiologist, he had spent the war at Walter Reed Army Hospital in Washington. What evil fate had brought him to Hiroshima, he confessed, he didn't know.

He had entered the city a month after the bomb, with the first team from the Manhattan Engineers Investigating Group. Their mission was to determine, for troops which would occupy the city, levels of residual radioactivity. They had cruised the ruins with Geiger counters, placing red flags at the hotspots, yellow at the marginal, and green flags at those which were safe.

"You walked from one green flag to another, at first. Wish we'd had lead-lined jockstraps. SCAP wouldn't even let us tell the Japs the stuff was hot."

"Did you ever treat a Caucasian survivor?" asked Josh.

"No." The army surgeon sat back in his swivel chair. "There were supposed to be ten American POWs in the city jail, but there was nothing left to treat. *Treat* a survivor?" he snorted. "We don't *treat* anybody!"

"Then why are you here?"

The doctor tossed a bulging binder of records across his desk.

"To keep score, Captain. Serology. If they don't come in, we go and get them. We got to have their blood. We're a team of goddamn vampires!"

"Blood? For what?"

"We write reports. All secret. Forget all this, Captain,

understand? Christ, we're not allowed to *talk* about them. *Treat* 'em? Hah!''

"Why *can't* you treat them?"

"Ask General Groves." The colonel looked sick. He slammed the binder with his palm. "He just wants to know what happens when . . ."

His voice trailed off.

"When *what*, Colonel?" Josh asked softly.

"When one gets dropped on *us!*"

There was a knock on the door and a dark, broad-shouldered MP entered. In his hand was a well-used thirty-five-millimeter camera, with a flash gun.

"Colonel, we caught him again."

The colonel sagged. "Well, this time let the Aussies deal with him."

Rab McGraw, hot-eyed and flushed, burst into the lab. On his gnarled, varnished cane, he limped to the doctor's desk. His jutting nose was red with cold, and his CORRESPONDENT tabs black with tarnish. He wore a U.S. Army field jacket and the same Australian bush hat he had worn on Guam. He looked even more worn, like his camera on the desk.

"What *is* this bloody shit?" McGraw demanded.

The doctor looked up wearily. "We went through it all last week, Rab. You can't *take* pictures here."

"You're wrong! The British Commonwealth occupies Hiroshima, this is a Red Cross Hospital, I'll take pictures any ruddy place I please!" He snatched his camera off the desk and checked its counter.

"You still have to deal with SCAP," shrugged the doctor. "You'll never get your pictures out of Tokyo."

"Then that's *my* problem, isn't it?" McGraw glared at the MP and spotted Josh. "Well, I'll be blowed. You landed anyway! War's over, mate: I told you that on Guam."

"Hello, McGraw," Josh muttered without enthusiasm. As the Australian limped out the door, Josh thanked the doctor and followed. McGraw was packing his camera into a canvas bag.

"That bloody quack is right, you know," McGraw said moodily. "I'll never get them through."

"I'm glad you won't," said Josh. The victims and the rubble had rubbed his conscience raw. The less the public knew about the mess the better off they'd be.

McGraw spotted Josh's collar bars and smiled. "I see they posted you as captain."

"And I'm still a Jew," Josh said. "Christian charity triumphed in the end."

"That's not certain, if they sent you *here*." McGraw hoisted the camera bag to his shoulder and fell in beside Josh as he started down the hall. "Why?"

"Looking for a Jap army major. And a girl," Josh said, and regretted it instantly. The Chichijima investigation was secret: he had better watch his tongue.

"A girl? Aren't we all, now? Last week I saw the girl you used to have, on Guam."

"Corky? I *still* have her. How is she?"

"Oh, she's a beauty, that one. You'd best get back there, mate."

"She'll keep," said Josh.

"Good . . ." McGraw eyed him strangely. "So why would a clean-cut lad like you be up here looking for a sneaky female Jap?"

"No comment."

"War criminal, like as not," McGraw speculated. "Another Tokyo Rose?"

Josh said nothing.

"Japanese Mata Hari? A collaborator from Guam?" grinned McGraw. "I plan to cover those trials down there: I hear you'll hang the lot."

"They'll get fair trials, you can bet your ass. After that, you never know."

An elderly man, draped in a white sheet and leaning on a cane, was shuffling down the corridor toward them. Half of his face was gone, and the other half was melted into a hideous, mirthless grin. He bowed as they approached. Josh avoided his eyes.

"Looks a proper leper, that one," said McGraw. "He needs a bell."

"Take his picture, then, you fucking ghoul!" blazed Josh.

McGraw shook his head. "Why? If you blokes saw it in the paper, you'd only turn the page."

Something snapped: Josh had had enough. He grabbed McGraw and pushed him to the wall.

All day long he had passed cripples on the streets, glimpsed monsters in the wards. He had looked away from children

covered with what seemed to be giant living crabs; avoided
teenage girls with devil faces, tots with balding heads, little
boys running between the beds, waving stumps for arms.

McGraw's eyes held his. From somewhere down the corridor a woman shrieked in pain. A nurse's aide brushed by: on
her neck was a keloid scar. Josh winced.

"Easy, mate," murmured McGraw. "You'll learn you just
can't look away, but I know where there's a beer."

Josh and McGraw bellied to the bar of the bleak Australian
non-com club: McGraw claimed that the officers' club was
full of leather chairs, Pommie bastards from the RAF, and
UK brass from Singapore. "I'd rather swill beer with the
masses than Scotch with horses' asses, any day."

Josh had released his driver, for McGraw had conned a
jeep from the Australian Press Officer and promised to drive
him back to Iwakuni.

The club smelled of sweat and beer and was jammed with
corporals and sergeants of the Australian Army. Josh sucked
at his lukewarm bottle of Lions Head beer. It slashed at his
stomach with claws of fire and relaxed him wonderfully.

"Sorry," he said. "About getting red-assed in the hospital."

"Hiroshima does that." McGraw studied the beer in his
bottle and swirled it thoughtfully. "You feel guilty. Though
mind you, if you'll remember, Aussies didn't cry much when
you dropped the goddamn thing." He surveyed the room.
"*These* blokes still fancy it the greatest invention since their
first bloody piece of ass."

When McGraw had landed with the first U.S. forces, he
was one of two—out of two hundred—correspondents to
ignore the surrender ceremonies on the battleship *Missouri*.
He had headed southwest by train instead, armed only with a
forty-five, surrounded by homeward-bound, sullen Japanese
troops, carrying his own food.

He and Wilfred Burchett, of the *London Daily Express*,
were the first Allied correspondents to arrive in Hiroshima.
"Carp in the castle moat were all belly-up. Everything stank
of sulfur, and dead bodies." They had filed their stories
successfully, somehow getting their copy past censors before
the iron gate of MacArthur's Press Code slammed shut.

"Bloody commies, they call us now. Nothing else got out.
Songs, poems . . . quashed. Jap newsreel footage: confis-

cated. *Nippon Eigasha* shot a documentary: thirty thousand
feet of film. Every foot's in Washington now, in a U.S.
Army vault. Freedom of the press: the Russians must be
laughing at the whole damn bloody do.''

Josh stirred uncomfortably. That wasn't his problem: Colonel Kondo was, and finding Alicia Bancroft and Major Fujihara,
and he had failed. He studied McGraw for a moment. What
had he to lose? McGraw tracked down sources every day:
Josh needed professional advice.

"Rab, can I tell you something, off the record?"

"Sorry, mate. 'Off the record' ties my hands."

Josh shrugged. "Well, it's classified secret, and I need help."

McGraw thought for a moment and relented. "Okay, cobber," he shrugged. 'You *did* drive me in from the airstrip that
day. 'Off the record' then."

Josh told him of the atrocities on Chichijima. McGraw
listened intently, and ordered them more beer.

"Cannibalism? Christ, I never heard of that! And *whites*
lived on the island?"

"Since 1831."

"Citizens of *Japan?*"

"Since before the First World War."

"You sure?"

"Rab, I've *met* some. The girl I'm *looking* for is white.
Evacuated here last year."

"Here?" McGraw stiffened. He frowned, searching for
something in his memory. "Speaks Japanese?"

"And English. Sure."

"Wears kimonos?"

"I guess. Why?" His pulse quickened.

"Blond sheila, is she?"

Josh wet his lips. "Yes. Alicia Bancroft is her name."

"Quite beautiful?"

"So her uncle says. Jesus, have you heard something?"

At a table in the rear a group of corporals and sergeants
were singing:

Oh, they say there's a troopship a-leavin' Bombay,
Bound for the land I adore . . .

"You know," McGraw mused, "there's a bloke I talked to

yesterday . . . Called Rhodes? A corporal? No, sergeant!''
He began to scan the room.

Bless 'em all, bless 'em all,
The long and the short and the tall . . .
Bless all the sergeants and their bastard sons.

McGraw spotted someone, and was off like a shot, stump-
ing with his cane across the empty dance-floor. For a moment
he was in conversation with a florid, potbellied sergeant. He
clapped the man's shoulder and started back.

For we're saying good-bye to them all,
As back to their nurses they crawl . . .

McGraw's eyes shone. "*Got* her, mate. The fat bastard at
that table? Met her at a party. All done up in a kimono. She's
a prostitute on Miyajima Island. Started a bloody riot Christmas Eve.''

"Thank Christ," breathed Josh. "She's alive."

"Body like Hedy Lamarr's, he says, and a face like Carole
Lombard!''

"Charge!'' belched Josh. "We're on our way!''

In three minutes they were bouncing along a rubble-bordered
concrete road, heading for the ferry to Miyajima Island,
which McGraw said was off the southern coast of Hiroshima
Bay. Josh began to sing:

There'll be no promotion
This side of the ocean . . .
So cheer up my lads, bless 'em all.

It was growing dark. He was half-drunk, and didn't care. It
was still a long, hard road ahead, but at the end of it sneered
Colonel Kondo, laughing with his eyes.

CHAPTER 7

Alicia Bancroft stood on the porch of Yuko's family home on Miyajima Island and watched the lights come on in stores along the waterfront below. She had escaped out here to mourn.

Today her last faint hope had fled. She had written Mickey-san at his Tokyo address a month ago, in the hope that if he had survived Hiroshima, he would have gone home.

This afternoon the postman had brought the letter back: NO HOUSE THIS ADDRESS. His residence in Marunouchi had probably perished in the fire raids, like everything and everybody else.

The atom-bomb sickness was returning to her body and her mind. It came and went. Last week she had been well enough to swim in the Seto Sea, from a secluded cove she found southwest of Daigan-ji Temple. But this morning, she had barely found the energy to crawl from her futon and had felt chills and fever all day long.

The sun was sinking over Hiroshima's ruins. High above the rubble, from the nearby base at Iwakuni, three U.S. Navy fighter planes—Matt would have known their names—crawled toward her, each drawing a double contrail across the golden sky. The war was over, the city was gone, but they were always flying past, as if proud of the wreckage below. The contrails were turning slowly red, and the apricot sky was ruined, skin clawed by a vicious cat. She touched the keloid on her shoulder.

"Alicia!"

Yuko was calling from far down the street. Her friend's face seemed white as a Kabuki dancer's. Flanking her were two *gaijin*, one a wide-shouldered American—a marine officer, she thought—and the other a lanky Australian with a cane. They seemed a little drunk.

She could not believe it. If Yuko was coming out of her shell, she was much too close to home. Suppose her grandfather wandered out and saw her?

She stepped to the rail and leaned over. "Yuko!" she called in Japanese, as loudly as she dared. "What are you doing with *them?*"

"They came to my uncle's store . . . Come down!"

"No!" She remembered Christmas Eve. Never again.

Yuko pointed to the marine. "I think this one is saying he has seen your *uncle!*"

Her uncles, so far as she knew, were dead, or they would have found her. All had lived in districts hit by the great fire raids.

"*Which* uncle?" she called to the officer in English.

"Noah!" the marine called back. "Please, may I talk to you?"

Weariness forgotten, she pulled open the *shoji* screen and flew past Yuko's grandfather kneeling on the tatami reading a newspaper. She stumbled down the stairs, jammed on her *zori,* and ran out the door. On the cobbled street, she almost fell.

The marine was even bigger than he had seemed from the porch, and his shoulders even wider. She caught a whiff of beer. Drunk? He was regarding her with wide gray eyes, mouth open, a half-smile on his face. Something deep inside her seemed to melt.

"My God," he breathed. "So this is *Alicia?*"

"You saw my Uncle Noah?"

"On Chichijima."

She believed him instantly. He took her hands in his. His own were warm and firm.

"Alicia Bancroft," he mused, "of Chichijima Island." His eyes were gentle. "Where can we talk alone?"

Alone? Impossible, unheard of . . .

"Yes, sir," she heard herself say faintly. "Her uncle's store . . ." His face began to swim before her eyes. "We'll go to her uncle's store . . ."

She heard Yuko cry out, and the street lantern lamp above her grew dim. She was crumpling to the pavement. She felt herself lifted like a child in a father's arms.

Her consciousness returned, and faded, and returned again: she was in Yuko's home, on the ferry, in a speeding jeep, then somehow between the sheets of a high warm Western bed.

A fat American nurse gave her a shot, and she slept.

Josh leaned on the record desk at the end of the ward in the tiny Iwakuni naval dispensary. He ran his hand across the stubble on his jaw. He had been up all night, arguing his case: first with marine sentries at the gate, then navy corpsmen, now with this medical duty officer. McGraw had left long before. Only a tubby navy nurse, a jg from UC Hospital in San Francisco, had given him a kind word all night long.

His nisei driver from the 41st Division in Kure had returned with news. Fujihara had survived the holocaust: the ration board had found his name in the Bunkyo-ku district in Tokyo, and the staff sergeant in Kure was checking with Tokyo police to find his address now.

Finally, buttressed with a sheaf of dispatches, Josh was arranging to have Alicia sent to Guam. She was part of the Guam war-crimes prosecution, though she did not know it yet.

The doctor, who had first objected to admitting a Japanese civilian, white or not, was objecting now to sending her: she was too sick.

"Guam? By air?" The doctor shrugged. His glasses sparkled in the morning light as he glanced at Alicia's chart. The problem, he said, was that he didn't know how to treat radiation victims: nobody did, even the experts across the bay.

He studied her chart. "Her white count's down. What was she doing in Hiroshima, anyway?"

"Long story, Doc. Anyway, how long? One week? Two?"

"We're going to give her whole blood, but you better count on two."

The nurse swished down the corridor. "She's awake," she told Josh. "She'd like to see you."

And I, thought Josh, would like very much to see *her*.

He told his driver to check with Kure to see if they had found Fujihara's address yet. Until he interrogated the girl, he would not tell her that the major had survived: if she knew that she might have to testify against him she might not say a word.

Quickly, he picked up his scratch pad and moved down the corridor. His mouth was furry from the Aussie beer, and his uniform was rumpled.

Whatever Alicia Bancroft was, she was certainly no prostitute, and he wished that he'd bothered to shave.

He found her propped in bed under gray U.S. Navy blankets and smiled down into her eyes.

Gorgeous, just gorgeous . . .

"You *saw* Uncle Noah?" she begged. "Where is he now?"

She had wide emerald eyes, golden hair, and a little bridge of freckles across her straight firm nose. When she smiled two tiny dimples showed. Her eyes, like no girl's he had ever met, held steadily on his own.

Enough, he had work to do.

"Your uncle's on Chichijima. He arrived illegally, but he's quartered in our barracks, acting as interpreter."

Her eyes filled. She told him that her brother had died at Honkawa School, and that Major Fujihara, her foster-father, had been killed in Hiroshima Castle. Her last letter to her Uncle Noah had come back, undelivered. "I thought *everyone* was dead!"

He had a crazy urge to ease her mind and tell her that the major lived. But if she knew he was alive, she'd never admit to an American that he'd interrogated the POW on Washington Beach.

She seemed so vulnerable that he wanted to take her into his arms and comfort her. Instead, he took her hand. "Your Uncle Noah is fine, Alicia. So are Harlan and Abner and Isaiah."

"Thank you," she murmured. "But why were you looking for me? And why did you bring me here?"

He studied her for a long moment. He had planned on an accusation of complicity, a frontal attack to jar loose the truth. He couldn't do it.

"On Chichijima, we learned that Colonel Kondo tortured American pilots. . . . You know him?"

It was as if a steel gate crashed between them. Her face became a blank.

"No."

"But you *met* him? On Washington Beach?"

She looked away. "No."

"Alicia," he said gently, "I know that is not true."

"I do *not* know him." Her face was closed. "I have *never* met him."

She must still be frightened of the *kempeitai*.

"Alicia," he explained, "he's a prisoner in our stockade. He can't hurt you or your Uncle Noah. We know that he forced you to question an airman on Washington Beach. A very young one, just a kid. We're sure you had no choice, and we only want to know—"

"Your story is not true," she murmured softly. "Not true, not true at all."

Who was she trying to protect? Fujihara? Josh took a deep breath. "And Major Fujihara was there, wasn't he?"

"He is dead," she said in a monotone. "Mickey-san is dead."

"And so he can't be harmed," he prodded, "if you tell me what you saw?"

"I saw *nothing!*" she insisted. "I was never *on* that beach." She met his eyes, finally. Her own were wet. "And neither was Major Fujihara."

She was trembling. Again, he wanted to take her into his arms. With an effort, he stood back.

"That boy was excecuted, Alicia. And the pilot. Murdered, that same night."

"Oh, no!" she breathed. "No!"

He explained to her that they needed their names, to inform their next of kin.

"*Whoever* they were," Josh persisted, "their parents are waiting. The war's been over four damn months, and we don't know who they are!"

"There are many such parents in Hiroshima," she reminded him softly. "We were beaten, Captain. You must have known it. Why did you drop the bomb?"

How do you answer that?

He moved to the window and looked out at the runway. Two marine Corsairs were lined up for formation takeoff, their gullwings poised for flight. Their engines blasted suddenly, making the window shiver. They roared down the strip, tucked up their wheels, and thrashed off together over the Seto Sea.

"I thought we dropped it to save lives. Now I'm not so sure." He turned back to the room. "But those guys on the beach didn't do it. And neither did their folks."

For a long while she studied her hands. She looked up. "Captain, when one makes a promise one must keep it."

A promise? To whom? Kondo would have needed none, the *kempeitai* dealt in threats. Fujihara, perhaps? *"Who'd* you promise?" Josh stabbed in the dark. "Major Fujihara?" Feeling like a monster, he continued:"You've said he's dead. So tell me what happened, okay?"

She studied him and took a breath.

"You do not know the young man's name?" she asked. "No."

She swallowed. "Hamilton. Jerry Lee Hamilton."

Thank God! At least he had that!

"Go on, Alicia."

"I think he worked the radio in one of the big gray planes."

"Yes? And his pilot?"

"I do not know."

"Chow time!" The door swung in and the tubby nurse rattled through, rump first, with a breakfast tray.

Jesus Christ, the timing!

"Eggs up, toast, marmalade, coffee," she chirped. She looked intently at Alicia's face, and turned on Josh: "Whatever's going on, Captain, could you delay it till she's fed?"

Josh nodded, seething. "Alicia, help yourself."

The woman left and Alicia stared at the tray as if it held the Holy Grail. She licked her lips. Shakily, she spread marmalade on a piece of toast and began to wolf it, smearing her cheeks like a child. In a moment she turned pale and put it back on the plate. "It's so much *food!"*

The door swung open. His nisei driver stuck in his head.

"Later," Josh said swiftly.

"Okay, sir." Oblivious to Josh's glare, he blundered on: "But counterintelligence confirmed Fujihara. He's living in Tokyo: Thirty-four Hongo-dori Avenue, Bunkyo-ku. They'll fly you up ATC."

His heart plummeted. As the door shut behind the nisei, the tray crashed to the floor. Alicia was staring at him.

"He's *alive?*" she whispered. The emerald eyes were piercing him. "And you *knew?*"

He swallowed. "I wasn't sure!"

Her legs flashed suddenly over the side of the bed. He saw an ugly keloid on her shoulder, as the hospital gown fell away. She covered it quickly. "You must get out, sir. Where's my kimono? Where have they put my clothes?"

"Where are you going?" he demanded.

"To Tokyo!" She stood, lurched, and almost fell. He caught her and lifted her back. Her skin was silk, her flesh was firm, and he felt his pulse beat fast.

"I'll bring him to Guam, and you'll see him there. We just can't let you go."

She gave him a long, long look. *"Why* Guam?" she murmured. "Why do you need me there?"

"To testify, of course. To tell us what you saw there on the beach."

Her eyes were suddenly empty. "What beach, sir?" she asked. "What beach is it you mean?"

Silently, he cursed the fat-assed nurse and the stupid army nisei. But most of all, himself . . .

"Okay," he growled. "You'll be there anyway. You can perjure yourself if you want!"

She suddenly began to cry. He moved to the bed, and touched her hair.

"Don't cry, Alicia," he said. *"Please!"*

"I shan't!" she said fiercely. "I don't *know* very many men, you see, and I thought we could be friends."

"I *am* your friend, Alicia," he said thickly. "I really, truly am."

"No. I was a goose. You are no friend at all."

She closed her eyes.

He stood for a long time watching her before he realized that she had fallen asleep. He picked up the mess on the floor, wet the napkin in her water glass, and gently rubbed the marmalade from her cheek.

Then he crept from the room. In an hour he was on a flight to Tokyo.

CHAPTER 8

*M*att Bancroft was very cold on New Year's Day.

Last night at midnight, temple bells all over Japan had pealed, one hundred eight times, in the *joya no kane* ceremony to welcome the new year. Now a biting wind slashed Tokyo from the northwest, swirling dust and ashes in the streets and forcing the beggars into subway stations. In the air was the threat of rain. Few Japanese in Tokyo had the food, sake, or beer to celebrate the New Year, except *yakuza* gangsters and black marketeers.

This morning Matt squatted by the litter that he and Hashimoto had erected of scrap-lumber to keep Mickey-san's futon off the damp tatami mat. His *sensei* had spent a feverish night, thrashing and turning in the freezing, drafty hovel.

Matt himself was ill. Along with half the people one saw on the street or in the subway stations, he wore a flu mask; many, in this time of shortages, wore a simple kerchief pulled over the mouth and nose.

His mentor seemed asleep, but Matt knew that he was not. He felt his brow. Even to his own feverish palm, it seemed hot. They had no thermometer, nor any aspirin. Hashimoto had gone out to try to steal a lump of charcoal from a taxi: the doctor up the alley had suggested that, dissolved in water, it would help Mickey-san's diarrhea. Looking at his foster-father in the dim light of the sleeping room, Matt doubted that the major could get it down.

Mickey-san's eyes were suddenly open, bloodshot and bleary. His eyesight had stopped improving. The doctor, who had two other patients from Hiroshima in his practice, seemed to think that he was doomed.

"Lorna was here," he whispered in English. His voice was hoarse.

"Yes, *sensei*," Matt muttered, startled.

Oh, Mama, help me now . . .

"She said . . ." Mickey-san shook his head and tried to smile. "Dreaming," he decided. "I loved her. Did you know that?"

"Yes sir." He dipped a cloth into their water drum and laid it on Mickey-san's brow. "Everyone did. And loved Alicia, too."

Mickey-san smiled. "When your father died, I would have married her."

More, then, had been between them than he'd known. Though surprised, he didn't care. He touched his mentor's arm. "She would have made you happy, sir."

"And I would have adopted you. There is nothing now to leave you, but you would be my son."

"I *am* your son, *sensei*."

Mickey-san peered at him in the feeble light. "Then follow my path."

"If I can."

"Do you think of General Sumi sometimes?"

How could he have known? "Well . . . When I read of those veterans' societies, I wonder if somewhere he fights on."

"He and his kind are death. Choose life! *Build*, Matt. Do not destroy."

Matt bowed deeply but said nothing. He could hear Hashi-moto drawing aside the panel they had propped at the entrance: without hinges, or a proper *shoji*, they had to make do with a plywood sheet for a door. It was probably the most valuable possession on the property.

The stocky ex-soldier entered. He seemed disturbed. He smelled of beer: somehow, on this New Year, he had found a drink. He had found a lump of charcoal, too.

Together, they ground it down and stirred it into water.

Matt tried to get Mickey-san to drink it, without success. Hashimoto put a can of water on the hibachi, to mix it into a kind of soup: perhaps he could swallow it warm.

While it was heating, he drew Matt aside.

"Tanaka called to me as I passed his *koban.*"

Tanaka was Hashimoto's friend, the policeman who manned their neighborhood *koban* box. He was responsible for a four-block domain running almost to the Yasukuni Military Shrine. Like most *omawari-san* police, whose very name meant "he who walks around," he was beloved and knew everyone and every secret in his ward.

The mystery of Hashimoto's beer was solved.

"Yes?"

"We must tell no one that he told me this, but—" Hashimoto hesitated, and glanced toward the sleeping room.

"Told you what?"

"His captain asked him yesterday whether Major Fujihara still lived here."

Matt froze. "Why?"

"The Americans wanted to know."

"*Americans?*"

"*Hai.* Their *kempeitai,* their CIC."

MacArthur's Counter Intelligence Corps was well known in the streets. It was said that it scooped up POW prison guards, ex-*kempeitai* policemen, and Imperial General Staff officers even in the dead of night. Tokyo police cooperated fully.

"Why do they care where *he* lives?"

Hashimoto shook his head. "They asked also about your sister. Alicia, was it?"

"Let them ask the man who dropped their *pika-don!*" His fists clenched. "Did they ask for my mother? Or my father? I could tell the Americans about *them.*"

He was frightened. He went to the entrance panel, moved it aside, and looked out. "*Why?*" he demanded again. "What do the *gaijin* bastards want with *him?*"

"The Kure bunkers?" suggested Hashimoto.

He was right! Mickey-san had drafted the fortifications. The Yankees must have discovered that, at the end, he had been on General Sumi's staff! Perhaps they thought the major had been *kempeitai* himself!

"What is it?" Fujihara called from the sleeping room. Matt

went to the door. Mickey-san was struggling to sit up. Clutching his blanket close, he peered across at Matt. "What *gaijin?*"

Matt shook his head. "Nothing, *sensei.* Please lie down."

His mind raced. He had seen Sugamo Prison, where General Tojo—with a bullet hole in his chest from a suicide attempt—and the rest were in cells, awaiting charges before MacArthur's International Military Tribunal. The newspapers, censored by the Occupation and devoid of other news, had no reluctance in telling the public about *that.* Sugamo seemed a grim and dismal fortress, reeking of death. Two American guards stood stiffly in gleaming white helmets at its entrance. He would die before he saw his *sensei* taken there.

Mind whirling, he managed to get Mickey-san to try the charcoal soup. When his mentor slept—he seemed to sleep continually—he squatted by the fireless hibachi with Hashimoto.

"We must get him out," he whispered.

"To where?"

"Where did we send the women?" shrugged Matt. "Somewhere, anywhere."

After the surrender there had been a mass evacuation—*sokai*—of young women to the far prefectures of Japan because it was thought that the Americans—who some Japanese seriously believed had descended from monkeys in the trees—would rape every girl they could find. The prospect was terrifying to parents. To pollute the family register—a careful chronology of the generaions kept in every home—with a mixed-blood *ainoko* baby was unthinkable. To provide for one afterward would be a legal obligation a clan could never endure. Some fathers, unable to evacuate their daughters, had provided them with poison: they would rather lose the girl than lose face.

The GIs had arrived, whistling as they went, scouting the streets with carbines slung and heavy boots, which they even left on inside. All looked precisely alike to Japanese eyes, and all seemed giants. There had been no one but old *baba-sans* and young children—who had begged for chewing gum until stopped by their elders—to greet them. The troops had been frightening enough, but had acted well.

The precaution of the *sokai* had been needless—Americans were mostly good-humored. They did not rape, but seemed to prefer to buy their women with Lucky Strike cigarettes. Informed of the conquerors' magnanimity, the evacuees were returning now.

They reported that the northern districts, compared to Tokyo and the Kanto Plain, were almost free of American troops. "I wonder if he could stand the cold of my village?" Hashimoto murmured. "And if we could get him there?" His tiny hamlet on Hokkaido would be freezing in January. "He is going to die, you know," he added sadly.

Matt stared into the ex-private's bloodshot eyes. For the first time his voice dropped into the register of a senior addressing a subordinate. "Not in Sugamo Prison!" he growled. "Do you hear?"

Hashimoto sucked in his breath and his eyes widened in surprise. Then he smiled faintly, bowing low.

"I hear, sir," he murmured, and the two began to plan.

CHAPTER 9

*C*aptain Josh Goldberg, USMCR, regarded the crowd in front of MacArthur's headquarters as he crawled from the back seat of the wood-burning taxi. Beneath his trenchcoat he shivered in his tropical worsted, the most formal uniform he had.

The Dai Ichi Building, Supreme Commander Allied Powers' headquarters, was seven stories tall. It faced the Imperial Palace grounds across a boulevard and a moat. In the moat, swans were preening proudly: in front of the alabaster headquarters, MacArthur's honor guard, in stainless steel helmets and silken scarves, were preening too. Not a man was under six feet tall.

With the emperor's renunciation of divinity, the Dai Ichi seemed to dwarf the palace. The crowd of Japanese stood back from the pavement as if held by an invisible rope. They were excited, agape, here to catch a glimpse of the American general who suddenly ruled Japan.

It had been a scary ride from the Yuraku Hotel, where Josh had been billeted last night, along windswept streets through heavy morning traffic. The driver had squeezed at breakneck speed into openings Josh would hardly have tried to bicycle through.

"Kamikaze?" he smiled, pointing at the driver. "You?"

The driver stared at him with eyes of stone. Tokyo was apparently not a city to joke in.

The meter read one hundred yen—about a quarter. Josh fished an oversized hundred-yen note, with an ornate picture of the emperor, from his wallet. He added another and handed them to the driver.

The driver glared at him, thrust back the tip, and was gone in a cloud of wood smoke.

Josh heard a siren whir, saw traffic pull off the boulevard. A razor-sharp army shavetail barked "Ten-*shun*."

An MP jeep sped up the street, followed by an olive-drab staff car, waxed and polished and flying five stars from each front fender. The entourage squealed to a stop. An MP yanked open the rear door of the staff car and braced to attention, eyes on infinity. The Supreme Commander Allied Powers unfolded to the world.

MacArthur wore his battered fifty-mission hat, a raincoat, and pink slacks. Despite the gloomy day, he wore his dark sunglasses.

"Present *arms!*" cried the lieutenant. Josh, braced at attention, saluted; the general noticed him and touched a finger to his visor. Behind him, Josh heard the slap of hands on leather carbine slings.

The Japanese bowed low. A child in the front row waved a tiny Japanese flag and squeaked "Banzai!"

MacArthur nodded in return, and very nearly smiled.

When the general strode up the steps, and the honor guard was dismissed, Josh fell in beside the lieutenant.

"You do this *every* morning?"

The shavetail, straight from a recruiting poster, regarded him with clear blue eyes.

"That's *all* I do, Captain. Morning, when he gets here, twice at noon for lunch, and quitting time, when he leaves."

"Jesus, they call *us* bellhops!"

The lieutenant glanced at the crowd. "He thinks they need a god, I guess, and we fired the one they had. You want my job?"

Josh shook his head and asked him where he could find G-2.

Special Agent Hector Foss, of the Counter Intelligence Corps, was a chubby, red-cheeked officer with a runny nose and blond tousled hair. On his collar he wore no rank: only two gold insignia: US, like a correspondent. He might be a lieutenant or a colonel, for all that Josh could see.

Foss had obviously not expected him, and seemed miffed that the Marine Corps deemed it necessary to send assistance for an arrest exactly like those he was making every day. With no diplomatic way to explain that marines didn't trust the army, Josh simply smiled and shrugged.

"They told me to come, so I came."

"You don't have a sidearm?"

"Not with me, sir." What was his rank, and why keep it a secret? His age was indeterminate, behind the fat. "We shouldn't have any trouble, he's just an architect."

"Okay. We'll pick up the local cop, anyway. You want an interpreter?"

"No." Noah Bancroft had told him that Fujihara spoke English well.

Foss had hardly glanced at the paperwork he had brought from Chichijima. Josh asked him if he didn't need a warrant.

Foss snorted. "We're running this country. All I need is this."

He took a forty-five hanging in its holster-belt from a hat rack, buckled it on, and shrugged into an Eisenhower jacket that hugged his belly.

"*And* this," he added. He removed a small gold badge from his wallet and showed it to Josh. It was emblazoned SPECIAL AGENT, U.S. ARMY COUNTER INTELLIGENCE CORPS.

He pinned the badge on his jacket and moved to the door. "I got three more to pick up before lunch. So let's move it, Captain, okay?"

As they climbed into a jeep parked on the street, a steady rain began.

The roof of the hovel began to drip. Matt, sniffling from his head cold, cursed the weather. The wind had shifted southeast, bringing a drumming rain. If they slid aside the plywood over the entrance for more light, the belongings they had stacked near the door would get wet; if they left it closed, they were likely to miss something in the gloom and forget to bring it.

Hashimoto had stolen a wheelbarrow from the groundskeeper's shack at a nearby park. In it, they would carry what little they had—bedding, hibachi, rice, and Fujihara's brief-case—to the subway line. Everything would get soaked.

Hidden in the bedding was Mickey-san's ancestral sword, known to be two hundred years old. Bundled with it was his short-bladed *wakizashi* knife. Razor-sharp, of tempered steel, the blades—along with the study of martial arts—were forbid-den in postwar Japan.

The urn with his son Tohru's ashes had been secretly buried days before, among stately elms in Yasukuni Jinja Park, where his name was already enshrined with those of two million other military heroes. He would be worshiped in the spring and autumn festivals, when a palace messenger—if the Occupation allowed it—would present the imperial offer-ings and read the imperial message to Tohru and the rest of the deities.

All was ready for departure. Now it was time to tell Mickey-san. Matt took a deep breath, adjusted his flu mask, and entered the sleeping room.

In the faint light through rice-paper panels that had escaped the flames, he could see that Mickey-san was awake. As briefly as he could, he told his mentor what they planned. "We think they are coming for you, and we think it is because of General Sumi's 'underground,' sir. I have read the Occupation is chasing down everyone who—"

"No," said Mickey-san. His eyes closed. "It is not that."

"What, then, *sensei?*"

Mickey-san sighed. "A thing that happened on Washington Beach. With your sister, and Colonel Kondo. The Americans have learned of it, and they do not understand."

Matt gaped. "Washington Beach? With *Alicia?*"

"I cannot explain now . . . Believe only that I was true to Bushido." Mickey-san's eyes snapped open and he struggled to sit up. "I cannot run away. But *you* must. The time has come: you are 'Christopher Hart.' "

"Sensei—"

"You wanted to be a soldier: this is an order. Now, bring me my writing case, and go. Hashimoto will stay, for a while."

"Sir, I can't leave you—"

"My writing case, Matt-san! Now!"

Hashimoto called quietly from the other room. "Bankloft-o!" Matt whirled and ran in. In the gloom, he could see Hashimoto tugging at the bedding. "They have come! Two *gaijin*, and Tanaka!"

Matt stumbled to the panel and peered between its edge and the doorpost. In the rain, a short, fat American, followed by the little *koban* policeman in blue and a tall American in khaki, were making their way through the puddles in the garden. The tall American wore a globe-and-anchor insignia on his overseas cap; from propaganda posters he recognized the insignia of the dread U.S. Marines.

He tensed. His father might well have seen the globe and anchor in his last few hours on Iwo. Well, this marine would not steal Mickey-san's last days. They would have to kill *him* first!

"Here!" grunted Hashimoto. All at once the sheathed *wakizashi* was whirling at him. He caught it, heart pounding. The razor-sharp samurai sword, drawn, glittered suddenly in Hashimoto's hand.

"I'll take the first," whispered Hashimoto. "And if I have to kill Tanaka, then I will."

"Matt-san!" called Fujihara from the other room. "Are you getting my writing case?"

"A moment, *sensei*," Matt answered. His hand was shaking so badly that he almost dropped the *wakizashi*.

Cool, like a lily floating on a pool. Calm, as a swan in a castle moat . . . His father's spirit watched over him: his mother's, too, and Alicia's: he would not flinch.

His trembling ceased.

There was a pounding on the plywood panel. "Open up!"

Behind him, the water dripped into a rice bowl they had set to catch the leak. He could hear Mickey-san arising from his couch.

"Matt-san?" Mickey-san cried from the other room. "What is it?"

Matt shrank against the wall. Hashimoto, eyes intent on the door, slowly raised his sword. Pudgy fingers from outside had appeared around the panel. Matt had a crazy impulse to slash them off.

Patience . . .

The plywood slid open with a squeal of dampened wood. Matt squinted; the fat *gaijin*, blinking in the gloom, stepped in, hand on his holstered gun.

"Fujihara?" he called. He moved forward uncertainly. The

little policeman, reluctantly, followed him. The marine stepped in, even more cautiously, at last.

"You in here, Fujihara?" the fat one demanded.

"Fujihara-san," repeated the policeman, uncertainly. *"Doko desu ka?"*

There was a stirring in the other room. Mickey-san, a skeleton with a bald skull and shriveled limbs, appeared, clinging to the doorpost, peering blindly into the light.

"Who calls?"

Hashimoto struck, silently and surely.

The blade crashed diagonally through the right collarbone of the fat *gaijin* and opened up his torso to his belly. There was a sound like cracking bamboo; then he simply whimpered and was dead.

The policeman jammed his whistle into his mouth and scrambled, shrilling, for the door. Hashimoto hacked again, half-severed his neck, and he fell on the fat American. Blood began to pour across the tatamis on the floor.

The marine dived for his comrade's gun. Matt stabbed at him as he passed, and felt the blade go home. Hashimoto's foot flashed out in an *aiki* kick to the jaw, and the American fell without a sound to the bloody, slippery mats. Matt dropped to his knees, the *wakizashi* short sword raised to pierce his chest again. A stain of blood was spreading across the right side of his tunic.

"No!" shouted Mickey-san. He stumbled across the room. "Matt-san, no!"

Slowly, Matt lowered the blade. He felt Mickey-san's hand clutch his shoulder. He arose. His mentor's eyes looked deeply into his.

"This was very wrong." He looked down at the marine and paled. "Hashimoto, strip his coat." He looked into Matt's eyes. "And now you *must* go, my son. You have the passport?"

Matt's eyes filled. *"Hai.* But, sir—"

"I have said that you must go," growled Mickey-san, "now, go!"

Hashimoto stripped the marine of raincoat, tunic, and shirt, baring his chest. Blood seeped from a wound between his right nipple and his shoulder. The captain stirred and groaned. "Bind it," Mickey-san ordered him.

"Better we kill him," Hashimoto muttered.

"Bind it!" barked Mickey-san. "Use my belly-band, and bind it well!"

He took the *wakizashi* from Matt, and the sword from Hashimoto. His eyes were filled with tears. "I have need of these, this morning."

Seppuku? Matt chilled. "*Sensei*, no!"

"I must. They will be in Hashimoto's care for you, if ever you return."

Matt bowed. Voice trembling, he said: "Let me stay to help you. I'll be your *kaishaku*."

"No. You will not." Mickey-san's eyes were swimming. "So, sayonara, Matt-san. 'Since it must be so.' "

Hashimoto had bound his belly-band tightly around the captain's chest. He covered the captain with the raincoat and told Matt that the blades would be forever in his village of Wakannai, in Hokkaido, safe from harm.

"So, my son," urged Mickey-san. "Go quickly to the Red Cross!"

Matt knew that he must obey. He bowed to them both, fighting back tears. He overcame the urge to embrace his mentor: in front of Hashimoto it would only be an embarrassment to them all.

He stepped into the rain. An army jeep nuzzled the stone wall, blocking the way. They had left its engine running against the chill.

He wanted no curious policeman to notice it there, for Mickey-san and Hashimoto must not be disturbed. He drove it a half dozen blocks, keeping to the side streets. Then, fearful of being seen in a U.S. Army jeep, he abandoned it in an alley. He threw the keys into a canal as he passed over a footbridge.

He had no subway money, and a long walk before him, to the YMCA Building near Meiji University in the Surugadai District. As he trudged along, he passed more and more GIs and saw more American cars with every block.

Ahead, if Mickey-san was right, lay a new life. He knew that by the time he reached it, his *sensei* would be dead.

Michihiko Fujihara kneeled in the light from the open ply-wood door, writing his statement, and confession. He wrote slowly and carefully, in English, for he wanted no half-educated nisei to blur the meaning of his words. With this document he could formally cover Matt's tracks to America and explain his part—and poor Alicia's—in the executions on Washington Beach.

The smell of blood in the hovel was nauseating. This, or a recurrence of his bone-deep fever, made his hand tremble, and he feared for the clarity of his handwriting, which had always given him pride. He wrote slowly and carefully, as befitted the last words he would write. When he was finished, he stamped the document carefully with his *hanko* and folded it.

He moved feebly to the marine on the floor, and stuck the paper into the pocket of his slashed trenchcoat. The bleeding had stopped. The American's face was gray with shock. There was no way to know if he would live or die.

In a few moments when Fujihara joined the gods, he would beg them to save the captain: otherwise Matt's soul would bear the burden of murder through all eternity.

Hashimoto, squatting soldierlike by the hibachi, was frowning. "Sir, suppose he saw young Bankloft-o, before he made the thrust?"

"I think not."

"With *me* it does not matter," shrugged Hashimoto. To *gaijin* all Japanese looked like minnows in a school. "But if he saw Bankloft-o, Major, we must not let him live."

Fujihara waved his hand. "I doubt he did. It's dark in here, and he wore a mask."

"But those eyes of green!"

Fujihara studied the marine. He thought of the boy on Washington Beach, as helpless as this one here. He loved Matt more than life itself, and prayed he would escape. But in his own last moments in this world, he could not kill again.

"We shall *not* kill him. And when you're safely gone, you will phone the police. If he survives, so be it."

So now it was time. Fujihara fingered his *katana*. Forged by the house of Masamune, it was said to have been given an eighteenth-century ancestor by his master, a great lord of Kyoto during the reign of the Tokugawa. With the *wakizashi* blade it was all that remained of the family heirlooms he had accepted so casually as a youth.

He felt its cutting edge. The mirror-smooth steel glittered with tiny crescent moons from its last sharpening. Its *tsuba* hilt-guards were cast as silver panthers.

The sword would not fail, nor would Hashimoto.

He sent him out first to wash the blades in the ruined garden pool. No foreign blood, even in death, would pollute his own. His belly-band was stanching the marine's wound, so he could not bind his stomach and would have to do without. He donned his only kimono. His heart began to beat.

A lily, floating on a pool . . .

Hashimoto returned, handed him the *wakizashi*, and stationed himself with the *katana*. Fujihara kneeled, tucked his flowing sleeves beneath his knees so that he would not fall backward if he flinched. Before his eyes, a red haze covered all: the trussed marine, the rice bowl beneath the leak. He looked up into Hashimoto's taut face, and somehow smiled.

"Pray for my spirit," he reminded Hashimoto.

"Hai." The soldier's lips were trembling, but his hand seemed firm.

His own heart was pounding in his head.

A lily, floating . . .

He touched the hilt of the *wakizashi* to his temple, as ceremony demanded. He slowly placed its point against his abdomen, felt the prick.

Grandfather, give me your strength today . . .

He sucked his breath and jammed in the blade. He felt a searing, grinding pain, as if his bowels had burst.

Father, give me yours . . .

Left to right, then up . . .

He could bear the agony no longer. "Now!" he grunted to Hashimoto.

Lorna . . .

He heard the whistle of the ancient blade. Beckoning him, beyond all pain, was the glow of a great white light. Joyfully, singing inside, he let go of life and joined with the radiance, merged in its blessed warmth.

Matt Bancroft walked all the way in pouring rain. By the time he reached the Red Cross Office, his army shoes were filled with water. He had removed his flu mask, which he had seen no other whites wearing, and the downpour had washed the blood from his trouser knees.

An American girl at the information desk, puzzled at his clothes, finally directed him upstairs. He told his story to a startled, bespectacled Red Cross worker, then a U.S. Army chaplain, and finally to the director of the YMCA, in that order, presenting his passport to each.

Dispatches were sent and phone calls made and it was found that his family was indeed listed as missing, by the Episcopalian Overseas Office and the State Department. Everyone seemed enthralled at his story, which he told modestly and sparsely. His efforts to lead his dead father's flock in the slums of Asakusa thrilled them: tears came to their eyes because he had failed. The congregation, he told them, had dispersed in the great evacuation, and very few returned: most had become like *etas*, sleeping in the streets.

To his amazement, they believed his every word.

He discovered that, as Christopher Hart, he could be sincerity itself. Hating their doughy white faces, he radiated love; despising them all, he shone with respect. At six o'clock he sat down in the YMCA cafeteria, to a meal so rich that it almost made him sick. That night in a dormitory, after prayers in a Lutheran chapel with a dozen Japanese converts, for the first time since Chichijima he slept between sheets.

In ten days, in custody of the pregnant, homeward-bound wife of a Lutheran missionary, he was on a U.S. President liner, bound for San Francisco and an Episcopalian orphanage in LA.

Near the Date Line, as Christopher Hart, he was invited to the captain's table to celebrate his fourteenth birthday. His own birthday, just three days later, passed unknown to all but him. He thought of it in passing, and of his mother, unavenged and trapped in torment in her grave.

CHAPTER 10

Josh Goldberg, wearing a gray army bathrobe, sat miserably in the sun room of the Army General Hospital in downtown Tokyo. He watched the counterintelligence lieutenant colonel dig into his briefcase.

Outside, traffic rumbled past: here, spring sunshine beat on the dirty windowpanes. It was stuffy and he wished he were back in his room.

The last months had been hell. He was leaving for Guam tomorrow, but pressure on him as the only survivor of the Bunkyo-ku murders had not eased.

He had been found in the hovel after a man with a Hokkaido accent had called the Tokyo police. Army MPs and medics had arrived minutes later, and found him with the dead agent and policeman, mysteriously bandaged but very nearly dead himself from loss of blood.

The blade, striking under his armpit, had missed his lung cavity, but had half-severed his pectoris major and slashed his axillary nerve. Army neurosurgeons had sewed and stitched and somehow patched him up. He had lost motion in his arm, so they cut and stitched again.

The doctors had protected him from investigators during the first twenty-four hours, and sometimes afterward, but the murders in Bunkyo-ku had struck at the heart of SCAP, and

CIC agents swarmed on him. Face had been lost: only the blood of the killers would atone.

The murders were an embarrassment to SCAP. They were the only sign of Japanese underground resistance the Occupation had encountered since the first troops marched in five months ago. So G-2 classified the crimes as "secret."

Major Fujihara—it was found—had served on the staff of General Toshio Sumi, an intelligence officer of the Second Army, in Kure. Perhaps he was ex-*kempeitai* himself, or perhaps the murders had to do with the Black Dragon Society. Maybe the U.S. Marines, with their makeshift war-crimes investigation, had unearthed a nest of ultranationalists after all. The trouble was that Josh was not much help. His inability to provide CIC with clues infuriated them. With counterintelligence in Tokyo, Josh was not a popular man.

Now, in the sun room, he regarded the counterintelligence officer warily. Unlike his previous inquisitors, the lieutenant colonel wore his rank, two silver leaves on his shoulders. He was an impressive, florid West Pointer with a chest full of ribbons and football scars on the bridge of his nose. His name was Jack Tallman, and Josh had lost a dollar betting on Navy against him in a 1934 Army-Navy game. To Josh he glittered with past fame, but now his image was tarnishing fast.

"Why'd you go in unarmed?" the colonel demanded.

"I'm not an agent, sir, I'm just a legal officer."

The colonel's lips tightened. He scanned Josh's initial statement, taken when he was half-unconscious from pain and codeine. The report was tattered from half a dozen previous sessions.

"'Suspect number one: Stocky Japanese, five foot six to five foot eight. One hundred sixty pounds? Age, about thirty. Brown eyes. Brown IJA uniform with no rank.'" He looked up angrily. "Hell, every beggar in the subway station looks like that!"

"That's because," Josh explained acidly, "he looked like every beggar you see in the subway station."

"Is that sarcasm, Captain, or what?"

"I've been through this a dozen times, sir."

"And tomorrow you're leaving Tokyo. And we've got nothing." The colonel drew a photo of the scene of the crime from his briefcase. He regarded it with distaste. "Look at

Foss! Wife and two kids.'' He sighed. ''Whoever killed him handled the sword pretty good.''

''And his foot good, too.'' Josh's jaw, broken in the attack, was healing, but not the memory of its pain.

''Probably a soldier. Trained in judo, karate, jujitsu, who knows? Now, suspect number two.'' The colonel inspected another report. ''Can't you do better than this?''

Josh told him wearily what he had told the others: it had been dark, his assailant had come from the side, he'd been wearing a flu mask.

The colonel looked at him coldly. ''Nothing distinctive? Nothing at all? The first one's twin?''

Josh moved painfully to the window and looked out. His jaw, chest, and shoulder ached, and he'd lost ten pounds. Even inside, the smell of Tokyo depressed him. In Guam, there would be ocean breezes, at least in the afternoon.

And Corky . . . And Alicia . . . He had dreamed of Alicia last night, instead of Corky, but with equal passion.

''A twin to the first one, Captain?'' the colonel pressed. ''Are we back in the subway station?''

''No, sir. *Not* his twin. Slimmer. Faster-moving, as I've said before. Younger, I'm pretty sure. There was—remember, I just glimpsed him—something different.''

The colonel looked at the report and remarked that Josh hadn't given the agent the color of the second Jap's eyes.

''I didn't?'' Josh took the report. ''Well, I was just coming out of the ether.''

He inspected the form the first agent had filled out. The colonel was right: *Suspect #2: Eyes* . . . The slot was blank.

''Brown?'' demanded the colonel. ''Or black?''

He couldn't recall. Not like the other's eyes, certainly, but brown, or black?

Had he seen those eyes again? In his dream, last night? Were they *green?*

Confused, he shook his head. ''Green?'' he offered.

''A green-eyed Jap? Come on!''

''I'm sorry, sir. I just don't know.''

The colonel shrugged, snapped his briefcase closed, and stood up. ''Okay, son. Good luck with *your* war-crimes trials.'' He managed a smile. ''We haven't been hospitable, but at least we sewed you up.''

Josh went back to the room he shared with an army lieuten-

ant, who had a broken leg and had hobbled down to chow.
He wasn't hungry, himself: he might as well pack.

He regarded his gear in the closet. They had sent his
clothes from the Yuraku Hotel. The blouse and shirt he had
been knifed in had probably been cut off him, and were
nowhere to be found. The raincoat, apparently delivered by
the CIC, sat in a bundle on the closet floor. Curiously, he
picked it up.

It too was ripped past all repair. It seemed incredible that
any blade that had sliced so easily through the heavy twill had
spared his life. Idly, he felt in its pockets for gloves, addresses, military scrip, or forgotten yen.

He felt something in the left pocket, drew out a folded
sheaf of rice papers. Surprised, he stared at it. The handwriting was neat, tiny, and certainly not his own. The papers had
not been in his trenchcoat when he had gone to make the
arrest: someone had slipped them in afterward.

He wandered to an easy chair in the light of the window.
With rising excitement, he began to read.

The first paragraph seemed to be of legal matters. It was
dated on the day of the murders in Bunkyo-ku.

LAST WILL AND TESTAMENT OF MICHIHIKO FUJIHARA

My own son and my two loving wards having
perished, I have no heirs in this world above. I have
few properties save worthless stock. I nevertheless be-
queath all that does remain to my revered Emperor and
the State. My family's swords, so regrettably bloodied,
have been given into the care of a suitable guardian.

Josh skipped a passage dealing with ancestral matters and
shrines, his attention dropping to a section headed: TO THE
OCCUPYING POWER: A STATEMENT OF CERTAIN
EVENTS ON CHICHIJIMA ISLAND.

Josh's eyes were riveted on the page. How had Army CIC
missed this?

An auto horn blasted outside the hospital. Josh heard the
distant clatter of a food cart in the ward. He read on.

On Washington Beach, after the morning air raid

on Chichijima September 1, I discovered that Alicia Bancroft was being forced, entirely against her will, to translate questions and answers in the interrogation of a young American Navy airman tied to a scaffold used for bayonet drill.

Another American, who Fujihara thought was an officer, was tethered by the waist to a nearby tree.

Josh found that his hand was trembling. He smoothed the paper.

Colonel Yasushi Kondo, General Tachibana's Acting Chief of Intelligence and head of the Secret Police, was interrogating. The flier gave his name as Jerry Lee Hamilton. He said that he was a radioman in one of the planes shot down.

The major recounted his own protests and his dismissal of the girl. At least, Alicia's innocence was confirmed.

For ten minutes Josh read, and when he was through, sat thinking for another ten. Finally he moved to a bottle on his bureau and poured himself a shot of bourbon. He went to the window. Traffic below was jammed in the purple, falling dusk.

He'd damn near lost his arm, and Foss had lost his life, and the policeman had died too. But his mission was accomplished. He raised his glass to Fujihara: "Mickey-san," Alicia called him. He had finally killed the radioman to prevent his torture. Josh thought he would have liked the major, if they'd met. He thought of Kondo's laughing eyes, taunting and jeering, and of MIAs, and parents and wives—and squadron mates like Bush—waiting for names that only Kondo knew.

"All Yankee names sound the same to me. I could not pronounce them if I knew them."

We have you, Kondo, you sonofabitch! You'll talk or I'll see you hung.

Josh had somehow lost his appetite for dinner, so he folded the flimsy pages, and began to pack his gear.

Former General Toshio Sumi kneeled on the tatami in his family farmhouse near Osawa, ten miles north of Tokyo. He wore his best kimono. His wife had been killed in the fire raids of General LeMay, and his daughter was serving him and his visitor tea.

The house was chilly from lack of fuel. The visitor was a brother of the Order of the Carp, a rising young Tokyo detective named Kazuo Nagano. Nagano was an unprepossessing man. He had protruding teeth and wore a shabby prewar business suit and a motheaten army muffler, but he was a ruthless and brilliant police officer and a fervent nationalist. He was stationed in the Marunouchi district of Tokyo, and he was here with information for Sumi.

Sumi was lucky to be home. Some months after the Occupation had begun, he had been interrogated, as a former Japanese general officer, on his activities preceding the war. Obviously, the Yankee CIC had intelligence on him: they had talked harshly of his membership in the Black Dragon Society. This he had not bothered to deny—the society was illegal now, but with ten thousand members during the war, there were not jails enough to hold them all.

MacArthur's list of Black Dragon leaders was hopelessly out of date. Of the seven he ordered arrested, two had never belonged, a third had died of old age in 1938, and a fourth had been forced by Tojo to commit suicide two years ago. Three others had renounced their membership in their youth and served as cabinet ministers.

The Yankees obviously knew nothing of the Brotherhood of the Carp, and Sumi would not have admitted membership had they torn his tongue out by the roots. Its roster, with the name of one princely member carefully cut out at the emperor's request, was buried in a canister in the grounds of a temple down the road.

Nagano, whom he was beginning to groom as his chief of staff, had been a member for three years. Despite his frail and faintly ludicrous appearance—or because of it—he was an expert in the martial arts. He had a superb memory. Now the detective was locating those members who had survived the war, to bring them back into the fold.

It was not easy. A Japanese could disappear without changing his written family name, simply by altering the pronunciation of it, and thousands of militarists had. But Sumi intended to track down his brothers, one by one.

For now that CIC pressure was easing, Sumi was readying

the Brotherhood of the Carp to resume its time-honored function. It had not historically been a military organization, although its roots lay in the Black Dragon Society and the Army of Kwantung. Civilian members, holding commissions in the Imperial Army Reserve, had always been placed overseas as industrial spies. Long before Pearl Harbor they had photographed assembly lines at Ford and radio circuitry at RCA, shipyards in Boston and airfields in Maine.

Sumi and Nagano agreed that the emperor had sounded the call for a revitalized Brotherhood on New Year's Day, in his thirty-one-syllable *tanka*, which launched the annual poetry contest:

> *Courageous the pine*
> *That does not change its color*
> *Under the winter snow.*
> *Truly the men of Japan*
> *Should be a forest of pines.*

When the Occupation relaxed its grip on emigration from Japan, brothers of the order would be sent again to German industrial drafting studios, the Stockholm embassy, the London Exchange, and all across America. Acting in the tradition of the venerable Japanese spies who had stolen the secrets of the Lancashire cotton factories a half-century before, they would feed their information directly to the great *zaibatsu* industrial conglomerates: Kawada, Yamashire, Mitsutomo.

There was plenty of time. Dependent financially on industrialists who themselves had lost everything they owned, the network would not be fully operational for ten or fifteen years. But time did not matter: it would take that long, anyway, for Mitsubishi and the other industrial giants to struggle back to their feet. Then the next war—of corporate titans—would begin. First steel, then shipbuilding, then electronics, finally autos: these wars Japan would win, if it took a hundred years.

Sumi sipped his tea and studied the notes he had made. Nagano, from the Marunouchi district, had already tracked down twenty-seven brothers of the order previously lost in the welter of the jumbled city.

Marunouchi . . . Sumi recalled that Major Fujihara had

once lived there. Nagano was bowing deeply, ready to leave, but Sumi raised his hand. "One moment, please, my brother?"

He asked him if he could locate one other person, not a brother of the order, but important: "Major Michihiko Fujihara, a well-known architect . . . ."

The detective sucked in his breath. "Sir, he is dead. He committed seppuku in a hovel in the Bunkyo-ku." He told Sumi that the American CIC officers had for some reason tried to arrest him, and been assaulted by persons unknown.

Sumi knew instantly the reason for the Yankees' interest: the affair on Washington Beach.

So General Fujihara's gentle son had almost been arrested for a war crime, while he himself had escaped with a harmless interrogation?

That was the way of the world. Sumi had another reason for pursuing the details. "The CIC officers were assaulted? By whom?"

The detective shrugged. "No one knows. My friend Tanaka—a *koban* policeman—was killed, a fine old man who helped me when first I was in uniform. We think a CIC agent was killed also. The Americans roped off the area and will say nothing, even to us. They are afraid of inciting the 'underground.' "

" 'Underground'?" snorted Sumi. "There is none, unless it is us. Did they miss the emperor's speech?"

"Americans are a stupid people," agreed Nagano. "But that is all for the best."

Sumi thought for a moment. "There is in Tokyo, from a tiny island five hundred miles south, a *gaijin* boy, about thirteen, tall and fair-haired. With green eyes. He was Fujihara's ward. Perhaps he is one of the 'persons unknown'!"

The detective seemed surprised. "Caucasian? But *Japanese?*"

"*Hai.*"

Nagano's eyes grew cold. "Could *he* have killed our *koban* policeman?"

"He is tall and strong. But whether or not he did," Sumi ordered sharply, "you are *not* to arrest him."

The detective did not like it. "Sir, if he killed Tanaka—"

"The Brotherhood has use for this boy. He must not be wasted in jail!"

Nagano bowed. "As you order. And I shall try to find him,

sir. But I've heard of no such person in Marunouchi or Bunkyo-ku, and I know the districts well.''

Sumi sighed. ''His name is Matthew Bancroft.'' He was struck by a thought. Suppose Fujihara had lied, and the passport survived? ''He may have an American alias, Christopher Hart. If you find him, bring him here.''

Sumi touched his eyes and lips in the secret countersign— ''Eyes for the emperor, lips sealed to all''—and Nagano automatically did the same. Sumi watched the detective drive off in his seedy police car.

Though Nagano was a good man, there was little hope that he'd find the boy. Sumi sighed, remembering Matt's white skin, native English, and loyalty to the emperor. Placed in Washington or another sensitive area in America, Bancroft would have been worth a dozen recruits with brown eyes and wheat-colored skin.

Sumi regretted not having acted more decisively in the bunker above Kure. Now the lad was gone as if the gods had snatched him from the streets. If ever he found him again, he would never let him go.

Josh Goldberg squirmed in the rattling R-4D courier plane from Atsugi Naval Air Station to Guam. His back was to the bulkhead, his feet stretched into the aisle. Iwo Jima lay four hours astern.

The plane had been a troop transport: the cabin, like half the cargo in it, was bilious jungle green. A navy courier officer and a draft of marines for the States slept sprawled along the seats. Across the piles of luggage and crates he saw an army captain reading, mouthing the words as he went.

He glanced at his watch. His butt ached from sitting eight hours in a bucket seat. He felt moist warm air of the tropics from the cabin ventilators and knew that they were descending, approaching Guam.

He would see Corky within the hour. He shivered; why, he did not know.

His stitches had long been removed, but his jaw throbbed and his shoulder and chest ached miserably from hauling his duffel aboard. He wore fatigues. He had been too short of funds in Tokyo to buy a new set of tropicals, and could probably not have found one anyway. He had been dozing all the way south, freezing in the half-empty, vaulted transport, which trembled with age, as if it had flown in every airborne troop movement from Guadal to Iwo itself.

He turned to look out the window. In the green paint above it was scratched a picture of the ubiquitous Kilroy, peering over a fence: *Kilroy was here.*

Now Guam was off the wing tip, and the plane was banking toward it. The army captain put down his book and moved across the aisle to peer out.

"Going to be hot down there?" he asked Josh.

"You're damn right," nodded Josh.

He looked at the army man curiously. He seemed too old for his rank, a small, wiry blond, with short-cropped hair and utterly blank gray eyes. There was something strange about him, as if he were wired with steel.

"Born in Maine," the captain said. "Don't like it hot."

"Too bad," Josh said. "You reporting for duty?"

The captain nodded, and slid into the next seat. His name was Harry Kendall. He was on temporary additional duty to the marine barracks' War Criminal Stockade.

Odd . . .Why an army man, TAD to a bunch of marines?

"Sounds grim. Who'd *you* piss off in Tokyo?"

The captain smiled. He had a gentle smile, but there was nothing behind the eyes. "Won't be bad. I'm used to prisons. Spent two years in Bilibid, after Bataan."

Josh guessed that he had learned Japanese as a prisoner and been assigned as a language officer for the war-crimes trials. He was the first ex-POW he had ever met.

"Jesus!" he breathed. "Why aren't you home?"

"Been home, came back. Ex-National Guard. They gave me a regular commission, so I re-upped."

Josh thought for a moment. He didn't want to disturb old hurts, but he simply had to know: "I'm investigating war crimes in the Bonins," he said carefully. "Is it stupid for me to ask you how they treated you in the Philippines?"

The captain grinned. Still no sign of life behind the eyes, but a pleasant grin. "No, it's okay." Speaking quickly, he ticked off his points on his fingers: "Bataan Death March: late coming out of the tunnel, and got trucked most of the way. Bilibid Prison: worked on a rice-growing detail, did a lot of bowing to the guards. Almost starved, but so did the Japs. They tried to ship a thousand of us to Japan on the *Oryaku Maru*. A *sukoshi* bit crowded in the hold. Might say, a little short of air. Hoisted the dead up through a hatch; maybe that's why I don't like heat.''

"Jesus!" breathed Josh.

"Do not take the name of our Lord in vain," smiled the captain.

Jolted, Josh murmured. "Sorry. Go on."

The captain shrugged. "Our own navy sunk us off Subic Bay; Japs machine-gunned some guys on the beach, rescued others. No way to figure which, so I didn't do much waving to the boats. Me and two other guys floated ashore, found us a Philippine guerrilla, and rode a U.S. submarine back to Espritu Santos.'' He paused and thought. "How'd they treat us? Well, Japs aren't my favorite people, but you got to turn the other cheek.'' He shrugged. "That was my war. How was yours?''

"Not *that* bad," admitted Josh. "By the end of it, I wanted to kill 'em all. Until I saw Hiroshima, where we damn near did." He regarded the captain in awe. "How do *you* live with it?''

The captain reached into his Eisenhower jacket and pulled out his book. It was a khaki-colored, tattered Bible, scratched and worn.

"All in here," he said. "All you need to know."

Josh, embarrassed, looked into the pale blank eyes. They were placid and calm. "Seems to have worked," he said. "For you.''

The plane's wheels thunked down, the flaps whined, and the cabin grew more quiet as they slowed. The seatbelt light flickered on.

"What are you going to be doing in the stockade?" Josh asked idly. "Translating, investigating, what?"

"I'm a hangman," smiled the captain. "I hang Japs."

CHAPTER 11

Alicia Bancroft sank back on the white Guamanian sand of Nimitz Beach and covered her eyes with two pink scallop shells. She let the Marianas sunshine seep into her skin, welcoming it to the marrow of her bones.

Today was her twelfth Sunday on the island. Her Uncle Noah, employed by the navy as an interpreter for the war-crimes trials, had welcomed her and she lived with him. Except for the horrid keloid scar on her shoulder and recurrences of nausea and fatigue, she was apparently well. She swam here, on the officers' beach, or at a little crescent strand below her uncle's Quonset, almost every day.

Josh had returned to Guam. He was off the beach swimming with his bride Corky now. He had told Alicia how Mickey-san died, and invited her to the wedding at the Navy Chapel. It had been a short, dazzling ceremony: white summer uniforms, brass buttons, and a glittering arch of swords; later, beer, for Guam had no champagne.

She had felt empty and cheated for weeks after the wedding, knowing that she was being unreasonable: there was nothing between Josh and her but a debt—he had found her dying, and she was sure that she owed him her life.

Here in the sun, the hurt seemed less.

"G'day, luv!"

Alicia sat up. Rab McGraw was limping across the sand

from the thatched "gedunk" stand by the road beneath the cliff. He wore a wild blue pair of Hawaiian swimming trunks, like an American, and a wide *chamorro* hat. The vicious scar along his thigh glowed red: Alicia was sure that it was a war wound, but he never spoke of it.

"Rather *hoped* you'd be here, child." He handed her a beer. "When do you testify?"

She wished he had not asked. She could not overcome her fear of Colonel Kondo.

"Wednesday." She lay back and looked at his profile, against the blazing sky. Hawk nose, searching eyes that saw everything, dimpled jaw . . . A sweet man, who seemed to like her well enough, and who welcomed silence. He was like a Chichijima islander: you never had to talk.

He was gazing down the surf line. Josh and Corky were emerging from the water. Corky tipped her head, smiling up at Josh, and banged water from her ear. Tanned and glittering with droplets, she was beautiful.

"Bit of a handful, that one," murmured Rab.

A compliment? Alicia didn't know.

Rab glanced down at her. There was such tenderness in his eyes that she felt her cheeks grow hot.

"You're far the lovelier, you know," he murmured.

She could not imagine a Japanese saying such a thing, and she had to look away.

Josh sat with Corky at their favorite table in the officers' club. Her lips had got tight; they always did when she drank too much, which was often. In a while her soft amber eyes would harden.

"I hate Guam!" she scowled. "Everybody's going stateside! Why not us?"

"We've been through this," he said tiredly. "I want to prosecute Kondo."

"What for?"

"For a couple of fliers—"

"That you never even met!"

"And a guy named Pappas, who thought I was Jesus Christ."

"Let Boscalli do it himself!" She frowned at her drink, finished it, and began to look for the steward.

Commander Boscalli was the staff legal officer, and was prosecuting the Chichijima war criminals: at Josh's request, he'd assigned Josh to the Kondo case.

"Boscalli's an idiot," Josh said tiredly. "He'll get him hung, but he'll never find out what he knows."

"That goddamn *Hodding*," she breathed. "First he gave you Pappas and that platoon of clowns, and then he stranded you up in Chichijima with Rixey, and now you and I *stay* on this rock, and he and the regulars all go charging home to their goddamn wives and kids."

"It wasn't Hodding's fault. Somebody had to take that platoon. Then Rixey needed a lawyer."

"A lawyer," she nodded wisely. "That's why Hodding put you in the bush, too, you know." She was drunk. "That's just exactly why."

She wasn't making sense, and he said moodily: "I always thought it had something to do with 'disobedience of orders under fire.' "

"No. Because you were a lawyer and he thought you'd beat the rap."

He might as well humor her. "Well, he was probably right."

" 'A smart *Jew* lawyer,' to be exact." Her eyes had grown hard as rocks.

Shocked, he blurted: "What?"

"He *said* that," she insisted. "He really did."

He felt his anger rising. "Hodding?"

"Lieutenant Colonel Frederick de Melville Hodding, sitting right there in that chair!"

Someone started the juke box, to a rumba beat.

"And what," he asked softly, "were you doing with Hodding?"

Corky toyed with her wedding ring.

"Having a drink."

A navy lieutenant guided a high-rumped Australian girl from the bar to the dance floor. He placed a hand carefully on her haunches and began to rumba, out of synch.

Josh studied his fingernails. "You do a *lot* of that while I was up there? Drinking with Hodding?"

"Until he told me that, I did."

He looked up. "Just with Hodding?"

"Yes." He could hardly hear her answer.

He could not keep it in.

"Well, hell," he said sarcastically, "poor bastard was pining for his wife: you're trained to give comfort; whoever could blame you, after all?" His mouth felt dry.

"Everybody in Com Marianas knew we were dating," she flared. "Are you saying you didn't *hear?*"

"On Chichijima? In Hiroshima? In Tokyo? How *could* I hear?"

He remembered Rab McGraw in Hiroshima: *"You'd best get back there, mate."*

He stared at her. Something was very wrong. "Did you *sleep* with him?" he murmured.

"You sonofabitch," she whispered.

"Did you *sleep* with him?" he lashed out. "Goddamn it, *answer* me!"

She stared into her glass for a long while. Finally she looked up. "Once," she whispered. "I got plastered. Only once."

"Only—shit!" In his hand, the glass had shattered. Amazed, he looked at a bloody finger. She grabbed it and tried to press it to her lips. He yanked it away.

He stumbled to the entrance, flagged a passing navy bus, and checked into a BOQ tent at the marine base. No one was there, but a bottle of Three Feathers Scotch sat on a field chest. He uncapped it. For a long while he studied it under the light of a single swinging bulb.

A night-fighter section took off, drumming the canvas above him. He put the cap back on the bottle. Booze wouldn't erase the image of Corky, rutting with Hodding. It would only make it worse.

He was weak from his stay in the hospital, his side and shoulder ached, and he needed rest.

He lay down on his bunk, tossed for a while, and soon drifted off to sleep.

Josh sat in his jeep with Alicia on the bluffs over Tumon Bay, a hundred yards from her uncle's Quonset in the witness compound. The sun was dropping past a tangantangan tree toward a razor-sharp horizon; the navy's five-o'clock gun boomed distantly from Apra Harbor and echoed from Mount Lamlam to the south.

He was coaching her as his witness in the Kondo case, out

of the presence of her Uncle Noah, who was a court translator and who might be challenged by Kondo's defense if he had prior knowledge of her testimony. She would be the last nail in Kondo's coffin, corroborating the Korean laborer Kim Hong Yong and Major Fujihara's written statement, placing herself, Fujihara, and Kondo all on Washington Beach.

She glanced back at the POW compound, beyond her uncle's quarters. "And Kondo is still in there?"

"In a cell, behind barbed wire and forty-five marines."

"I'll be frightened." She remembered how Josh had almost tricked her in the Iwakuni sick bay. She looked into his eyes. "Josh, this time you *are* to be my friend?"

Impulsively, he squeezed her close. "Your friend, in court and everywhere."

Without willing it, he brushed her lips. Uncertain, trembling, they were suddenly moving beneath his own. He pressed her close, pulling her taut body to his chest, his fingers running down her back. He forced himself to pull away. What was he thinking of?

"I'm sorry, Alicia."

"My fault," she murmured. "I'm so ashamed!"

"Alicia, it's nothing," he lied. He discovered that he wanted her, badly. He tried to make light of it: "Alicia, come on, now. Am I the first guy who ever kissed you?"

Her chin went up. "Of course not!" He realized with a shock that she was lying when he saw the glorious eyes begin to fill with tears. She was all at once out of the jeep and fleeing toward her uncle's Quonset hut.

Thoughtfully, he drove past the ramshackle, tin-roofed shacks of Agana. He parked outside the BOQ tent for a moment, fingers drumming on the wheel, thinking of Alicia. Though his marriage was in sudden limbo, he was an idiot to stir her up, and himself.

But something bothered him more: her emerald eyes. They evoked a memory, through a mist of fear and pain. The attack in Tokyo! The eyes above the mask had been green!

Impossible. Noah Bancroft had said Alicia's brother was a child, only twelve or thirteen: besides, he'd died at Honkawa Middle School. Josh remembered passing its site in the rubble. No one could have survived.

CHAPTER 12

*T*he next morning Josh was astonished to find himself begging for Kondo's life, facing a raging navy commander. Commander Xavier Boscalli stared at him from across his desk: "You want to offer Kondo *what?*"

Josh said doggedly: "Life imprisonment. Even drop it to thirty at hard labor, if we have to."

In the din of a half dozen typewriters in the legal office, the commander was blazing. A web of alcoholic blood vessels glowed on his cheeks and he was soaked with sweat. He mopped his brow. "Jesus, just when we had these cases licked!"

The secretary of the navy had yesterday dispatched approval for both General Tachibana's and Major Matoba's sentences, and they were to hang tonight. Josh knew that Boscalli, who was taking full credit for convicting the general, had got a free ride, for Matoba had broken in court. Question to Matoba: *Then by your own admission, you are a cannibal?* Answer: *Yes, I was a madman due to the war and that is the only reason I can give for being a cannibal.* And then, with some inconsistency, Matoba laid it all on the general: *General Tachibana said that supplies would diminish and men would have to eat their own comrades fallen in battle and the flesh of the enemy should be eaten.*

Free ride or not, Boscalli was tasting blood, and was not going to let any of his prosecutors plea-bargain.

"Let me get this straight! You want to let *Kondo* cop a plea?" the commander exploded.

Josh slapped the letter from the ex-navy pilot—George H. W. Bush—onto the desk. "I want names, sir! Let me use this trial for something useful! We lost eighty fliers on those strikes!"

"If Kondo won't talk," shrugged Boscalli, "he won't talk."

"Why *should* he if we're going to hang him? If we offer him thirty to life—"

"Up in Chichijima you were screaming for his ass! That's why we're trying the bastards! What happened, Captain? Christ, he made his surgeon into a butcher! He's a goddamn *cannibal*."

And we have surgeons at Hiroshima sucking blood like werewolves, and I'm sick to death of killing.

But Boscalli would never understand, for he'd sat the war out on Guam.

"We offer him life for those names," insisted Josh, "or I'll quit the goddamn case."

Boscalli snorted: "Then I'll frigging well court-martial *you!*"

Josh looked into the angry bloodshot eyes and knew that his pleas were futile. All right. If Boscalli wouldn't let him plea-bargain, maybe Josh could try an end run. If he got Kondo sentenced to die, and *then* offered an exchange . . . The POW names for a commuted sentence? Life imprisonment in Sugamo Prison?

He might even get help from on high. He had read that Bush's father was connected politically in Connecticut and considering a run for the U.S. Senate. Perhaps, for information on his son's crewmen, the senior Bush would get to the secretary of the navy, or even President Truman.

At least he could hint at it to Kondo, when the trial was done. Who knew what he might remember, under a swinging noose?

He scooped up the letter and left.

Josh drove at dusk to Noah Bancroft's Quonset at the witness compound, above the cliffs of Tumon Bay. He was to pick up a translation of some Japanese Army papers from Noah.

Tomorrow, the Kondo trial began. It would be his first

prosecution—civil or military—of a capital case. He was nervous. And Alicia was probably nervous too.

"How's she holding up?" he asked Noah. "Where is she, anyway?"

"Down at our little beach," said Bancroft. "She likes an evening swim."

"Rab's a lucky man," he murmured.

"Rab's not with her. He's gone to Melbourne for a bit."

"She's swimming *alone?*" Josh stiffened. Tropical twilight was swift as a gull, and the sun was dipping now. There were horny GIs on the island, and renegade Japs in the hills. Guam wasn't Chichijima: she and her uncle were innocents, even after all they'd seen. "You shouldn't let her do that, not this late."

"She's a lass with a mind of her own."

Josh's own lass, with a mind of her own, had written him a single note, delivered by yard mail, yesterday. She was shipping out tomorrow on an eastbound hospital ship, and would file for divorce in San Francisco. Commander Boscalli was calling it the longest engagement and shortest marriage in all of World War II.

Well, let her go. In her note, she'd made no overtures. It was she who'd slept around, not he.

"I'll send Alicia home," said Josh. His heart was drumming strangely. "I can't afford to lose a witness to the sharks."

He worked his way down the cliff by moonlight, to the crescent of sand at its foot. He could see her plainly, in her white bathing suit. Emerging from the gentle surf, she paused to study the sand. She stooped and picked something up. Carrying it like a nugget of gold, she saw him, and ran across the sand.

"Josh!"

"It could be anybody! You shouldn't be down here alone!"

In the yellow moonglow she was all curved shadows and gleaming golden flesh. In her hand she held a seashell.

"Josh, it's a *textile* cone, Rab calls them. See the picture on its shell!"

"Be careful!" he warned. Some cone shells at Guam were poisonous; the venom was squirted from the animal inside through teeth at the cone's small end.

"Rab says to hold them just like this." She grasped the shell by its thicker end. She turned it in the moonlight. "Look! The range of peaks, and there's a princess, in her kimono, and her lord the *daimyo*, see? He's beaten Kaminari, the thunder god, and now the war is done!"

He took it carefully. She was right; in the delicate, sea-lacquered mosaic sketched on its surface by nature, a Japanese woman bent like a spirit over a seated samurai. She had truly made a find.

She looked up into his eyes, toweling with the bedspread. "Who paints the seashells, Josh?"

"Neptune? Mermaids?" he shrugged. God, she was beautiful. "*You're* a mermaid, you should know."

"My father gave me a book of Hans Christian Andersen, in English," she mused. "There was a picture of 'The Little Mermaid.' She was sitting on a rock, watching her prince sail off, with sails all gold in the sunset." She looked out at the sea. "I'm sorry about you and Corky. When are *you* leaving, Josh?"

His mouth went dry. He licked his lips. "After the trial."

Her skin was smooth as the seashell, and glittering in the moonlight. The ugly keloid rode her shoulder like a curse. Gently, he took the bedspread and blotted at the scar. "Does the damn thing *hurt?*"

"Not in the dark." She looked up at him with such longing that he dropped the spread and took her into his arms. They sank to the sand, with her moist lips searching, and her breasts thrusting. The only sound on earth was her breath and the ocean's, sighing in the night.

"I love you, Josh, I love you."

He touched a finger to her lips. "No, you don't."

"Oh, yes I do. And you *are* the first."

When the tide brought the ocean to lick at their toes, they dressed and left the beach.

CHAPTER 13

On Com Mar Hill at the narrow waist of Guam, surrounded by shade palms, stood a great white elephantine Quonset, the Com Marianas Auditorium. In it, by the third day of the Kondo trial, the Guam War Crimes Tribunal had been sitting for almost six months.

Josh watched from the prosecutor's table while the remaining Chichijima war criminals—Admiral Mori, Colonel Kondo, and the rest—were led into the prisoners' dock.

The auditorium was a cavernous structure, crowded with spectators. High on a dais, under a huge American flag draped across the end of the Quonset, sat the judges: a commander, an army lieutenant colonel, a colonel of marines, a lieutenant commander, an air corps lieutenant colonel, a commander in the Navy Dental Corps, and—in the center— the president of the court, an admiral with two stars glittering on his collar. He was a silver-haired regular with a high forehead and piercing, inquisitive eyes.

Below the dais sat Noah Bancroft, as official translator. He wore marine khakis without rank.

The accused Japanese sat in three rows in the prisoners' dock behind the tables assigned the defense and prosecution. They were represented by Japanese lawyers or—for those of them who wished it—U.S. Navy legal officers. Two marine MPs from the island provost marshal stood above them, billy clubs in their canvas belts, white helmets gleaming, braced interminably at parade rest.

Coming to court this morning, Josh had seen the hospital ship *Mercy* in her great white majesty, steaming out of Apra Harbor, heading for Hawaii and the States. His throat had tightened as he watched the ship sail off. Corky had not even phoned to say good-bye and he had been unable to bring himself to call her.

Now, as the prisoners filed in, Josh met Kondo's eyes. They were still gleaming with scorn and laughter, as if he knew a secret. He did: the names of the POWS. Josh wondered if he would have the guts to take them to his grave. The colonel took his seat befitting his rank, next to Admiral Mori in the front row.

Josh rose. He put the Korean Kim Hong Yong on the stand to testify as to Washington Beach. Now he moved to the bench, presented Fujihara's last statement to the president to be entered as Exhibit A. Returning to his table, he saw Rab McGraw in the press section. Rab jerked a thumb toward the spectators' seats. Josh stared.

Sitting in the first row, dressed in a tropical print, was Corky. Her lips parted and she mouthed, "Good luck."

Kondo's lawyer was chattering loudly in Japanese, demanding through Bancroft that the statement be authenticated. Josh would have to call Alicia to the stand next.

Shaken by the sight of Corky, he asked for a fifteen-minute recess. The gavel banged, and within moments he was outside with Corky, under a rustling palm.

"I saw the *Mercy* leave—" he began.

She shook her head helplessly. "I was all moved into my stateroom, Josh. And I love you, and I couldn't frigging *go!*"

She was Corky, and he loved her, and that was that. He framed her face with his hands and kissed her on the lips.

Alicia, sequestered as a witness in a waiting room near the entrance, glanced up from *Forever Amber* as she heard someone enter. It was Rab.

"Recess, school's out. Fifteen minutes. Freshen up, you're soon on stage again."

She fumbled with her pocketbook, and took a mirror out.

"Child," he smiled, "don't worry, you're quite smashing, for a funny-looking Jap."

She chuckled. She had been happy all week long; she just hoped she would not fail Josh, who was so busy she hadn't seen him since the night on the beach, except in court.

"Well," she said, applying lipstick, "I'd rather be a funny Jap than a gimpy kangaroo."

Rab had just come back from Melbourne. She wanted to show him the cone shell and maybe—although he mightn't approve—tell him that she was in love with a married man. He might even stop calling her "child."

"Corky's out there," he said offhandedly. "Watching her lad fight the dragon."

Her lipstick froze halfway to her mouth. In her mirror, her eyes seemed frozen too.

"No!" she heard herself mumble. "She left on the hospital ship!"

"I reckon she changed her mind. Look!"

He nodded out the window. Josh and Corky stood in the shade of a palm. He took Corky's face in his hands and kissed her. For a moment, Alicia stood transfixed.

"Alicia? What's wrong?" She shook her head dumbly. As he watched, his face grew thoughtful.

"I see . . ." he murmured. He put his arms around her and awkwardly patted her back. "Child, child! I didn't know. But I don't doubt it'll pass."

He stayed with her in the witness room until she was called to the stand.

With Alicia sworn and in the chair, Josh handed her Fujihara's statement. "Miss Bancroft, do you recognize the writing on the document you hold?"

"Major Michihiko Fujihara's."

"And how is it that you recognize his hand?"

"He wrote a note in English to us when he left Chichijima. And we lived with him in Hiroshima for a year."

Josh took a deep breath. Someone had to read it, to get it into the record: no one could make a greater impact than the girl. "Alicia," he said reluctantly, "please read your foster father's statement to the court."

She knew its contents and she stared at him for a moment. *"Read* it?"

He nodded. She dropped her eyes and began. When she paused, her uncle translated for the accused. Kondo stared at her, eyes glittering with hate. Each time she looked up and saw him, she faltered. Kondo could not have been making a worse impression on the bench if he had tried.

She turned a page. Fujihara was back on the beach now, alone with the dying boy. " 'I clapped my hands, having need of my own gods, and drew my sword. I asked my ancestors to witness that my act was one of merciful *kiashaku*, in the code of Bushido, to stop pain and hasten death.

" 'My blade struck him at the neck. My family's sword is a keen one, and it killed him instantly.' " She looked up at the dais. The members of the court were mesmerized. The auditorium was silent, except for the soft clack of the yeoman's stenotype machine.

She looked at the admiral. "Sir, it is true. He *was* indeed a *kiashaku*. He was a *gentle* man!"

The admiral sat stone-faced, but nodded. "All right, miss. Go on."

She continued. " 'And now I must write here, before I end my life, a thing that occurred which shames me for our Gracious Emperor's name. I am dishonored as a Japanese to write it, but must in all conscience do so, that the colonel's shame be known.

" 'When I visited Colonel Kondo's quarters on Miyano Hama Beach, to plead for the young man's life, there was a party there. General Tachibana, Colonel Kondo, and Major Matoba were in Colonel Kondo's quarters, kneeling at a table while Kondo's cook prepared sukiyaki in a large iron pot.' "

Grimacing, Alicia read of Kondo's waving the meat and bragging that it was from an American flier: " ' "Try this, Fujihara. It will make your stomach strong."

" 'I decided they were insane, and ran outside.' "

When Bancroft translated into Japanese, the prisoners in the dock stirred. Admiral Mori sucked in his breath and rubbed his broad jaw, shaking his head, as if he did not believe his ears.

She was finished. For once, Kondo's lawyer had no questions. Josh reached up to help Alicia from the stand. She looked into his eyes, and shook her head.

"Good-bye, then, Josh," she murmured. So, he thought, she knew that Corky had not left . . . Heartsick, though he knew his case was won, he started back to his table.

Suddenly Colonel Kondo jumped to his feet.

"Yankee hangmen!" he called. "You hear *me!*"

Jesus, he speaks English!

The instant froze in black and white. Somewhere a car backfired. Josh found his voice: "Sit down, Colonel! *Now!*"

"Drop the curtain," Kondo jeered at the bench. "The play is done!"

The admiral slammed his gavel. An MP grabbed the colonel's arm, but he tore loose.

"*I* shall write a statement! Now!"

"Grab him, Corporal!" Josh yelled, hurtling toward him from the stand.

Kondo snatched a long, newly sharpened pencil from beside Josh's legal pad, grasped it in both hands, and plunged it into his chest. The scar across his jaw twisted as he rammed it into his heart. Josh rounded the table. The colonel fell from the grasp of the guard.

Josh dropped to his knees beside him.

"You stupid sonofabitch, I could have got you life! Give me some names and I *can!*"

Kondo's eyes widened. "Names?" he grunted. "No. You would hang me anyway!"

He groaned, the black pupils rolled back, the body tensed, shuddered, and was still.

A flashbulb popped. Josh looked up. Rab McGraw had vaulted the press rail. "Got a statement, counselor?" he asked coldly. "For Reuters?"

Josh shook his head.

For a long moment, Rab studied him. "Then, I'd best pick up the pieces of Alicia, don't you think?"

A siren wailed distantly. Josh watched McGraw guide Alicia through the milling crowd, hugging her very close. He started after them, then stopped.

In the Iwakuni hospital bed, with marmalade smeared on her cheek, she had looked at him with wounded eyes: "*You are no friend at all.*"

He hadn't been. Rab McGraw, if he could get her, was a very lucky man.

Josh worked through the swarm of spectators. He threw Bush's letter into a GI can as he left. He had failed the navy pilot and the rest.

Corky was waiting for him. Their war had lasted far too long, and they were going home.

CHAPTER 14

Christopher Hart—born Matt Bancroft—lingered at his drawing board in the San Diego schoolroom. The bell had jangled half an hour ago. Only Mr. Barker, the mechanical-drawing teacher, still remained, checking assignments at his desk in the front.

Through the open window Matt could hear the band on the football field: the school was playing La Jolla High today, and the halls had blazed with banners and posters all week long.

It surprised none of his classmates that he had not broken for freedom at the bell. In the two months he had been here, he had never joined the herd.

He had arrived in his first American classroom wrapped in rumor and legend: a gossipy secretary in the principal's office had seen to that. Who else had seen bombs drop on Tokyo, or heard air-raid sirens scream? He had probably—although he never mentioned it—been tortured by the little yellow bastards in their camps. It was known that he spoke Japanese, although he never bragged of it, and a nisei classmate who tested him reported that he'd shrugged him off.

At first, when he answered a question in class, he would stand and bow, but he soon stopped that.

He was so tall, contained, and handsome that he seemed older than fourteen. Girls eyed him, but he seemed oblivious.

Although he was only a freshman, a blond senior with a Plymouth convertible offered one afternoon to drive him home. She parked in Balboa Park instead, and introduced him to the joys and strains of French kissing. He liked it, but avoided her afterward.

No Japanese girl—even if her parents would trust her with a car—would think of picking up a boy in it from off the street. American girls were amusing, but his mind was occupied with more important things.

Mechanical Drawing 1A was one of them. Now he sneaked a look at Mr. Barker, wishing he would go. The teacher was a football fan: why didn't he leave for the game? No sign of it.

Carefully, Matt untacked a corner of his assigned project, a simple, three-view scale drawing of a stupid steam pump, copied from the course book. He peeked underneath.

Hidden there was his secret drawing: a low, sweeping profile of a mythical structure—a library, or scientific center, or medical lab, perhaps—set in the crown of Point Loma, at the entrance to the harbor. He had cycled to the Point on Sunday, and sketched the building of his dreams: low-lying, blending with the sweep of Loma, which lay like a slumbering dragon across the harbor's mouth. Lying on the wind-swept grass of the bluff, he had finished his sketch and begun to watch the planes—Corsairs and Hellcats and newer ones he had never seen—endlessly landing and taking off from North Island Naval Air Station across San Diego Bay.

You would never know the war was over, from Point Loma.

A TBM Avenger drummed above the cliffs, and he was suddenly on the quay at Omura, running toward his mother . . .

He found himself curled into a ball in the grass, protecting his sketch book, trembling with fear and hate and guilt.

Shaken, he had pedaled back to his foster home near Old Town, into which a gentle Episcopal couple—a childless landscape contractor and his wife—had taken him on a subsidy from the orphanage within a week of his arrival.

As a missionary's son who was rumored to have tried to tend his father's flock when his father died, he was known to be devout and quickly was made an altar boy. Though he was strangely clumsy at first—considering his upbringing—he learned quickly.

Now the teacher spoke from the front of the room. "Chris?"

He came back from his reverie and hurriedly let the drawing paper drop.

"Yes, sir?"

Mr. Barker was approaching his drafting table. "I'm shoving off. Aren't you going to the game?"

Mr. Barker had let him work here late before, and now Matt tried again: "Could I stay and lock the room myself, sir? I want to finish this."

Mr. Barker leaned over him, squinting at the drawing of the steam pump. "You're pretty well along, son." He lifted the magnifying glass dangling from his neck and peered at the inked junctions: he insisted on perfection in the linking of lines, and long ago, on Chichijima, Mickey-san had shown Matt how to join them flawlessly.

"You're getting to be a draftsman, Chris. How's geometry?"

Matt blushed. At the school in Omura, such a question would have been answered: "I am stupid, *sensei,* and lazy, but shall try hard." Here, it was different: you had to tell the truth, even if you boasted: he was getting A's, in geometry and everything else.

"Pretty good, sir, I guess."

"Are you in college prep?"

"Yes sir. Four solids and this."

"Next year take trig. There's plenty of time, but I think you should consider architecture."

Matt, who had never considered anything else, nodded. He wished the teacher would go: he had longed for this moment all day, when he could finish rendering the hidden building, bring it soaring to life over the waves below.

But Mr. Barker lingered. As a recently discharged veteran, he wore a Ruptured Duck in the lapel of his white work-coat. He was said to have flown a fighter off a carrier in the South Pacific. Mr. Barker's classes were all male—girls didn't take mechanical drawing, they took fine arts, and typing, and home economics—and a fighter-pilot teacher was a hero to his students.

"Somebody said you were born in Japan, Chris," Mr. Barker said suddenly.

Go, leave, let me draw . . .

"Yes, sir."

Mr. Barker seemed disturbed. "I heard your parents were killed."

He nodded. "In the firebombings."

The teacher grimaced and lit a cigarette. Matt noticed that his hand was shaking. "Where?"

"Tokyo."

Mr. Barker seemed suddenly relieved. So, thought Matt, he had not flown over Tokyo itself. Then where?

The teacher glanced at the clock on the wall. "Look, Chris, the game's about to start. You're ahead of the class, why don't you go?"

"No, sir. I—"

"With me?"

"Yes sir," he smiled. "I'm much obliged."

Planning buildings was fun, but he had a far more pressing dream. He had never known an American carrier pilot. He had lots of them to meet, he knew, and he might as well start now. Because every week or so, he awoke sweating from a nightmare.

His mother was struggling in her grave, crying to be free.

PART THREE

Kamikaze

CHAPTER 1

The last Imperial Army troops on Chichijima Island were repatriated to Japan in 1946, as the 3rd Marines prepared to leave.

But the Bonins, strategically too valuable to the U.S. to resettle with a potential foe, would remain an American protectorate for the next twenty-two years. It seemed for a while that they would continue as the "Islands of No Men." No Japanese, it was thought, would ever be allowed to return to the chain.

The "original settlers," as those of white blood came to be called, were exceptions. As the 3rd Marines embarked for Guam, Noah Bancroft's petition to the Supreme Commander Allied Powers, carrying Colonel Rixey's endorsement, was approved by MacArthur's headquarters and by Washington. The Bancrofts, the Savorys, the Washingtons, the Gilleys, the Robinsons, the Gonzaleses, were allowed to return to what was left of their homes. They would have to leave behind, in Japan, spouses unrelated to the original Caucasian settlers of 1831, and anyone who had ever joined the Communist party. None of the seven thousand Bonin Island pure Japanese who had been evacuated under American bombs were permitted to resettle.

Almost all the descendants of old Nat and Elias's colonists decided to return to their childhood homes. They had been soured by life in Japan proper. The war had been even more miserable for them than for the average Japanese. Farmers had refused to sell them food, and they had been forced to forage in the fields and paddies after dark.

Jefferson Bancroft, traveling in wartime Japan for a company he worked for, had been imprisoned as a spy for forty days. Luke Robinson had almost been killed by farmers with bamboo spears who thought he had parachuted from an enemy plane. Hester Gilley had been questioned by *kempeitai* and only released when she lied and told them that she was Italian.

So 129 islanders were allowed by the Americans to resettle. All bore Caucasian blood. They were of all ages and various shades of skin. They arrived on a creaking island freighter on October 21, 1946. Most found their homes destroyed, and moved into Quonsets that the 3rd Marines had left. They had disappeared from the outside world.

For the Cold War was beginning and a veil of secrecy was suddenly drawn over the Bonin chain.

When the North Koreans slammed across the border of the Republic of Korea in June 1950, only a U.S. weather station remained on Chichijima. A succession of officers-in-charge began to arrive. They were often changed—one turned out to be an alcoholic—but they always seemed to wear the entwined golden dolphins of the submarine service. Some U.S. Marines—only fifteen of them, but heavily armed—appeared. Submarines began to visit, tying up to a sub-tender, safely anchored in 120 feet of water over a perfect hard-sand bottom, protected by towering peaks.

The island became a secret atomic storehouse for the Pentagon. Under the terms of the Japanese-American Peace Treaty of 1951, nuclear weapons were forbidden on Japanese soil, but Chichijima—only five hundred miles south of Tokyo— was no longer exactly that, though under "residual sovereignty" of the emperor.

Massive egg-shaped objects—always draped with canvas covers—began to be craned ashore from supply ships. They were trucked up the mountains, to be stored in the Imperial Army copper-lined cave, constructed originally to hide the national archives of Japan. The weapons being stored in the caves were obviously atom bombs, but the mixed-blood islanders were taciturn people, the Americans were an economic godsend, and no one ever asked.

American personnel, hunting for Japanese army souvenirs in the bush, sometimes wandered to the graveyard on the ridge, so the Bancrofts were glad that Noah had planed the curse from Lorna's cross.

In the Tokyo Press Club, correspondents occasionally asked what had become of the Bonins. Some even applied for permission to visit and do a story. From the public information officer at the headquarters of Commander Naval Forces, Far East, they got only smiles. The islands, for all the navy would admit, might have sunk into the sea.

By 1953, as the Korean War dragged on, Commodore Perry's century-old dream of a U.S. naval base in Futami Harbor—and old Nathaniel's fondest hope—had come true. If it was decided to unleash atomic bombs on the North Koreans and unyielding Chinese, at least Chichijima was well stocked; and the U.S. Navy owned a base where none had been before.

In the late spring of 1953, seven years after he had first sighted Chichijima from the bridge of the USS *Trippe*, Major Josh Goldberg, USMCR, found himself arriving again on a U.S. Navy frigate up from Guam. His mission was a secret one, and so unlikely that for the past few days when he awoke in the morning he confused it with a dream.

Two weeks ago, courtesy of Colonel F. D. M. Hodding of the Office of Naval Intelligence—seducer of his bride-to-be six years before—the corps had recalled him to active duty for the Korean War.

Ablaze with anger, five thousand miles from Corky and his Berkeley home, he was entering Futami Harbor once again.

CHAPTER 2

Matt Bancroft moved out of the blazing Arizona heat into the cool halls of the Matthews Library at Arizona State College at Tempe. Finals for the spring semester of 1953 were close, and the place was jammed.

Holstered on his belt was a slide rule, disguising him as a student.

Kimiko Yamamura, a freshman exchange student from Tokyo working at the reference desk, noticed him approaching and knew that she was blushing. They seldom spoke, but when they did, her voice shook and her tongue grew thick. She had seen him half a dozen times this semester. He was a puzzle to her: the slipstick labeled him as an engineer, but the only books she ever got him from the Special Stacks had to do with World War II.

Green-eyes stepped to the desk and opened his binder. "I need Morrison's *History of the U.S. Naval Operations in World War II,* volumes eight and fourteen, and Robert Sherrod's *History of Marine Corps Aviation in World War II.*"

She slid him a call slip and watched him fill it out. As usual, he left his name off at the top. She knew that he would retreat to his usual table by the window, and be there for an hour, and disappear quietly, and she would not see him for a week.

For some reason today, she had to know his name.

"You have to fill it *all* in."

He hesitated for a moment, then printed "Chris" on the line at the top. She looked at it disconsolately. She wanted his last name, too, but it seemed too transparent to ask.

"Could I see your library card?" She knew that she was blushing.

He seemed surprised. "Gosh, I must have left it in my room."

"That's okay," she muttered.

She stuffed the slip into the pneumatic tube and sent it to the stacks.

She spent half of every shift fighting off men, and couldn't even learn the name of the one she wanted to meet.

Matt looked at his watch. By four P.M., he would be due back at the Taliesin Fellowship, Frank Lloyd Wright's wild, sprawling complex, done in stone and canvas and redwood, on Maricopa Mesa near Scottsdale. As one of sixty architectural apprentices studying under the Grand Old Man, he had kitchen duty at five, and then planned to draw in the studio until dark.

But he had work to do here first. All the books at Taliesin dealt with architecture, and he had another project, even more important to his life.

He glanced at the reference desk. The beautiful Japanese girl at the counter was handling another student. He did not think that she was nisei, somehow, although she spoke perfect English. Her tiny bow had told him that she was native Japanese, perhaps a student from Todai University, here for library studies.

He opened his binder slowly. Hundreds of hours of research lay within.

It held sheet after sheet of neat, carefully drawn outlines and itineraries, and hundreds of U.S. Navy air unit designations: VC-61, VF-22, VMF-12, Carrier Air Group 50, Fasron 12. There were maps and diagrams and dates. There were code names for operations, air strikes, locations.

He leafed through the pages systematically, and looked up.

The girl was still busy.

He flipped through the index: 1942, 1943, 1944 . . . Tracking the squadrons and their carriers was difficult. The larger, glamorous actions were well covered, but seven years after

the surrender, a shroud of secrecy clung to the Bonin strikes.
Historians seemed unable to draw it aside. He wondered if the
Bonins—which America still occupied, despite the Japanese
Peace Treaty—were still being used as a base.

Truk, Midway, Yap, were easy. He knew which carrier air
groups had hit Tarawa and Guam. If you dug deeply enough, you
could unearth the names of squadrons that had struck at villages
on Leyte and Samar. *Every* place, it seemed, but Chichijima . . .

His work had hardly begun.

His eyelids were heavy. He dozed. A hand on his shoulder
awoke him. Startled, he whirled. The girl was standing over
him with his books, staring at the sheets.

"Nani-oshite imasuka!" he growled, slamming his binder
shut. *No* one saw these pages, ever. "What the hell are you
doing?"

"Domo sumimasen," she gasped. "I'm sorry."

She dropped the books on the table and turned to flee.

He caught her arm, sorry that he'd frightened her, and
forced a grin. "It's okay. I was half asleep."

"How is it you speak Japanese?"

"Born in Tokyo." She still seemed scared. "Look, you
didn't *do* anything. Simmer down." The hell with Taliesin,
he'd ask her out tonight. "Hey, what time do you get off?"

She dropped her eyes. "No, I . . ."

"What time, damn it?" He'd found little trouble with
women, and became impatient when he did. He softened, and
flashed his best smile. "Come on, please?"

"At five," she murmured feebly.

"The Casa Vieja," he smiled. "For dinner?"

She looked at him numbly, and nodded.

He watched her return to her desk. She bore herself like a
model. He'd phone Taliesin and find someone to stand in for
him in the kitchen: say he had a flat tire on the desert.

She was from a good family, he could tell. At Casa Vieja
the first thing he must find out was her name.

He took her after dinner to Taliesin West, and she met
Frank Lloyd Wright himself. That night, on the way back to
the campus, Kimiko peered ahead at the speeding highway,
bathed in their headlights. Chris's voice droned on.

She glanced at him. In the instruments' glow, his face
seemed thinner, even more mysterious. She liked to hear his

voice. Anyone else would have bored her to death. She hung on every word.

"We need architects in Japan."

"I'm *gaijin*. I'd never break in."

From the sketches she'd seen, she knew he had talent. Her father would recognize it, too.

"My father is with Mitsutomo Bank in Hiroshima. He could help!" she exclaimed.

Suddenly she realized her stupidity. She doubted that her father would ever accept a white as her suitor: Japanese-born or not, budding genius or not. Not in a thousand years.

Matt glanced at her from the wheel. He was certain from her bearing that her father was a wealthy man. She liked him very much. And she was of such classic Japanese beauty that a nisei waiter in the Casa, when he thought they were not looking, had snapped a picture of her in the mirror above the bar.

Next week Matt went back to ask him for a print. The waiter, grinning and shuffling, admitted taking it. But he said it had not come out at all, for the light had been too low.

CHAPTER 3

As ordered by the call-up letter which dragged him into the Korean War, Captain Josh Goldberg had reported to the Pentagon first. He had pushed through the glass swinging doors at the River Entrance of the building, and blundered up stairs and ramps through what seemed like miles of corridors. Finally he reached the Brass Ring, on the Potomac River side.

The corridor was decorated with paintings of naval derring-do, from Decatur taking HMS *Macedonian* to a U.S. cruiser off Korea shelling Wonsan just last year. He glanced at the slip of paper in his hand, matching door numbers.

He found Colonel Hodding's office, returned the orderly's salute, and was admitted into the presence of the deputy chief of naval intelligence.

Colonel Fred Hodding wore eagles on his shoulders in place of silver leaves, but otherwise had hardly changed. He stood behind his desk, slim and erect and determined, the image of a battlefield marine.

"Josh," he beamed, rounding the desk. "Hello!"

Josh ignored his outstretched hand and took a seat. Hodding smiled grimly and retreated behind the desk. "Anyway, it's good to have you aboard."

"It isn't good to be here. Confusing, and not good."

Hodding smiled. "The confusion we'll take care of here and now. We owe you an explanation, that's for sure."

You might explain why you sent me north and screwed my fiancée, thought Josh. Aloud, he said: "It's a little late in the goddamn war! Did *you* get me recalled?"

"No. President Eisenhower, in a way."

"I asked a civil question," said Josh tightly. "I hoped for a civil answer."

"You got one," replied Hodding. He called for coffee and said: "Sit down, Josh, relax, and I'll tell you why you're here."

"Tell me one thing, first. Am I going into the line?"

"No."

Josh sipped from his cup to hide his relief: he hadn't realized how frightened he'd been. The coffee was pure marine: almost undrinkably strong. "That should save a lot of lives. But I'm also not an intelligence man, so what am I doing here?"

Hodding clearly didn't like his attitude but just as obviously had to accept it. Josh hoped to learn why.

"You got a spot promotion this morning, Josh. In absentia, so to speak. You're a major now. Congratulations."

"You're very kind. *I* want to know why I'm not a *civilian*."

Hodding sat back. "How's Corky?" he asked suddenly.

None of your fucking business, Josh thought, but answered: "Okay."

"Nursing?"

"Yes."

"She told me once you know Rab McGraw. The Australian correspondent."

"When did she tell you that, sir?" Josh asked quietly. "In the Com Mar officers' club?"

Hodding stiffened. "Yes."

"Or afterward?" Josh studied his face.

Hodding's eyes never wavered. "In the club." He swirled his coffee. "So far as I know, you two were not then married?"

"*You* were, Colonel."

"Then that was *my* business. And it was, what? Seven years ago?"

"Yes."

"Then, shall we go on?"

Oh, the hell with it. "Go ahead."

"Now, as I remember, McGraw helped you find that girl for a witness? The white Japanese, for the war-crimes trial?"

"Alicia Bancroft. Yes." Jesus, Hodding knew everything. It must go with his new job.

Hodding asked him what McGraw was like.

Josh shrugged. "Good journalist. Married the girl."

"Do you trust him?"

"More than some people I know."

Hodding flicked his eyes at him coldly. "Do you think he's loyal to the U.S.?"

"To the U.S.? Hell, he's *Australian*."

"Well, Australia's in Korea too! Is he loyal to Australia?"

"How would I know?" He told Hodding that McGraw had fought at Gili Gili with the Aussie 16th Brigade, and almost lost his leg in the Port Moresby attack.

"Yes," nodded Hodding. "But he also wrote that sob story from Hiroshima. 'Atom-bomb sickness.' He *still* writes that crap."

"Why not? He *saw* Hiroshima. His wife's got a scar from it!"

Hodding regarded him narrowly. "Yes, we'll discuss that later." He walked to the window and looked across the Potomac. Beyond him, Josh could see the Washington Monument gleaming in the sun. "I'm afraid I have to set you straight. McGraw's in Panmunjom now. He's just about the only Western journalist accredited to the Chicom Army."

That was news to Josh. He kept his face expressionless.

Hodding turned back to the room. He told Josh that McGraw had broken a story that the U.S. Army had killed Communist prisoners of war while quelling the riots in camps on Koje-do Island. "We were trying to soft-pedal it, and we yanked his accreditation. So now he files out of the *Communist* press tent. He's got the confidence of Kim Il Sung and the *Chinese* commander, too. He's supposed to be a correspondent for INS, but *I* think he's a full-fledged Communist hack."

"I don't believe that."

Ignoring him, Hodding went on. "We want to use him."

"*And* me?" guessed Josh.

"Well, yes."

The shadow of Senator Joe McCarthy, pounding the Army

and State Department in his hearing room across the Potomac, fell across the room: it was a bad year for Jews. Fuchs,
Gold, and Greenglass had been exposed for feeding Los
Alamos secrets to the Russians, and the Rosenbergs awaited
execution as atomic spies.

"Where do *I* come in? Am I a Communist too?"

"Come on, Josh!"

"Why not?" flared Josh, "I know McGraw. And I'm
Jewish: don't I *have* to be a little pink?"

"If we thought that, you wouldn't be here now."

A ship's clock on the wall struck eight bells. It had been
years since Josh had heard one. He calculated swiftly: noon.

Hodding got up and stretched. "Despite your enthusiasm,"
he murmured dryly, "I'm going to take you to lunch with an
army general. You met him when he was a colonel, in
Tokyo. He's with army counterintelligence. We'll see if we
can't inspire you, because we have a job for you to do."

"I *had* a job," growled Josh. "A law practice in San
Francisco. An important job, to my clients."

For a long moment Hodding gazed at him.

"Not as important as this."

"Bullshit."

"No, Josh. Not bullshit." He stared down at him. *"This*
one could end the war."

The three sat at a window table in the Pentagon's general
and flag officers' mess. Across the river Washington baked in
the heat.

The silverware was spotless; the table linen snow-white;
the conversations hushed. Black stewards flitted everywhere.
The scotch in Josh's glass, he was sure, was Chivas Regal.

He'd recognized the army man instantly. He was Jack
Tallman, General Tallman now, the army counterintelligence
agent who'd questioned him in the Tokyo Army Hospital.
Today he was full of smiles: perhaps the two stars on his
shoulders had made him a happier man.

"The last time I saw this young man," Tallman murmured, "he was mad as hell at me. Some Jap had skewered
him like a pig, and I was blaming *him*."

"It was never solved, I take it, sir?" asked Josh.

"No." Tallman squinted at him. "You were at Chichijima,
right?"

"Yes, sir." Christ, they must have gone through his service record with a vacuum cleaner.

"You know of Copper Cave?"

"Yes sir."

"You ever hear of a cannon named Athena?"

"I don't know too many cannons, sir."

"Good. You weren't supposed to know this one."

Tallman, with a glance around, began to talk. When the waiter came to take their order, he stopped. When the waiter was gone, he began again, very quietly, so that Josh had to lean forward to hear him.

It seemed that Athena was a unique artillery piece, the largest in the U.S. Army, perhaps the largest in the world. "She's our answer to that 'ballistic missile' thing the Air Force wants to build."

Athena fired a projectile almost five feet long, 280 millimeters—eleven inches—in diameter. Packed into the shell was an atom bomb. It had never been tested, but its yield was estimated to be fifteen kilotons, almost three quarters of the charge that had leveled Hiroshima. It would surely annihilate the sort of massed Chinese attacks that had broken MacArthur's drive for the Yalu.

"And knock out half the batteries they got on those Chosan peaks," added Hodding, "all at once."

As part of a secret program to familiarize infantry with atom warfare, Athena would be tested at Frenchman Flat in Nevada in two days.

Hodding, playing with his drink, cut in: "Troops have a certain fear—"

"I wonder *why?*" exclaimed Josh bitterly. "For Christ's sake, didn't you go look at Hiroshima?"

Neither had. "Hiroshima's the sticky wicket," admitted Hodding. "Bad press, starting with your friend McGraw. Our boots believe what the papers print, and ignore their own field manuals."

"Let me read you this," interrupted General Tallman, pulling a magazine from his briefcase. "This is the *Infantry School Quarterly*. My God, we had to print this for *officers*, just to cool things off: 'The facts are: Your troops can move into or leave an exposed area a few minutes after an air burst. A soldier is not a casualty until he requires treatment. Even though he has been exposed to a lethal dose of radiation, he can perform his combat mission until symptoms appear. Radioactivity does not permanently affect sexual potency. Men exposed to radiation can have normal children. Radiation sufficient to produce permanent sterility or impotency would also be lethal.' ''

Tallman put down the magazine and shook his head. "It's a problem, Major, let me tell you. *You'll* see, when you're there."

Slowly, Josh put down his drink. His heart began to pound. "Where?" he asked politely.

"Frenchman Flat," said Hodding. "Athena's going to lose her cherry, so to speak. Shot 'Grable.' Named for Betty."

"That's cute, sir." He had a horrible thought. "You don't fire it at the *troops?*"

"Near them. They're entrenched. Two birds with one stone. Test the weapon, test the man."

"You're playing atomic *chicken?*"

"Not really. Perfectly safe."

Josh studied his drink. "And how close to ground zero do you put these heroes?"

"Hell, twenty-five hundred yards from IP," shrugged Hodding. "The AEC won't let us closer until after impact."

"And then?" asked Josh incredulously.

"You're just an observer," said Hodding. *"You* stay in the trench if you want. The snuffies attack."

Josh stared at him. *"Toward* ground zero?"

"That's right, Major. *Semper fi.*"

"With their officers?"

"Led by their officers. What did you think?"

"Attack? To how close?"

"Grable's only fifteen kilotons. Fifty yards, I think."

He couldn't believe his ears. He felt like the innocent traveler in a Gothic horror movie.

"Why, for Christ's sake?" demanded Josh.

"Baptism of fire," shrugged Hodding. "Maturity rite." He told Josh that the army and marines were going nuclear, and the corps wanted one hundred percent of its personnel qualified in atomic weapons.

"From artillery to demolition charges you can carry on your back. Everybody! From cooks to company clerks! They have to *love* that mushroom, or we're screwed!"

There was a long silence. Josh sighed. "Might I ask if *you* gentlemen are attending this exercise?"

"Nope," said Hodding.

"Why not, pray tell?"

"I've already been," Hodding said. "Shot 'Dog' in 'fifty-one. An airdrop. Quite an experience." He smiled at Tallman. "How about you, General?"

"Not yet. I scheduled myself for 'Priscilla,' in the fall."

Josh could only shake his head.

"What's the problem, Major?" asked Hodding, irritably. He claimed that 42,000 men had watched 'Crossroads' at Bikini. "We've had twenty thousand troops crawling around the Nevada Proving Ground since the tests began: we plan to qualify sixty thousand more in the next two years. Christ, you talk like some of those fairy scientists down at the AEC!"

Josh slapped his hands on the table. "I'm not going to sit in a trench while our own army lobs an eleven-inch shell at me! Atomic or not! I don't want the goddamn oak leaves, just give me a company in the line! I'm no guinea pig!"

"We've got special plans for you, and the President's approved!" growled Tallman, suddenly losing his cheer.

"I heard. Since I've never met the gentleman, it's a little hard to swallow." He paused and added: "Sir."

"You don't *have* to swallow it," barked General Tallman. "You'll goddamn go, or else."

Hodding held up his hand. "General, the major and I *had* this kind of argument once on top of a cliff on Guam." He sighed. "I'm afraid that Major Goldberg is likely to pick 'or else.' "

Josh nodded. "You're reading me pretty good, Colonel. You couldn't be more right."

Hodding looked at the general. "I think we better tell him *why.*"

"Did his clearance go through?" the general asked.

"Yes sir. This morning."

"Okay. Now, Josh, you *listen,*" said Tallman gently, and began to brief him on reasons for intentionally leaking top-secret data, and the methods of doing so.

At Panmunjom, the general said, the North Korean delegates were screaming to the world, protesting prisoner deaths and

U.S. brutality. On Koje-do hard-core Communist prisoners seemed not to care if they lived or died. The war had all gone very badly, and was getting worse.

UN allies were wavering: Canada was on the verge of pulling out.

Thirty-three thousand U.S. soldiers and marines had died in Korea, and another 103,000 had been wounded. Five thousand had been captured. President Eisenhower wanted them home. Now.

He demanded that the Pentagon force the Chinese and the North Koreans to sign an armistice. The Pentagon would try to comply.

Its scheme, as related by General Tallman, was simple.

Athena was the U.S. Army's single atomic cannon. It was classified top-secret. It would be shipped to Japan next week. Atomic rounds would follow under separate cover. Josh would be their shepherd.

"The shells, of course," General Tallman said acidly, "must never touch the virgin soil of our dear ally Japan." That would be a violation of the Japanese Peace Treaty and Japan's constitution. So they would be stored in the secret U.S. submarine base on Chichijima, in the Copper Cave, "with the fly-boys' atomic stuff." Athena's presence in the Far East—and that of her atomic shells—would be leaked to the North Koreans and Chinese.

The leak must remain secret, and the reason was simple. Two years ago, the People's Republic of China had gained instant prestige in the minds of Asians by stopping the UN drive to the Yalu. The Pentagon was sure that they would never sacrifice their newfound splendor by signing a truce under public threat of a single weapon—even an atomic one.

President Eisenhower, Tallman remarked bitterly, and the State Department pinkos, had decreed that Chinese face be saved. An Oriental "Golden Bridge" must be provided them. Secrecy was the bridge. Athena was unknown to the world, and the U.S. threat to use her must remain a secret between the United States and the Communists. But it must be proved to the Chicoms to be a *real* threat, not an empty one.

"Rab McGraw of INS is the contact," said Hodding, "and you're the conduit."

"*I* leak it to McGraw?" asked Josh. "That's insane, sir. We're not that close!"

"I'm sorry. He's cut his Pentagon ties, he doesn't trust us. He won't believe anyone we sent him who he doesn't already know. We've searched our files, and you're all we have."

Josh, he said, would be armed with knowledge: he would have seen the cannon, and witnessed the test, and delivered the shells to Chichijima. He would have photos with him that would prove these things.

"Specifically, sir," Josh asked pointedly, "how would I go about leaking it?"

It was all very military, and precise. "One: When you find McGraw, you have a few drinks and tell him why you looked him up."

"Okay, *why* did I look him up?"

"Because you noticed this item in the *Stars and Stripes, Far East*."

He passed Josh a clipping.

WIFE OF LEFTIST CORRESPONDENT DENIED VISA.

Melbourne, June 18: Mrs. Alicia McGraw, wife of Rab B. McGraw, INS correspondent at the Panmunjom armistice talks and occasional critic of U.S. policy, today was denied a visa by the American consul to enter the U.S. for medical attention. She is a survivor of Hiroshima. U.S. consular sources refused to confirm or deny the report.

General Tallman explained: "She wants to see one of the plastic surgeons at Johns Hopkins that worked on those 'Hiroshima Maidens' they sent over here last year. She has a scar—what do they call them?"

"Keloids," murmured Josh. He felt a rising rage. "They call them keloids, General. It comes from the Greek: *chele*—'crab's claw,' which they invariably resemble." Without trying to keep the anger from his voice, he added tightly, "You'd find them most disfiguring."

Hodding shot him a warning glance, but the general seemed pleased by his tone.

"That's the very note I like, Major. That's why you're there with McGraw: your country's guilty, you were at Hiroshima, you know the woman."

"Why are they keeping *her* out?" Josh demanded.

"Because we asked them to."

"Jesus," flared Josh, "you can't do that!"

"Yes we can," the general said pleasantly. "You're appalled? Stay that way. That's step two: You tell McGraw you know a Congressman Durkee on the Foreign Affairs Committee, so maybe you can help them, just for old time's sake. Durkee's already briefed."

Josh stared at him. How did G-2 get a congressman to lie?

"Three: By now, you're getting a little drunk. You're angry and bitter. So you tell him you were recalled and sent to the Far East to help us with an international legal problem. Ironic, because the problem is an atomic cannon on Japanese soil. Which we intend to move to Korea, if Kim Il Sung and his friends haven't signed by July thirtieth."

"Look—" protested Josh.

"Four: When he doubts there's any such animal, you show him your briefcase." In the briefcase would be pictures of Josh at Frenchman Flat, on Chichijima with atomic shells, and pictures of Athena herself.

"General, you're describing the biggest story of the war. Why wouldn't he put it on the wire?"

Tallman sat back. "Hell, you're a lawyer. Convince him not to."

"How?"

Hodding shrugged. "A choice between the Pulitzer Prize or the scar on his wife? You'll think of something."

It won't be *that,* thought Josh. He shook his head. "So he runs to the North Koreans. And Kim Il Sung says 'Print it, tell the world, or *we* will!' "

Tallman smiled. "The Chinese won't let Kim do that."

"We hope," Josh said, unconvinced.

It was an impossible mission. McGraw was not an idiot; Josh couldn't con him. It was all too transparent, they must know that.

"Suppose it doesn't work? Suppose they *don't* sign?"

Josh caught a quick look between Tallman and Hodding. Tallman shrugged. "Then we mount our summer offensive, chase the slopeheads back to the Yalu, and we've won the goddamn war."

The room was very quiet. Suddenly all was clear. The Pentagon plan was a sop to keep the President happy, but the army would like it to fail. Especially if they could pin it on a poor reserve marine.

A stalemate wouldn't do: they wanted a win.

To test his theory, Josh said: "I have a better plan."

"We don't need it," Tallman said coldly. "Just use the one you've got."

"But sir, I'm not an actor. He'll never believe that crap! I'll give him Athena *straight*."

Hodding looked him straight in the eye. "Don't do that, Josh."

"Why not, sir?"

"Because I'm ordering you *not* to. In front of a witness. Forget the 'Awkward Squad.' This time it would be a general court!"

There was a long and deadly silence. From across the dining room, the black steward sensed tension, and moved even farther away.

"Well," said Josh quietly, "I have one more question. If they *don't* sign, how *do* we chase them back to the Yalu? With Athena?"

There was a long silence. Tallman wiped his lips delicately.

"There's a saying in the MPs, Major, and lawmen say it too. 'Never draw your sidearm if you don't intend to use it.' "

"Jesus!" breathed Josh. "Half the world already thinks we burn babies. We can't use atomic shells!"

"We'll use Athena," said Tallman, "if we have to. You can count on that."

Josh shook his head and sighed. "One last thing. If I try to play out this script of yours, does his wife get her visa *then?*"

General Tallman rolled his napkin and carefully inserted it in a silver ring, which bore his name and the West Point crest.

"Of course she does, Major." He rose. "What do you think we are?"

Josh huddled in a sandbagged bunker at Frenchman Flat, Nevada, with two dozen army, navy, and air force doctors who had been ordered to observe the shot. He had seen Athena from the bus en route.

The cannon was an enormous, sleek-bodied weapon with a massive barrel, crouched behind a dune ten miles from here. She looked as if she belonged in the turret of a battleship, and made the artillerymen swarming over her seem like ants. On her breech was painted a mushroom cloud.

A single shell, ready for loading, was almost as tall as the soldier setting its fuse.

Twenty-five hundred yards across the desert from him now stood a great white marker. This was ground zero. Between the target and the observation post, World War II army trucks, jeeps, and staff cars were strewn across the sand, each with an enormous sign on it defining its distance from ground zero. In the shadow of the target lay a marine amphibious tank.

Josh saw dozens of live pigs, tied to steel posts, wearing carefully tailored army khaki. Someone had pinned general's stars on one. Some were lashed behind sheets of glass. A burro was staked further out. A monkey was strapped to a wooden structure, arms stretched out, like a little brown Christ on a cross.

A loudspeaker like the voice of God thundered from somewhere down the line: *"Kneel on your left knee, and remain in this position. Do not stand. I repeat, do not stand."*

Josh jammed on his helmet. His hands were shaking. He felt as he had in his last combat on Guam, with the cave obscenely beckoning, filled with mystery.

"Athena has been fired, the live round has been fired. We have one minute."

Josh's left knee, with the weight of his body on it, rested on a pebble. He could not bring himself to move it. Faintly, he heard the burro braying from the target.

"Place your left forearm over your eyes. Close your eyes tightly and do not open them. It is now H minus thirty seconds and counting . . ."

Someone coughed in the still desert air. Josh was sweating now. What the hell was he doing here?

"Ten seconds!"

Insane, insane . . .

"Five, four, three, two, one . . . Incoming mail!"

He squeezed his eyes more tightly shut.

He heard the rumble of an artillery shell gurgling in from the west. It carried a note of fearsome frolic, like a Japanese 250-millimeter howitzer's.

"Zero!"

On the back of his neck, as if a new sun had peaked, he felt a blast of heat. At the same time, with his eyes still closed, he saw the bones of his forearm in ruddy X-ray. In a moment he heard a rattling, rising rumble, like an approaching locomotive: the shock wave from the blast. The earth began to wobble, and he could not keep his balance. He fell against the sandbagged forward wall.

He heard Captain Ralph Feathers, a black air force psychiatrist, curse next to him.

Josh, rising, fell again as the ground slipped out from under him. His helmet had fallen off; he found himself on his hands and knees searching for it. The sound returned like a clap of thunder, hurled back by the dun-colored peaks. He found his helmet and jammed it on.

The dust was settling.

A voice thundered from the loudspeaker: *"Okay! Over the top, men! Move out!"*

Stunned, Josh arose. Doctors, white with dust, were slowly arising from the dirt. The pudgy black psychiatrist shook his head, scrambled up the sandbagged wall, and disappeared toward ground zero. Josh would not have followed him for a million dollars. He climbed to the rim of the sandbagged parapet and peered out at the desert.

An enormous column of creamy smoke was rising from ground zero. At its base, spreading for a mile across the desert, churned a roil of dirty white cloud. At the top of the column sat the mushroom: a giant clenched fist of darkened smoke. A bracelet of fire glowed at the wrist, then disappeared. The fist rose higher, brandished at the sky from the foaming earth below. Somewhere under the boiling smoke lay burro, pigs, monkey. An overturned truck, not far away, burned on the desert floor.

Josh smelled an acrid odor, and his own sweat.

As Josh watched, men began to appear from adjoining trenches, hesitating, carrying their rifles at the port. Soon they were jogging toward the plume. They were followed by more and more, until the desert floor was alive. He could see the psychiatrist, legs pumping like a high school track man's, disappearing into the haze.

Someone tapped his shoulder and he turned.

An Army Signal Corps photographer, armband grimy with

dust, stood behind him, a press camera in his hand. He posed him on the rim of the sandbag, against the rising cloud, and shot three pictures.

A week later, in Futami Harbor on Chichijima, a Navy photographer did the same while three of Athena's shells were craned from the frigate to the old Imperial Navy dock.

In Tokyo, he phoned the correspondents' club and found that Rab McGraw—no longer accredited by the UN Command—had moved to a rented home in the Marunouchi District. There was no phone installed yet, but he got the address. At his quarters in the Dai Ichi hotel, he took a shower, dressed, and picked up his briefcase. At the front desk he had the clerk write the address on a slip of paper in Japanese. Then he hailed a cab and left.

CHAPTER 4

*E*x-general Toshio Sumi, former intelligence chief of the Second Army, sat uncomfortably in conference. He shifted on his chair at a low coffee table in his grimy corporate office in Hiroshima. He was facing a revolt in the Brotherhood of the Carp.

"For seven years," he tried to explain, "each of our brothers who serves in the United States has carried Hart's description, and at last we have found him. And now this!"

Across the street a rivet gun chattered, high in the structure of one of the new office buildings sprouting in the blasted city. Sumi broke off to wait for the noise to stop. The hammering had given him a headache, and this meeting was making it worse. He longed for his quiet country home outside town. But he was suddenly fighting for his life as leader of the Brotherhood, and must not let the headache dull his brain.

By Japanese business standards, the tone of the confrontation had become unthinkable. Belly-language crackled in the tiny office. In a land where no one took a stand until the issue had been decided, the effect was almost laughable: breathing became heavy, brows glistened with sweat, and everyone was trying to drop his voice to the traditional pitch of verbal dominance. To Sumi his subordinates were beginning to sound like a cageful of hungry lions.

Yohji Osada, a stubby little retired colonel, leaned forward in his seat. "To admit a *gaijin* to the Brotherhood," he snarled, "is to piss on Prince Kuni's memory, and the dead of the Misty Lagoon."

The men around the table sucked in their breaths. Prince Kuni, long departed to the World Below and father of an empress of Japan, was the father of the Brotherhood as well: his officers of the Misty Lagoon, royal fliers of the imperial house, had plotted the Manchurian War in the thirties and the attack on Pearl Harbor. Sumi had known them all. For the colonel to invoke their memory was a measure of the threat against him. There were men here trying seriously to depose him, and all because of a *gaijin* young enough to be his son.

He lifted his eyes from his teacup, studying the others. All had followed him faithfully through the awful postwar years. They had risen to his general staff, although in the files of his corporation—International Marketing Research, Ltd.—they were merely listed as directors of the board.

None had wavered, none had balked, no matter how uncomfortable or far-flung his mission was. One, a prewar research chemist, had left his wife and children on Sumi's orders. He had taught in Germany at starvation wages while he lifted polymer secrets from the labs at Heidelberg. His wife had divorced him, but the secrets—sold to a Japanese chemical conglomerate—had funded the office here.

Another, an ex-commander in the Imperial Navy, had survived MacArthur's CIC and U.S. naval intelligence checks to somehow get a job as a janitor at the Commander Naval Forces Far East headquarters in downtown Tokyo. For months Sumi had channeled the man's reports to Japan's embryonic Self-Defense Force, free of charge. The ex-commander had risked much—perhaps his life—to enter U.S. Navy vaults, and all for a Palace that, Sumi suspected, did not really care.

Osada, the squat cavalry colonel, had commanded a tank regiment. Now he was rising to the top of the tractor division of a new motor company planning a plant in Hiroshima. Surrounded by liberal businessmen and apolitical engineers, fighting the last of the U.S. Occupation laws that still restricted heavy Japanese industry, he had the most to lose of any man in the room if his membership in the Brotherhood were known.

The reward for all of them, since the emperor must disavow them, lay only in the World Below, with Prince Kuni, the men of the Misty Lagoon, and their own dead ancestors.

Sumi's clerk, who was his bodyguard as well, refilled their cups. Sumi waited while he drifted past the *shoji* screens to the other end of the office. The clerk had keen ears, worshiped Sumi, and would be taking notes in shorthand. Later, Sumi would want to know who had not supported him when this minor revolution failed.

Conspiracies did not suddenly occur full-blown to conspirators: someone in the stifling room had sparked it. He turned to a man he could truly trust, Kazuo Nagano, his chief of staff. It was Nagano, buck-toothed chief of the Tokyo Police Identification Section now, who had unearthed Matt Bancroft's asylum.

"Perhaps if we let Nagano speak?" Sumi suggested. "He'll tell you how he's found him. Then this crazy meeting could end. We are acting like Italian politicians at a wake."

Nagano peered from behind his thick glasses. He looked, Sumi had often reflected, like an American wartime caricature of an idiot-Japanese, and had a brain like a filing cabinet.

"I've found him, all right, or one of our brothers has," Nagano assured them. He explained that the brother, an aeronautical engineer working as a waiter in an Arizona restaurant not far from a rocket test range, had heard a *gaijin* speaking Japanese to a Japanese girl. "With no accent!" Nagano lit a cigarette. "He even snapped a picture as they left. The boy's a student of the architect Frank Lloyd Wright."

"It's Hart," said Sumi, stirring his tea. "Or Bancroft, if you wish. Or Bankloft-o, if it pleases *you*, Colonel."

"None of it pleases me," muttered Osada. "I'll never mix my blood with a *gaijin*, no matter what his name."

"I named him Hart myself," observed Sumi. "We hoped to use him as a saboteur. I had the passport forged by the *kempeitai* in 1945."

"And then," Osada growled, "he used it to forsake his emperor's land for steak and eggs and butter? I can smell him across the Pacific. I do not want him here."

Osada, Sumi decided, was the one who was sparking the revolt. Sumi leaned back and lit a cigarette himself. He had not reached the top of the Brotherhood by fighting useless battles.

"*I* want him here. That is enough. But he need not enter

the Carp,'' he said softly. "Not yet. Does that satisfy you, Colonel?''

There was a moment of surprise. Sumi had risked losing face, but the anger had fled from the meeting. Everyone looked relieved except Nagano, who was always impossible to read.

"How much will it cost us to bring him here, then?'' the colonel wanted to know. He was the Brotherhood's treasurer.

Sumi shrugged. "How much does your company pay architects at your Kyobashi River plant?''

"Not enough to attract a student of Frank Lloyd Wright.''

Sumi shook his head. "You are wrong. I know him. You are starting a trade war with America, and he hates his kind. They killed his mother.''

"Well, he's used to soft beds and soft ladies by now.''

"No, I suspect he is still in combat. He will some day be of use. *You* will bring him here, Osada. You must not hint that you know who he is, or that he is Japanese. Or hint of the Brotherhood . . .''

The colonel drew in his breath as if he had been slapped. "The Brotherhood? Are you mad?''

"Domo sumimasen, I am sorry. I need not have said that.'' Sumi arose and walked to the window. "Tell him of your troubles on the Kyobashi with the *gaijin* from the U.S. Army Engineers, and that the fight goes on. I think he will come.'' He looked out at the city. The hammering had stopped. "This place needs all the help it can get, from white or brown or black.''

The poetic justice appealed to them all, and the colonel shrugged. "It's true, the *gaijin* dropped the bomb. Let a *gaijin* clean it up.''

Sumi snuffed out his cigarette, closing the discussion, and bowed precisely thirty degrees. He watched the colonel. The colonel bowed forty-five degrees, so Sumi had won, for now.

They touched fingers to their eyes: "Eyes for the emperor.'' They touched fingers to their lips: "Lips sealed to all.''

They all bowed again, and the meeting was adjourned.

CHAPTER 5

Alicia McGraw regarded her son across the dinner table in their newly rented Tokyo home. He was toying with his Jell-O, which meant that he wanted to go out and play. The next-door neighbor's child, the tubby, spoiled son of an American steel importer, was screaming for him now.

"All right then," she capitulated. "Go ahead."

Americans were no longer among her favorite people, but you shouldn't blame the sons for the sins of the fathers, and Cobber, yanked protesting from his mates in Melbourne less than a month ago, needed all the companionship he could get. He refused to let her teach him Japanese.

He was seven years old, with her own green eyes and straight white teeth and Rab's sandy hair and freckles.

She told him to stay within calling distance. She moved to the window to watch him scurrying down their front steps. On the quiet street below, a noodle vendor piped mournfully on his flute.

The house was Western-style, a pretty place with a rock garden, set high above the street behind a stone retaining wall. They had leased it furnished. The rent was enormous, but Rab had been lucky to find it at all. It was owned by the chief flight instructor of the new Japan Air Lines, a tall, gangly American pilot who had been sent back to the States for six months to recruit others. Japan Air Lines, like other Japanese enterprises, was crawling to its feet.

She wished they could afford to buy the place, but with Korean War inflation its price was astronomical.

She had come up from Melbourne two weeks ago, with Cobber, when she'd been mysteriously refused a visa to the United States for medical treatment. Rab had found her a job in the Tokyo INS office as a translator. He was back and forth to the peace talks at Panmunjom almost every week.

The elderly maid she had hired came bowing in from the kitchen to clear the table. She reminded her of Baba-san, in Hiroshima.

Alicia turned on the radio for the day's news of Panmunjom: Rab had told her confidentially that the pressure from Washington on the U.S. delegation was becoming enormous.

The doorbell chimed. She waited a moment for the maid to respond; then, when she didn't, Alicia rose to answer it.

She stood rigid in surprise.

He wore an olive-green trench coat, with oak leaves on the shoulders. He carried a briefcase. For a moment she felt dizzy. He seemed as shocked to see her as she was to see him.

"Josh!" she murmured. "Josh Goldberg?"

He looked into her eyes. "I didn't know *you* were in Tokyo."

She felt unready. Her hair was a mess. "You might have called first—" She remembered suddenly that they wouldn't have a phone for weeks. Just the same, what gave him the right to drop into her life, like another *pika-don?* "What are you doing here?"

"I came to see Rab."

"He's in Korea." Her voice was shaky. "Panmunjom." Where, she thought bitterly, he practically lives.

In a Japanese doorway, Josh's cap almost touched the top. He was even more solid than she remembered, and as tall as Rab.

"How's Corky?" she asked, as coolly as she could. She was almost afraid to let him in.

"Well, okay," he said, though a shadow crossed his eyes. He smiled, almost sadly. "You're as beautiful as ever."

The Tokyo mist had drifted up from the street. Cobber and

his friend were having a distant, strident argument. The noodle flute wailed softly. She could not simply leave Josh here in the fog, not after seven years.

"Come in," she said. She called to her maid for coffee, and they sat down to talk.

To Josh, she had grown even more lovely.

"I never thought," she said, "I'd see you again. In uniform, anyway."

"Well, the bastards called me in."

"And why do you want to see Rab?"

He toyed with his coffee cup, wondering how much he should tell her. He decided he might as well level, from the start.

"Would he pass up a story the Pentagon leaked—a *big* story—to help to end this thing?"

She looked unhappy. "He's a bitter man. He thinks the Pentagon kept me from getting a visa—"

"They did," said Josh.

"We thought so. So why would he believe a thing they told him now?"

"Would he trust *me?*" he wondered.

"He's so bloody dinkum square himself, mayhaps he would." She looked him squarely in the eye and said bluntly: "*I* don't."

"Really?" He arose, moved to a bookcase by the wall, idly read the titles. Many were books on seashells. On one of the shelves was scattered a beautiful display of scallops, cones, and pink-eared conches. "Why *don't* you trust me?"

"You tricked me years ago about Mickey-san in Iwakuni—"

"I'm sorry."

"On Guam, you made *me* read his statement on the stand! To play on the emotions of a bunch of angry men—"

"I said I'm sorry!"

He'd done what he had to do, unfortunately. His eye fell on the cone shell she'd found on the moonlit beach. Idly, he held it to the light of a reading lamp. He squinted at it to find the *daimyo* they had seen there, or the princess hovering close.

She was suddenly at his side. "That's the one, Josh, yes. You can't see the figures, can you, in the light?"

"No."

She snapped off the reading lamp, and somehow, in the dimness, they appeared.

"Too *much* light," she said, "seems to frighten them away."

"Oh?" he murmured. She seemed very close. "And scares the mermaids, too?"

"There was too much light in that courthouse, Josh, and the gold sails never came."

He stared into her emerald eyes, and took her into his arms. He could feel her sobbing gently, and he held her very close.

The front door opened.

"He won't let me ride his skateboard, Mum!" A little boy stamped in and stopped, confused.

Josh stepped back. Flushing, Alicia introduced them. "Cobber, this is Captain Goldberg, an old, old friend of ours."

"He's a *major*, Mum, not captain!" cried Cobber, recovering himself.

Josh bent and shook his hand. "It's okay. Just Josh."

Cobber nodded and scampered upstairs.

"I'm sorry he found us the way he did," said Josh uncomfortably.

"My problem, Josh, not yours. And he never will again." She put the shell back on the shelf. "That's something you do to me, Josh Goldberg, but I do love Rab." She looked up at him, defying him to deny it. "I love him very much, and I mustn't see you again."

All right, he'd had his chance, a thousand years ago. He put on his trench coat, squeezed her hand, and left. As he climbed into a cab on the street below, he looked back up.

She was standing at her window. The frame concealed her mouth and chin, but he glimpsed the emerald eyes, full of tears.

The old, old vision returned.

In Tokyo?

Emerald eyes, above a mask . . .

Crazy . . .

He returned to the hotel and took a taxi to Haneda Airport. He checked in at MATS Operations. Then, briefcase in one hand, duffel in the other, orders stuffed in his trench coat pocket, he ran for the morning courier plane to Seoul.

• • •

Josh peered from a window in the belly of the Piasecki Flying Banana. The huge twin-rotor chopper circled Panmunjom. The pitiful hamlet seemed, from this altitude, a sorry spot at which to have centered the hopes of half the world. It lay on the road between Kaesong and Pyongyang, in the center of a flat, bleak plain. Five large tents, two olive-colored and three white, fronted a ramshackle conference hall built by the North Koreans. Four sentry boxes, two for UN sentries and two for Communist, faced them.

Columns of trees had been planted at the sides of walks which led to the latrines and the helicopter pad. Four immense silver balloons floated on the thousand-yard perimeter of the neutral zone, to warn off U.S. tactical aircraft.

The chopper landed in a great whirl of dust. Briefcase in hand, Josh ducked his head and braved the hot, moist gale. The place smelled of night soil from the fields.

There were photographers wandering everywhere, American and Oriental. A U.S. Navy movie crew was setting up for an interview with a navy press officer; bored journalists, denied access to the conference hall, were pitching pennies in its shade.

Josh headed instantly toward the Communist press tent: back at Munsan-ni, in the apple orchard where the U.S. delegates lived, a *Life* photographer had told him that this would be the most likely spot to find McGraw.

He passed a scowling North Korean sentry in a box, and an equally unhappy U.S. Army MP in another. He glimpsed a sign: ACCREDITED U.S. CORRESPONDENTS ARE ADVISED NOT TO CO-MINGLE WITH COMMUNIST CORRESPONDENTS. U.S. ARMED FORCES PERSONNEL ARE FORBIDDEN TO DO SO. The man from *Life* had told him that the editor of *Stars and Stripes*, the army's own paper, had been sent back to Tokyo for talking to McGraw at Panmunjom.

Josh passed into the tent. Standing at the center of a circle of ragtag American newsmen stood Rab McGraw. He had changed hardly at all in seven years, though his muttonchop sideburns were touched with white. He was pointing to a map with his walking stick, briefing his colleagues on a trip to the site of an alleged U.S. truce violation on the Communist side of the line.

His eyes widened as he saw Josh: "What the bloody hell!" They shook hands. "Don't often get to shake hands with a major any more, at least an *American* one. What are you doing in the Far East?"

"Looking for you. I found your home in Tokyo. Alicia told me you were here."

"You saw Alicia?" His eyes grew cool. "And you're looking for *me?* I wonder why?"

"It's a long story. Where can I tell it to you, alone?"

A Chinese photographer was sidling up, nervously fitting a bulb into his flash gun.

"Not here, mate," McGraw said swiftly, drawing Josh away. "He'll splash you on the *Daily Worker* in a flash."

They stepped outside and moved to a row of command vehicles and North Korean armored cars. As usual, McGraw had found himself a jeep. Josh tossed his briefcase in back and they climbed in.

They were parked next to a black seven-passenger Chrysler, expropriated, according to Rab, from some businessman in Seoul. Two Korean soldiers were polishing it in the hot summer sun. General Nam Il arrived in it daily from Kaesong, smoking his long cigarette. "Saving face," said McGraw. "*Your* blokes all come in choppers, and the Chrysler's the best he can do."

He pulled out and drove down the dusty road, fronting the conference. He beeped at the Japanese crew of a Fox Movietone camera truck. The crew waved back. They passed the conference hall. McGraw looked at it in disgust.

"A circus that never pulls its stakes. The clowns perform inside, to no one's applause but their own."

"Park somewhere we can talk."

"My gooks will probably shoot you if we leave the demilitarized zone." He drove to a leafless tree on the perimeter, stopped in its skimpy shade. "So what's this all about, mate? And why are you still in?"

"I was called in just for this." Josh sat for a moment, thinking. He pulled out a pack of Luckies and offered one to McGraw. He drew the ancient Zippo from his pocket, lit their cigarettes, and flipped the lighter shut.

"You called them *your* gooks, Rab. Have you really crossed the line?"

The smile left McGraw's face. He reached for the key, switched it on, and pressed the starter.

"I don't want a fucking lecture, Goldberg! Who sent you here?"

Josh reached across McGraw and turned off the ignition. "I have to know. Are you a Communist?"

"I'm a journalist," said McGraw softly. "I hate lies: American, Russian, Chinese. You're all lying, and I'll bloody well write what I see." He faced Josh, and his eyes were cold as steel. "Now, I asked you a fair question! Who sent you here?"

For a moment Josh eyed the scratched and battered globe and anchor on his lighter. He was about to disobey Hodding again. He took a deep breath, wondering whom he'd get to defend him in a general court.

"The Pentagon sent me," said Josh. He set his briefcase on his lap and began to talk.

For a long while, when Josh was finished, McGraw stared across the empty plain. A huge bluebottle fly, probably fresh from the latrines, landed on his cheek, and he hardly seemed to notice it. Finally he brushed it away. He looked again at the photo of Athena, turned it over, smiled tautly at the TOP SECRET stamp.

"Do you really think," he said finally, "that Eisenhower will let them *use* this bloody thing?"

"If the Chinese don't sign," said Josh, "I think he will."

McGraw handed back the photo.

"What did they *really* tell you to do?" he murmured. "*Not* simply spill your guts to me, that's certain."

"No," Josh shrugged. "The scenario was complicated, let's forget it." He dug into his pocket, pulled out the clipping about Alicia's visa from the *Stars and Stripes*. "But this was supposed to be the trigger."

Rab glanced at it. "The bastards! I knew that's why they wouldn't let her in."

"She can go there now, that's for sure."

"You're bloody right, unless I print it." Rab smiled thinly. "Right, then. I'll give it a go, your way."

"Take the pictures," offered Josh. "That's what they're for."

Rab nodded, took them, and drummed the steering wheel.

He reflected for a moment, and looked at Josh. "It isn't to save the world, or get Alicia her visa, either." He looked distantly out at the barren land. "Remember that poor bloody bastard at Hiroshima Red Cross? With his face all melted down? And *I* said he looked like a leper and needed a bell?"

"Hell," Josh shrugged, "you were bushed. You'd seen a lot."

"Well, he's the one I seem to remember now."

McGraw drove him to the helicopter pad, and carried his gear to the Piasecki. As the chopper thrashed into the sky, Josh waved at him from aloft.

That night in his room at the Dai Ichi Hotel, Josh fought with himself. With all his heart he wanted to see Alicia. He settled for the bar below, got sodden drunk, and staggered up to bed. The next morning he left for the States.

Twelve days from the time he had left the Pentagon, he entered Colonel Hodding's office once again.

The colonel was unsmiling. "You stick to the script?"

"No comment, sir."

"I didn't think so. How'd it go?"

"Does his wife get her visa?"

Hodding nodded. "Yes."

Josh went to the window and looked out. Pentagon workers, civilian and military, were breaking for home: the beltways were jammed. He turned back.

"He said he'd tell Nam Il Sung. Whether the Chinks believe him . . . Hell, who knows?"

"*We* know," Hodding said. "Look at this."

It was a top secret dispatch from ComNavFE—Commander Naval Forces Far East.

It announced that on July 27, at Panmunjom, Marshal Kim Il Sung, supreme commander, Korean People's Army, and General Peng Tai-huai, commander, Chinese People's Volunteers, would sign the Armistice Agreement, and that repatriation of U.S. prisoners would be accomplished at Panmunjom in sixty days.

"Athena's on her way home now," said Hodding. "And so, my friend, are you."

Hodding reached into his outgoing basket, and handed him a set of orders, releasing him from active duty. "Well, that's real George of you," Josh nodded, moving toward the door.

"Josh?"

"Yes sir."

"The President's very happy. We told him who we sent."
Josh paused and turned. "But *you're* not happy, are you?"

"We could have won, who wants a tie?" shrugged Hodding.
"Well, next time."

"Next time?"

"French Indochina: Vietnam. The French will lose their
asses there, and it'll be up to us."

CHAPTER 6

Matt Bancroft stood by a little hillside shrine in the park on Ogon-zan Hill, gazing down at the mouth of the Kyobashi River, where it joined the Seto Sea. It was a sparkling day in April 1960. In the gleaming new Fucho-cho district of Hiroshima at the foot of the hill, and across the Kyobashi too, glittered the Yamagawa Motor Plant complex. Its long white buildings swept for three miles along both sides of the river, eastern branch of the languid Ota. At the northernmost edge of the factory lay the big Yamagawa Hospital, for employees and their families.

Matt had been the only white executive in the company for almost seven years.

A new Hiroshima had risen from the ashes of the old. The ancient city, so fortunately sited as a port, had been thoroughly modernized by the atom bomb. That which was important had been restored. An exact replica of the ancient castle had been completed, with government funds and private contributions. Even the carp in the moat had been replaced. Asano Park, near the castle, was replanted. Relics of the bombing were saved, for a museum in Peace Memorial Park. The twisted framework of the Peace Dome at ground zero had not been touched, despite the complaints of some that its skeleton disturbed them as they drove to work.

Past Hijiyama Hill lay a freeway built over the East Drill

Field, where he, Mickey-san, and Private Hashimoto had sheltered when all to the west had been rubble.

This noon Kimiko's father—Matt's prospective father-in-law—had asked him to come here alone to view the cherry blossoms. The two men had been deposited at the entrance to the park by a Mitsutomo Bank limousine, standing now at the gate to the shrine.

Matt knew that they were not here to view cherry blossoms. He braced himself, knowing what was coming.

Daiji Yamamura—Mitsutomo's executive vice president for western Japan—was a quiet, gray-haired man and a member by marriage of the Mitsutomo banking family. He was a major stockholder in Yamagawa and an interested adviser in all things pertaining to Matt's career. Matt had designed him a home high on Hijiyama Hill. The residence, cantilevered over the city, seemed to grow naturally from the wooded mountain and was Yamamura's pride. He squinted toward it now.

"It is so clear with the wind from the south that one can see my home, Hart-san. See? Framed by the *sakura?* We should surely have brought our cameras." He paused. "One might believe that the site below mine—where the stream goes through—might be almost as suitable as my own."

Matt's pulse quickened. He longed for a chance to build on the site: a structure already was growing in his mind. "A fine investment, sir."

"Not an investment. A present! For Kimiko's birthday." He was looking directly at Matt now. "She will be twenty-seven."

"I know."

Yamamura shrugged. "Well, it is probably overpriced." He sighed. "Have you thought of what we talked of, Hart-san?"

There it was: the goddamn matchmaker again. Yamamura, nagged by wife and daughter to allow Kimiko to marry him, was on the verge of surrendering. But on one matter he had not budged: though the marriage would be *ren-ai*—a love match—he wanted a traditional *nakodo* matchmaker to check Matt's family roots.

Now Yamamura persisted: "The matchmaker I would hire would be very discreet. And he has contacts in the United States. His wife is Christian. Episcopalian, like your parents!

She can search your church's records. She need only have your permission.''

Matt braced himself and produced a lie he used when people sniffed too closely at his background. He told Yamamura that his parents had left the Catholic Church to become Protestant missionaries, that they were disowned by their *own* parents, and that his grandparents had broken his mother's heart. "If they are living, I do not want them to know that I exist."

"Still . . .'' Yamamura looked up at him. "Hart-san, the matchmaker is all I ask."

Yamamura was pleading with him now. Matt marveled at the change, but suspected the reason, too. Kimiko's father would for the first time gain face, rather than lose it, if Matt became his son-in-law. For Yamagawa Motor was poised on the brink of international fame and Matt had become its rising star.

Yohji Osada, the squat ex-tank commander who had hired him out of the Taliesin school, had been a good mentor, though strangely hostile in private conversation. He had already proposed Matt as vice president for plant construction, despite his fair skin and round eyes.

To be white was no longer a burden. The company was liberal and progressive. It was suddenly building not only three-wheel trucks and tractors, but passenger cars as well. There were rumors that Ford would like to buy in. All at once there were American auto men in Hiroshima, and Japanese executives seemed to be spending half their time in San Francisco or Los Angeles.

Matt stood fast on the matchmaker: there was no choice.

"I would dishonor the memory of my parents if I let the matchmaker proceed."

The older man moved off, lost in thought. He gazed out over the city. Matt could hear a sparrow chirping in the brush.

Yamamura turned and approached him.

"Then you may marry her anyway," he said softly. "You and the women have won."

Matt felt a leap of joy. He bowed deeply. "You are most generous, sir. I am grateful beyond words. Kimiko will be overjoyed."

"Good," nodded Yamamura. He glanced at his watch.

Having surrendered, he seemed anxious to be gone. "I will buy you that land for your home. You must pay for the house yourself." He looked into Matt's eyes. "Now, since the three of you have beaten me, will you grant a single wish?" He tried his English. "Tat for tit?"

Matt hid a smile. "Anything, sir."

"Bring me a grandson."

"Hai," grinned Matt. "It shall be done."

The old man's eyes twinkled. "I thank the gods that you haven't already."

So he had known of their lovemaking. Matt blushed but his heart was singing. Backed by Yamamura's money, his search for his mother's murderer could not fail.

The wedding took place on a Saturday, so that it would not interfere with production at Yamagawa, in the Marriage Room of the Hiroshima Grand Hotel. The hotel was crowded with Yamagawa and Mitsutomo executives in morning clothes. Mr. Yamagawa was an honored guest. Kimiko was spectacular. Her *tsuno-kakushi* headdress—meant to cover the bride's horns of jealousy—had been worn by her great-great-grandmother in the era of the shoguns. Matt was too tall for any of the Yamamuras' samurai clothes, but had the *montsuki* overgarment for his kimono made for him by a very ancient tailor in the Yamamuras' home village, west of Tokyo.

They stood before the Shinto priest, in their costumes. Kimiko in her headdress seemed almost as tall as he. The priest purified them, and heard their wedding vows, and watched while they exchanged their rings.

The wedding moved to the reception room, where *shugi-bukuro* envelopes, with cash in them, had been left by each of the hundred guests. Each envelope was tied with gold and silver strings, in knots impossible to undo, to symbolize the permanence of the union.

Kimiko changed her costume twice during the reception, looking more lovely at each change: from her *uchikake* to a long-sleeved kimono to, finally, Western dress.

At the rear of the reception room, Matt saw a stocky man with iron-gray hair. He wore no carnation: only an expensive dark suit and a silk tie. He seemed vaguely familiar, and somehow both at ease and out of place. A gold tooth gleamed as he flashed him a sudden grin.

Matt saw his father-in-law approach the man, bow stiffly, and escort him to the door. Matt, turning back to accept congratulations from the Yamagawa comptroller, thought no more of him. Perhaps he was a hotel guest who had drunk too much sake at the bar and wandered in.

That night, in the Hiroshima Grand bridal suite, as Kimiko packed for Tahiti, he began idly to slit the *shugi-bukuro* donations. A plain white envelope, larger than the rest, attracted his attention. He opened it and gasped.

Inside was a half-million-yen banknote: over three thousand dollars.

Within the bill were two business cards clipped together. One was faded, formally embossed with the old insignia of the Imperial Japanese Army: LIEUTENANT GENERAL TOSHIO SUMI, SECOND ARMY STAFF. On the back, in awkward Western letters, he read: "To Mr. 'Christopher Hart' many happiness this day." Under it was Sumi's *hanko,* stamped in red.

The other card was a modern one with a compass-rose at the top: TOSHIO SUMI, PRESIDENT, INTERNATIONAL MARKET RESEARCH, LTD. It bore addresses in Tokyo, Hiroshima, Osaka, Los Angeles, and Washington, D.C.

As he stared, perplexed, Kimiko wandered from the bedroom, modeling a bikini she had got for the South Seas. She whirled for him, and noticed the envelope. "*That's* a big one, Chris. How much?" she asked, posing in the glass.

He stuffed the bill into his pocket. "A couple of beers tomorrow, on the Papeete quay."

He followed Kimiko to bed. As always, their love was good. But afterward, in the light from a neon sign outside, she traced a finger down his jaw.

"Chris? What's wrong?"

"Nothing. Why?"

"You're sorry we finally got married?" she teased.

"No, glad."

"Good." She nibbled his ear. "Why aren't you sorry?"

"Because you own the Imperial Mint."

She giggled and tried to throttle him, and soon they were entwined again, and when they were through, she drifted off, but Sumi hovered still.

"*Do not trust him and promise him nothing,*" Mickey-san had warned in the bunker above Kure. "*The war is over.*"

Matt knew that *his* war would never end; and if General

Sumi felt the same? Sumi had once said: *"I shall find you in Tokyo and we'll speak of this again . . ."*

In the quotes around "Christopher Hart"—and the ridiculous size of the gift itself—Matt had sensed a message, all quite Japanese. Mickey-san had suspected that Sumi was a member of a powerful secret society: the Brotherhood of the Carp. Suppose it had survived the Occupation? What if the general could help him in his quest?

Matt's father-in-law, knowing nothing, had quietly shown Sumi the door at the wedding reception, losing him great face if anyone had seen.

At least Matt could apologize for that. When they got back from Tahiti, it was the first thing he would do.

Ex-General Toshio Sumi sat opposite Matthew Bancroft—"Christopher Hart," he reminded himself—at a table in the rear of his favorite *ikizukuri* restaurant in the Nagarekawa district of Hiroshima.

"I have," continued Bancroft, "binders with the squadron history of every navy torpedo plane attack in September of 'forty-four, and many of the pilots' names. Except in the Bonin Islands. All those strikes are secret. Still!"

General Sumi nodded. Bancroft had not lost his anger: good.

Sumi had ordered *koi*—raw carp—carefully sliced so as not to kill it. It was arranged quivering on a bed of garnishing in its natural state. Gasping gently in shock on its side, with its organs and stomach intact but its flank filleted cleanly, it had been a favorite Hiroshima dish for generations. He plucked at it delicately with his hashi sticks, then paused to study the young man.

He liked what he saw. He had observed at the wedding that Bancroft—"Hart"—was handsome for a Westerner, and tall, now that he was grown. In Sumi's downtown office, where the young man had come to tender an apology for his father-in-law's discourtesy at the wedding, he had towered over Sumi's clerk, who was almost six feet tall. The clerk had not liked it at all.

Sumi wanted Bancroft more than ever in the Brotherhood of the Carp. Within the order, Osada's silent rebellion continued. It was not the time to bring the issue of Bancroft to a head, but he could wait. What mission he would assign him he didn't know. First he must get him to stop his private research into the U.S. Navy or else—untrained in intelligence—he might stumble and lose his cover before he would be of use.

Sumi searched for a grip on him strong enough to make him wait.

"In compiling these books, these binders you have made," said Sumi, "you found no intelligence on *any* of the Bonin Island raids?"

"No sir."

"*I* can," Sumi said bluntly. He knew why Bancroft had failed: the U.S. used the island for an atomic arsenal and had classified everything to do with Chichijima as top-secret since World War II. He sat back, chewing at the sweet raw fish. "If you give me time. In the bunker, we spoke of the carp."

Bancroft nodded. " 'A brave and stubborn fish,' you said."

"And patient." He prodded the *koi*. "This one hates me."

"At least he knows who to hate," mused Bancroft, in belly-talk. "*I* have no one. Only *kataki-uchi* eats at me."

"Your time will come." Suddenly Sumi thrust his forefinger at the mouth of the carp. The jaws opened and he felt a stab of pain. He did not flinch, but tiny drops of his blood fell on the lacquered table.

"Did you know," he said idly, "that they will put him back in their tank to keep him fresh? He will swim on his side, but refuse to die for a very long, long time. And if I come back in a week, and dangle my finger in the water, he'll attack me again and again."

"I understand," said Bancroft. He took a deep breath. "Can you truly help me, sir?"

Sumi hesitated, as if deep in thought. Finally he looked into Bancroft's emerald eyes. "Did Fujihara tell you of the Order of the Carp?"

"He thought you were a member, sir."

"I am," Sumi sighed softly, violating his oath without a qualm. "And in time we could find your man. But are you Japanese enough to wait? As the Forty-seven Ronin did?"

"I can wait for *kataki-uchi*," swore Bancroft, "until the day I die."

The hook was baited, Bancroft was pleading, Sumi need only jerk the line. "You would be the first *gaijin* to join," Sumi muttered, as if doubtful.

"In my gut I am Japanese."

Now!

"All right. There are others to consult. They will object. It will not be soon, but some day I shall see if I can get you into the Brotherhood of the Carp."

Tears of gratitude came to the young man's eyes.

Sumi, with his hashi sticks and the little pool of blood, sketched the outline of a fish on the lacquered table, and began to speak of the steely discipline that a brother need endure.

CHAPTER 7

*T*he home that Matthew Bancroft built on Hijiyama Hill was the envy of his fellow executives at Yamagawa. Matt was constrained in its design only by his father-in-law's proximity on the slope: a more impressive dwelling would have cost Yamamura face.

Kimiko had indeed been pregnant when they were married, and the boy was born eight months after the wedding.

Two years later, the boy had a little sister. They seemed quite Japanese; the emerald eyes were gone. Both children were bright and active, and good athletes. On summer evenings Matt would play catch with them in the little rock gardens to the rear of the home hanging high on the slope.

The gold and silver strands on the wedding envelopes held fast; Matt and Kimiko lived happily on the hill below Yamamura-san and the children thrived.

Though his oath on his mother's grave never left him, Matt was true to his promise to Sumi and did no more research on the Pacific strikes. Sumi had asked him not to mention their friendship to anyone, but they met quietly in the Nagarekawa restaurant every few months.

In the winter of 1977, ex-General Toshio Sumi was summoned by telephone from his Hiroshima office to the Imperial Palace in Tokyo.

He disliked flying, and instructed his bodyguard to get them seats on the *shinkansen* bullet train. Staring out at the lights of the bleak coastal countryside as they sped east, he knew why he had been called.

One of his agents at the Electric Boat Company, in Groton, Connecticut, had bought pictures of a submarine missile-launching console from a draftsman. The photos were intended for transmittal by Sumi to Japan's Defense Ministry. The draftsman had been apprehended by the FBI, and confessed.

The American had been quietly fired and Sumi's agent deported: the material was classified, but unimportant. Japan, like Israel, was a client nation, to be treated politely, even when its spies were caught. But obviously the emperor was embarrassed; hence the summons.

In the morning, Sumi was picked up alone in a palace limousine from the driveway of the Imperial Hotel. Through a heavy morning mist, he was was driven across the street, over the moat, through a massive gate, and into the palace grounds.

He had been here thirty years ago, just before the first of MacArthur's troops set down at Atsugi's battered airstrip. Then he had been summoned by a minor prince who was a brother of the order. The man was a captain in army intelligence and a distant cousin to Hirohito. It had been a hurried, secret meeting, in which the prince demanded that his name be taken safely off the Brotherhood's rolls.

With inner scorn, Sumi had assured him that though the rolls were safe enough, this would be done. Revering the throne, he had already lost what little faith he had in the Westernized palace advisers. They had deprived him of a chance to die for his emperor.

Now, crippled with the arthritis which struck him in such weather, he was going to meet again with the same nonentity. Like all but the emperor's closest relatives, the man had been stripped of his title by the Occupation, but retained his palace sinecure, as a liaison between the Imperial Marines and Japan's Self-Defense Force. Having once distanced himself from the order, he had not seen fit to reenter the Brotherhood even when the Occupation left.

Sumi looked out of the limousine window. When last he had seen these grounds, they had been scorched by a wind-whipped "dragon tail" of LeMay's fire-raids. Then he had glimpsed the gabled, Tudor-styled Pavilion of Concubines, where the empress and her ladies-in-waiting had lived, and the Pavilion of the Frosty Brocade, but now it was too misty to see either through the trees.

Today the limousine drew up in front of the immense new palace, completed ten years ago. He had heard that inside was a banquet hall which could seat three thousand. He knew that for him no banquet was in store.

He was ushered into the office of his erstwhile brother, bowing just low enough to acknowledge his princely blood and not low enough or long enough to show esteem. The man, who bore the hook nose of a patrician, had greatly aged and had deep pouches beneath his eyes. It was to be expected: the new commoners of the House of Fushimi, still subsidized by the Diet, had not given up their dissolute, womanizing ways and never would.

The man seemed to sense Sumi's disdain. Though he arose behind his desk, he barely bowed. He nodded toward a chair. They hardly inquired of each other's families: both were widowers. Then the prince got to the matter at hand.

"The Brotherhood has drawn criticism," he said bluntly.

Meaning, the emperor is displeased.

"For what reason?" asked Sumi.

"Do you know the head of the CIA?"

Sumi looked at him, amazed. "I know *of* him, of course. Mr. Bush?"

George H. W. Bush, son of a U.S. senator, head of a Texas oil company, ex-congressman, who had served as representative on the United Nations and chairman of the Republican National Committee, had distanced himself from Watergate sufficiently to be named chief of the U.S. mission to Communist China, and finally become director of the Central Intelligence Agency. The Brotherhood had a dossier on him, as it did on all known intelligence professionals—if Bush could yet be called a professional. Sumi had skimmed his dossier once, as a matter of interest. He had noted that the man had flown a navy plane against Japan in World War II.

"Well," said the aristocrat, "Mr. Bush knows that the Brotherhood still lives."

Sumi tensed. "That cannot be."

"He knows of it, I tell you! Because of your fiasco in Connecticut!"

"How can he? Our brother in Groton was under interrogation, but he said not a word of the Brotherhood. *You* know he would not."

"*Your* brother, Sumi. Not mine."

"I had forgotten," Sumi said acidly, "that *you* have forgotten."

"The brother said nothing," admitted the ex-prince coldly. "Nevertheless, Bush knows."

Suddenly Sumi understood. It was the palace which had leaked, not the Brotherhood. It must have seemed better, under CIA pressure, to point to an ancient, secret society, than to admit that the Japanese Defense Ministry itself would engage in espionage against the United States. This deposed noble, violating his sacred oath to the order, had doubtless spilled it himself to some American embassy officer over tea and crumpets. And there was nothing Sumi or the Brotherhood could do.

The "Voice of the Crane"—the emperor's presence—was clearly in the air.

Sumi sucked in his breath. In a bitter monotone, he said: "*So desuka*. I am responsible for the 'fiasco.' Is it desired that I take my life?"

The aristocrat snorted. "That would only embarrass the palace. But there is something you *must* do."

"What, then?"

The former prince tapped his pencil, studying him. "Mr. Bush is said to be an angry man. He had made his peace with Japan, though he lost crewmen over the Bonins in the war. Now he feels that a trust has been violated. The palace does not desire that he be tempted to expose the Brotherhood to the press." The prince moved to the window and looked into the fog. "In America, while Bush holds power in government, the Brotherhood of the Carp will sleep."

Somewhere in the inner palace, a temple bell began to toll.

"No!" exploded Sumi.

This was stupid! The palace was cutting off the Defense Ministry's source of American intelligence. And what of MITI, the Ministry of International Trade and Industry? The Brotherhood serviced *it!* And the great cartels and *zaibatsus:* electronic industrialists, chip-makers, shipbuilders, supranational banks, muscles of the nation? The order's network pulsed with their very blood!

"Only a fool," protested Sumi, "pokes out his eyes to save his face!"

The prince swung sharply around. "Whom," he asked softly, "are you calling a fool? His Imperial Majesty?"

Sumi labored to his feet, breathing hard. "Of course not!"

"Then me?"

"Certainly." Sumi bowed low, and drew in his breath. His head was pounding. "If the Carp are to sleep, then what is *my* task?" he asked thickly.

"*Your* task is to put out the lights."

The former prince and brother nodded and Sumi was dismissed.

He noticed that the limousine which drove him back to the hotel was smaller and that its chauffeur wore a shabby cap. He was departing with less face than he had brought.

"While Bush holds power in government" was the key. Bush was director of the CIA at fifty-three: his political potential seemed enormous. But there were ancient ways to eliminate politicians who threatened their secret society. Prince Zuni and the men of the Misty Lagoon had understood them well. Prime Ministers Hamaguchi and Inukai, and countless Chinese incumbents, had learned this in the 1930s, lying in their own pooled blood.

Crossing the moat, Sumi gazed at its emerald water. Carp might sleep in sunlit pools and streams, but they were a tireless breed. He would watch Bush and wait, and strike when he could. But strike with whom?

For Bush, the killer must not be Japanese, brother or not. The outcry in America would ruin the very industries the Brotherhood served. And if Sumi proposed a white professional—and trusted him—his staff would think him insane.

The mist was burning away. A *koi* took an insect in the moat, and he caught a flash of gold.

Inspiration struck him. Bush had been a U.S. Navy pilot. He lost crewmen *over the Bonins* in the war, the ex-prince said, and the palace's sources of information were very good.

The gods were with them! His instincts had not failed him. It was time to swear Matt Bancroft into the Brotherhood of the Carp.

Matt Bancroft kneeled, sitting on his heels, in the Brotherhood's lodge room. It lay in Sumi's wooden, tile-roof home on a peak above Kure, not far from where the bunker had been. The initiation was very nearly through.

He wore the formal black *montsuki hakama* half-coat he had been wedded in. Below his shoulders blazed the crest of the Yamamura family, there being none for Hart. In his hand he held his *sensu* folding fan.

General Sumi, kneeling on a tatami dais, wore a *haori* kimono and no family crest at all. Before him lay his glittering *katana* and *wakizashi* blades, both bared. Sumi was flanked by two brothers on each side, dressed in *shinobi shozoko* costume, all in black, and wearing the ancient hooded masks of ninja warriors, symbolizing stealth. From his week-long instruction by the Brotherhood's Shinto priest, Matt knew that they and Sumi were called "the Five." Only Sumi was known to the rest of the order.

Matt had been told that if he glimpsed their faces he would die. Their brown slit-eyes regarded him coldly. One wore glasses. From him he sensed hostility. He felt that he knew another—a squat figure with burly arms. Osada, the man who had brought him to Yamagawa Motors? It was possible, but he did not know, or care.

He had fasted for twenty-four hours, and meditated in Sumi's private shrine for six. He felt clear-headed and powerful as a god.

Sumi motioned him and he crawled to the dais. He prostrated himself before the *katana* for a moment. He arose to his knees and picked up the *wakizashi* and an ancient blue Noritake bowl, stained inside with blood. He handed bowl and blade to each of the black-costumed men. Each pricked a finger, squeezed three drops into the bowl, and handed it back. He did the same and gave blade and bowl to Sumi. Sumi pricked his finger and mixed his blood with the rest, holding the bowl in two hands and rotating it slowly. He put it down.

"The way of the samurai is death," he intoned.

"*Hai*, master," whispered Matt. "It is true."

"Is the spirit of Prince Kuni in you?"

Behind the *shoji* screen the priest tapped a prayer bell, and a sweet, long note floated across the room.

"His spirit is in my heart," murmured Matt, as instructed.

"And the men of the Misty Lagoon?" asked Sumi.

The bell sounded again. "They are gathered there as well," said Matt softly.

"And do you swear before your ancestors to die in the Brotherhood's cause?"

"I so swear."

Sumi and the others touched their fingers to their eyes: "Eyes for the emperor," they chanted. They touched their lips: "Lips sealed to all."

Matt did the same, and bowed his head to the mat. The smell of the straw was sweet. He waited until the bell rang out, and raised his eyes.

He was alone. He sat back on his heels. His throat was tight, but his heart was full of joy.

At last he was Japanese.

Afterward Sumi walked under the pines with the new recruit. His clerk trailed closely behind. Fear of assassination lay heavily these days on the general's mind. The Brotherhood felt emasculated, and blamed him for timidity in retreating from the States. It would be ironic if he, doomed by his emperor to walk like a *ronin* with sheathed sword, was murdered before he could act.

The resistance to the *gaijin* acolyte had not waned: Sumi had simply ignored it. He smelled anger on the dais and sensed it afterward in the secret vestibule through which the other four departed. Colonel Osada had barely bowed. Nagano, the taciturn detective, had looked deeply into his eyes. "Some day you must ask our new brother where he was when Tanaka the *koban* policeman was murdered in cold blood."

Sumi glanced back at his bodyguard. The man was near. He relaxed.

"I am grateful," Bancroft said softly, "for what you have done for me."

"It is all for the Brotherhood, in the end," said Sumi. His arthritis pained him, and he winced. "You were not brought in like the others, to snap pictures overseas. You have your own mission."

"I shall fulfill it when you find my mother's murderer, and the Brotherhood's missions too."

The old man smiled, his gold tooth catching the wintry sun. Bancroft, he reflected, did not know how close to the mark he was. He pointed toward the peak, where the bunker had been.

"You were brought in because one day up there you told me that you would fight on. Perhaps your spirit saved me from seppuku. I am grateful. It has been a good life, and prosperous. I am almost seventy years of age, and near the end."

"I hope not, sir."

Sumi put a cigarette in his mouth. His hand trembled when he tried to light it, so Matt took his lighter and held it for him.

"You have been patient, Bankloft-o. I once told you we could find him and we shall." He looked into Bancroft's eyes. "But now you have a family: You have taken 'hostages to fortune,' as the English writer said. Would you risk all that you have?"

"I swore it on my mother's grave," said Bancroft.

He sounded firm, but Sumi was not sure.

CHAPTER 8

*F*or ten years after Bancroft's induction Sumi waited, without agents in the United States, like a *ronin* waiting his master's word.

In 1979 he had a stroke. He began to walk with a cane. He felt that he would lose control of the Five unless he quickly recovered.

He had watched, with curiosity, amazement, and finally anger while Bush picked his way through political minefields to become—in 1980—Vice President of the United States. By 1987—despite a stupid scandal over Iran—it looked as if he might become President.

Bush was known to have a long memory. He was said still to be enraged at the Connecticut espionage incident, and at the politics which had sealed the lips of his CIA. In his dreams, Sumi saw him installed in the Oval Office, forcing the palace to smash the Brotherhood—still active in Europe and Southeast Asia—as one might swat a fly.

As the American campaigns heated Sumi grew nervous. He had counseled patience for Bancroft but was far from it himself. He ordered a worldwide culling among the Brotherhood for intelligence on Bush. A brother in San Diego—working as a TV repairman and quiescent in espionage for the last ten years—sent him a clipping from the *San Diego Union* describing a bombing raid the Vice President had flown against the Bonins. Sumi's clerk, who read English, translated, as Sumi drank his tea across the *kotatsu*. As he listened, Sumi's hand trembled. "Did you say *Chichijima?*"

"Yes, master."

He suddenly felt the presence of Prince Kuni and the men of the Misty Lagoon. He had files that he must doctor, to motivate Bancroft, but the gods remained with him!

All at once he was ten years younger. He ordered his clerk to bring him more tea and the yellowing Second Army intelligence reports from Kondo on Chichijima. Then he dismissed the man, whom he seldom let out of his sight.

He lifted his cup, leafing through the memories, whiffing a musty island smell. Kondo, Tachibana, Matoba . . . all dead now, in the service of the emperor. He had known none of them but Kondo; still, their names, read so often so long ago, spoke to him as out of the World Below.

Colonel Kondo's field summaries were intact. Sumi called for *katagana* brushes and special inks he had learned to use at the Imperial Army Intelligence School, and had not seen for fifty years. He wanted no one on his staff to know of his plot: not yet. Nagano, later, if he must. His clerk he could trust, too.

His fingers were twisted, but his skill remained. He altered Kondo's report for the week of September 2, 1944, the day Matthew Bancroft's mother had died on the quay on Chichijima. No one would ever know who had strafed her. It was obviously not Bush, but Bancroft would never discover that, for when Sumi studied the paper under a glass, he found his forgery quite good, for a man of eighty-one.

Now he put down the docket, sipping his tea.

At the Military Academy, he had become a *kendo* master, second class. With his *shihan* bamboo sword, he had been quite famous: a whirling, leaping, peasant boy, slashing classmates who scorned him for the night soil on his feet.

He was still a *kendo* master, though his blade was flesh and blood.

It was time to unsheath Bancroft from his family, if he could.

It had poured all night. Matt awoke with a feeling of dread which he could not shake. Kimiko and his son and daughter were flying to Tokyo to the wedding of her niece. He could not make the trip: he was scheduled for a preliminary meeting in the Yamagawa boardroom between a delegation of Japanese auto manufacturers and the U.S. consul general for Japan.

He drove his family to Hiroshima Airport over freeways slicked with rain.

The Hiroshima-Tokyo shuttle flight was, as always, crammed. He clasped Kimiko's hands and suddenly, in plain sight of the public and while his daughter giggled in embarrassment, kissed her full on the lips, Western-style. After, he could not think why.

On the ramp, waving good-bye to the howling jet, he felt the fear in his stomach once again. The raindrops danced on its wings. He wished suddenly that he were going with them.

One half hour north, and thirty miles off course from its line of flight to Haneda Airport, the aircraft crashed on the wooded slope of Mimuroyama Mountain, in a fiery sheet of flame. There were no survivors.

Later, it was found that the pilot and copilot—who had breakfasted together in the Hiroshima terminal—had called Haneda Tower on an emergency frequency, complaining of stomach cramps. It was first thought that they had been distracted or actually paralyzed by fish poisoning. Public health officials investigated and the terminal manager, though cleared, resigned in mortification.

A waitress reported that a tall Japanese in the uniform of a flight steward had joined the pilot and copilot at their table, but though Hiroshima detectives and Detective Captain Nagano, all the way from the Tokyo Identification Section, investigated, no such man was ever found.

Matt, to everyone's astonishment, took his bereavement well, even better than Yamamura and his wife. It was as if he were not *gaijin* at all, but had a core of rolled steel, like a samurai sword. He buried his family's ashes in the rock garden on Hijiyama Hill, where he and the children had played.

The night of the burial he dreamed of his mother in her grave.

He seemed detached, driven by some inner force. He disappeared for a week—factory rumor placed him inexplicably on a somewhat seedy tourist island in the Bonins, named Chichijima, which had recently—and belatedly—been returned to Japan—but three days before his vacation was over, he was back in his office overlooking the Kyobashi.

He was the vice president of Plant Design. Outwardly, all seemed the same. At fifty-five, he was still young enough to sire children. Besides, his house, by Hiroshima standards, was enormous. Everyone hoped he would marry again.

Matt knew better, and thought he knew why the plane had crashed.

His marriage and his little family had diverted him from his oath. He had abandoned his mother in her grave, placed too much faith in Sumi's network, used the Brotherhood of the Carp as an excuse for inaction.

The gods had spoken. And now they spoke again: Sumi called him on the phone.

Ex-General Toshio Sumi sat across from Matt Bancroft at the general's favorite table in the Nagarekawa restaurant. Sumi no longer dined on *koi;* for a year he had been unable to eat raw fish, let alone the trembling flesh shorn from one still alive. He suspected stomach cancer. Still, today he was content. Bancroft had been freed to act, and in his own briefcase was the spur to prod him on.

"My brother," the general murmured, "at last we've found your man."

Matt froze, his bowl of *miso* broth held almost to his lips. He slowly put it down.

"*Found* him?" he asked hoarsely.

Sumi regarded him, squinting in the dim light. Bancroft's face was white as snow. "Yes, Bankloft-o-san. There is no doubt."

"Who is he?" he demanded. "Where is he now?"

Sumi sipped his tea for a moment, looking into the emerald eyes. Then, with twisted fingers, he fumbled with the clasp of the briefcase he had used in World War II. He extracted the copy of the intelligence report from Kondo he had falsified. Clipped to it was an article, quite genuine, dated August 25, 1985, from the *San Diego Union.* He hesitated, holding the papers.

"There is help that your brothers can give you, but you must kill the man yourself."

"I would not have it otherwise. Who is he?"

Sumi reached across the table and placed the papers by Bancroft's plate.

"Mr. George H. W. Bush," said Sumi softly.

"What?" gasped Bancroft. His face fell, and his shoulders drooped. He put the papers down.

Obviously he thought Sumi senile, or suddenly insane.

"Pick that up and read it!" Sumi whispered, thrusting the papers at him. "The man who killed your mother is Vice President of the United States."

Without hope, Matt picked up the newspaper clipping. On it was the headline: FOR LT. (JG) BUSH, FIRST THE MISSION, THEN A FIGHT FOR LIFE.

It was a feature story two pages long, condensed from *Washingtonian* magazine. The byline was Ernest B. Furgurson, chief of the Washington bureau of the *Baltimore Sun*. Furgurson reported that Vice President Bush, a seasoned torpedo-plane pilot at the age of twenty, had been launched from the carrier *San Jacinto* for a strike on Chichijima Island in the Bonins.

The time was 7:15 A.M.; the date September 2, 1944. The day his mother died.

Matt's hand began to shake. He heard Mickey-san's voice: *"Think of a lily, a water lily, afloat on a dark mirrored pool . . ."*

He looked at Sumi. The general smiled, and nodded. "Read it, Bankloft-o, read on."

With three other TBMs from his own ship, eight Helldivers and a dozen Hellcat fighters from the *Enterprise,* Bush had taken off for Chichijima before the carriers turned south for strikes on the Palau Islands.

Furgurson wrote:

> George Bush today is reluctant to talk publicly about all this. To do the natural thing—to bring it up in routine conversation—would be for him like putting on an American Legion cap and flaunting his wartime service. Critics would call such behavior a political effort to assert his manhood, as they did some of the wisecracks for which he was derided during last fall's campaign.

But Bush had described his feelings when he was hit by Japanese antiaircraft fire.

> I realized I was in serious trouble when I saw the flames moving back along the crease in the wing, where

it folds aboard ship. That's where the fuel tanks were. . . .
I couldn't see the instruments for the smoke.

Furgurson quoted another pilot from Bush's squadron:

Bush got hit and went on in, smoking. I pulled up to
him, then he lost power and I went sailing by him. My
gunner was the only one who could see behind him, and
he called out "Chutes!"

Bush's Distinguished Flying Cross citation for bombing the
Yoake Radio Station read:

for his courage and complete disregard for his own
safety, both in pressing home his attack in the face of
intense and accurate antiaircraft fire and continuing in
his dive on the target after being hit and his plane on
fire.

Bush had parachuted into the sea and crawled into his life
raft. "The chute," wrote Furgurson, "blew off toward the
island . . ."

Matt was suddenly back on Chichijima, forty years ago,
with the wind on his cheek, urging it to freshen from the
northeast.

Blow, wind of Chichijima, blow. Divine wind—kamikaze—
blow.

The breeze had ruffled his hair and ignored his stupid plea.

"And then," wrote Furgurson, "out of the depths, barely
100 yards away, poked a periscope, followed by a shiny
tower. Within minutes he was aboard, and the ship slid
silently back below."

Just as little Susumu had described it. Still, the article
proved nothing by itself. It mentioned no strafing of the island
freighter or the Omura quay.

Matt looked at Sumi. "How do you know that this was the
plane I saw?"

"Because Colonel Kondo tells us, from his grave."

Sumi handed him a folder. It had a musty smell. Matt
leafed through it quickly. It was a series of weekly intelligence briefings, summarizing bombing raids, neatly written
in *katagana* characters: if any typewriters had remained in

island headquarters by the end of the war, Kondo had not had one.

REPORT OF AMERICAN TBM DOWNED 9/2/44: One TBM "Turkey" aircraft which strafed the freighter was seen to bank steeply and return for another run on the dock area. It fired its wing guns at the dock and continued over Futami Bay in a northerly direction. There was a single casualty on the quay: Mrs. Lorna Bancroft, a civilian of mixed blood, wife of Superior Private Lemuel Bancroft, Imperial Japanese Army.

Matt swallowed, fumbled for his sake cup. He drained it and went on.

The TBM then bombed the Yoake Radio Transmitter. Passing over a battery of the 308th Machine Gun Battalion, Major Sueo Matoba commanding, it began to smoke heavily. One parachute was observed. It landed at sea. Thereafter a flier was observed in a raft, blowing toward Washington Beach. Two fishing boats manned by naval personnel were dispatched to capture him. They sustained two casualties from American Hellcat fighters and failed to complete their mission (see Imperial Navy Intelligence Summary #90244). Before the flier could be captured, a U.S. submarine was seen to surface and pick him up. This office is conducting an investigation at the naval base to assess blame for the pilot's escape.

Matt looked into Sumi's eyes. "What can I do, sir? How can I reach him?"

Sumi smiled faintly. "You will be breakfasting with him in Washington next month."

"How can that be?"

"The Brotherhood moves slowly, but your brothers are everywhere." Sumi lit a cigarette, and blew the smoke across the alcove. "In JAMA, for example."

The Japan Automotive Manufacturers' Association, with delegates from Nissan, Toyota, Subaru, Mazda, and Yamagawa, was meeting with the Vice President in Washington next month. Matt knew that Osada, his mentor, was a delegate.

Was the colonel the brother? Matt had suspected it in the lodge room.

"Osada-san told me of the delegation," Matt said. "But I am not likely to attend. Only he."

"He may decide his English is too poor," shrugged Sumi. "Has a present been selected for Vice President Bush?"

During President Reagan's first term, the U.S. Vice President had endeared himself to Yamagawa and the other Japanese auto manufacturing companies by convincing President Reagan that Japan, having voluntarily quit its industrial spying, could be trusted with voluntary export quotas. The JAMA delegation would of course bring him an official gift.

"Not so far as I know, sir."

"If you were at that breakfast," mused Sumi, "you could carry no gun or blade. But if—because of your English—you were chosen to give the gift?"

Belly-talk, but very clear. Matt nodded. An idea was forming.

Sumi sat back, wincing at the pain in his knees. "We have certain explosives experts—" he continued, but Bancroft held up his hand.

"No, sir, you've done enough. I shall handle that part myself."

Surprised, Sumi guessed that he was thinking of Hashimoto, the sapper Fujihara had chosen to blow their bunker. So his accomplice in the murder of Nagano's *koban* policeman still lived on? Nagano would be interested in *that*.

Bancroft was bowing deeply, his head almost to the table. "I thank you, sir," he murmured, "from the bottom of my soul."

Sumi was suddenly very tired. "Thank Prince Kuni and the men of the Misty Lagoon," he sighed. "Remember that, when you lie dying. It is all you need to know."

CHAPTER 9

On August 5, 1987, Josh Goldberg checked into Hiroshima's Silk Plaza Hotel. It was jammed with delegates to the Peace Rally, but on eight previous trips he had found it to be convenient lodging, close to the Peace Park and cheaper than the Grand.

When he traveled to Japan he practiced all the economies he could. Each August 6 he was invited to speak at the A-Bomb Anniversary Peace Rally by the Japan Council against A and H Bombs. Each year he swore that he would never come again. He was always broke, and the yearly trips helped not at all. By the nature of his practice, his clients died like flies, leaving destitute widows and unpaid legal fees. The council never paid his way to Hiroshima, and each year the yen went up. But each year he returned.

He had become the leading American advocate for the rights of American nuclear veterans. In 1971, ex-Captain Ralph Feathers, the black army psychiatrist who had watched the Athena shot with him, had visited his Berkeley office and retained him to file a claim against the army. Feathers seemed to have shrunk by half. His ebony skin was moist, and there were pouches under his eyes. He was dying of leukemia, and angry. Josh was angry too, and had found a cause to fight for.

Feathers had died before his suit could come to trial, but the dam of Defense Department secrecy was breaking, and there seemed hope at last for those that the nuclear tests were killing. Josh became counsel for the Atomic Veterans' Legal Aid Center, a nonprofit organization in Washington, D.C.

For a while the tide had seemed to be turning in favor of the veterans.

The government could not keep civilian casualties secret. Ninety-one of 220 members—forty percent—of the cast and crew of *The Conqueror*, an RKO historical extravaganza filmed near Frenchman Flat a year after Shot Grable, had suffered cancer. Half of those affected had already died, including Susan Hayward, Agnes Moorehead, Dick Powell, and John Wayne. The lid was off for Nevada and Utah residents, and they were fighting to be heard.

In 1979 Josh became the veterans' aid center's director. He found a flat in Washington, and began to commute across the country. Corky was alcoholic, and whenever he was gone too long from Berkeley, she would disintegrate, so finally they sold their house and bought a place in Arlington, Virginia.

He helped organize the Committee for U.S. Veterans of Hiroshima and Nagasaki. He fought for veteran's compensation for many of the ten thousand marines who had been exposed when they occupied Nagasaki, and the army troops from the 41st Division he had seen in Hiroshima. He litigated and lobbied in vain. Congress seemed paralyzed by the fear of potential health claims from a quarter of a million irradiated personnel. The NRC and the Nuclear Defense Agency fought him at every turn. On some days he faced fifteen Department of Justice and Defense Nuclear Agency lawyers, alone in a federal court.

Corky, in and out of AA, and nursing—when she was sober enough to work—in an Arlington pediatric clinic, never came to Hiroshima with him.

Josh hoped that his yearly speeches here had not got him on some CIA hit list. But by now—having fought anonymous bureaucrats and arrogant government lawyers for sixteen years while his clients dropped dead—he didn't give a damn.

He wrote off his travel for business. Perhaps some year he'd learn something from the other speakers that he could use in court.

As he signed the register, a Hiroshima lawyer named Kazuo Habu joined him. Kazuo—"Kaz"—was a charming ex-Imperial Army lieutenant who—quartered in barracks here—had somehow survived the blast. Half his face was scarred with keloids. For years he had been a Peace Rally host, and they knew each other well. He invited Josh to his downtown club for a drink, while they discussed tomorrow's slate.

Alicia sat in a booth in the second-story bar of the Suntory Club, a private membership affair in the center of Hiroshima. Tomorrow at dawn the crowds would gather for the forty-second anniversary services in Peace Memorial Park. Rab was covering it for Melbourne Channel 7. They had arrived with a film crew from Australia yesterday.

This, she hoped, would be their final roost of the evening. They had dined at the Shingetsu *ryotei* restaurant, served in a private tatami room by kimono-clad waitresses. The food was delicious, and her energy had held up well.

Then, because the network's liaison man insisted, the crew had begun a tour of the Nagarekawa and Yagenbori districts, gulches of glowing neon, where every other doorway led to a bar in which she was invariably the only female—outside of hostesses—in the place.

On this Memorial eve, the places were jammed. She had had too much sake at dinner, and too much whiskey afterward. She was dizzy and a little drunk. And she was afraid that her fatigue and weakness—recurrent for forty years—was returning. She had an appointment next week at Johns Hopkins, where her keloid had been removed years ago, but where they had never got at the root of her tiredness.

She sat back. The Suntory Club was quieter, and a haven in the storm. At the bar, a customer was singing into a microphone, and the other booths were crowded, but the disco music was muted, and at least she could hear herself think.

A waitress brought a bottle of whiskey. Their network liaison man, a diminutive Japanese who had been drinking far too much, picked up the bottle and began to trickle it into her glass. Rab warned her with a glance—and he was right—but to refuse in Japan was to deprive their host of face.

She bowed and lifted the glass: *"Kam-pai."*

Josh Goldberg had noticed Alicia and Rab the moment they entered the club. Sitting at a table in the rear, he had started up, then settled back.

His host looked at him quizzically. "Someone you know, Goldberg-san?"

He nodded. "Someone I knew, long ago," he said softly. "Long ago, and not so far away."

His heart was beating fast. She was beautiful, still. He longed to cross the room and draw her into his arms. An ache began in his chest, of loneliness and regret.

He suspected that, like him, Rab was in Hiroshima for the peace rally. Perhaps for some feature story? He had noticed before that the bomb reached across decades and continents, touching all who had seen the thing or the ruin it had spread. Whether scarred physically like Alicia or Kaz, or wounded in spirit like Rab or himself, they were all in it together, and for life.

"I mustn't see you again," she'd said, in Tokyo. All right.

He decided not to join them. It was unlikely that they would notice him in the crowded, half-lit room. If they heard him speak tomorrow, so be it, but he saw no reason to face her now, knowing that she would leave with Rab.

His host had followed his gaze, and was looking at their party. "He is a well-known Australian newscaster, Josh. But I have forgotten his name."

"McGraw," murmured Josh. "Rab McGraw."

"I met them at the Peace Rally office. Do you know she speaks *Japanese?*"

Josh nodded. His host looked at him curiously and signaled a waitress. "My friend, you need another drink. She is a most beautiful woman. There is more to this, I think."

"Nothing at all, Kaz," Josh smiled wanly. "Nothing at all any more."

"If I had you on the witness stand," Kazuo smiled, "I could impeach you on *that* statement in a flash."

Josh nodded. His host filled his glass and they sat back to listen to the music.

Matt Bancroft sat at the Suntory Club singalong bar with his colleagues. They had appropriated the section far to the rear, as they did almost every night.

He came here often, on business parties. There was much one could not say at the factory, where anger was unheard of. With a few drinks warming one's belly, it all came out at night.

But there were few grievances this evening—few directed toward him, at least. Tonight he was a hero. He had dined with four top Yamagawa executives, their Mitsutomo bankers, and two of his fellow Japan Automotive Manufacturers' Association delegates from the team which would visit Washington next week.

Today's meeting of the association in the Yamagawa boardroom had gone well. Everyone—Yamagawa, Mazda, Nissan, Toyota, Honda, Subaru—was awed by his originality in conceiving the gift: a gold-plated model of the warplane Mr. Bush had flown when he was young. It was nearly finished. Matt had seen it in the Yamagawa model shop, and reported that it was beautiful.

So Hart-san was the hero of the day. But he was not enjoying the evening, nor the Scotch everyone was pressing on him.

The anniversary evenings always depressed him. Forty-two years ago tonight, he had stood in a bedroom in Mickey-san's quarters, watching his sister brush her golden hair.

By midnight Alicia was tipsy.

The microphone had left the bar and was making its way toward their table. Rab, who had no ear for music at all, succumbed and sang "Waltzing Matilda." Alicia, who had spoken not a word of Japanese all evening, sang "The Coal Miners' Song," a folk chant from the North. When she finished, there was a moment of silent astonishment from the Japanese, and then applause. Someone called in English: "More!" and the rest took it up, urging her on.

Drunk for perhaps the third time in her life, she got to her feet.

She was suddenly seventeen, standing by her window in Mickey-san's quarters, and her brother was leaving for school. The sun was shining brightly and the world was full.

Oh, what a beautiful morning . . .
Oh, what a beautiful day . . .

Matt was listening to the complaint of the local Mitsutomo Bank comptroller on the expense of helmets, shoulder pads, and jerseys for the company American-football team.

And then he heard the voice, clear and true . . .

Alicia?

I've got a wonderful feeling
Everything's going my way . . .

Matt felt as if he had turned to stone.
*He was driving away from the curb with Mickey-san, and
she was watching from the window, She was blowing him a
kiss . . .*
Trembling, he put down his glass. Alicia was dead, he had
heard her screaming in the flames . . .
Slowly, he turned from the bar.
She stood by a booth, near the entrance to the club. The
customers had twisted on their barstools to watch her in the
dim light. She was tall and slender, dressed in a plain black
dress. Her hair was as golden as ever. She swayed slightly—
perhaps a little drunk. Her teeth were white and even, and the
eyes . . .
Alicia? *Alive?*

All the sounds of the earth are in rhythm . . .

Their eyes met, and hers were as green as his own. Her
voice faltered, and trailed off, as if she had forgotten the
words.
He turned swiftly back to the bar. She could not have
recognized him, it would be too much, not now, when he was
closing on their mother's murderer, no, she had not . . .
Uncertainly, someone in the audience clapped, and the
others joined in. The Mitsutomo banker went on with his
complaint. Matt wanted to escape, but there was no way to
get past her table. His hand shook so badly that he was afraid
to try to lift his glass.
He must get ahold of himself. Whatever happened, she
must not be allowed to ruin his plans.
The banker was staring past him. Matt felt a touch on his
shoulder and turned.
His sister, face white as a geisha's, was staring into his
eyes.
"Matt?" she whispered. *"Matt?"*
He took a deep breath and smiled. "Pardon me?"

•   •   •

Alicia's knees were wobbling from the shock of seeing him there. The eyes, the emerald eyes!

"Matt!" she whispered. "It's *you?*"

He looked at her pleasantly. "Have we met?"

She took a deep breath. What was wrong with him? "Matt!"

"Sorry, Mrs. . . ."

"McGraw," she said feebly. *"Alicia* McGraw. You're not *Matt?"*

He shook his head, smiling. "Chris Hart, of Yamagawa Motor." He showed her a business card. His emerald eyes stayed blank, and very cold. "I'm sorry, ma'am."

She had made a fool of herself, and lost enormous face. She somehow summoned a smile and turned. She lurched for her table, but the room began to spin.

All at once a man stepped from the shadows, grasping her arms before she fell. His grip was solid, but quite tender, and it was a moment before she recognized him.

"Josh?" she whispered incredulously. "What are *you* doing here?"

"Peace Rally. Alicia, are you okay?"

"Oh, Josh, oh, Josh . . ."

She felt herself drifting away. She glimpsed Rab, as if in freeze frame, half out of his chair, moving to grab for her, and then everything went dark.

She awoke in the taxi. Rab was rubbing her temples, and they were pulling into the portico in front of Hiroshima Grand Hotel.

"Bloody habit," he said dryly.

"I'm so *sorry,* Rab," she murmured. "I'm *mortified!* Did you see Josh, or am I crazy?"

"I saw him," he said dryly. "Answer to a desperate maiden's prayer. You passed out in Miyajima, too, about forty years ago."

"I'm so ashamed," she said. "That poor damn network man. He can never go back to his club!"

"He's the one who filled you with booze," shrugged Rab. "Do the blighter good." He peered at her curiously. "Who *was* that bloke you spoke to at the bar? Anyone we know?"

"I thought I saw my brother," she said simply. She ached with disappointment, and her throat caught. "Liquor! I was wrong."

• • •

Josh Goldberg sat at the table, trying to concentrate on his host's story of a bankrupt client before Hiroshima Prefecture Court.

The encounter with Alicia had shaken him. He had had a lifetime of experience with a drunken female, unfortunately, and was sure that Alicia had rarely been that tipsy, but he wondered why she had tried to meet the man at the bar. Someone she thought she recognized, perhaps.

It was even stranger that the man had rebuffed her. He seemed American. A diplomat, maybe, or a businessman: he was talking now to his companions and seemed to know Japanese.

Josh peered through the smoke toward the bar. He caught the flash of emerald eyes. Like Alicia's?

Or another's? The eyes above the mask, some forty years ago?

Ridiculous. He realized suddenly that he was being impolite. He turned back to his host. "So you moved to quash the motion?" he prompted.

"Yes," chuckled Habu. His eyelids were sagging from the Scotch. Japanese could not drink, admitted they could not, and tried to prove it every night. "And when I turned to bow to the bench—you will not believe me—I found the judge asleep!"

"I believe you, Kaz, believe *me!* I see it every day."

When he turned back to the bar, the green-eyed man was gone.

Services in Peace Memorial Park would begin at seven A.M., with a hymn. Alicia had left a call for early breakfast, and they were up before dawn. Rab planned to narrate a full thirty seconds on camera, and while he ate he studied the schedule of events.

"Alicia," he called into the bathroom, "have a look at this!"

She emerged, brushing her hair, and took the schedule.

On the list of speakers he had encircled a name. Between a professor of radiology from Tokyo University and the director of the Australian Nuclear Veteran's Association, she found: "Mr. Joshua Goldberg, Attorney: Atomic Veterans' Legal Aid Center, Washington, D.C."

She felt her cheeks go hot. She turned away, ashamed of how she reacted to his name. She must not let Rab sense it. Guilt was a Judeo-Christian vice, she reflected, and shame—guilt discovered—Japanese. She was less *gaijin* than she thought.

"I wish he hadn't seen me there last night!" she murmured.

"I'm sure you do," he said dryly. "But, as I remember Corky, he's used to drunken sheilas. And he did keep you from falling on your bum."

"You have a sweet way of putting things," she commented, touching lipstick to her lips. She still loved Rab, she reckoned, but was sick to death of his foreign-correspondent coolness, which he wore like a mask, on screen or off.

He would be filming all day, and tonight he was leaving with the crew to videotape the lesser anniversary at Nagasaki in three days. She planned to hear Josh speak.

As they were leaving the room, the phone buzzed. Rab picked it up.

"Hotel valet," he said, handing it to her. "For you."

Strange. She hadn't sent clothes to the cleaner. She took the phone, while Rab went to press the elevator button.

"Mrs. McGraw?" asked a voice in English. It was familiar, but she could not place it.

"Yes?"

Now the voice changed to Japanese, quickly and positively. "You are to show no expression, no surprise. Your husband must not know."

"Who is this?" she faltered.

The voice came back in English. "The man last night at the bar. You are to meet me tonight, at the floating of the candles on the river."

"Well, I shan't!" Her heart was beginning to pound.

"You *have* to. You must come *alone*, at eight. Tell no one. On the bank of the Honkawa, at the Charnel Mound." He paused. "Do you know where that is, Alicia? Across from Honkawa School?"

She sat suddenly on the bed.

"Matt? *Matt?*"

"Yes," he said, "it is." The voice was cool and distant. "And you must not tell your husband, or I'm in danger. So, *alone*, Alicia, you understand? Tonight."

She heard a click and slowly replaced the phone.

Rab's voice echoed down the corridor: "Alicia, there's an elevator-full. Shall we get a move on, then?"

She somehow pulled herself together and they left for Memorial Park.

To U.S. photo-reconnaissance pilots who had photographed Hiroshima before the attack forty-two years ago, the island between the Honkawa and Motoyasu branches of the Ota looked like a skinny turkey, hung from the Aioi T-Bridge—ground zero—by its beak.

Now all was green and lush. On the turkey's beak and head lay the Peace Memorial Park. It stared across the Motoyasu at the steel framework of the Peace Dome—once Hiroshima's Industrial Exhibition Hall—and beyond that, at the Municipal Baseball Park, home of the championship Hiroshima Carps. At the turkey's head lay the long, wide Peace Museum, full of relics of the bombing. Fronting the museum lay the Peace Fountain, a massive spout surrounded by four lesser ones. Two hundred yards away from the museum, at the turkey's eyes, was the concrete Memorial Cenotaph, like a covered wagon open at both ends.

Across the park, but framed by the cenotaph's open ends, burned the eternal Flame of Peace.

Rab's press credentials had got Alicia a seat precisely in the center, close to the speaker's stand. From her wooden folding chair—one of thousands placed by the Peace Committees in the Peace Park—she could see, beyond the podium, the Tower of a Thousand Cranes, the children's peace monument. It was covered with paper cranes, folded by school children, in memory of the little *hibakusha* girl who, dying of leukemia, had been told that if she folded a thousand of them she would get well. At eight hundred, she had died.

Behind Alicia, all the way back to the museum, sat row upon row of spectators: the morning paper had announced that over twenty thousand had come to pray for an end to nuclear armament. There were hundreds of peace groups represented, from every continent. She had seen Indian saris, Sikh turbans, Turkish caftans, German lederhosen.

She had been in a daze since Matt's phone call, hardly following the ceremonies. Matt lived. Why had he lied last night? And why could he not come forward openly today?

Why was he "Christopher Hart"?

It was a hot sunny morning, like that of forty-two years ago. The skies were a bright blue. She spotted Josh Goldberg, trim, broad-shouldered, hair graying now, in the first row of the speakers. As always something moved inside her.

Rab was going to ask him to dinner tonight—she sensed jealousy there, but comradeship, too, between the men, from their days at the end of the war. Somehow she would have to escape them both to go to the river.

Alone . . . But *why?*

The services began with a prayer by a Catholic priest in English, another in Japanese by a Buddhist. The city officials spoke, and then the speakers from the Japan Council against A and H Bombs.

Josh was introduced as the director of the Atomic Veterans' Legal Aid Center and a former major in the U.S. Marine Corps, the last drawing hisses. He ignored them. His words floated over the crowd in English and then—translated poorly by a high school English teacher—into Japanese.

He spoke of the nuclear rubble he had seen on this spot forty-two years ago. "Some of us welcomed the bomb—*I* was one—before we saw what we had done. Our *own* disasters came later and have not stopped yet . . ."

It was very hot, and he paused for a drink of water and spoke of the 135,000 U.S. servicemen and passing Japanese fishermen who were exposed to atomic radiation during the seventeen years of U.S. testing in the Marshalls.

"Our organization forced the U.S. Defense Department to open a radiation hot line. Forty-seven thousand U.S. veterans have phoned it in one year, with their questions, their fears, and their symptoms."

He removed the microphone from its stand and stepped to the edge of the podium, closer to the audience. The park was very still.

"Many U.S. veterans are dead of radiation poisoning and more are dying. The U.S. Defense Department denies responsibility even toward its own soldiers. Washington seems not to care. Neither do Paris or Moscow."

Josh paused for translation.

"We, here today, *do* care," he continued. "We in America have been punished. We have our own *hibakushas*." He swept his eyes across the thousands, and for a moment she thought he had spotted her. "We are all *hibakushas*, every one!"

There were no hisses now. Thousands rose to applaud him. The choir sang, a children's band played, and three hundred doves were released. They ascended in a pulsating, shimmering column, wings flashing in the sun.

As they rose from the mass of people below, they dispersed like a mushroom cloud.

Alicia found herself trembling. It was almost noon. She had eight hours to wait for the floating of the candles on the river.

When she arrived at the Charnel Mound by the Honkawa, it was growing dark. She had left Rab and Josh at the Hiroshima Grand, telling them that she had promised to meet her old friend Yuko by the river for a few short hours alone.

The crush by the embankment was immense. The evening was balmy, and the breeze was from the west. Mixed with the scent of candle wax she could smell the mountain pines.

The Bell of Peace behind the Memorial Cenotaph was tolling. Thousands of those who had lost relatives had gathered in the dusk to launch their little lanterns: two crossed sticks to float a candle, inserted in a paper sack turned upside down, with the bottom cut out, to protect the flame from the breeze.

Some were floating away from the concrete-lined bank of the Honkawa now, moving serenely downstream on the current. As the summer darkness fell, more joined them, and soon thousands of little lights were winking by, spirits of loved ones heading for the Seto Sea.

It was seven o'clock, and Alicia stayed close to the mound, searching the faces heading for the river. But when Matt came, she did not see him, for he approached from behind.

"Alicia?" she heard him murmur.

She whirled. He wore a sport shirt, carried a camera, and looked like an American tourist. He had bought a lantern from one of the stream-side vendors, and carried it in his hand.

"Matt!" she cried. "Oh, my God!"

"*Sh . . . ,*" he whispered, and took her into his arms.

Matt looked into his sister's face. It was the last time he would see her, and he must forget nothing.

Last night, in the bar, he had noticed lines around her eyes, of age and pain. In the dusk, he could see them no longer. She was as he had remembered her, that last night in her room.

They sat on the bank while the crowds streamed by. They spoke in English, holding each other's eyes, then gazing into the night. She told him of her husband, and Cobber—whose real name was Matthew, after him.

"He's a barrister, now, in Sydney, and you have a grand-niece, too."

He told her of Kimiko and his own children and she wept.

She nodded toward the place where Honkawa School had stood, across the river: "I came back when I could, and there was nothing." She pointed toward the Memorial Mound. "Yesterday, I decided that your ashes were in there."

"I thought you had burned in our quarters," he told her.

They decided that it was Baba-san he had heard screaming, in the flames. He told her of Mickey-san's death, and found that she already knew. She had gone to Guam, he learned, where she had married the Australian newsman. "You will like him, Matt."

He would never see him, but could not tell her that, just yet.

"But why," she demanded, "are you 'Christopher Hart'?"

He sat thinking for a moment. He had spoken to no one else of the murders, not even General Sumi, who surely suspected; not in forty years. Quietly, he told her of the attack in Tokyo. He had been in contact recently with Private Hashimoto, who still lived in his little village on Hokkaido, but he did not mention him by name. "I only wounded the American: perhaps he lived."

"He lived," she murmured. "I know him, and he's here."

He could not believe it. "In Hiroshima?"

She told him of meeting the captain, of her hospital stay, and the trial. "He'd seen Hiroshima just after the bomb. He spoke today at the ceremonies. Forget the American, he's all right. So you don't have to live this *lie!*"

"I was an accomplice to two murders, Alicia! You can't tell anyone! Not your husband, not your son. You'll ruin my life if you do."

"*You* didn't kill anybody, Matt! And you were just thirteen!"

She began to weep again, and he gave her his handkerchief.

"Promise me," he said grimly. "Promise me now."

"I promise," she said. "I wish we'd never left Chichijima!"

He told her that he had returned to the island last month, to visit the graveyard on the hill. At fifty-five, as an American tourist, with camera, graying hair, and a full mustache, no one had recognized him, though he had seen and avoided their Uncle Harlan and Uncle Isaiah, and George Gilley, on the street. He had stayed in a hotel, built where Yankeetown had been. He had climbed to the cemetery on the ridge, and found their mother's grave badly overgrown with pandanus bush and vines.

"Forget Chichijima," he told her.

"But hardly anyone," she sighed, "ever knew that it was there. We were safe in the tunnels! Why did they make us leave?"

"The gods failed us on the day we did," he agreed. He stared into the night, and said softly: "The gods and the northeast wind." He turned and looked into her eyes. "I know where that pilot is," he murmured.

She stared at him. "*What? Where?*"

"In Washington. I've found his name."

She was very frightened.

"Why did you bother? It was war, Matt!"

"War was strafing the freighter. He circled and came back. That was murder."

"But you'd never try to . . . *do* anything?"

He had told her far too much. He forced a smile.

"This is 1987, I'm a wheel at Yamagawa Motor. Do you think I'm a goddamn *ronin* on the loose?"

She gazed at him for a moment. Finally she smiled back. "I'm glad. We've been through quite enough. Leave *that* bloody bastard to God."

She watched him pick up the lantern from the grass. He looked at it and gestured across the river, toward where his school had stood. "This is for my classmates," he said, "and I want to launch it now."

He scrambled down the concrete bank to the water.

The river was alive with bobbing candles, twinkling in the ebony stream. She felt suddenly that if his light joined the others, he was lost to her forever. Hurriedly she followed him down the sloping concrete bank to the water's edge.

From somewhere in the dark above, a Buddhist priest was chanting for the souls in the tiny flames.

Matt struck a match, and lit the candle. She grabbed his wrist. "Matt, don't."

"Why not?"

"I don't know."

"I have to, Alicia." He set it on the water. She started after it, and he yanked her back. She was suddenly in his arms, and his lips were hard on hers. He turned to watch the lantern. In his eyes, she saw anguish, and fear.

"Shall I see you tomorrow, Matt?"

"No. I have to go to Hokkaido, and then the States."

Her throat grew tight: "When *will* I see you, then?"

"Alicia," he said softly, "your brother Matt is dead. Don't look for him again."

Then he was up the bank, lost in the crowd and the darkness. She yelled after him and scrambled up herself. Fighting fatigue, she searched through the mourners on the bank. It was no use; he was gone.

She returned to the bank of the river. For a long time she watched his tiny candle, bobbing in the breeze. Abreast of Honkawa School, a cluster of lanterns swirled in some errant current. Matt's stayed apart for a long, long while, but finally joined the rest. In a little while she could not tell it from the others any more.

She arrived at the hotel drained and exhausted. Rab had already eaten and left for Nagasaki with the crew: he would pick her up on the way back to Melbourne.

As she passed through the lobby, she saw Josh Goldberg, surrounded by a group of Japanese from the peace movement. Most of them, she knew, were intellectuals from Hiroshima University and the medical school.

Their eyes met across the room. She conquered an urge to go to him. She headed for the lifts, but he left the group and joined her while she waited. She congratulated him on his speech.

He shrugged. "A yearly rerun. Does no good, but gets it off my chest." He studied her. "Rab told me you'd be on your own tomorrow."

"I'm going to sleep all day."

"No," he said firmly. "There's a tour to Miyajima, and I need an interpreter."

A warning jangled in her head. She glanced at the group he had left. "There'll be plenty of interpreters, Josh. And you know it."

His eyes were warm and gentle. "Alicia?"

"Josh, I can't."

"Please?"

She felt as if she were dissolving in an *onsen* hot springs bath. Feebly, she fought.

"Why Miyajima? You've *been* there."

"Look what I found there last time."

The gray eyes melted her, again.

"What time, then?" she murmured. "When do we go?"

"The bus leaves from the lobby at ten A.M."

When finally she turned off the light that night, she slept as if she were drugged.

CHAPTER 10

Matt Bancroft stood waiting in the cluttered little yard behind Hashimoto's machine shop, while Hashimoto—white-haired and still rock-hard—worked at his bench inside. After a month's experimentation, the ex-Imperial Army sapper was completing his task. He was inserting a fuse he had devised into a World War II Japanese twenty-five-millimeter shell. To Matt, it seemed an appropriate charge in the model plane.

The operation was apparently dangerous, for Hashimoto had refused to let Matt come into the shop to watch.

Matt shivered with cold. Here in Wakkanai Village, a north wind had been sweeping in all afternoon from Russia's Sakhalin Island, visible only twenty miles away across Soya Misaki Strait. His blood, used to Hiroshima's summer breeze, was too thin for northern Hokkaido.

It was Matt's third visit in the last month. On the first, he had brought the plans for the model airplane, on the second, a balsa mock-up carved in the Yamagawa model shop. This morning, having stayed in a hotel in Asahikawa last night, he had driven north in a rented car with the model itself, for the final fitting. Carefully, Hashimoto had cut and drilled, machined and polished, and now the model, hollowed, was ready to receive its charge. Tomorrow Matt would leave with the delegation for Washington.

"Hai!" called Hashimoto. "You may come now, Bank-loft-o-san!"

Hashimoto, the only living being besides his sister or General Sumi who knew his name, apparently found it impossible to think of him as Hart. It hardly mattered, any more: in a week, it would all be over.

In the cramped work space, he smelled hot oil and metallic filings. Hashimoto turned from his bench. His face was shadowed in the light from a single dusty window. His snowy hair was still cut short, and his wide flat face unlined.

On the bench sat the golden airplane, wings folded back. Next to it lay two brass twenty-five-millimeter cartridges, scribed deeply in a diagonal grid pattern like grenades. The projectile had been removed from both. The base of one cartridge was painted red. Hashimoto picked up the other and moved close to the window.

"Like this, sir," Hashimoto said. He pointed to a ring which protruded from the unmarked cartridge. "This cartridge is powderless, for practice. And when one pulls the ring it extracts the safety device." He pulled it. "Then . . ."

He unscrewed the model's nose. He slipped the cartridge into the fuselage. It fitted perfectly. He screwed back the model's engine nacelle. "Now, Bankloft-o-san, unfold the wings, and listen carefully."

The wings lay back along the fuselage, like those of a resting gull. The only way to spread them was to point the nose at one's chest and use both hands. Matt pulled them forward. They moved easily: the unwitting Yamagawa model makers were heirs to centuries of skill, and known for their artistry throughout the industry.

As the wings clicked into the flying position, there was a loud snap from inside the fuselage. Hashimoto smiled.

"The blast will channel through the nose. With the other cartridge, that click would have been your end."

He unscrewed the nacelle, removed the dummy cartridge, and screwed the nose back on. Carefully, Matt polished Hashimoto's fingerprints from the plane and the red-ringed cartridge. He would not need the practice cartridge, and told Hashimoto to destroy it.

He packed the plane into its fitted, felt-lined rosewood case, while Hashimoto wrapped the red-ringed cartridge in a clean dustrag. He looked into Matt's face. "And so, Bankloft-o-san, now it is done. For whatever purpose . . ."

Matt had seen no need to burden him with the immensity of the deed: he would find out from the newspapers or TV, soon enough. But the hint was plain, and required some sort of a reply.

"It will be used," he answered carefully, "to avenge a woman much beloved of Major Fujihara."

Hashimoto bowed deeply, in respect to Mickey-san. He had flatly refused payment, and now he asked Matt into his tiny house, adjoining the shop. They removed their shoes and kneeled on the tatami. He was an honored guest, and had to wait while Hashimoto's sturdy wife performed the *sado* tea ceremony. He was anxious to leave for his plane, but he watched her pour the hot water with her *hishaku* ladle into the *chawan* cup, then stir the green tea with the *chasen* brush. As ceremony required, he bowed and received the cup with his right hand, placed it on the palm of his left, rotated it clockwise three times, and sipped it. It was properly bitter. He wiped the point on the rim that his lips had touched with the fingers of his right hand, rotated the *chawan* counter-clockwise, bowed, and returned it to his hostess.

He had brought gifts, a case of Johnny Walker Scotch for Hashimoto, and a bolt of the finest *yuzen* material he could find for his wife, who probably sewed her own kimonos.

He and Hashimoto spoke of Mickey-san, and the awful days in Tokyo. Reluctantly, Hashimoto realized that the time had come for Matt to leave. The old soldier arose and moved to the *oshiire* cupboard. From it he took, reverently, Mickey-san's *daisho*—his matched *katana* samurai sword and the shorter *wakizashi*. He laid them on the tatami mat by the table.

"You remember that the major gave them to my keeping?"

"*Hai.*" Matt nodded.

Hashimoto unsheathed the shorter sword. "It was with this that he began to take his life . . ."

"I know."

Hashimoto unsheathed the other. He touched its blade to the hairs on his wrist. "And with this, I finished. Like a razor," he murmured, "and I have not touched the blade to stone in more than forty years. *I* was his *kaishaku,*" he said proudly. "I am boasting, but no samurai could have struck cleaner."

"I am sure."

"I think these blades are very old," mused Hashimoto. Obviously, parting with them was a struggle. "Well, at least they were kept safely for you." He sheathed the blades, caressed the scabbards, and murmured: "So . . . Take them!"

"The *wakizashi*, yes," Matt smiled. The time had come for the greatest gift of all: with the *katana* Hashimoto could buy the village, not that he ever would part with it. "The long sword is for you."

Hashimoto's eyes shone, and then dropped. "I cannot, sir. To take *wakizashi* from *katana* is to steal the father's son!"

"His own blood is on both of them, old friend, and he would want it so."

Tears squeezed from Hashimoto's eyes. Kneeling at the door, he bowed deeply to Matt in farewell, then peered into his face.

"We shall not meet again?" he asked.

"Not in this world," said Matt.

CHAPTER 11

*M*iyajima Island glittered in warm sunlight after a summer shower. Alicia wandered with Josh along the waterfront to the Itsukushima Shrine, nibbling on a stick of charcoal-grilled *yakitori* temple meat Josh had bought her at a handcart stall by the ferry landing. They stood on the beach gazing out at the great vermilion Torii gate, rising out of sapphire waters a hundred yards from shore. A sacred deer strayed over and nibbled at her lunch. Alicia felt better than she had in weeks: the afternoon fatigue which always overtook her had not struck.

They had quickly lost Josh's tour group, which had taken the rope railroad up Misen Peak to see the sacred monkeys.

They strolled up the alley where she had fainted on the night they met, outside Yuko's house. Alicia did not want Yuko to see her here: they had already met two days before, in Hiroshima, and traded news, and wept at parting. Now she found that she wanted to be alone with Josh.

They roamed through the endless wooden halls and verandas of Itsukushima Shrine, and found them crowded with naval cadets from the academy on nearby Eta Jima. They moved along beaches she had discovered after the *pika-don*, past Daigan-ji Temple and pine-shaded shrines and sanctuaries in the woods that tourists seldom saw.

At last she found a wooded cove in which she'd swum,

when the keloid on her shoulder was so livid that she could not bear to have other bathers see. The water was blue-green, and the sand was purest gold. It was dead-high tide, and the wavelets lapped at the roots of pine trees climbing the slopes behind. There was no one there, only the old trees gossiping in the breeze from the Seto Sea. A sacred monkey glared from the shadows, as tall as a five-year-old child.

"You're not to stare back at him," she warned. "They've been spoiled quite rotten for a thousand years, and he'd just as soon attack."

Josh waved his arms and the monkey scurried away.

"Now you've done it!" she told him. "Mayhaps he'll get his friends."

" 'Mayhaps,' " he grinned. "It's like listening to Maggie in *The Mill on the Floss*. You're an anachronism, Alicia. You always have been."

She smiled. "I say 'bloody,' and 'make out.' " She gazed up into his face. "What era do you place me in?"

"Eighteen-fifty?"

"Thanks," she said. "It's what every woman wants to hear, when she has to dye her hair."

He sat in the shade of an ancient tree and, when she sat beside him, drew her close. His arm felt strong as steel: Rab seldom embraced her, except in bed. "You were born in Shangri-la. You're still so beautiful, and young."

"Not young. Not now."

"Young," he insisted. "And I could look into your eyes the whole day through."

He leaned toward her, her face in his hands. They kissed.

"No sea shells?" he murmured after a moment. He still held her, but he was gazing far away. The beach at Guam seemed to be all around them.

"Not here. Mayhaps offshore," she whispered. They stripped in the shelter of the tree. The water was shallow, and warm as blood. Because he'd said she was young, she fought the weariness creeping over her.

They swam to a huge rising rock, some fifty yards from shore. Sheltered from land, he put his hands on her waist. Their eyes locked. She kissed the graying hair on his chest. Beneath the surface, she could see his legs, tanned and firm from tennis, shimmering like twin columns beneath the surface. He was rising, like the rock above them. Her fingers traced the scar on his shoulder, which she now knew Matt had made. Now, since her surgery, hers was smaller than his.

"We match," she murmured.

"Same war."

"If you hadn't got me my visa, that scar would still be there."

"Rab got you your visa, not me."

"You helped," she said. She did not tell him that she was going back for treatment. Evil thoughts plagued her nowadays: what if she were dying? So many others had.

She looked at Josh, imagining how it would have been if Corky had taken the hospital ship home.

The wasted years, for him and her, when they could have had each other.

She looked into his eyes and saw regret, and melted into his arms. She felt him entering her, and growing in the gentle surge of the water. In the clear warm sea they merged. She threw back her head in delight. Shards of sunlight were falling on her hair, she was of the sun, a part of it . . .

Afterward, a gull winged overhead, jeering; Josh cawed back. Hand in hand, they sloshed ashore. They found a flat, smooth rock in a patch of sunlight, and sat for a long time, drying, without a word.

Josh abandoned the tour and that night took a room for them at a *ryokan*, on the waterfront. At dawn they saw the great *torii* gate as it rose from the sea at low tide.

It was at breakfast *gohan* in their room that he spoke of Corky. The maid, smiling and bowing, served their dried fish, raw egg, miso soup, pickles, and rice. He said: "She's been bored since she was six. She's an alcoholic, Alicia. You could see it coming, back on Guam."

"Mayhaps if she'd had a child she wouldn't have been bored."

"She didn't want one until too late. And then I didn't, so . . ."

He shrugged and got up from the tatami, effortlessly. Most westerners his age, she thought, had to struggle to rise from a mat. His body filled the tiny room. He looked out at the *torii* gate. He came back, kneeled beside her, and kissed her on the cheek.

"Alicia, Alicia," he sighed, smiling. "Child of a different age. Do we mayhaps have another day?"

She hadn't intended to stay, but she looked into his face and nodded. "Rab won't be back in Hiroshima until tomorrow."

That afternoon they swung up the funicular cable car to Shishiiwa Station on Misen Peak. From the crest they could see the Shikoku Mountains and the islands of the Inland Sea. There were ancient tombs about, and she found her eyes filling with tears. "What's wrong?" he asked.

"My mama looks down like this, on Futami Bay."

"From the ridge," he said. "I know."

She stared at him. "You've seen that place?" she asked.

"The first day I landed, I saw her grave." He told her how shocked he'd been when Captain Ohta had read him the inscription. "I didn't know how much you hated us."

She was confused: "*Who* hated you?"

"Your brother, for one."

"Well, yes, can you blame him?" She looked at him sharply, suddenly realizing what he'd said. "But how could you know?"

He quoted the curse that Captain Ohta had read him, word for word: "'Her only son forever swears on her grave . . .' Something. In Japanese." He groped for the word. "I forget. 'Revenge,' or 'vengeance'?"

"*Kataki?*" she breathed. "*Kataki-uchi?*"

"Yes." He was staring at her. "Alicia! What is it?"

She remembered Matt, rigid as the cross itself, hanging back after the funeral, lingering at the grave. He must have carved it then, for he hadn't joined them on the quay for almost half an hour. And by the Honkawa, the other night, he'd said he returned to the grave last month! To renew his oath? Why else? And he'd found the pilot! And he was going to America, perhaps already there?

"He carved *that* on her cross?" she breathed. "And 'Forever'?"

He squeezed her hand. "I'm sorry. I thought you'd know."

"I *didn't* know!" She jerked away, and started down the trail to the funicular. "And I've got to go!"

"Alicia, wait!"

"Come, or stay. But I have to go!"

She refused to tell him why. They made the next car on the funicular, and dashed for the hydrofoil back to Hiroshima, and as she ran up the dock in the Ujina district, to get a cab, he could hardly keep up with her.

She raced into the Hiroshima Grand. Josh still had a reservation for his flight home tonight: she begged him to go. She could afterward barely remember saying good-bye. She fumbled with the key to her room. When she opened the door, she found Rab shaving in the bathroom, getting ready to go out.

Thank God she hadn't stayed in Miyajima for the extra night.

"You're back early!" she said shakily. "Is Nagasaki wrapped?"

"I spoke *my* lines, the crew's still there." In the mirror, his pale eyes met hers. Something was wrong.

She could not stand the strain. She would have to confess, and very soon. To delay was cruel, and cowardly too. She hated herself for waiting, but first she must talk to her brother: now was not the moment for a clash.

"Where are you going?" she asked shakily.

"Out."

"What time will you be back?" she asked.

He shrugged. "Local network. Big party, I imagine," he said, checking his tie in the mirror. "Gorgeous bloody geishas, vying for my body. Why?" he asked, straightening his tie.

"Why *what?*"

"What difference does it make?" He centered the knot. "Josh left today, I take it. You've no one *else* in mind?"

"What do you mean by *that?*" she asked weakly.

"I wonder?" he said, and left without kissing her good-bye.

So he knew. She started to call after him, and stopped. It was five minutes to five. Matt's office would be closing.

She lunged for the phone, dialed Yamagawa corporate headquarters, and asked for Christopher Hart.

There was a long delay. His secretary had left already. They switched her from office to office. She finally reached a draftsman who worked for him.

"I must speak to Hart-san," she said in Japanese. "It is very important."

"*So desu ka?*" the draftsman said, condescendingly. Japanese men were always amused by anxious women. "But you see, it is impossible. He has gone with a trade delegation to Washington."

"Will you please find where he is staying there?" she begged.

"That is impossible too. His secretary has gone home."

"I must have his schedule!"

"*Everyone* has left, and I must leave now too."

He hung up, and she called Japan Air Lines. There was a flight for Washington from Narita International at ten tomorrow morning. She could reach it on the shuttle flight to Tokyo, if she left at seven.

She packed, left a call for five A.M., and went to bed. Staring into the darkness, she tried to think what she would say to Rab. To tell him that she was going to Johns Hopkins Hospital in Baltimore seemed best.

At five A.M. the phone rang. An emotionless voice greeted her in Japanese and English and wished her a happy day. The drape across the window was gray with dawn.

Rab snored beside her, smelling of sake and beer. She lay for a moment gathering strength. She had never been more tired. Finally she got up and dressed, creeping around the room, afraid to flush the toilet. She closed her suitcase, and gazed at Rab. She dreaded disturbing him.

What if she left him a note? No, that would be cowardly: there was too much between them.

Gently, she shook his shoulder. As always, he awoke instantly, red-eyed but alert.

"What the bloody hell?" he growled, grabbing for his watch.

"Rab, I'm leaving. It's all set up."

He struggled up, threw his feet over the edge of the bed, and sat fingering his eyes. "Leaving? When? For where?"

"Now. For Baltimore. Johns Hopkins. I'm getting sick again."

His eyes burned into hers. Softly, he said: "No, you're going to Washington. I've seen it coming, for thirty bloody years. Not a week's gone by I haven't thought about that night."

"About *what* night?"

"The night in Tokyo when he saw you and I wasn't there."

"You were never there, Rab."

"I was there when you needed me in Guam."

"But afterward?"

"I had a job to do." He looked into her eyes. "Cobber told me, you know. Comes in and finds his mother in a goddamn major's arms."

She swallowed. "And you kept it in for thirty years?"

"Couldn't rat on my own son for telling tales." He shrugged. "And can't cry over spilt milk, can we, now?"

"No milk was spilt, believe me."

"Not then?" Suddenly he was shouting. "Or the bloody night before last?" He got to his feet, limped to the dresser, and picked up his cigarettes: "I called from Nagasaki! Where were you at two in the morning? And three? What do you fucking take me for?"

He pulled out a cigarette. She tried to light it, and he slammed away her hand. He went to the window and pulled aside the drapes. From the fiery sky she could tell that the day would be hot.

"We'll talk about it later," she said. "Not now. I'm going to Washington. But I'm *not* going to Washington for Josh."

"For the cherry blossoms, then?" He smiled tightly. "In August? You're just a little late."

She must break her promise, or her marriage was finished.

"My brother—" she began, and choked.

She could simply not go on.

"Your *brother?*" He turned from the window. "Your bloody brother's dead."

What was the use? "All right. Yes, I spent that night with Josh."

"I know," he murmured tonelessly. "So perhaps you'd best be off."

She touched his lips with hers. It was like kissing a statue. She turned, picked up her suitcase, and left.

As the airport bus crossed the Honkawa she glanced at the site of the school. Rab was wrong, and so was her brother. Her brother had *not* died there, and need not die now.

She had lost Josh once, and Cobber was grown, and Rab would leave her now. Her brother was all she had left.

If only she could reach him, and in time.

CHAPTER 12

*T*he delegation from the Japan Automotive Manufacturers' Association glided through the heat of a Washington August afternoon in three air-conditioned cocoons—cream-colored stretch limousines provided by the trade division of the embassy. They were bound from Dulles International to their lodgings in the Hilton Hotel.

Matt Bancroft—Hart-san—rode in the first. Colonel Osada had indeed resigned from the delegation, and Matt had indeed been selected as spokesman for the group. He spoke unaccented English, and had after all conceived the gift. He had coordinated its manufacture in the Yamagawa prototype model shop, using the finest model builders in the automotive industry. It seemed only fair to let him have the honor of presenting it.

The consensus had not come without some exquisite private maneuvering on his part. From the first, he had known that nothing could be more disastrous than to hint that he wanted the job. Ambition must always be hidden in corporate Japan.

The proper veil had been a subtle deference to Honda's delegate Ohkawa-san, oldest and most experienced of the group. And so, over the past weeks, at board meetings and after-work parties, he had carefully shunted aside the first suggestions that he, as a *gaijin*, should be chosen to speak for the body. Around conference table and cocktail bar, he had continually reminded his fellows that he was only an architect, a plain-spoken draftsman with no claim to political skill: if a polished presentation was desired, there were several in the group more qualified.

He had pointed out that he had been lucky, nothing more, to have stumbled on the choice of gift.

He had even suggested others: Ohkawa-san, or Nakashima-san, an articulate, rising star in Toyota sales; Ohga-san, of Nissan, who was a graduate of Tokyo University in International Law.

When his modesty had been overridden and the choice was made, he demurred: he should like, at least, to contemplate his qualifications for a day or two before he accepted, to make sure that he was worthy of the task. This had cinched the voting and gained him face. So at Dulles, the people from the Japanese Embassy had insisted—though he was among the younger delegates—that he ride in the first limousine.

So he would make the presentation personally, look into the eyes of his mother's murderer at the instant of retribution, and die—he hoped—in the instant after the blinding flash of powder and Imperial Army brass.

He was surprised to find himself quite calm.

The little cavalcade rolled into the circular drive of the Hilton and deposited them at its entrance, apex of two curved wings dominating the city above Embassy Row.

The Secret Service agent called from the lobby. Matt was unpacking his clothes.

He invited the agent up, then swiftly unlocked the rose-wood box and opened it. He drew the golden airplane model from its nest and put it on the bureau. From his suitcase he took a polishing cloth of tan flannel. He draped it on the fuselage, as if he had been interrupted while polishing the plane: he believed that it would survive careful inspection, but the more he could inhibit the man's handling it, the better.

The agent was a lean, white-haired man in a seersucker suit. He wore a laconic smile and teeth that were too perfect to be real. He showed his wallet at the door, and Matt caught the flash of a small gold badge and an ID card. ''Rick Lambie, Mr. Hart. I'm assigned to Mr. Bush's detail.''

With him was a Japanese with iron-gray hair, protruding teeth, and thick eyeglasses. The agent introduced him as Detective Captain Nagano, of the Tokyo Identification Section. The Japanese Embassy had brought him over to handle security for the JAMA delegation. Matt stiffened, apprehensive at the slightest change in plan. No one had told him of this.

They bowed and shook hands; Nagano bowed just low enough to be polite. Matt sensed that he spoke little English, and felt ill will behind the glittering glasses. Perhaps Nagano resented a white delegate on a Japanese mission, or—like many of his countrymen—did not like any *gaijin* who spoke Japanese at all.

Lambie swept the room with a slow gaze, and Matt felt that he had missed nothing: suitcase open on the rack, rosewood model box and model on the bureau: briefcase on the writing table. Matt offered them chairs, which they declined, and asked if they would like drinks from room service. Lambie smiled and shook his head. "I have just a few questions, Mr. Hart."

Steady, steady . . . He had expected this from the outset, was only surprised that they had waited so long.

"Sure, shoot."

The agent felt in his coat and drew out a list. "You have to understand, with the Mideast thing, we're very tight just now."

"We should be."

Lambie handed him the paper. On it was listed, in Japanese and English, the names of the visitors and their corporations.

"You're carried as head delegate, I thought I'd have you check this. Did they all fly in with you?"

Matt scanned the names. "Yes."

"Were you acquainted with them in Japan?"

"Some. I know most of them by reputation, at least."

"No 'Red Army'?" smiled Lambie.

"Jesus, I *hope* not," said Matt. "They're corporate executives, but you've cleared them with their embassy, haven't you?"

"Of course, and with the National Security Agency. But NSA don't exactly bat a thousand, do they? I'm glad their embassy brought in this gentleman: takes some of the heat off us."

Nagano, sensing that they were talking about him, glanced at Matt, who translated. Nagano bowed, but did not smile.

"Anyway, it's nice to have an American we can ask." Lambie folded the list and put it back in his coat. "You were born in Japan?" he asked idly.

"Tokyo," said Matt. "Before the war."

"CIA and State had a hell of a time on *your* background. Methodist missionaries' son?"

"Episcopalian."

"That's right," nodded Lambie. "And you studied under . . ." He snapped his fingers as if he could not remember. "The architect?"

"Frank Lloyd Wright."

"In that Arizona commune?"

Matt grinned. "Commune? Well, we weren't exactly hippies."

"We know that," said Lambie blandly. "Well, you've done very well in life." He got up and moved to the window.

Matt shrugged: "You can get a long way on two languages. I'm their token white."

Lambie was looking down at the street. He seemed to have lost interest. "Right down there," he mused. "I could have got my ass blown off."

"What?" asked Matt, confused.

"Hinckley. When he shot Reagan. And hit the poor old Bear." He smiled wryly. "Got me sent to the Bush league, you might say." He became suddenly brisk. "Now, about the model airplane. We may have a problem, there."

Matt's heart plummeted, but he kept his face blank. "He'll *accept* it, won't he? I mean, it's a matter of face." He moved to the bureau. Holding the model in the flannel rag, he brought it to Lambie.

Lambie clicked his teeth. "Beautiful!"

"You can't beat the Japs," Matt enthused. "Every rivet perfect." He touched the fuselage below the cockpit. "You almost need a magnifying glass, but his name's printed there: 'Lieutenant (jg) George Bush.' " He pointed at the nose. "He called his plane Barbie, for Mrs. Bush: here it is, see?" He pressed the model on him, handing it to him in the cloth.

Lambie took the model cautiously. "Hollow inside?"

"I guess."

The agent gripped the nose and twisted it. It screwed off.

He held it to the light, peered inside, held it upside down, and shook it. Nothing fell out. Carefully, he screwed the nose back on. The cloth was slippery, and he did not risk trying to unfold the wings. It was, after all, the Vice President's gift.

"Cast iron, and gold plated?" the agent asked.

"I imagine. Metallurgy's not my thing." He took the model back.

"How much did it cost?" asked Lambie.

"About five grand."

Lambie looked uncomfortable. "*That's* our problem. Mr. Bush doesn't want to hurt their feelings, but there's a law on the books—"

"The Gift Act?" Matt relaxed. "Hell, the Japs know he can't *keep* it."

"Good," said Lambie. The press would be informed, he said, that the model would eventually go to the National Air and Space Museum on the Mall.

Matt put the model back on the bureau and showed them to the door. When they were gone, he repolished the model lightly with the cloth and put it back into its case. Unless they invited a bomb-sniffing dog to the breakfast, it had apparently passed.

He wondered if Nagano would be at the meal. Behind the shimmering glasses, the detective troubled him.

CHAPTER 13

Alicia found herself jammed in a window seat on the JAL Jumbo, next to a squirming Japanese three-year-old, his doting mother, and all of his toys.

Shortly after takeoff at Narita, she became nauseated. And when she rose to go to the toilet, somewhere over the western Pacific, at twenty thousand feet, she had to cling to the back of a seat for a long moment before she could trust herself to move.

As they landed at Dulles she felt deathly sick. The occasional nausea she had endured all her adult life was returning. She had been twelve hours in the air to Kennedy, and another hour down the east coast on New York Air. She'd had no appetite for lunch or dinner yesterday, but had somehow ingested two leaden doughnuts and a cup of coffee as dawn broke over Winnipeg—the stewardess having assumed that she wanted Western fare.

She stumbled as she boarded an FAA shuttle lounge that took passengers to the terminal.

She had never understood what happened when one crossed the International Date Line, but discovered that she had arrived at Dulles on the same day at the same hour she had left the Hiroshima Grand Hotel. Had the world stopped while she flew?

Jet lag, or something, had thrown her mind off track. Her

eyelids felt like sandpaper, and it was an effort to move her limbs. She changed her money from yen to dollars and hurried to a pay phone. She called the Japanese Embassy. A security guard told her, in a patronizing tone, that the offices would not be open until nine thirty. He had never heard of Hart-san, Christopher, and knew nothing of a trade delegation, or where they might be staying.

Suddenly she knew that she could never find Matt without help, in a strange city, sagging with fatigue and jet lag. She needed help.

She looked up Joshua Goldberg, Attorney-at-Law, and called his office. She heard his voice on tape: *"Law Offices, Josh Goldberg, and Washington Office, Atomic Veterans' Legal Aid Center. Please leave a message after the beep, and we'll get back to you during office hours."*

His voice brought warmth to her body. She found herself babbling: "Josh, it's Alicia. I'm at Dulles Airport. Oh, Josh, my brother's alive, I should have told you, he was at Yamagawa Motor in Hiroshima all the time, now he's here with a delegation, he's found the man who killed our mother, remember what he carved? Suppose he tries to *kill* him? Josh, Josh, what shall I *do?*"

She recoiled, staring at the phone. She must be mad! Suppose a secretary, or a law clerk, heard the message? What would they ever think?

She wanted to erase what she had said, tell the machine to ignore it, spit it out. "I'll call back," she said.

Now she *must* reach Josh, and quickly. He'd said he lived in Arlington. She found the number and dialed. The phone rang and rang. Suppose he had not returned from Japan? Had stopped en route, in LA or San Francisco? Then where was Corky?

Phone to ear, she blinked back tears. She had never felt so helpless or alone.

"Hello?" The tone was husky.

She almost broke down. "Corky?"

"Yes." She could hear the rustle of sheets, and a slurred and muffled voice. Then: "What time is it? Who *is* this?"

"Alicia."

"Alicia *who?*"

"Alicia McGraw, Alicia *Bancroft!*"

There was a long silence. Across the airport terminal, Alicia heard a plane announced, and then another.

"Corky," she prodded. "Is Josh there?"

"Gone to work," Corky mumbled.

There was a *clump* as if the phone had dropped to a rug, and no matter how Alicia called into the mouthpiece, Corky didn't answer. When Alicia tried to call again, the line was busy.

She wrote down Josh's office address, checked her suitcase in a locker, and flagged a Virginia cab discharging a passenger outside.

It was, the driver warned her, a good forty-minute drive.

CHAPTER 14

*T*he little cavalcade of limousines, waved on by a sweating policeman, drew up in front of the brand-new Far East Trade Center on G Street in Washington's Chinatown. The chauffeur of the lead vehicle moved briskly to the rear door and opened it. Matt, rosewood box clutched in his hand, stepped into the steaming morning air.

Today was the opening of the center. On this first day, admission to the celebrations and exhibits was limited to foreign diplomats, VIPs, celebrities, and the press. JAMA's own breakfast with Vice President Bush, in a private dining room in the rear, had apparently been quite upstaged.

Good. They would hear about it soon enough.

Matt followed the welcoming committee through great columns supporting the pagoda-roofed entrance, blazing with new vermilion paint. Banners in English, Japanese, and Chinese, announcing the beginning of the First Japanese Summer Festival today, hung from staffs projecting from the façades of stores facing the street and along the central promenade.

The party passed guards at the entrance, and trailed into the blessed coolness of a water garden, planted with greenery, where streams meandered down rocks to quiet pools of lilies. The liaison man led them into a vast, airy atrium crowded with people. From ceilings hundreds of feet above hung huge Japanese lanterns. Throughout the central court were restaurants and stalls vending Chinese, Japanese, and Eurasian dishes. Already they were doing a heavy breakfast business, and the sushi stands were mobbed.

A young Japanese in traditional peasant dress was touching up Nebuta, a huge god of sleep from the Aomori region, made of paper stretched over a bamboo frame. A juggler tested the balance of a tall structure of forty-six lanterns suspended from a tall cross, a tradition of the Kanto festival in Akita. A *dashi* float from the Hanagasa-Matsuri festival of Yamagata City blazed with flowers and dolls, and a huge dragon from the Okunchi Festival of Nagasaki was twisting past the food stalls.

The Namahage demon, who chastised the lazy, stamped about already, horned, masked, dressed in a shaggy coat. A troupe of Kabuki actors hurried by; two padded *kendo* swordsmen sparred with bamboo *shinai;* in a sumo ring, a strutting, bloated wrestler tossed salt to purify the area while his opponent watched impassively.

The party was led across the atrium. At the door to the last banquet room at the end of the building, Matt saw Lambie, the Secret Service agent who had visited his room. The agent spotted him and moved over swiftly. The rosewood case became suddenly heavier in his hand.

"Mr. Hart, I'd like you with me as your colleagues pass in," he murmured. "Just a last-minute check?"

"No problem," breathed Matt.

They stood by two enormous agents, wearing dark glasses and identical gray slacks and blue blazers, checking pictures from a list as the delegates filed in.

When the last delegate had entered, Lambie held out his hand to Matt. "Now, just let me take that box."

Matt felt a jolt of alarm. He handed him the case. Lambie told his agent to turn off a metal detector and they entered.

The breakfast room was intimate and cheery. There was greenery everywhere, and a little brook and pool. On the stereo, a muted flute backed by the Tokyo String Orchestra touched the place with magic: "Sunlight Shining through the Trees."

Near the entrance stood a tall, candy-striped *yagura* festival stage, hung with *chochin* lanterns. On it sat a brawny *taiko* drummer wearing a headband. Past the stage, in the center of the dining room, an oval Japanese rock garden had been laid out, with a raked sea of sand. On one side was a wide flat slab, probably representing America; on the other, a chain of smaller rocks, the islands of Japan. Between them lay a lacquered Japanese bridge.

At the far end of the rock garden was a kidney-shaped breakfast table, laid for the delegates, so that the Vice President and senior delegates overlooked the little seascape. Behind the table were rice-paper *shoji* screens. Suits of samurai armor guarded the screens. Lambie skirted the rock garden, placed the rosewood box at the head of the table, and opened it.

Matt tensed. He reached into his pocket, found the handkerchief, groped in it for his cyanide pill. Lambie drew the model from its case and placed it on the table. He beckoned to a wispy little photographer in the corner.

"Shoot this for Aviation and Space Museum, Jeff, before he gets here."

The flash gun fired. Lambie nodded to Matt.

"Chris, you want to unfold the wings?"

He felt sweat start to his brow. "Not before the Vice President . . ."

But Lambie was looking past him, toward a rear entrance. "Never mind," he muttered. "Too late." He raised his voice: "Gentlemen, the Vice President of the United States!"

A tall, pleasant man with glasses entered the room. Those who would sit at the speakers' table shook his hand, one by one, while the flash gun fired.

Matt was the last to pose.

For a moment, while the photographer focused, he looked into the eyes of the man he must kill. He saw friendliness there, and a certain humor. The handshake was firm, and the eyes held steady.

Bush glanced at the model by the microphone. "They told me the Turkey was your idea. It's a lovely model, Mr. Hart."

"Well, thank you, Mr. Bush."

"Thank *you!*"

The flash gun flickered and they sat down.

Matt glanced around the room. Detective Captain Nagano was seated with the Yamagawa delegation. Their eyes met. It seemed to Matt that Nagano's were glistening with hate. The detective stared at Matt, removed his eyeglasses, polished them on his napkin, and gently rubbed his eyes. Then he touched his mouth, replaced his glasses, bowed and began to eat.

Eyes for the emperor, lips sealed to all . . .

A brother! Matt swallowed. A *kaishaku* to help him die as a samurai? Not this man. He read it in his eyes: he had simply been sent to kill him before he could talk. The countersign was a warning to be silent, nothing more.

He doubted that the detective would try to bring in a gun. A poisoned *fukiya* dart from a six-inch blowpipe, like a ninja? Or a nine-inch throwing knife?

Matt felt an awful deadness in the bottom of his soul. To Sumi he was a *gaijin*, still. The general did not trust his courage, nor his silence if he lived.

CHAPTER 15

Alicia sweltered in the backseat of the aging taxi. The air conditioning did not work, and all the windows were down, letting in the stench and smoke of traffic and the moist Potomac heat.

She blew the hair from her face. The morning sunlight glared from the river, hurting her eyes. Far in the distance, she could see a massive, ugly building she took to be the Pentagon. They had been stopped twice in heavy traffic. Now the cab coughed as they finally inched onto Arlington Boulevard. She was becoming nauseous again.

The driver turned on his radio as they skirted a huge statue of marines raising the flag at Iwo.

". . . along George Washington Parkway, we have a stalled vehicle in the number one northbound lane. Traffic on Arlington Memorial is bumper-to-bumper, but moving . . ."

He glanced at her in the mirror and said: "Key Bridge and Roosevelt Bridge be jammed for sure. We gonna try Memorial."

She dozed. When she awoke they were stopped in the middle of a stately concrete bridge. A double line of traffic stretched ahead, shimmering in the harsh sunlight. The radio was braying the morning news.

". . . And in other local events this morning, Vice President George Bush breakfasts with Japanese auto makers at

the new Far East Trade Center on the first day of the Japan Festival.''

It took her a moment to get her bearings. Japanese auto makers? Matt's delegation?

"A spokesman from Yamagawa Motor Company will present him a model of an airplane. It is the plane from which the Vice President parachuted in World War II, off the Bonin Islands near Japan, to be saved by a U.S. submarine. Elsewhere . . ."

She sat up straight. A spokesman? Matt?

And all at once she knew. He *did* intend to kill. Submarine? Bonin Islands? The *Vice President* was his target!

Panicked, she clutched at the driver's shoulder. "Take me to the Far East Center!"

"We gonna be *here* quite some time."

She lunged forward, reaching past him to blast his horn. As it sounded, he grabbed her wrist. "No *way* you gonna make this traffic move!"

"How much?" she cried suddenly. "How much to here?"

He turned off his meter. "Twenty-two dollars, so far."

She thrust a ten and a twenty into his hand, jumped out, and sidled through the line of traffic to the curb. Far ahead, she recognized the Lincoln Memorial. She had visited it from Johns Hopkins years ago. Cars encircling it seemed to be moving well, and she was sure that taxis were among them, so she began to run.

In his second-floor law office opposite the General Hancock statue on Market Place, Josh Goldberg hung up his jacket and sagged into the worn leather seat behind his desk. He reflected that he spent more time lately staring at the rump of the general's horse below, waiting for clients, than he did in court.

The accumulated mail on his desk depressed him because it bore, he knew, the usual burden of pain. His chair groaned as he swiveled to gaze across the street. The dingy façade of the Children's Emergency Home stared back at him. He wished he had never left Berkeley.

Today would be hot. He was exhausted from his flight back from Japan.

His part-time secretary, a black law student at Georgetown University Law Center, would be in class all morning. He moved to her desk in his tiny reception room and glanced at his answering machine. Seven messages: less than one a day. He'd surely starve to death. He began to listen to them. The first half dozen were from atomic-veteran clients or their widows.

Then Alicia's quiet, desperate voice began. He froze where he stood.

"My brother's alive . . . He's found the pilot who killed our mother . . ." He heard the message through. He had no idea where she was now. Instantly he called his home, and got only a busy signal. Corky, stumbling around the house with a hangover, had probably knocked the phone from the cradle again.

Alicia had said she'd call back, but when?

Heart pounding, he tried to read his mail. He found himself staring out the window. Across the street General John Hancock, on his bronze charger, exhorted his Army of the Potomac to hold fast to Cemetery Ridge.

On Chichijima was a cemetery on a ridge, and an oath of vengeance. Vengeance against an unknown American flier, whose soul would burn in hell? A pilot who still lived, and was here?

"He's found the pilot who killed our mother . . ." His thoughts were jumbled and he could not quiet them.

Below, a pigeon fluttered from the general's sword arm to the ground. It began to peck at litter by a bush.

Something plucked at Josh's subconscious, but he could not pin it down. On his desk lay a yellow legal pad. He began to doodle with a sharpened pencil.

Her brother worked at Yamagawa Motor, she had said. And was in Washington with a "delegation." Perhaps the Japanese Embassy would know where he was.

But he must have changed his name: young Matthew Bancroft had disappeared: neither Josh nor MacArthur's CIC had ever found a trace. Why *had* he disappeared? One rainy afternoon, in a fetid, darkened hovel, could he have attacked— and almost killed—a full-grown man?

Josh stared at the doodles on his pad.

Two eyes glared out above a mask, the pupils round with hate. Emerald-green, the eyes of the woman he loved.

Josh fumbled with the phone and called the Japanese Embassy. He spoke with a consular clerk, claiming to be an auto-parts distributor who had met a Yamagawa delegate last night and lost his business card.

"He wasn't Japanese," said Josh. "Caucasian, with green eyes?"

He heard the man suck in his breath.

"Ah . . . Hart-san! Mr. Christopher Hart, head delegate."

"Thank you." He swallowed. "And where can I find him today?"

"I shall look." He heard papers shuffling. "A breakfast meeting! With Commerce Department committee, at Far East Trade Center. Do you know where that place is?"

"Yes." It was six blocks away.

He locked his office. The elevator was fifty years old and moved like glue, so he dashed down the stairs instead. He caught a departing bus on Seventh, heading north.

CHAPTER 16

*A*licia argued with a black, round-faced guard beneath vermilion columns outside the Far East Trade Center.

"Can't I *buy* a ticket, then?"

"Sorry, Miss." The guard checked a pass and passed a well-dressed couple through. "Tomorrow's general admission: today it's passes only."

"But I have a message to deliver!"

The guard shook his head: "They should have gave you a pass."

Behind him, inside the arcade, she spotted a Japanese gentleman in a black kimono and *montsuki* half-coat, emblazoned with a family *mon*. He wore big black glasses and was obviously of managerial importance. Throwing manners to the winds, she called to him in Japanese and beckoned: "Sir, I have need of help."

He looked shocked and walked over. She bowed deeply. "I am sorry to trouble you, sir."

"But you speak perfectly!" he marveled.

She bowed again. "*Domo.* I am from Yamagawa Motor, with an urgent message for Hart-san, of the automotive delegation . . ."

She felt dizzy and unsteady, as if she might pass out.

The Japanese studied her face. "*Hai.*" He nodded. To the guard he said, "Let her through."

He led her through a water garden of plants, apologizing for the confusion of this first day of the festival. They entered the vast atrium. The place was swarming with people; a *shishimai* demon with a black cloak and a red lion-face was dancing from food stall to food stall; *awaodori* performers from Tokushima Prefecture with red underskirts and great flat hats were flowing among the visitors. A Bunraku stage was set up, and a *shamisen* player on the side was tuning, while the black-hooded *omozuki* puppeteers—in plain sight—worked their man-sized wooden puppets: three puppeteers to a puppet.

The Japanese pointed to the rear, half a city block away.

"There, at the end of the atrium," he said. "In the Imperial Breakfast Suite. But the Vice President is there, and the Secret Service has been there since last night. I fear you will not get in."

She thanked him, bowed again, and hurried through the swarming crowd. She was afraid that he was right.

Matt sat next to the Vice President of the United States as the breakfast drew to a close. Ohkawa-san, on the other side of Bush, spoke good English, and monopolized the Vice President's attention, much to Matt's relief. He and Bush would die together, that was enough: he had no desire to speak of Chichijima, except at the final instant, with the man who had murdered his mother.

Matt pleaded a hangover and ordered only tea: Under Bushido, one did not eat before destroying oneself. Bush had diplomatically picked dried fish, green tea, raw egg, pickles, *miso* soup, *nori* dried seaweed, and rice, and was eating it with the ivory hashi sticks provided.

They were entertained by traditional Japanese performers from the festivities in the atrium: ancient *gagaku* court music plucked by a pretty geisha from a long stringed koto: a wailing flute solo by a mendicant priest with his head hidden in a basket. Matt's hands were shaking so badly that he feared to lift his cup. He caught Nagano studying him from his place near the speaker's table. His moment was approaching fast: waiters in peasant costume, wearing *tabi* sandals and black linen coats with Japanese characters on the back, were clearing the dishes now.

The door opened and he could see, past the Secret Service,

a group of folk dancers in festival kimonos. He glanced at his watch.

Nine fifty-three. He was to present the plane at ten.

The Vice President had seven minutes to live.

Alicia saw quickly, as she approached the Imperial Breakfast Suite, that she would not be allowed in. A bulky man in dark glasses blocked the door.

But a half dozen girls in the bright kimonos of Shikoku Island were clustered at the entrance. She could tell from their chatter that they were to perform their regional dance for the Vice President inside.

She turned to the oldest of the girls. *"Ohayo gozaimasu!* I'm from the embassy, sent to translate for you."

"Domo arigato gozaimasu," beamed the girl, bowing deeply.

So far so good. She managed a smile for the Secret Service agent. "We're ready to go in, sir."

He motioned her through. Inside, she peered past a festival stage, over a rock garden to the head of the table.

She recognized Vice President Bush. On one side of him sat an elderly Japanese, on the other side her brother. In front of the Vice President stood a model airplane, dazzling in gold. Except for the fact that its wings were folded back, it looked exactly like the one that had strafed them on the quay.

She suspected instantly that the gift was charged to kill. But suppose she was wrong?

She would ruin his life. She must somehow get her message through, for him alone.

Matt's mind grew fuzzy with sound of the *taiko* drum. He stared at his notes, not really digesting them, trying to pass the next seven minutes with his mind a total blank. The notes, typewritten in English by his secretary in Hiroshima, blurred before his eyes: "Mr. Vice President Bush, distinguished members of the Department of Commerce, fellow delegates of the Japan Automotive Manufacturers' Association . . ."

The *taiko* drum was beating from the stage, and a *shakuhachi* flute began to wail. He became aware that across the rock garden, girls were dancing around the platform. Their hands waved in the restrained, intricate choreography of their home prefecture, Tokushima, not far from Hiroshima on the Inland Sea.

His eyes wandered across the room. Rick Lambie, the Secret Service agent, was standing by the *shoji* screens which lined the walls. He was relaxed, but ignored the dancers. His eyes moved everywhere.

Surreptitiously, Matt removed the cyanide pill from his pocket and placed it under the rim of his saucer, handy to his reach. When the blast went off, he knew that he would be jumped instantly.

Suddenly he heard a voice—*Alicia's* voice—drifting clearly across the room.

He stared at the high, canopied stage. Alicia was standing at its front. Behind her the drummer had fallen silent.

"Gentlemen," she said, "Japanese folk dances all tell stories. This one tells a simple tale with a moral at the end."

He could not believe his eyes. He barcly restrained himself from leaping to his feet.

"It is the story of a little boy who was told by his father to take some eggs to market, in a village by the sea . . ."

No! he wanted to yell. But he was speechless.

"But on the quay the wind came up and blew his cap away . . ."

Matt could only stare at her. *Stop!* he cried silently. *It's too late!*

Now her eyes found his, and her voice dropped. "And when he chased his hat, he dropped the eggs."

That wasn't what happened, at all!

Her voice went on: "He was angry and thought he had disgraced himself before his father, so he vowed to kill the wind spirit in revenge."

He found himself sitting with clenched fists, pulse pounding in his head.

Alicia's eyes were full of tears: "But when his family heard, his father said: 'It was not your fault: give up your search. One cannot find the wind.' "

Across the room, their eyes locked.

"And, gentlemen," Alicia murmured, "that is all."

The Americans clapped, but Matt sensed puzzlement on the faces of his colleagues: a folk dance was a folk dance, nothing more. The dancers kneeled, bowed to the floor, and filed out. He waited for Alicia to leave the stage, but she did not move.

He arose, heavy with dread. "We thank you, ma'am." He

looked at his watch. "Now, since Mr. Bush has a tight schedule . . ."

If she would not leave, all right. But she could not stop him, not while their mother lay twisting in her grave.

A lily in a dark, dark pool . . .

He cleared his throat. "Vice President Bush, distinguished members of the Department of Commerce, fellow delegates of the Japan Automotive Manufacturers' Association . . ."

Using a parking lot pass for the Court of Military Appeals, Josh talked his way past the front door guard and into the Far East Trade Center.

Inside, he surveyed a sweeping, vibrant atrium, kabuki players, sumo wrestlers strutting. There were hundreds of performers on the floor. The place seemed more foreign to him than Hiroshima.

A bespectacled Japanese in a kimono seemed to be in charge of the entrance foyer. Josh flashed the pass, which had the U.S. eagle on it, and told him that he had to see a delegate from the trade meeting: Where was it?

The Japanese bowed slightly. "They are breakfasting with the Vice President." He pointed to the end of the atrium.

"Vice President Bush?" He had not expected this.

The man nodded. "And I don't think they will let you very close."

His mind was fluttering around a memory. A letter, signed by a lieutenant (jg) in the navy, bucked to him long ago. "George H. W. Bush, LTJG, USNR." *And the jg had bombed Chichijima! The letter had given the date!*

"Jesus Christ," he breathed. "Holy jumping Jesus Christ!"

He cut blindly across the atrium floor, darted past a flute player, stumbled between two sumo wrestlers, and made a shouting *kendo* swordsman drop his bamboo stave.

A bellowing ten-man dragon blocked his way. He ducked beneath it and went sprinting toward the rear.

Matt stood at the head of the banquet table. The words he heard were his own, but it was as if he were listening to someone else. "In this time of strain, in appreciation for Mr. Bush's past attempts to bolster free trade, we have brought a gift."

For a moment, reaching for the model, he scanned the

faces of his colleagues, saddened by the disgrace and shame they would endure.

He faced Vice President Bush, who was rising to his feet. The model was cold in his hands. He turned its nose toward Bush. "The airplane itself," he heard himself say, "is one in which the Vice President distinguished himself in action . . ."

As briefed, the Vice President held out his hands, eyes twinkling behind his glasses.

"In action," Matt repeated softly, "against an island called Chichijima, in the Bonins."

He heard his sister cry: "Matt, no!"

At the door to the banquet room, Josh's parking-lot pass failed him. "Sorry, sir," said the agent, 220 pounds of meat, "and please clear the corridor, too."

It was time to declare his hand. If he was wrong, so be it. "The Vice President's in danger," Josh warned.

"What the hell do you mean?" the agent exclaimed. He drew a walkie-talkie from his pocket, spoke into it, listened, shook it, and tried again. "White Control from Station One! I got a willy-willy!" A blast of static answered him and he shook it again. He spoke to Josh: "What do you mean 'in danger'?"

Josh could not wait. He lowered a shoulder and charged. It was like hitting the side of a steer, but he caught the man in the solar plexus, and the agent dropped to his knees.

Josh burst in. The man from the Suntory Bar was on the podium, handing Bush a golden airplane.

He glanced toward Josh. His eyes were emerald green.

"Don't, Bush!" Josh screamed. "Don't touch that god-damn thing!"

In an instant Matt's world overturned. Someone yanked Bush from the microphone. A gray streak—Lambie—vaulted the table in a crash of cups and glasses. Matt glimpsed Nagano rounding the podium, whipping something from his coat. It was the *musubinawa* garroting rope of a samurai: a braided three-foot line of woman's hair with an ivory ball in the center to crush the windpipe.

He felt a Secret Service agent grab him from behind. He had waited too long to snatch the pill from beneath his saucer. Nagano was on him now, and behind him, and the *musubinawa* was searing his neck, tightening. The world was turning red . . .

Someone shouted faintly: "Asshole, you'll kill him with that thing!"

"For Tanaka," hissed Nagano in his ear. "You *gaijin* swine."

He could not breathe or think. His eyes started from his head. Hands grappled for the model, bending his thumbs backward, but he would not let it go.

He had failed, and could not face the shame. Clinging to the plane with all his strength, he forced the nose toward his own chest.

He heard Alicia scream as he jerked the wings apart.

There was a blast like the *pika-don*'s. It blew him from the grasp of those behind him and slammed him against a *shoji* panel under a samurai shield. Fire licked at the rice paper around him. Men cursed at him and flailed at the flames and tried to drag him away. Through the smoke he glimpsed Nagano, with an ivory hashi stick extended, struggling with an agent to get close enough for a *kunoichi* thrust through the eardrum to the brain.

He heard a roaring in his head, and Alicia's helpless wail. For a long while it seemed to him that he heard nothing more.

CHAPTER 17

Word of the failed assassination reached the Brotherhood at noon, Hiroshima time, from Detective Captain Nagano, though there was nothing in the paper or on the news.

At ten P.M. Toshio Sumi, ex-general, Imperial Japanese Army, kneeled in his formal kimono before the three masked, black-clad men on the dais of the lodge hall. He had been cold all day. In the darkness of the night outside, he could hear the southeast wind off the Seto Sea, setting the pines to creaking. There would be rain. The summer storms were late in coming, but now his bones need not endure them. He was almost glad.

"Sumi-san," said Osada, behind his mask. "You have heard the verdict of three of the Five. How do you say, yourself?"

Traditionally, he must agree. Consensus meant everything: he had ignored this in plotting the assassination, and see what had transpired? To trust a *gaijin* with the killing had been stupid. He had driven the Carp beneath the sea for another fifty years.

He bowed. "I concur. But I have a request."

Osada nodded. "Yes, Master."

"Master," still. But for the last time. So be it.

"May I wait for Nagano-san to be my *kaishaku?* We've been comrades for over forty years."

Osada frowned behind his mask. "Should I tell him, brothers?" They nodded and he continued almost regretfully: "Sumi-san, Nagano is in Washington."

"I know. I think you sent him, Osada, because you did not trust the *gaijin*. You were wrong. Bankloft-o would never have talked. I swear he has not talked now. If the Brotherhood is exposed, it will be Bush who will expose it. I was stupid, but Bankloft-o will not betray you, even if he lives."

"All that may be true," said Osada. "And Nagano is on his way home." Osada's eyes fell. "But you would not want *him* to send your spirit to the World Below. Let *me* be your *kaishaku*."

Sumi stared at him. "Are you insane? You have plotted against me, Osada. Do you think I'm too old to know? You will be the master. You have won."

Osada looked at him with something like pity. "No, Sumi-san." He glanced at the other two for guidance, and they nodded. "Nagano will be master. It is agreed."

Sumi sat back. So the leader of the insurrection had been Nagano, all along. He felt nothing, only cold, implacable anger in the pit of his stomach, anger against them all.

Before his empty place on the dais lay his swords, one long, one short.

Nagano was out of reach, and could have disarmed him anyway, but the rest? Sumi was still a *kendo* master, one never lost the skill. His legs were old and his fingers twisted, but if he attacked now . . . To kill the three would save his face. Let Nagano rule the Brotherhood alone.

He said contemptuously: "I need no *kaishaku*. Could any of you say the same?"

With an effort, he rose, moved to the dais. He glanced down at his *katana*. A lightning movement now, Osada first, then the chemist, then the aging ex-commander-janitor, in a flash of whistling steel. He ached to do it, and knew that he could.

No. He was not a treacherous peasant, smelling from the fields. He was a samurai, and would not die a murderer of his brothers.

He took his place between Osada and the chemist. He arranged his flowing kimono sleeves beneath his knees. He opened the garment, bared his belly-band, and grasped his *wakizashi* in both hands. He touched the hilt to his forehead, touched the point against his shriveled belly, and pressed home.

"Sayonara, brothers," he muttered. "Since it must be so."

The pain was no worse than that he had known for months. The blood gushing down his stomach warmed his skin. He smiled, his gold tooth glittered, and he died.

CHAPTER 18

*M*att Bancroft was said to be failing fast by the time Alicia was allowed to visit him, in a guarded room in the prison ward at the U.S. Navy Medical Center in Bethesda, Maryland. Thoracic surgeons had done what they could. He had been slipping in and out of consciousness for almost two days, while Josh fought with the Secret Service for her right to see her brother one more time before he died.

In the bleak corridor outside his room, she met the agent who had been assigned his case. He had questioned her all the day before. His name was Rick Lambie, and he was very kind.

"There are things I want to tell you before you go on in."

"He's going to die," she murmured. "What else do I have to know?"

He shrugged. "That he was tricked. If he was after the pilot that strafed your dock, Bush wasn't his man."

He handed her a manila envelope. In it were pictures of Matt and herself and their father and mother, and Mickey-san, on the beach at Chichijima. They were found in her brother's room. "There was a newspaper clipping about Bush's wartime record, genuine. And a fake Imperial Japanese Army report, fingering him as the pilot who strafed the Omura quay. The ink's less than a year old."

"But why would anybody trick him?"

Lambie spoke of a secret branch of the Black Dragon Society, and Matt's involvement in it. He searched her face, as if he expected her to deny it.

She could not. She didn't know the man inside the room; her brother had not survived their stupid war. She kept her silence.

Lambie went on: "The Brotherhood of the Carp, Mr. Bush called it. Run by an ex-general who wanted Bush out of the way. He committed hara-kari yesterday in Kure. We scooped up one of his agents in an auto plant and one in a tire factory this morning. The Tokyo detective who tried to strangle your brother may be another. Or he may just have been trying to save the delegation's face: we'll never know. The Japanese government is supposed to be moving against the rest."

She thanked him and entered the room.

Matt lay in a jungle of tubes with his eyes closed. His skin was gray. A plastic cone covered his nose. She moved to him, and took his hand.

His eyes opened. "Alicia?"

"Oh, Matt!"

"I was wrong . . . *He* didn't kill Mama . . ."

She shook her head. "No."

"*I* did!"

"You didn't!"

"Bullshit!" he murmured.

"No!"

"Bunkum, then?" All at once he smiled, and they were young, in golden sunlight in her room on the last day of the world. She felt him squeeze her hand. "Bunkum, Alicia?"

"I *said* it was the wind!" she wept. "Damn it, weren't you listening? I said it was the *wind!*"

He closed his eyes, and squeezed her hand.

"All right," he breathed, "the wind."

She stayed until his hand grew cold and then she called the nurse.

In her room at the Hilton she called Melbourne: Rab should have arrived home from Hiroshima last night. She caught him as he was leaving for the studio. She told him that her brother had indeed been alive, but was dead now, and told him of the assassination attempt. The wire services, he said, had had nothing on it. She knew that at the request of the palace, the

Japanese delegation had sworn secrecy, and even Commerce Department security had held. It would leak out, she was sure, in the end, though Matt was the only casualty.

"Will *you* use it?" she asked.

"Not yet, if you say no."

"He was my brother, Rab."

"I shan't. And I'm so very, very sorry. And I've gone fairly round the bend," he said hoarsely. "Whatever happened, you should've trusted me. But I need you. Are you quite all right?"

"All right," she murmured. "And coming home." She paused. "Is *that* all right?"

"All *right?*" he choked. "My God! Tonight! Unless you can leave before!"

She hung up, and the red light began to flash on the phone. It was Josh.

Josh waited in the bar of the Gazebo Restaurant, under the sweep of the Hilton's eastern wing. A breath of wind stirred the elms above, and when she approached across the lawn the breeze made her hair shimmer.

They sat at a table under the trees. They nibbled cheese and sipped some wine. The evening grew cooler; he could feel autumn in the air.

She did not ask him to stay and dine, for she knew it would be too hard to face Rab on her return. And they did not speak of times to come; he suspected there were none. He finished his wine, and looked into the emerald eyes. In his lifetime, he thought bitterly, he had seen them seldom enough.

They strolled through the trees toward the entrance drive. Hand around her waist, he guided her through the hedge. He paused in the loom of a great sighing pine.

When he stepped onto the pavement, she'd be gone . . .

"Josh?"

"Yes?" he whispered.

She smiled into his eyes. "I *hoped* we could be friends, and so we were."

She kissed him lightly and he watched her cross the lawn, fragile as a dream.

"Alicia!"

She turned. He moved back across the lawn. He took her in his arms and looked into the emerald eyes.

"Life's too damn short," he muttered. "So let me stay tonight?"

"No, Josh." She smiled and touched a finger to his lips. "But someday mayhaps we'll meet again."

He stepped to the pavement, called for his car, and drove home.

Acknowledgments

So many helped in the research that it is hard to list them all. But to the following persons the author—and the reader— are especially indebted:

On Chichijima, besides the erudite Jerry Savory, the charming present-day Nathaniel Savory, mentioned in the dedication, and the kind, shy Jeffery Gilley, there are Arthur Gilley, with whom we shared many brews on the Chichijima ferry *Ogasawara Maru*; Nobuhisa "K. C." Shiozaku, clerk at Chichijima's Hotel Kanko; and Herbert Washington, Lynn Webb Ohira, and her husband Sado, all of whom helped to acquaint us with the forgotten island's life and history. Jimmy Savory, of Los Angeles, is a good friend and a wonderful source of Chichijima family history, and Jessel and Vicki Savory of Las Vegas have been most kind.

We're indebted to: Mr. Hasagawa, of the Ogasawara Island Administrative Office in Tokyo, whose kind contribution of historical charts and data were invaluable; the energetic, multilingual Yoshiaru T. "Tom" Yamane, whose friendship, translations, and guiding hand through Tokyo were essential; Volker Boy and his wife Akiko, whose hospitality and love for Chichijima meant so much; Osamu "Sam" Aridome, whose pride in Japan and friendship we treasure; and Mrs. Mary T. Shepardson, who has made a lifelong study of

336

Chichijima and was kind enough to send us her article "Pawns of Power," as a historical source.

Those in Tokyo who took us under their wing: Shozo Tsujiyama, of the *Gensuikyo* Council Against A and H Bombs; Manami Suzuki, of the similar *Gensuikin*; Teruaki Minami; Naoko Itoh; Yoshinori Ito; Dr. Zenshiro Hara, Japan Scientists' Association; Miss Fumi Yamashita; Dr. Ikuro Anzai, Department of Radiological Health of the University of Tokyo, whose tireless energy sustained us in the frantic swarm of Tokyo; and Jack and Nona Landers, of Wakayama City, for their advice and support.

Those who led us through the new Hiroshima, and helped us find survivors of the old: Professor Naomi Shono, Hiroshima University; Keiko Ogura; Kunio Asakura, who guided us through Kure; Professor Kan Katayanagi, Women's College at Hiroshima; Sumiko Obinata and Somo Yamoto, two gracious ladies of the new city; and the lovely Kyoko Yoshida, unequivocally the best interpreter in all Japan, whose intelligence, diligence, and warmth sustained us—as Americans— through painful interviews in Hiroshima with those who had suffered the bomb.

And some of those who survived: ex-Lieutenant Hiroshi Oda, Imperial Japanese Army, now manager of Hiroshima's fine Hotel Silk Plaza, whose story of the bombing broke our hearts; Hisao Doi, an ex-Imperial Army enlisted man barracked at Hiroshima Castle, whose memories of that awful day live in his eyes today; Mrs. Kazukye "Kaz" Suyeishi, who survived the bombing as a child and graciously gave us her time in Los Angeles.

Dr. Howard Hamilton, MD, whose efforts at the Radiation Effects Research Foundation in Hijiyama Park continue, and who—in our view—wages a valiant battle to overcome the past image of the "Fish Cake on the Hill."

To those in the U.S., too, who have not forgotten Hiroshima and Nagasaki, some of whom lost loved ones: Jean Ralph, whose husband, an ex-marine of the 2nd Marine Division, was sent into Nagasaki soon after the bombing and died for it of radiation sickness; Ellie Mills, of the National Association of Radiation Survivors; Vic Tolley, of the 2nd Marine Division; Tom Saffer, who as a lieutenant of marines crouched in a trench during one of the Pentagon's ill-advised shots at Frenchman Flat, and whose book *Countdown to Zero* was one of our finest sources; Peter Wyden, whose book *Day One* is a bible of the Hiroshima bombing, and whose advice on Hiroshima was invaluable; Kanji Kuramato, President of the Atomic Bomb Victims in America.

To those U.S. Army, Navy, Army Air Corps, and Marine veterans of Hiroshima, the Chichijima Occupation, and the Guam war-crimes trials who gave their time for interviews and entrusted photos and diaries and memories to us, we owe a special debt, and regret that—for some—the novel may be disturbing. It is binocular vision, after all, which shows us a world in three dimensions.

General Rixey's daughter, Mrs. Ann Boyd, gave generously of her time; the general's monograph on solving the war crimes on Chichijima—"Camouflage"—was essential source material. General Rixey himself, with his good recall, did much to make this novel come alive. His younger brother, Lieutenant Colonel Palmer Rixey, USMC (retired), an Annapolis classmate of the author, contributed memories of Guam and the war-crimes trials.

There were many others: Captain Lloyd Smith, USN (retired), and Commander Harold Hall, who landed at Nagasaki after the second bomb was dropped; Lieutenant Colonel Dan McGovern, USAF (retired), one of the first cameramen into Hiroshima; Lieutenant Colonel Fred East, of army counterintelligence in Nagasaki; our good friend Colonel George Suzuki, USA (retired), of army counterintelligence in Tokyo; Colonel Dmitri Evdokimoff, USAF; William Derby; Ken Ito, who was so kind in analyzing background material; Yuri Sato Silber, who caught every misspelled word in Japanese; and Mary Ohigawa Rose.

George Avakian, who visited Hiroshima as a new second lieutenant shortly after the bombing; James Russel, of the *Marine Corps Gazette*, and Ben Frank, the Marine Corps historian; ex-Lieutenant Barnette Greene, who flew B-29s with leaflets from Saipan; Cal Cavalcante, of the Navy Department, a treasury of information and a tireless archivist who found us the combat log of *Finback*, the submarine which rescued Vice President Bush.

Lieutenant Colonel Robert D. Shaffer, USMC (retired), whose unsung board of investigation on Chichijima Island helped to break the war-crimes mystery, and whose help on this book was essential; ex-First Lieutenant Wilburn Caskey,

Rixey's intelligence officer; John Kusiack, an officer on Rixey's staff; Ms. Anita Coley, who helped us get a record of the Guam war-crimes trials.

Captain Frederic T. Suss, USN (retired), who prosecuted General Tachibana, Admiral Mori, and Captain Yoshi in the war-crimes trials on Guam and provided us with transcripts of his arguments and pictures of the trials; Commander Ed Horne, who reviewed the trials.

Ed Howard, whose wife was executed by the Japanese on Guam and who recalled his fight to survive as a prisoner in Japan; Bob Hill, of Fort Mill, South Carolina, who remembered Chichijima and the war-crimes investigations; Major John Goar, then a young marine corporal, who served as a guard at the trials; Frank Ferris, who helped repatriate Japanese at the war's end.

Dr. Mitchel Covel, MD, Dr. Grant Gould, MD, and Dr. Gerald Wilkes, MD, for their help on medical passages.

Ex-master sergeant John Watson of the 41st Division, which occupied Hiroshima; Colonel John F. Minclier, USMC (retired), who recalled Guam during the war-crimes trials; Captain Vince Cassani, USN (retired), executive officer of the USS *Trippe*, which brought Rixey's staff to Chichijima; George Quinn, engineering officer of a landing craft which anchored in the harbor.

Many who knew Chichijima under U.S. occupation after the war: John Clunie, Jim Westwood, Ed Gunderson. And my good friend James William Holzer, the writer, an expert on Japanese martial arts.

Leo Nadeau, Vice President Bush's turret gunner during the Bonin Island strikes, who gave generously of his time and recollections.

While we prefer oral history to library research, we owe a special debt to Ernest B. Furgurson, chief of the Washington bureau of the *Baltimore Sun*, for his article in *Washingtonian* magazine—reprinted in the *San Diego Union*—on George Bush's mission and rescue off Chichijima Island. Lieutenant Colonel John Shotwell, USMC, and Major Don Kappel, USMC, were able, forty years after the fact, to put us in contact with officers of the board of investigation on the Chichijima war crimes.

To Vice Admiral Bob Baldwin, USN (retired), dear friend and classmate, we owe the naval aviation color, and to John

Ballough, of the Washington Information Group, we owe thanks for his research on Washington settings.

Thanks, also, to Scott Meredith and Jack Scovil, my longtime friends and agents, for their support, and to Leslie Meredith, my editor at McGraw-Hill, who revitalized an overresearched overwritten manuscript, and cut it down to manageable size.

And to Berna Ann Searls, truly a co-author, without whom this novel—or any other we write—could hardly have been done.